T0354496

Kathy, Wait For Me!

Morelle Forster

BALBOA
PRESS

A DIVISION OF HAY HOUSE

Balboa Press books may be ordered through booksellers or by contacting:

Balboa Press
A Division of Hay House
1663 Liberty Drive
Bloomington, IN 47403
www.balboapress.com
1 (877) 407-4847

Because of the dynamic nature of the Internet, any web addresses or
links contained in this book may have changed since publication and may
no longer be valid. The views expressed in this work are solely those
of the author and do not necessarily reflect the views of the publisher,
and the publisher hereby disclaims any responsibility for them.

The author of this book does not dispense medical advice or prescribe the use
of any technique as a form of treatment for physical, emotional, or medical
problems without the advice of a physician, either directly or indirectly. The
intent of the author is only to offer information of a general nature to help you
in your quest for emotional and spiritual well-being. In the event you use any
of the information in this book for yourself, which is your constitutional right,
the author and the publisher assume no responsibility for your actions.

Any people depicted in stock imagery provided by Thinkstock are models,
and such images are being used for illustrative purposes only.
Certain stock imagery © Thinkstock.

Print information available on the last page.

ISBN: 978-1-5043-3850-9 (sc)
ISBN: 978-1-5043-3851-6 (e)

Balboa Press rev. date: 10/06/2015

Chapter 1

─────◦⌇⊙⌇◦─────

Waiting for the Bus

It was because she wanted to impress Gary that she had bought the shoes. She realized that now. And they had cost a lot! They had cost all the money that Mike had been carefully putting in her jam jar, week after week.

Gary, the boss of the gang in this part of west London occupied a good part of her thoughts. It was upon understanding him, not making a mistake around him, that she invested her hopes of survival. She had seen how he had bullied many of the boys in the gang into fear and submission and she had observed how deferential the few girls were to him. She had understood from one or two of them, Tina in particular, that you had to be very careful of Gary. But it was not just fear that Gary used to control his territory; he could also be very affectionate and protective, and actually encouraged affection among the whole gang. Once you were in the gang then loyalty was asked of you.

Loyalty, once you were properly accepted, was assumed. The whole gang was based on loyalty, she felt. It was demanded. Kathy wondered how you knew when you had been accepted, how you knew when you were part of the gang – not that she had any thoughts of joining any gang. She was just riding the tide for the moment. So far she had met about twenty of the gang members – the Twickenham Boys, they called themselves – and they had been interested in her background and her plight and had asked many of the right questions, and, for all their lack of education and their undoubted dysfunctions, she felt she had been welcomed. And this was a new experience for her in London.

Tina had met Gary while she was in the detention centre for juveniles. He had procured cigarettes for her. Kathy had been introduced to Gary through Nick, the oldest resident, by a few months, in The Haven, the children's home where Kathy now found herself residing.

Kathy had had another depressing encounter in the home after returning from her school. Mrs. Buller, the cleaner and part-time manager, had run her vacuum at her, shouting she was a rude and stuck-up young girl, and she better get the 'hang of things around here, real quick; Miss Too-good will soon learn which side her bread is buttered on,' she had sneered. Kathy had not had a very good day at her new school either. Most of the other girls looked down on her ('She's in a children's home, did you hear? Uugh!' 'My parents told me there's always trouble round those kids,' said another. 'Best avoid her,' said a third). Lonely and depressed Kathy had returned from school to the taunts and bullying of Mrs. Buller. Containing her grief about her lost family and family life, and managing the trauma of the move from her own territory in the N.E. of England, was more than her fifteen years of psychological development could handle. On top of this it was clear she would never make out in the new school. It was just too middle-class; the girls all looked to be from good backgrounds, and with little experience of the 'other side of things'. They were not able to perceive there was a normal, regular girl behind the few facts they'd been given or heard rumoured about Kathy. They put two and two together, like most kids, in their own way, and had silently agreed she was an outsider, and best let her remain that way. True, one or two had tried to be kind to her, but it was never going to be enough to change things.

Sitting on her bed in her room, which was painted in a dingy cream, depressed and momentarily angry with Mrs. Buller, Nick had knocked gently on her door. A big, strong lad for his fifteen years, but with a slimness about him that suggested he would be tall, his black hair falling over his eyes, he appraised Kathy's face understanding immediately her mood. His dark blue eyes surveyed her for a moment or two, registering her dejection. Something told Kathy he was attractive, but all she knew of him was his sullenness at the dining table, his refusal to join in any conversation. The adults who supervised these meals made efforts to engage all the children in conversation, but Nick always obstinately rejected any encouragement if efforts were directed to him. Now he was revealing quite a new side to him.

'Kathy, want to come out with me tonight?' he invited.

'No thanks!'

'You better, Kathy; you can't stay here all your free time. You gotta get outta here – a lot; this place's a dead end! I'll introduce you to my mates; they're a much better lot than the lot here - and them girls at your school, I'll bet! They're rubbish!'

Kathy did not need much persuading. She rose and put on her old jacket she had had at home, a pretty purple one with a zipper front and a hood at the back.

'We can't,' she said, taking her jacket off again. 'I'm under supervision for my homework.'

'To hell with homework,' said Nick. 'There's far better things to do with my mates.'

'But we can't just walk out; someone will see us,' objected Kathy.

'No, they won't; they never know when I'm gone! Look, put a CD on your player and turn the volume up just enough so the supervisor will think you're here doing your homework.' Kathy did as she was told and put on some old Beatles music.

'That's right,' said Nick. 'That'll fool him – if he does come up and check.'

'But how do we get out without being seen?'

'Follow me,' said Nick. They tiptoed warily along the landing to the end where there was a sash window. Nick gently and noiselessly slid it up, climbed through and disappeared into the September evening. Kathy looked out and saw he was climbing down a tree, which grew very close to the house. She climbed out too and, after quietly closing the window, she descended to the ground. It was warm with a slight breeze blowing, and they made their way cautiously across the little bit of lawn to the front gate, crouching along in the shadow of the thick hedge as they went. They quietly let themselves out of the gate and proceeded up the street. 'Put your hood up,' said Nick, pulling the hood of his sweatshirt over his head. 'Why?' asked Kathy, 'it's not raining.'

'We don't want to be recognized,' grinned Nick. This was the first time she had seen any animation in Nick's face. It must be the thought of where we're going, she mused.

After about 10 minutes they came to a house in a terrace. It reminded her of her old home, that had been a terrace house too. But this one was bigger. It looked in good repair, which surprised Kathy. Having let themselves in with his key, Nick then said, 'Come and meet Gary, you'll like him!'

'Is this Gary's house?' asked Kathy.

'Naa, he just uses it from time to time.' They passed along a passage laid with a pleasing wooden floor and up a flight of stairs covered in a thick green carpet. Nick opened another door on the landing, and Kathy saw a room full of youths and a few girls. Unlike Nick, the boys all had very short hair, and so did the girls, except for one, who wore hers at shoulder length. Most of the boys wore their cropped hair greased up on the tops of their heads. 'These are punks,' thought Kathy, with a sinking heart. 'I can't stay here.' A youth at the far side of the room, suddenly extricated himself from the arms of one of the girls, rose and strode across the room to where Kathy was standing. Shorter than Nick, but immensely broad and strong he advanced towards Kathy, his pale blue eyes scanning her face, obviously making deductions about her.

'So, Nick,' he said without taking his eyes off Kathy, 'who've you brought along?' Nick introduced Kathy, and then went to sit beside some of his mates. Gary intimated that she should come with him. She noticed then that he had a deep scar running across one side of his forehead.

'We're having a party, Kathy. Come and join us,' invited Gary, his short fair hair greased flat on his head, unlike the other boys, and his pale eyes continuing to scrutinise her. Kathy sensed an intelligence behind those eyes, but not the sort of intelligence she was acquainted with. This was different; it was a raw, native intelligence, the sort she had come across in books, with plenty of cunning, she thought.

'Have some cheese straws, Kathy,' offered Gary, courteously. 'Some burgers are just coming,' and he poured some wine into a glass (a proper wine glass she noticed) and handed it to her. She had not drunk much wine in her life, but she too had a natural intelligence and she saw she'd better accept the glass of wine - and drink it! She could handle one glass.

The wine relaxed her, the hamburgers and chips and tomato ketchup arrived and she accepted another glass of wine from Gary. He was watching her intently, she noticed. The girl with the longer hair asked her where she was from, and Kathy found herself giving them a brief and matter-of-fact history of her recent life.

'Aw,' said the girl, whose name was Colette, and who seemed about the same age as Kathy. 'That's awful. You must've been so cut up. I hope the girls in your new school are nice; Do you like the children's home? I was in one of them once; I hated it. I got out soon as I could.'

'Yes, I hate it too,' confided Kathy.

From the other side of the room Gary suddenly called out 'You come here, kiddo, and hang out with us any time. We meet most evenings, not always here.'

'It's a nice house, here,' said Kathy diplomatically. 'Whose is it?'

'It's my boss' house,' Gary replied, but said no more.

She began to take more notice of the boys and observed some of them were as young as thirteen or fourteen, younger than she, with their voices hardly broken. They played a few games of cards, laughed a lot and told some dreadful jokes, some of which Kathy could not understand at all. At 10 o'clock Gary looked at what Kathy saw was a rolex watch on his wrist and announced she and Nick must get back to the children's home, 'to your residence,' he said in a mocking tone, which Kathy thought very funny, and laughed. 'Your awol will soon be noticed,' he added, 'and I don't want you in trouble with them.' Kathy felt a surge of gratefulness for this gesture of concern and left with pleasant, if mixed, feelings about Gary. Walking back to the children's home with Nick, she felt in the best spirits she had known since first coming to London. They shinnied up the old oak tree, whose leaves were just beginning to turn in the first hints of autumn, slid open the window, climbed in and padded softly down the landing into their rooms, Nick's in another part of the house - the boys' section.

Now, waiting for the bus, she felt again the bag containing the new trainers and hoped Gary would be impressed – Gary, boss of the Twickenham Boys, Nick had said. But was he the boss, she wondered. Gary had said the person who owned that nice house was boss. This was a complicated world, she thought, something her simple background had not prepared her for. In the sitting room of the home, at night, when the television was switched off and if no-one was around, Nick would divulge a bit about Gary and the gangs. He was very guarded, she noticed, and only dropped morsels but they did satisfy her for the time being. At one level she was horrified and distressed that she had met a gang leader and his boys and that she had implied agreement to further acquaintance, but the sensation of acceptance, the concern Gary had extended to her, the feeling that with these kids there was at least some sense of belonging, some return to her old way of being in the world, gave her some sort of hope. All this was too much to fight against; this way promised some progress, some comfort - a means to survival. She breathed a little lighter for finding herself in this avenue.

Traffic pulled slowly along the road – buses, cars, taxis; pedestrians too, many in saris, passed close by her on the other side of the bus shelter, which was festooned with graffiti. Shabby shop fronts faced each other on either side of the street, and old leaves gathered here and there on the side of the pavement. There was an air of dilapidation, of hopelessness, and the girl slid her hand into her jacket pocket, where it folded round her pack of cigarettes. The whole area had seen better days, but she was unaware of that. For her the place was filled with strange people - people with alien, closed faces; dead, inanimate eyes, all seemingly slotted into lives that somehow moved them along, albeit in some shabby, down-at-heel way, but nevertheless moved them along, gave them lives, a reason to live. And for a moment she was envious of them. But they were not of her kind and never could be. By the roll of the dice they belonged. She stood apart. They could act with intent and purpose. She could not; her actions now were only responses to situations. Perhaps she would become an outcast. She prayed silently to Becky. Becky Sharp! If she kept her mind fixed on Becky, she would win through. And on Gary; and she nudged her bag containing the trainers again.

Chapter 2

An Education

Kathy adopted Nick's style of attending his school some days and taking others off. This way she just kept herself enrolled at St. Margaret's, but it was a perilous arrangement. She knew that truancy was not tolerated at good schools. However, there was no alternative: at school she felt inferior and ostracized and without an identity. With Gary and the others some of her old personality returned, and she felt a certain relief about this.

One evening Nick again stole up to her room. 'Tomorrow we're doing a job; leastways Gary is. He wants me and you to go with him. Me and you, just us!' His deep blue eyes glinted in anticipation of something exciting.

The next morning Kathy swung her school bag on her shoulder and left the home, as usual, at 8.15 am to catch the bus to St. Margaret's. Instead, when out of sight of The Haven, she changed her direction and went to the Rag, a small bit of common land that had been left undeveloped, and onto which fronted a few shops, including a convenience store, a liquor shop and a video store, all of which did good business. Often the kids met here, mostly after school hours, but sometimes during the day also. They left an unsightly mess on the pavement after their longer meetings much to the annoyance of the shop owners who had to clean it up.

Kathy had been told Gary would be there waiting for her. He was not there when she arrived, but she was early and propped herself on a bollard to await Prince Hal, as he liked to call himself. She wondered if he knew anything about this son of Henry IV and of his fame acquired at Agincourt. Gary was a mystery she could not fathom at the moment.

Nick was the first to arrive and he too lounged on one of the several bollards, all of which had been placed there to deter 'hooligans' with their bikes and skate boards from doing damage to property. Kathy smoked the cigarette Nick had given her, and noticed it made her cough less. 'I'm getting the hang of this,' she thought with satisfaction, and was conscious that one more piece of this new puzzle was fitting logically into place. Her old self was slipping away, but another one, altogether leaner, sharper and more efficient was slowly developing. This is exactly what Becky Sharp would be doing in these circumstances, she thought consolingly. She survived; I'm going to survive! Becky, that wily, hard, ambitious young woman whom she had first met in the last term at her old school; the anti-heroine of Thackeray's acclaimed novel, Vanity

Fair, who was determined not only to survive but to survive very well by whatever means at her disposal.

In ten minutes or so Gary arrived and led them round the corner to his car. Kathy had not envisaged Gary having a car, but there it was – a spanking new, dark blue BMW and a big one!

'Get in,' he told them both. 'Kathy, you're sitting here in the front with me.' Kathy obediently took her place in the front, and gazed at the dashboard with its smart display of numerous dials and buttons, and admired the technological sophistication and the comfort of the car. She could understand why young men loved this sort of thing; in its own way, a masculine way, it was very beautiful, but nothing her father would have ever craved.

'Where are we going?' she asked politely, as if she were with a teacher or the father of a school friend.

'Brixton,' was all Gary said.

'To Bardo's place?' asked Nick from the back.

'Yup, Bardo's place,' returned Gary.

'What does Bardo do?' asked Kathy.

'You'll see, kiddo,' said Gary and was then silent. Kathy looked out of the window and watched the shabby houses and businesses pass by as they drove to Brixton. It was certainly all very different to the place she had come from.

Bardo was a black man who seemed to own a clothes shop selling designer apparel very cheaply, some of which had spilled out of the shop and which was hanging on stands on the pavement. Kathy thought she detected a shadow cross Bardo's face as the BMW pulled up opposite, and they all got out. But the next moment Bardo was all smiles, showing big, white, regular teeth, and Kathy forgot that look of apprehension she thought she had first seen.

'Business,' said Gary, answering Kathy's question of some time ago, and strode into the shop, Bardo following behind obediently.

'Kathy, stay there,' said Gary. It sounded almost like an order, and so she stayed outside and inspected some of the designer apparel. Nick came over.

'That ain't no designer clothing,' he said in a low voice. 'But Bardo does well; very well.' Kathy looked to where Bardo was talking with Gary, and, at that moment, she saw him giving Gary a large wad of bank notes. Gary stuffed them in his pockets, said something more to Bardo, who was still smiling, and strode back to Nick and Kathy.

'Fancy a cup of coffee?' he asked. They assented and went into a smart little coffee shop a short distance away. A group of youths, all black, got up and left at the same time. Kathy could have sworn it was the sight of Gary that was behind their departure.

'Did you complete your business, then?' asked Kathy, trying to make conversation.

'Yup, I did, sis,' said Gary, staring at the coffee menu board.

'What was it?' she ventured politely.

'Girls don't ask no questions,' he replied gruffly, and that was the end of that conversation. Nick and Gary talked about the big soccer game of the previous evening, something that obviously peeked the interest of both.

After a short time they got up and went out, and walked further down the street, Gary sometimes disappearing into a shop to get more payments for some work he must be doing for these shop owners, conjectured Kathy. Finally, at lunch time, Gary announced he was finished and they would go home. But first he stopped at a newsagent's and bought the Financial Times newspaper. 'Just to keep up with things,' he said importantly, winking at Kathy.

After a quick lunch in a burger restaurant, they returned to the car. Bardo was standing beside his wares. Beside him another black man, quite elderly, was sitting in an old chair, smoking, and blowing rings. Bardo gave them a friendly smile and waved.

'Ganja rings,' said Nick proudly, recognizing the smoke rings. 'He's doing ganja rings.' Kathy remained silent, not wishing to appear naïve. 'Hemp, weed,' supplied Nick helpfully. 'He's the best in London!' Gary started the engine and they were soon cruising along the main roads back to west London. Rap music was playing on some CD and Kathy set herself to listen to the words, and was shocked by them.

"I like your shoes,' said Gary, without looking at them.

'Thank you,' said Kathy. 'I like them too,' and was satisfied Gary had noticed them at last. She looked at his shoes – white trainers – and then her eye was caught by something shiny sticking out of his pocket. It was a knife, a carving knife she thought. Upon getting into the car Gary had taken off his jacket, and now Kathy saw a huge, deep scar on his left forearm and another one lower down on the top of his wrist. The image of her parents unaccountably flashed into her mind. What would they think, she thought, if they could see her now?

It took some time to get back to Hounslow; Gary had another call to make in Clapham. Once more they all climbed out of the car and walked a block to a small parade of tawdry-looking shops. One of these was selling jeans and tee shirts and the whole shop front was open to the street. Gary disappeared inside and went to the back of the shop. Nick and Kathy had stayed back at the entrance, not sure if he wanted them with him. Kathy noticed a strong smell in the shop, not quite like cigarette smoke, but similar. It must be marijuana, she thought.

'Smell the weed?' asked Nick quietly.

'What's he doing?' asked Kathy.

'Drugs,' said Nick. 'He's buying weed and ecstasy and speed, I think.'

'Ah,' thought Kathy. 'He's paying for it with all that money from Bardo.' 'What will he do with it?' she asked. 'Is it for him?'

'No, stupid, he sells it on. God, Kathy, you gotta lot to learn!'

'Yes, I have,' she accepted readily. 'And what I don't understand is why Bardo gave him all that money.'

'Protection. Bardo pays Gary and his boys for protection; they protect him from thieving, violent criminals. There's other gangs there in Brixton and they would give Bardo trouble. So, Gary's lot – that's me too – give him protection.'

'But you're all far away from Brixton, how can you protect him?'

'Gary has tentacles,' said Nick knowingly, and would say no more.

'Who's Gary's boss?' ventured Kathy, sensing an opportunity to glean more information.

'Dunno, kid. To me, Gary's the boss.'

'But that house we were in; who owns that?'

'Like I said, kid, I dunno.'

They fell silent as Gary returned with a Waitrose plastic bag stuffed with something on top of which lay two bottles of coca cola. It looked like a bag full of regular shopping. They resumed their seats in the car, and Gary started the engine again.

'I'm just like Jamie Dimon,' he said, when the car was running smoothly on a main road. 'Know who he is? He's the CEO of JP Morgan Chase, and he used to run Citigroup – huge organisations. Quite a guy, eh?' Kathy remained silent not sure if he was addressing her or himself. 'I'm just like him,' he continued. 'I'm the head of a big organisation too. We're the same! We're both smart – that's what you do when you're smart – head up a big organisation. That's what we both do, but I'm smarter, because my organisation is outside the law. I have to run it *and* I have to keep the cops clear of everything, stop them sniffing around. The cops never bother Jamie Dimon and his kind. They only go for people like me. They're prejudiced, see! He does just as many illegal things as me, only he's above the law. The government decided he's not doing things illegally. So the police don't give him no trouble. So, his job's easy, really. I could do it, if I wanted, but I prefer *my* work!'

Chapter 3

———~w∘⊶⊙⊱⊙⊶∘w——

On the Moors

S he knew she shouldn't look at the sun, but she did it anyway. That ball of pulsating yellow, always there, if often hidden from view. How little attention she paid to it, but how much it changed things if it did shine, like today. How warm and relaxed she felt. How beautiful the moors looked. If there was a good summer her grandfather's raspberries and strawberries would do well, and he would be happy. If there was sun at the weekends, she would take her bicycle out and ride round the village, and sometimes ride to the next village, and feel exhilarated, which to her was the best form of happiness. If the sun was shining on a Sunday afternoon in the summer, the whole family would have tea in the garden, and the warmth and the chocolate cake would bring relaxation and a feeling of wellbeing to everyone; any tension would be dissipated, and her mother might laugh, which brought happiness to Kathy's heart. And Susie might relate some trivial incident that had occurred at school, which was of great importance to her, and her childish, blue eyes would be troubled by an uncharacteristic seriousness. Then they would all listen, and Kathy's mother would respond with a motherly, sensible suggestion, and Susie would lapse into her untrammelled and unchallenged innocence again, while their father would stretch out his long legs in his deck chair, turn his face to the sun, and make a joke of Susie's story, which, momentarily, confused the child, and caused her brow to pucker, while she considered this new, illogical angle. Granfy would still be eating his strawberries, pondering, with each mouthful, on the quality of the taste. But he would also be listening to Susie, and might proffer a comment, often facetious too, and which Susie was learning to ignore. It was called 'Granfy's leg-pulling'. Susie was not yet sure that she liked it.

Kathy continued gazing at the sun and wondered if she would go blind at some point. She noticed there were many rings or auras around it, and that the pulsating movement of the sun itself, that she seemed to see, always kept within its own perimeter. She gazed in a lazy way, noticing how the colours of this fiery star seemed to vary between yellow and white, and how there were distinct markings on it; it was not a blank disc; like the moon, there were contours. She closed her eyes; she was beginning to feel dazzled.

She was twelve years old and she was lying on the August heather, deep in the Northumberland moors. The heather too burned, but in a different way. It filled the landscape, as far as she could see, with a blazing purple, set off here and there by green bracken. Yes, that was it – the landscape glowed under that fiery sun!

Her eyes moved from the sun across the blue vastness that held it, a blue that seemed to recede into ever more blueness and space the more she looked at it. Someone had once said you got an awful lot of sky in Northumberland. She wondered why this should be. It did seem true, at least on days like this, when there was hardly a cloud in the sky; just a little puff here and there. Perhaps it was because there were fewer people in Northumberland. She looked across to the Cheviot Hills, an uneven mauve shadow in the far distance, and felt she could be the only one out on the moors.

She rolled over and contemplated the brittle roots of the heather going down into the hard ground and the small insects that crawled around down there, all engaged, she supposed, in purposeful activity, perhaps foraging for food, perhaps looking for a place for rest. The sheep's path that she had taken lay a few feet away, and this led onto the path that she had taken from her house. She loved to come out here, and it was not a long walk from home. She simply followed the path out of the back garden gate, up through the wood of oak and beech, over the fence, across a couple of fields and then into the wildness - land that had not been annexed by farmers, not cultivated – and on and up into the moors, till she felt deep in untouched nature. On these hot days, which only occurred in July and August, lying in the purple landscape, she could forget everything – all the minor stresses of her life; she could lay them aside, drowse in the balmy warmth, revel in this short time of aloneness, and dream strange, lucid dreams of people and enchanted places that she half remembered from her early childhood, from the books her parents had read to her, and from other strange memories.

It was hot! Even though the sun was well past its zenith, the afternoon seemed to be generating more and more heat that showed no sign of abating. She stood up, instinctively feeling that to continue lying in the sun would bring on a headache. She followed the sheep path, but before it joined the main path, she veered off on another one, tiny and indistinct, that wound a twisting route through the heather. After some minutes, she arrived at the burn. Sometimes her father would bring her here with Susie, and they would fish for minnows and sticklebacks with their fishing nets, and put what they caught in jam jars, and then at the end of the afternoon they would throw everything back into the water. And watch the little fish rejoicing in their freedom again and swimming quickly away.

Taking her plimsolls off, she climbed down the shallow bank, and, holding onto some round rocks, lowered herself into the water. It was cool and the water closed around her legs in a pleasing way. The bed of the little river was uneven and she had to be careful to find rocks around the deep holes, on which to place her feet. At last, near the middle of the burn, she found a large flat stone that was perfect to stand on, and, although the water was up to the top of her knees, it was only flowing gently, and she could balance without any difficulty, especially as the stone was not slippery.

She looked down at her legs in the transparent, brown water. About a dozen little fish had gathered there, and hovered, seeming to be inspecting her skin. She gazed down at them in the clear, clean water - little minnows, surprised by this strange intrusion into their world. Periodically, one or two would suddenly dart away and then return. What were they doing, she wondered. Susie did not like this experience and always moved her legs to be rid of them, or else climbed out of the water, but she, Kathy, enjoyed it, found it interesting. She edged off the flat stone and disturbed a frog, who leapt out of the water onto the next stone and then onto the bank. It was necessary now to bend double and keep her hands on the stones that were above water level, because the stones under her feet had become small and slippery and unwelcoming to groping feet.

Even so, in her bent posture and concentrated attention, she was aware of the hot sun beating down on the water and her back. The water, which surged and flowed round big stones, through narrow gaps, over flat stones, bending the river weed in a forward movement, pushed slowly and effortlessly past the banks on either side and took anything that was loose and unattached in its onward motion. A stick and a leaf flowed haplessly by.

She stood, like the rocks and stones, immovable, rooted, the flow unable to take her, but rejoicing in the energy all around her of this sparkling, pure water that was brown beneath and silvery above. The fish had now all departed from her legs, she observed, and she continued her tortuous progress across the burn. Suddenly, her foot, encountering a very slippery round rock, lost all hope of anchoring itself, and carried on down the far side into a deep hole. She found herself up to her neck in water and greatly surprised. She had not known there were such big holes, that the river was quite that deep. Panicking for a moment, she imagined strange, unfriendly fish lurking in those depths, and expected to feel a bite on her legs. But getting out of her predicament required her to think carefully, rather than give vent to her fears. Using a breast stroke with her arms, she was able to raise her legs, and, bending them against her stomach, she gradually propelled herself back to the bank she had climbed down minutes before.

Hauling herself up by bracken and river alder shoots, she attained the top of the bank, her clothes streaming with river water. She decided not to go home immediately (she was not supposed to go in the river alone) and stretched herself out on the grass on the bank.

The sun was lower in the sky, but still hot, and soon her clothes would be dry. They would be dry by tea-time, and, being Saturday, there would be scones. She listened to the lively stream, watched a buzzard overhead, and heard its strange, plaintiff call, and felt the heat of the afternoon drying her shorts and tee shirt, and fell asleep.

Chapter 4

—~∽∽◌⌇◌⌇◌∽∽~—

Gary and the Gang

I t was four in the afternoon. Kathy had been used to thinking of this hour of the day as tea-time, especially at weekends and in the holidays. Now it was a kind of free time, but also an uncertain part of the day, when there was usually no-one at the home properly qualified to supervise the kids. Mike had given permission for television to be watched. But, apart from one or two of the younger ones watching the usual soaps, no-one bothered.

'Coming up to the Rag, Kathy?' Nick approached her, as she sat, looking vacantly about her, on the sofa in the sitting room. Unsmiling, he beckoned her. Nick's style in the home was to be as unsociable and sullen as possible. The kids had been meeting here almost every day since the convenience store opened a few years ago, although numerous complaints by the public and a few interventions on the part of the police had sporadically curtailed their meetings.

Nick and Kathy arrived to find the group was all but complete. Nick went into the shop to buy cigarettes and chocolate. Kathy stood at the edge of the motley crowd of kids, youths with hoods pulled over their heads and a few girls, and observed the rows of studs in ears, the odd stud in the bottom lip, the stones that glistened on the sides of noses, and the steel ring in someone's tongue. One youth had his arm in a sling, and another his hand heavily bandaged. (Probably from a gang fight, thought Kathy.) Hair was greased in the usual way to stand up on the head. The girls all wore heavy eye make-up, and three of the four of them slouched submissively. The boys sniggered or laughed in high-pitched, unnatural voices betraying suffocated emotions. Like a herd of bachaelor animals, they knew their place, and stayed there diligently.

Kathy looked at Gary. In sweatshirt and jeans, but no hood over his head, he was busy swinging his body in a horizontal position on a bollard, which supported his weight, on alternating arms. Kathy watched, admiringly. 'He's strong,' she thought. 'and good at it; but then he would be for someone going to the gym every day.' One or two of the other youths took to imitating Gary, and started swinging too, falteringly at first, until they fell into some sort of rhythm. Like a gymnastic competition, thought Kathy, and wondered at the momentary beauty the boys were creating in this forlorn area, the Rag. The girls giggled and made appropriate comments. Tina, a bit bolder than the rest and festooned with ear studs, jumped onto a seat, which had been placed nearby for the public to sit on, mounted the back and jumped down. She ran round and repeated the movement, two others joining in. Soon the small shopping area was a flurry of activity and discordant sound, as the girls disported themselves on their apparatus, screeching with forced enjoyment, while the youths, watched, chortled, and laughed in their strangulated way. The few customers, making a wide berth around them, complained loudly and the more confident ones threatened to call the police. Kathy watched the scene with apprehension; the only girl not to be engaged in hurling her body up and down the seat, she stood out. She stood apart from the youths too. She was clearly an outsider. She had missed her moment; now it was too late. She could not even bring herself to snigger and laugh in the way the others did. She had never laughed or giggled in that way.

'What's up, little sis?' called Gary, still twirling himself, amazingly, on his arms.

'Nothin',' she replied, quickly and defensively. Regretting her slow-wittedness, she looked around for some face-saving prop, something that would restore her belongingness. 'You're not street-cred,' she thought with anxiety.

At that moment Nick emerged from the shop with his purchases stashed in his pockets. A bollard became free as a youth ceased twirling, nursing his aching arms, exclaiming. Depositing his purchases on the end of the seat, Nick jumped onto the bollard and began twirling. Not as big and muscular as Gary, he was nevertheless strong in his slim, wiry body, and his twirling was as impressive as Gary's. The kids who were not engaged in the activity giggled and laughed their appreciation at this new performer, standing warily on the pavement, drawing furtively on cigarettes.

'Right, that's it,' said Gary, jumping down from his bollard, not giving any indication that his arms ached, as surely they must, Kathy thought. Everything came to a halt. The ring master was back in his accustomed place. That is, everyone except Nick, who kept on twirling.

'Hey, f..... you,' shouted Gary. 'I said "stop".' Slowly, Nick brought his circles to a close with an elegant jump from the bollard.

'Great stuff, little Nick, great stuff,' and Gary cuffed him round the back of the neck, as the younger boy passed him. Nick flinched feeling a sharp pain on the back of his head.

'You're gonna get hurt one of these days, little Nick; you're gonna get really hurt!' Nick laughed nervously, a laugh of obeisance while he fumbled to re-find his place in the order of things. His moment of independence had not been worth it.

'And what's the matter with little sis?' Gary's gaze swung round to Kathy. Nervously, like Nick, having lost her place in Gary's scheme of things, she returned his gaze, carefully, deferentially, disguising her fear. 'Not afraid of me, little sis?' Watching his eyes for clues to the correct answer, she paused a second, then said: 'Course, I am, Gary.'

'Been at that school of yours today?'

'No,' she replied, aware there was some pride in her voice.

'Why not? You should go. You should be getting an education, like. Then you can help us here with all the f ..... forms we fill in.'

'Oh I couldn't do that,' she offered again.

'You having me on, little sis?' Gary narrowed his eyes and regarded her for a second or two.

'Never, honest,' she said, trying to sound like the girls, and aware that, although Gary often gave the impression he was stupid, those small, blue eyes, cold and hard as flint, were as wily as a fox's.

'Come here!' he commanded. He had taken off his jacket, revealing thick battle-scarred arms, decorated here and there with tatoos. 'Come here!' he commanded again. Kathy obediently stepped to his side, thankful for the new row of studs in her ears and her new training shoes, and hoped these would appease him. 'Little sis,' he said. 'You've no reason to be afraid of me. You're my little sis, my long-lost little sis, and you've come to help us, see. You're clever, see, and I've got a job for you.' And this great hulk of a youth, not yet a man - this big, strong lad, who would most likely never become a man - put his arms round her shoulders, and drew her protectively towards him. She felt the powerful muscles, the body of a great warrior; she smelled the odour of his sweat, and she knew the protection he was offering, the place in the pecking order – the pride of place, perhaps the number one place – and was comforted and safe. She relaxed into his great strength, felt a certain victory, felt strengthened for the next round of life.

Chapter 5

—⁓∽⌬⌬∽⁓—

The Fatal Divulgence

Nick and Kathy left the group. Beer and lager cans lay all over the pavement outside the shop. She knew they would not get picked up and that the shop manager would call the police again, who would come again, and tell the kids again to move on – to another place. And Gary would, of course, oblige (it was all part of a game the police and Gary played) and take his harem of females and eunuchs to another patch on his territory, the precincts of a new shopping centre about a mile away.

But for now the group dispersed, the kids went their separate ways, and Kathy and Nick walked back to The Haven.

'I like your shoes, Kathy,' ventured Nick, as they walked up the street, under the leafy boughs of a few harshly pruned trees. Kathy did not reply; she was aware Nick was angry and ill-at-ease with himself after this humiliation by Gary. She walked on in silence, conscious of the new disparity between herself and Nick. Certain sands had shifted, and she found herself on the right side of this quicksand of danger that lay all around Gary, while Nick, by an act of momentary negligence, found himself in a perilous position. Cognisant of the absolute necessity of maintaining her advantage, she continued in silence. Suddenly, Nick grabbed her hand, which had been swinging by her side. Kathy withdrew it instantly, angered by Nick's presumption.

'Kathy,' said Nick, in an imploring tone.

'Shut up,' she replied. 'Shut up, Nick. You're a fool.' Nick tried again. His strong, lean hand enclosed hers, tightly, pleadingly. Kathy felt the anger rise in her, and again she withdrew her hand sharply. 'Get lost! Or else I'll tell Gary you're bothering me.' Surprised and chastened Nick took up a position a pace behind Kathy, and fell into a sulk, or so she thought. However, a short distance before the home he caught up with her. They walked a few paces in silence, then Nick withdrew his hand from his pocket, revealing a small green shammy-leather pouch.

'Got some ecstasy,' he murmured slyly. 'Want some?' Kathy understood. Like a small child, he was flailing around for acceptance. She was disgusted.

'I don't do drugs, Nick, so get lost!'

'Don't you, Kathy?' said Nick in feigned surprise. 'Don't you?' And Kathy instantly felt he was locking this divulgence away in some secret part of himself.

*   *   *

It was late September, and the leaves on the trees were blossoming into their full autumn colour. Not the small leaves of the hawthorn in the street, which remained a dusty green, Kathy noticed, but the chestnuts and the oaks on the common. Wide branched and high, they were becoming a burnished gold from the distance; nearer to they were light brown and often full of insect holes. Here in the space of the grassy pasture of the common, untouched by pruning machine, they flourished and lent a rural presence to the townspeople, who, for the most part, unheeding, scurried across the green spaces, bent on their pressing affairs. Only the young mothers, who sat on the seats and watched their small children play on the grass, seemed appreciative of this haven of nature. And the old people too, who dozed in the gentle sunshine and who seemed to have come to a sort of reconciliation with life, seemed grateful to be there amongst the trees and birds.

Kathy sat down and watched the sparrows turning over the leaves on the path, and the blackbirds hopping in the grass, hunting for worms, and was suddenly reminded of Ma Riley and the time they had watched the little mouse in her kitchen. How free and easy her life had been. She seemed to have some secret others did not have; she seemed to have so much time to appreciate and marvel at nature; she seemed to be a part of it, like the animals and birds are, Kathy reflected. How did she, alone, have the time to be like this, when everyone else was always rushing around? Even the vicar, who people looked to as an example of the right way to live, was always hurrying, as though he too felt life must be caught, controlled and manipulated, before it got away. So little time to do everything!

How different Ma Riley, the old gypsy woman back at home, had been! She had always had all the time in the world! 'But she hasn't achieved much,' she could hear her mother saying. 'Poor Ma Riley!' How Ma Riley would have appreciated the beauty of these trees, how she would have enjoyed this gentle autumn sunshine, how she would have loved to see these young mothers, just taking time to be in nature with their babies. It was Ma Riley who had taught her to take notice of nature, to listen to the trees and the running water, to observe the little animals and the insects. It was Ma Riley who had first drawn her attention to the work of the Creator. 'The Creator is all goodness, Kathy, all love. Just think of that!' she had said. 'Just think of it, Kathy. Don't just hear it, like everyone else does; listen to it, make it your own.' She should have been at school, and a slight twinge of guilt hit her. To skip school was not an act of goodness. What would Ma Riley think of her life now, Kathy wondered. Would she understand the choices she was now making? Would she understand her predicament? 'Always be good, Kathy,' she had said. 'Take the path of goodness. It may seem difficult; it may lack glamour, but it is the way of the Creator, and it always triumphs in the end.' Well, the fact was Ma Riley was wrong. The fact was she did not have choices. The fact was the gang was the best way forward for her, the only way, and whether the gang was good or not was not something she could afford to be concerned about at the moment. Goodness, she saw now, was rather a luxury. The fact was she had to use her intelligence to get herself out of this mess God and the social workers had put her into, and she blessed the fact of her intelligence. Her intelligence would help her survive. No, she must turn her mind now to the important things of life, the most pressing things of life, the matter of her very survival. Ma Riley, it was clear, had never had to deal with such a chronic situation as she now found herself in.

Yes, she should have been at school, but too bad, she thought; it was more important right now to pay attention to her credibility amongst the gang members. Gary knew everything – who was doing what and where and who was trying to go straight. He must have spies everywhere, she thought. Who were they? The other kids? Who could she trust then? If Gary thought that she was trying to go straight, trying to do well at her school, she knew she would have to pay. They could be very violent, these youths, she was learning, and Tina had recently told her that Gary had killed someone in a fight with another gang. 'Last year,' said Tina. She had remained calm, while Tina had imparted this information, determined to take it like Becky would have done – unsurprised, searching for the opening, the opportunity for some advancement of her own cause. But, as so often now, there was nothing that Becky could help with here. Perhaps Becky had had an easier challenge. It was painful to think that might be true; what she sought above all was the reassurance that Becky's path had been hard and brutal; but certainly Becky had not had to deal with the fear and the threat of violence that underpinned her, Kathy's, world. But it was inconceivable that she abandon Becky. In some indefinable way, the image of Becky Sharp was profoundly helpful, and Kathy allowed the feeling of Becky to float pleasurably and inspiringly around in her mind. Becky Sharp, that flint-hearted anti-heroine of Thackeray's masterpiece, Vanity Fair, which had kept readers in Victorian England enthralled, as each new instalment came out in a weekly magazine.

Kathy had had a rather good week. She had counted her progress with Gary as a great success, and had almost forgotten her faux pas with Nick. She had also started at a new school. She had been asked to leave St. Margaret's due to 'chronic truancy' and was now attending Michael Mount, a much less privileged school and hosting many children from poorer families. Kathy felt herself much more comfortable in this less prestigious environment. Mike, the 'father' of the Haven, for reasons of his own, had decided to drive her to school every day, and, somewhat to her embarrassment, deposit her safely with her teacher. However, this minor humiliation was soon got over, as she joked and bantered with her class-mates. Her wit stood her in good stead here at school. And she was in the right set. A rough lot with a certain power in the school and including several bullies among them, Kathy was finding a comfortable place in the order of things here. There was not much leeway, but there was not a Gary in this school gang. There was not that challenge to be reckoned with and to manoeuvre around constantly. However, this was still Gary's territory. Those kids who lived in the vicinity of the school and who spent time on the streets automatically found themselves on Gary's turf, and had to adjust their behaviour accordingly, or face very unpleasant consequences. Most of the kids stayed indoors or mooched around small gardens.

Suddenly, the young woman on the bench opposite, who had been on her mobile phone for the last ten or fifteen minutes, got up and walked away, still talking into her device. 'Once upon a time,' Kathy recalled her mother saying 'people used to talk to each other on the trains. Isn't that strange to think of? Now they all talk with machines, as though no one else were there.' Her mother! There, she had done it again! Tears welled up in her eyes, and she felt her stomach melting into weakness. She tried to think hard about Gary and her present life; she tried to enjoy this warm September day; the common was serene and unthreatening, full of normal people with normal lives. But her thoughts did not obey her will. She wondered what was happening in her little village near the banks of the Tyne.

Chapter 6

———∿∾⌒⊙⌒∾∿———

Mickle Wood

Mickle Wood! It was a hamlet set around a green, containing a small, natural pond, fed by the several small gills or streams that flowed down from Kielder, and the Cheviot Hills beyond, into the Tyne. At one side of the green there was the beginning of a big oak and beech wood, which gave off a roaring sound when a strong wind blew from the north. Kathy had always found it strangely comforting; reassuring to know, now and again, that God or nature was in fact in control of things. Several houses and cottages were dotted around the green, including the rectory, which was still inhabited by the rector, and the old manor house, which had now been renovated and made into a smart residence for a rich young family from Newcastle, seeking to escape the barrenness of an upwardly mobile modern life. Mickle Wood had been lucky. In the sixties it had escaped the town planners' axe and had remained untouched, while many other villages had been abandoned, as the planners forced the inhabitants into new towns. The rest of the homes in Mickle Wood were old houses or cottages, which had been built for the wood mill workers in the nineteenth century. The rooms in Kathy's home were small and the ceilings beamed, and between the sitting room and dining room there had been a particularly low beam, on which her father occasionally banged his head.

Her father! Kathy remembered him with all the favour that grief for a dead parent can bestow. Tall and dark, she had worshipped him, and when she was little she would sit on his knee in the evening in front of the big, wood-burning stove in the living room, and be aware of his big, rough hands, calloused by his work, and feel the strength and maleness of his body, as she perched on his knee or snuggled close to his chest. He worked in the wood mill in the next village, and went thence every morning by bicycle. One evening he did not come home. Instead, a car had arrived at the front door, and the news was given to her mother by an ashen-faced man that there had been a terrible accident at the mill. Her mother had rushed off with the man in his car, leaving Kathy and Susie with a neighbour. But there was nothing to be done. Dick Miller was dead. The funeral was three days later.

That scene, in the early evening, had played itself out many times in Kathy's mind since then. Even though it had been a little over three years ago, it seemed like yesterday. That event had changed her life forever, had changed all the lives of her family irrevocably. Her mother had never recovered. Then, as the breadwinner, she found work in a baker's shop in Hexbury, a nearby country town. But she was always tired, and no longer slept well. Kathy loved her mother too, and when her death occurred just six months ago, her world of security, warmth, predictability and promise came to an abrupt and shocking end. Her childhood was over; family life was over. Normality was over - the promise of life gone. Her paternal grandfather who lived with them was found a place in a care home somewhere in Somerset. He had a surviving sister in that county and the social workers had deemed it best he live there, within easy reach of the sister. The social workers! Kathy felt bitterness towards them. They had descended on her family, and had carved them up. They had so much power. Granfy sent to Somerset, and she to West London because there was a second cousin of her mother's living there, who had undertaken some responsibility for Kathy. However, she had only been once to The Haven, the children's home, and Kathy was glad she came no more. She had formed a dislike of Eileen in that first meeting, and she had the impression that Mike, the 'father' of The Haven, did not think she was a particularly good influence on her. Susie, ten years old, and Kathy's younger sister by five years, had been found adoptive parents quickly. A round, blonde little girl with very blue eyes, and dimples in her cheeks, she was immediately appealing, and the adoption process had gone through easily. This stroke of good fortune meant that Susie could stay on at the same school in Hexbury. Momentarily, now and again, Kathy found herself jealous of Susie's 'luck'. She would not be uprooted from her environment; she would continue to have the same friends and see the folk in Mickle Wood from time to time; there would be continuity. By contrast, Kathy felt she and Granfy had been cast to the wolves. They had been ousted from home and county, and sent so far away it could have been to a different country. Numb with shock, and forced to give her full attention to making a survival plan, Kathy had not had much time to concentrate on the different turns of fortune that had befallen her sister. She had promised to write and telephone Susie, of course, but she had not. She had simply not felt like it. Six months ago that would have been unthinkable. 'It is amazing,' she thought, 'that I cannot bring myself to get in touch with Susie.' And she became frightened for herself. What was happening to her; what was she becoming? And what was to become of her? 'Granfy, Granfy,' she thought, 'I must find you.'

Chapter 7

———·—·—·—·———

Forming A New Identity

She switched on her walkman and soon the beat of modern music was thrumming through her head. She tapped her feet on the floor, beat time with her head and gradually the thoughts of what she had been, what her life had been, were dissipated in the insistent throb of the guitar and the drum and the tuneless screeching of the vocalist. But to Kathy it was solace. It drew her away from her memories and into the ever-demanding standards of her peers, into a value system that afforded no joy, but which did extend that belongingness of which she now felt a great need. She allowed herself to be bombarded by this clutter of sounds, by the dark pulsing of the instruments, and the persistent and explicit references to sex.

She pulled the ear buds out of her ears. She had long since been unaware of the music; she must have unknowingly turned the volume way down. But now in the total absence of background noise, and in the silence of her thoughts (because now she no longer thought) she listened to the noises in the children's home, noises with which she was becoming familiar: the other kids banging their bedroom doors, their strangled laughing and giggling, someone running up the stairs, Mrs. Buller, the part-time manager, downstairs, rattling around in the dining room. The noises subtly and subversively entwined themselves into her consciousness, like silently-creeping ivy, moulding and re-shaping some part of her awareness, so that one day, soon, those noises, stealing into her mind, would become a familiar, almost welcome part of her life. She listened to Mrs. Buller laying out the cutlery for supper on the grubby dining table. It would be a chaotic and ill-mannered event, but the sounds of the setting of the table contained some message of order. And then Kathy heard the filling of the kettle, and the responding gurgles in the pipes outside her room, near the water heater. Then she heard Mrs. Buller switch on her radio, low, to catch the evening news. All these sounds Kathy was aware of, and, on a new canvas in her mind, they were delicately embroidering themselves, organising the threads into the first, fragile attempts at creating a picture, a structure in which she could find shelter and solace, a sense of belonging, a new way of being. Certainly she felt a sense of relaxation, a new familiarity in her life, but she would have put that down to her recent success outside the home, her new position in Gary's gang. And the shoes had certainly helped with that!

Suddenly, there was a knock on her door, and before she could say anything a small, black child had entered. Angelina was about eight years old, and had recently come to the children's home, and had not yet learned the ropes of the system there. Even the small children had to learn the ropes - who it was desirable to associate with and who not, how to talk and how to laugh, and how to behave, especially at table, where it was necessary to display bad manners. Kathy was not entirely surprised she should have been selected by Angelina; she was gaining some status in the home through her persistent truanting. But she wondered why the child had come, what she could want of her. There she stood in the doorway, in her blue school dress, and her good training shoes, her black, springy hair done in two pigtails that reached to her shoulders and which were tied in red ribbons. She was smiling broadly and revealing big, white teeth, with a gap between the two front ones, in a face that Kathy thought very pretty. Once upon a time Kathy would have found the child very appealing, but now feelings like this felt out of place, and she had not paid much attention to Angelina, except to note her new presence. The small children were of no consequence in the home; they could not advance the causes of the older children. If any of the big ones paid attention to them it was because of a rare occurrence of kindness, or else to tease them.

But there Angelina stood, smiling and trusting, her big brown eyes fixed expectantly on Kathy's.

'Well?' said Kathy, not quite sure how to initiate things.

'Well, I just thought ……. I thought it would be nice to talk to you, Kathy. Can I come in?' The child spoke very nicely; she not yet learned to talk in the rough way that all the other kids did.

'Of course,' said Kathy, not sure how she should handle Angelina's sudden appearance. In her old life, she would have known automatically how to react and manage the situation. But here it was not normal for a big kid to be kind and sisterly to a smaller one; she might lose kudos. 'What do you want?' Angelina was not put off by the abruptness of Kathy's response.

'Well, I just wanted to see you. I thought it would be nice to talk to you.' And with that Angelina dried up. She began to be afraid that she had indeed made a mistake about Kathy and that she was not welcome. But Kathy softened; there was something about Angelina that reminded her of Susie, and despite herself she encouraged her to come in. Angelina carefully shut the door and came over to Kathy. She settled herself on the bed beside Kathy.

'Oh, Kathy, I do like your shoes,' said Angelina gazing with great admiration at Kathy's new trainers. 'I want a pair of shoes like that, but I don't suppose my mum would let me have them.'

'Why not?' asked Kathy.

'Oh, she doesn't like clothes like that. She always wants me to look 'proper".' Kathy laughed.

'I had a mother like that, once.'

'Did you?' said the child. 'What happened to her? Where is she now?'

'She died,' said Kathy, simply.

'Oh, how dreadful,' said Angelina. 'Were you sad?' Kathy considered this question.

'Yes, dreadfully.'

'I would be too', said Angelina. 'My mother's gone away, and I am very sad about that. But if she died ....' And Angelina suddenly looked very anxious, and stuck three fingers in her mouth, and her eyes filled with tears. 'If my mother died, I would just cry and cry.'

'Where has your mother gone?' asked Kathy.

'We don't know; she just didn't come home one night. I cried all that night, then some people came for me, and now I'm here. She will come home, and get me out of here. I know that. But I wish she would come home now. I don't know where she is. What has happened to her? What do you think has happened to her, Kathy?'

Kathy put her arm around the child, and drew her close, the way her father used to, if she was upset about something. Then Angelina, feeling this kindness and desire to comfort, burst into tears. She cried for a long time, and Kathy let her, knowing there was nothing she could say that would be of any great comfort. Angelina's tears splashed onto Kathy's jeans, and she was reminded of the last time she had cried for her parents and for all the life that she had lost. It seemed a long time ago. She had not dared shed tears for many weeks. It would take away the mood and resolve she needed to adjust to this new life.

'What does your social worker say?' said Kathy.

'She says they don't know where my mother has gone; that she might come back soon, and she might not come back soon; it might be a long time.' And Angelina started crying again, and sucked furiously on her fingers.

'Perhaps she has gone with her boyfriend,' suggested Kathy, not knowing if that was the best thing to say.

'She didn't have boyfriends,' said Angelina. 'She went to work every day, and every night there was just us. Oh, I want my mummy,' and the child wept again. Kathy stroked Angelina's hair, and felt deeply sorry for the child. She was so little to be having to cope with this tragedy. She wondered that the social workers had not been able to find foster parents for her. That would have been far better than a children's home.

As if reading her thought, Angelina said: 'Lynne – she's my helper - found a family who would take me, but, I don't know why, they didn't let me go there. I suppose it's because I must wait for my mummy. Perhaps it's best I wait for her here.' And Angelina, over the worst of her sorrow, turned her eyes to Kathy, and gazed hopefully at her. 'What do you think will happen, Kathy? Do you think my mummy will come back and get me out of here?'

'Yes, I do,' said Kathy. 'I think she has got lost somewhere, and the police will soon find her and bring her back. What you have to do is just be patient and never give up hope. Do you go to a nice school, the school where you were before?'

'Oh, yes,' said the child. 'It's a nice school – it's Rushy Hill; do you know it? I've lots of friends there, and the teachers are very nice. My mummy liked my teacher very much, and helped me with all my homework every night.'

'Well, you have to go on working well at school, and with your homework at night; that way your mummy will be very pleased when she gets back. It's very important that you are a good girl at school and work very hard, and do the sport that they have there.' Kathy listened to her own words with amazement. She was offering advice and a way of life that she herself now found no value in. How could she do this, she wondered. Why was she not honest, advising the child to do as *she* was doing – misbehave so that she could be a good member of a gang? She listened to herself as she firmly encouraged the child to be straight, and to be a good pupil at school. It was a strange feeling. She had never before experienced this dissonance between what she said and what she actually believed in. Was it because she actually did not believe in what she was doing?

The gong suddenly sounded loudly and stridently, throughout the house, responding to the stick wielded by the beefy-armed Mrs. Buller, who appeared to relish this opportunity of striking something with great force. Kathy kissed Angelina and the two of them stood up and went downstairs for their supper.

Chapter 8

—∿∘୧୨୧∘∿—

Memories

Angelina took her place next to Kathy. Kathy wondered how she could hold her own at the table, continue this exhausting ritual of status maintenance that meal times with the other kids demanded, with Angelina sitting beside her, watching her every move. Kathy wondered if she would be true to her word to Angelina or if she would misbehave and invent new and gross bad manners to impress the other kids. Mrs. Buller or Mrs. Tait would often sit with them and try to control the dozen children, but without any success. Supper here was an ordeal, and Kathy could not remember having enjoyed more than one or two meals since she had arrived. They were events usually embedded in the fear that stalked through life in the home. Mrs. Buller talked about the indigestion the kids gave her, and often would not eat with them, but took her meal afterwards. Today, the staff chair at the end of the table was not occupied, and Kathy, with anxiety, expected that supper would be another free-for-all, and that Angelina would be betrayed. Nick, sitting opposite, eyed Kathy and Angelina, with suspicion, confirming Kathy's fears that she was to be 'scrutinised', and knew that any good manners she might want to display to Angelina would have to be sacrificed. Just six months ago, when life had been normal, such a decision would have been unthinkable. To have no choice but to behave badly; what a bad and hopeless place this is, she thought. That was except for Barbara. There sat Barbara at the end of the row on the far side, stubbornly retaining her choice in the matter of behaviour, but also trying to be as inconspicuous as possible, yet standing out like a sore thumb in her aloneness and as a ready target for torment. The teasing of the weaker elements started, and Kathy geared up to defend her position, to survive. She was about to open her mouth and come out with some bad-mannered and tasteless joke, that would have Nick, Carla and the others roaring their approval with raucous laughter, when an awkward hush descended on the throng. Knives and forks that were poised mid-air as accessories to the bad behaviour descended quietly to their places on the table. Kathy closed her mouth, turned round and saw that Mike had entered the room. He took his place at the end of the table, and politely asked for good behaviour, and instructed Carla to start passing round the dishes of vegetables and stewed chicken. The kids maintained silence. None of them was going to break the code of honour by making polite conversation, but none of them was able to summon the degree of insubordination that would be required to challenge Mike. Mike had some quiet power over the kids,

Kathy thought, and she felt a wave of relief sweep through her body, and suspected all the kids were experiencing the same sensation. At least now it would be possible to enjoy supper. Angelina basked in the protective presence of her new friend, and Kathy was aware of it, and wondered how she was going to shake off this new nuisance.

Supper ended and Angelina and the three or four other younger children went off with Mike on some business. The other kids got up and went into the recreation room, where the stilted laughing and conversation resumed. Mrs. Buller came into the dining room and started clearing up the dishes in silence. Kathy watched her, thinking how lucky Mrs. Buller was to have a family to go home to, which she most probably did. She was in step with the world, while, she, Kathy, was out of step.

She rose from the table and went into the sitting room which lay at the end of the house next to the front door. It was a big, wide room with a wide window at the far side, and which was now draped over with thick, off-white, dirty curtains. The cream walls were scuffed and the woodwork chipped here and there from the comings and goings of children not imbued with a sense of care for their surroundings. In one corner stood a large television which, in the evenings, generally had an audience of most of the kids in the house, watching a soap or reality show. At first Kathy had shunned these programmes, but gradually she had felt herself drawn into them, and become fascinated by the stories and the antics of the characters, and now no longer noticed so much what her mother and father would have called 'the appalling behaviour' of the protagonists. She felt she needed relaxation, and this was as good as anything else she could think of. Besides, she was also picking up slang, and ways of using her voice that was proving useful to her in her new way of life, not to mention the new attitudes towards sex – a learning too that she felt was essential to her survival. It was all a far cry from Mickle Wood and her old school and her books - but this was life too. Vastly different, but life; another kind of life, whose rules and standards she had no choice but to learn, she thought.

But the television was off tonight. The kids were still in the recreation room, probably cavorting around the ping pong table, not daring to play properly and seriously. Kathy's attention was caught by a white and blue bowl of red apples. It looked out of place in this room, she thought, but there was still something lovely about it. It stood on a little wooden table in the centre, and seemed to change the room in some mysterious way. Perhaps, she thought, this is a concession to the new wisdom of the government that kids today were not eating sufficient fruit and vegetables. She sat down on the old chintz settee, with the broken springs and gazed at the apples.

Red apples! Her mother had always had a blue and white bowl of apples on the large dining room windowsill. They had looked best, Kathy thought, when they had been red apples. Behind the red apples in the blue and white bowl was the window, giving onto the small garden which ran to the woods at the far end. At the end of the garden were the raspberry canes which her grandfather had lovingly trained over the years. In June and July, when the berries were ready to be harvested, Kathy had secretly gorged herself. Plucking those large, full, red berries had been one of her delights, and she would steal into the rows of the fruiting canes after her return from school and the long bus ride. A few birds would be chirping here and there. It was not the season for the robin, but the chaffinch cheered her with its repeated call, and always there was, somewhere, the cluck cluck of the warning blackbird. To prevent the wildlife gaining access and feasting on the garden plants, particularly the lilies and the roses, a strong fence had some time ago been erected on all sides of the garden, and which was now screened by shrubs and trailing creepers.

Someone else lived there now, but Kathy refused admittance of this fact to her mind. She dwelt, in her memory, on those lovely, long June days, when the mid-day shadow of the house stretched only half way up to the raspberry canes, and the shadow of the canes did not reach the back fence. Beyond the back fence and the gate lay the woods. Often Kathy would go through the gate and wander among the trees, green and shady in the summer, and light and bare in the winter. Here and there grew yew trees, and their twisted, gnarled, wide girths gave the woods an altogether bewitching air. Whether you felt their presence to be malevolent or ancient and kindly, there was, Kathy thought, something compellingly powerful about them, witnesses to a different age, different times, perhaps to a time when magic had prevailed.

Here she would wander for some time in 'her' wood, as she liked to think of it, and then, refreshed, she would return to help her mother with the supper. Sometimes the blue and white bowl of fruit lay on the round oak table that stood in the middle of the small dining room, and Kathy would remove it to the window sill. Her grandfather would be sitting in the next room, which faced south, catching the late afternoon sun and reading his paper over and over - because he kept forgetting what he had just read, Kathy's mother confided to her. He spent the most time on the betting page. Or he listened to the radio, hoping to catch news of the day's racing results. He would have liked to smoke a cigarette, but the rule was he could only do this outside in the garden. Now, as Kathy put knife and fork and spoon onto the white and red check cloth that covered the table, she could hear the low murmuring of the radio in the next room. Often, in those minutes, she would go in and sit with her grandfather before her mother put supper on the table. Then Granfy would turn off the radio and ask Kathy how the school day had been. A tall man, like his son, Granfy's legs stretched out in front of him, one crossed on top of the other at the ankles, his feet clad in soft leather shoes. The grey hair was thinning on his head, but still thick enough, thought Kathy, and in his long face with the long nose and slate grey eyes and shaggy eyebrows, Kathy recognised something of her own face. His sunken cheeks and a certain tiredness betrayed his age and disappearing enthusiasm for life, and his great, bony hands revealed a life-time of manual labour.

'That girl still giving you trouble, Kath?'

'Oh no, that's over, all settled,' replied Kathy.'

'There's my girl; knows how to deal with difficult folks. But never let 'em put one over on you; they'll be up for more, see. One, two, three times, and the pattern's set; they enjoy it, see.'

'Yes, I know,' said Kathy, enjoying these confidences with her grandfather. 'Seems you always get girls like that. I think there's one or two in every class.'

'You'll always hold your own, gel; you're good at sport, like your Dad, and that always gets respect.'

'You were good too, Granfy,' said Kathy. 'Didn't you play rugby league for St. Annes in Lancashire?'

'Aye, aye, I did. Warrington, actually, but that was a long time ago.' And he paused in the conversation to feel the pleasure some memory now afforded him.

Then, at about this time, they would hear the front gate click and her father's footsteps, heavy, but deft, would proceed up the path of the tiny front garden to the door, enclosed in the small, green porch. His bicycle would be propped up against the hedge, and later on he would take it round the back and put it in the shed. Granfy's eyes would light up at the sound of the approach of his son, and six year old Susie would emerge, bouncy and happy, from the kitchen. Then Kathy's mother would come in, wearing her apron, and there would be a short family reunion. Her father would then sit down with a can of beer, which he dispensed into a glass, and would settle himself to listen to his family's news, his long, strong legs stretched out in front of him, so that his feet almost touched his father's. He had taken his working boots off in the porch, and was now wearing his soft, leather slippers. Underneath his thick, dark hair he too had the long Miller face, the long, slim nose and the slate grey eyes, and the thick straight eyebrows. Susie, Kathy reflected, was quite different, and not even like their mother, with her wavy blonde hair and forget-me-not blue eyes. Being neither as clever nor as athletic as Kathy, the family was nevertheless hoping she too would win a scholarship to the big school in Newcastle. For the moment she went to a school in

Hexbury, a few miles away, and, like Kathy, travelled there by bus. She's happy there, her mother had told Kathy. And Kathy had thought, with a pang, that Susie would have been happy anywhere.

'Move yourself, Kathy Miller. Get yourself off that settee, and go and do something useful,' snorted Mrs. Buller unnecessarily. Kathy felt that feeling again in the pit of her stomach; she was on guard again, on the defensive. Mrs. Buller looked at her with her small, piggy eyes set in a fleshy face. In the woman's expression Kathy saw a depressingly idiotic look that seemed to have led her into an habitual attitude of harassment, that made the lives of the more sensitive children one of added stress. And if she chose to favour one child over another it was to increase and enhance the discomfort of the disfavoured one. Mrs. Buller made no pretence of the fact that she had 'taken against' Kathy, and with what power she had she made her communications with Kathy as unpleasant as she dared, particularly when Mike was out of earshot.

'Get in the kitchen, where you belong, and give Annie a hand,' she ordered. Remembering Granfy's advice to stay out of confrontations until absolutely necessary, she was also aware, at an instinctual level, that to give in to Mrs. Buller would be to play right into her sadistic tendencies, and to encourage further harassment.

'No, I will not, Mrs. Buller. It is not your business to order me to work in the kitchen,' said Kathy in a voice as middle class as she could muster. Seething quietly, Mrs. Buller glared at Kathy and retired into the kitchen.

Secretly, Kathy would have liked to have helped in the kitchen, to do something that was quietly normal, familiar and basic, but life now was no longer a question of following the simple routines, but rather of calculating, assessing and manoeuvring. You had to be on guard here, she thought, every minute; careful, vigilant, defensive. That was with everyone except Mike. And she thought of him with gratitude. He was of another order, and his presence gave hope. And that *other* order, outside the home - the bullying, fearful world of Gary - what about that? Kathy knew that Gary's bullying was far more dangerous than anything that happened in the home, that there were no constraints on him, for he seemed to be beyond the arm of the law. He had a calculated cunning, Kathy thought, an animal wiliness that made him the undisputed leader of a large area of this part of London. She wondered if he had killed someone, as Lisa had said. Perhaps he had killed more than once. He seemed to know how people ticked, played on their weaknesses, undermined their strengths, kept them in harness. He seemed to know the consequences of his actions too – when to hold back and when to act and by how much. He was really, she thought, a brilliant tactician, and would have made an outstanding commander in war, possessing that instinctive quality that was necessary in battle. But his sadism and power frightened her. When she thought of him she could feel her chest tighten, and remembered the word 'psychopath' that she had come across in one of the last lessons in ethics in her old high school in Newcastle. She went up to her room and lit a cigarette.

Chapter 9

—∿⌒⊙⊙⊙⌒∿—

Turning Point

'The school has suspended you!'

It was a week later, two days after Kathy had skipped school yet again. The golden sun of an early October evening bathed the garden outside in a pale yellow, a glow that alighted on the tired shrubs and scrawny flowers and scrubby bit of grass that was the lawn, and which, inside, lay across Mike's desk in a gentle, almost a happy way, that lifted Kathy's spirits. The brass desk lamp shone in the reflected light; the water in the glass vase was bright with the light, and cast a white shape high on the wall, and the michaelmas daisies vibrated with colour. Also on the desk lay a letter, and that too was picked out with clarity, the black print highlighted against the bold whiteness of the envelope. Kathy could not understand why the sight of this room, and particularly the sun across the desk should affect her in such a positive way. But there was the matter of the school suspension, and she brought her thoughts back to deal with this new event, and now saw the white envelope, stark and too bright in the sunlight, and felt her spirits sink.

'The one day I did not take you to school.' Mike's voice was stern with authority, but at the same time Kathy felt that he was immensely tired, and, for a moment she felt a great surge of sympathy. He was doing his best, she thought, working to the highest standards that governed his world. But I too am doing my best, she reflected. I too am trying to make sense of my world and act as logically as I can. The difference was that Mike was rewarded and acknowledged for his efforts, was in tune and in step with something nice. There was an assuredness about his way; whereas her own way seemed uphill all the time and bore no illumination; it was a blind struggle impelled by her own inner reasoning. For a moment Kathy felt an overpowering anger with her family for so letting her down. Her father; why did he have to get himself killed in that stupid, undignified accident? Why did her mother let her anxiety get such a grip on her that she should soon afterwards die of cancer? And why could Granfy not rise to the occasion and care for herself and her sister, enabling the three remaining members of the family to stay together, supported in what was left of their lives?

She stood before Mike feeling bereft and betrayed of all she had known and all she had been. She only had three months of her new, burgeoning identity to rely on, and it seemed not enough. Anger gave way to self pity, and she noticed a weakening in her stomach and heart as a wave of grief swept over her. The very word 'orphan' symbolised the utmost in pity and wretchedness that she could imagine, and she recalled the picture of the little match girl in her old story book at home. She kept the tears at bay, and wondered if Mike could see the breaking down of her armour, the cracking of her structure, and the leaking away of something very important. Unveiled, she stood before him, aghast at how easily her front, her mask, had deserted her, and now in territory for which she had no compass. She felt the blood rising to her cheeks, in one of those embarrassing blushes she sometimes now experienced; she felt giddy and wanted to hold onto some furniture to steady herself; she felt quite disoriented and looked away from Mike in confusion, while she fought to quell the waves of emotion that threatened to engulf her. She felt like a trapped animal, but trapped by herself – by a strange, dark, unfathomable part of herself, and this terrified her. Is this a panic attack, she vaguely wondered, remembering that Jennifer, in her old school, had started these a short time ago.

Mike let the moment play out, believing it was a few moments of remorse and regret, perhaps hoping it might lead to an epiphany for Kathy, a realisation of her wrong direction. He gazed at her with encouragement and kindness; Kathy gazed at the michaelmas daisies, endeavouring to draw strength from them and an abatement of the uncontrollable storm that surged in her head and body. After what seemed an age, Kathy shifted her gaze and looked down and saw her shoes. Those big, flashy, macho shoes! She wiggled her toes in them, and with that, the tide of emotion started to recede. Kathy wondered what it was about the shoes that had been the key to her recovery.

She resumed the encounter once more, and looked at Mike with sullenness. For a second each saw into the other's soul; each saw a fellow traveller on the same, hidden path, but each separated by intractable landscapes. Mike wanted to draw her back onto the real path, the path of moral correctness, good behaviour, achievement in the system, but recognised only the vast desert that lay between them, and which was growing bigger by the day, with every new experience that Kathy now underwent in her new life. Like all the other kids in the home she was going the way he had fervently hoped she would not. Was it because she had no choice? Was there something about this life – life at the bottom of society – that made it inevitable that kids would turn out this way, the way of no hope, the way of sex and drugs? Should more money be thrown at the problem of all these problem kids, at the problem of problem families? He had already been through that experiment, and knew it was not the answer. He felt a wave of hopelessness about his job. Not one kid in the home over the age of fifteen was going to make it, except perhaps Barbara, and she looked more unconfident every week now.

And Kathy regarded Mike and felt he did not understand her world, her internal world that had to be made sense of every minute. Mike belonged, she did not. She was an outsider, an inhabitant of a country where there were no clear-cut moral answers any more. 'Oh why, oh why can you not see that, Mike?' She wanted to say. 'I do not choose this path out of perversity, simple naughtiness, or dull-mindedness, as you think; I choose it because I have no choice.'

The moment when she had understood that Mike did not understand and that he was and always would be inadequate to her needs, her strength started to return and the period of panic subsided completely. Perhaps it was the light of the sun that was now moving across the room and now partly resting on herself. It seemed to warm her and it illuminated her shoes. Feeling her confidence swell inside, she put her hand in her pocket and felt her mobile phone and pack of cigarettes, and the confidence waxed.

'If it's the bullying, Kathy, that is changing you, you can always tell me. We can fix that, you know.'

For a moment Kathy believed him. Perhaps she had been terribly wrong, and problems could be fixed. The fear of this life could be made to go away. But she rejected this line of thinking very quickly, and felt that Mike had made a rash statement, a hopeless promise. He was no match for the gang and its leader, Gary. Gary had an enormous power; all the kids in the neighbourhood felt this. Now she felt *she* was the adult, not Mike; she was the more efficient judge of things and life; after all she was learning through experience. No, she had been betrayed by people – her family, the social workers up north, her aunt down here who had not taken responsibility for her – and by the values she had been brought up with; they simply did not work now. No, Becky Sharp was a much better model for her. Becky had fought her way through things, and that's what she, Kathy, would continue to do. Fight and assess and manoeuvre. Strive for survival. 'I want to survive this,' she wailed deep inside herself. 'There must be something at the end; I must survive to find it.'

Mike knew that the moment for any understanding was now over, and drew the meeting to a close.

'Next Monday we will go and visit a special school and enrol you there,' he said quietly.

'Yes,' she said and turned and left the room.

Chapter 10

―――ﾏ∽っﾚ☉ヮﾟ‿―――

To the Bottom of the Hole

It was time to show up in Gary's gang again. She had not been for three weeks – the same amount of time she had been in her new special school. She had decided the special school was for very disturbed kids, and that if she stayed there much longer she would go crazy herself. She had decided it was not a school at all, but a mental hospital for teenagers, where the staff pretended to be teachers. The kids lay about all over the room - on the floor, on chairs pulled together, across the desks, one even had lain on the top of a cupboard – anywhere but at a desk; and the 'teachers' accepted this and carried on as though everything were normal - as if you could teach geometry and biology to people who had set themselves so implacably against the system and everything it offered. What a waste of money, Kathy thought.

But the experience was affecting her too. The system had judged this school to be appropriate for her needs. So this was what she had arrived at now – a holding place for outcasts. She was considered by someone or by a group of people, somewhere, that she was delinquent and that she must go to a place for delinquent children or mad children. She was also amazed - she had not known that her misbehaviour could be perceived in such a harsh way; she had not done anything very wrong, not broken any law. She had merely walked a line that was awkward for the authorities – at least that is what she thought. She had not chosen to walk a path on the edge, to be 'way out'; she had only meant to buck the system a bit in order to survive. How could these people, who held her future in their hands, condemn her to this? Mike was concerned for her, she knew; how could he have let this happen to her? Surely he knew she did not deserve this fate. How could they judge her in this way? There was not much lower she could sink. She supposed living on the street was the next step. True, her social worker had visited her and had 'talked' to her, but Kathy had no respect for her. She was unintelligent and inexperienced, and had demonstrated that she had no idea of the experiences Kathy was going through. She felt herself changing. The old, confident, smart Kathy was almost forgotten; she was now all at sea, she admitted; unsure, wavering. Unattractive, with unkempt hair, studs in her ears, the black clothes that all the kids wore, her large trainers, and that sullen look and attitude – she certainly looked the part and was the part she had set out to be. But she now began to feel that her plan may have been flawed; that she had perhaps omitted something important, and that that omission was now causing something to crumble inside her. Where was she going, she wondered. What had been the point of all her adaptation, all her skilful manoeuvring, her intelligent, quick adjustment? Her brilliance in survival tactics? What had she been thinking of, she wondered. What had been her aim deep down, what had she really wanted? Was it only survival?

Tired by these thoughts and misgivings that she had been rehearsing for days now, she turned again to her mental notebook and notched up all the things she had gained. She had achieved status and thus security in the gang; in a short time she had become a respected member of Gary's troupe. Nick left her alone. And the kids in the home all thought she was the role model to follow. But deep down, when she fleetingly thought of her home and her family, she knew the price she was paying was too high; that it was a terrible price, and that if she went much further down this path there might be catastrophic consequences. Not for her physical safety, she felt; that seemed now guaranteed; but for something far more important, that she could not at present name or describe. Something to do with her very essence, 'with my soul', she said to herself. 'My soul is dying.' And having articulated that thought, she realised it was the truth, and while feeling a great depression envelop her with this revelation, she also felt some strange release, as though, by finding that truth, a door had opened. She rested now in her depression and allowed her mind to wander down the same dead ends of the maze that her thought-life had become, but, now, without being part of it, without needing to find a solution down those well-trodden alleys. She seemed to be looking at herself from afar, and was amazed at this experience.

She roused herself slightly, and wondered what she should do. Some energetic, physical activity, she thought out of old habit. But now there were no exhilarating experiences like a hard game of hockey or netball to lift her onto another level of mental activity altogether, and to banish the previous thought-game as irrelevant, of no consequence. Her spirits were so low that she thought she must be very depressed. Her social worker had wanted to put her into therapy; she had mentioned 'grieving'. She had an appointment next week with someone. But somewhere, now, there was that image of a door, very faint; and there must be something behind it, she felt. How to get there?

Gary knew she had been moved to this school, and seemed to approve of the downward spiral her life was taking, and therefore he no longer constituted a threat, and she no longer felt the need to show up regularly in the gang. But she felt she needed to see the gang again. Why, she wondered. Did she actually like those kids? Did she find something nurturing about seeing them?

So, on this blustery Autumn day in the late afternoon, after school had finished, she walked to the Rag, instead of returning to the Haven, as was her official schedule. Through the little streets, with their white beam and hawthorn trees, turning autumnal now and beginning to drop their leaves; past the sad, little Victorian houses, mostly uncared for, with curtains hanging askew at the bleak and often dirty windows; and past the pocket handkerchief gardens; through the spiritless high street with the various Asian-owned, dilapidated shops; and on until she came within sight of the Rag at the edge of the common.

There they all were, lounging against the bollards and the one lamp post! About a dozen of them. Smoking, drinking cans of lager and beer. Kathy felt intimidated and knew she would have to drink a beer and smoke a cigarette to settle her nerves, and to signal her belongingness.

'Hey, kiddo, where you been all this time?' called Gary, as she approached.

'At James Arnold,' she said. 'I changed schools.'

'Yeah, I know; I heard.' And she felt his informants were all over his turf. He probably knew all about her experiences at James Arnold, and where she went truanting. 'Enjoyin' it?' he queried.

'Yeah, lots!' And she wanted to say: 'are you satisfied, Gary; pleased with me for losing my middle-classness and standards and respectability? Does that tickle you, Gary, reinforce your warped sense of self? You build yourself up on the brokenness of others. You are a king, yes, but a king of a stinking, dung heap.'

Gary, in a sleeveless tee shirt that revealed those thick, tattooed arms, came over to her and put an arm round her shoulders.

'My lil sis,' he said protectively, and now Kathy felt safe. She wondered at the fickleness of her emotions, and at the little control she had over them.

'You come just in time,' he went on. 'We just goin' to Tam's place – his half-way house. His house mate's away a few days, and we all goin' there to do dope.'

'What?' said Kathy, taken off guard by this unexpected turn of events.

'Yeah, sis; we're gonna take dope, and you're comin' with us.' And Kathy saw him wink at Nick. So, her faux pas had caught up with her. Her boasting with Nick that she did not 'do' drugs had boomeranged back on her. Seeing there was no escape, she sullenly agreed. Once upon a time she might have brightly agreed, but here sullenness was the code of conduct among the girls, and what rules she had learned she applied.

They all moved off, and walked away from the common – that airy, golden harbinger of some safety, across which shone the twilight sun – in the other direction, down a mean, little street of a few shops, that petered out in the usual small, semi-detached houses.

Eventually, they came to a street of larger Victorian houses, converted into flats; houses, like all the rest in the area, forlorn and unkempt, and home now to immigrants and the local ne'er do wells. Two or three of these apartments had been taken over by the council, as half-way houses for those considered able to 'return to society'. Tam, who looked to be in his early twenties, had recently, she learned, come out of mental hospital and had been placed in one of these flats. They passed up the small garden that had been concreted over, and stood near the front door. Tam produced his key and opened the door, and all the kids passed inside into the hall. As it was not yet evening, there were not many people around. 'Anyone seeing such a crowd of ill-behaved, ugly young people, as we are,' thought Kathy, 'entering this house, might well be alarmed, especially if they lived here.' But only an Indian woman and an elderly black man were around on the street to see, and they would not report them.

The gang of youths and girls shambled up the stairs, one following the other. Tam was leading and Gary behind him, Kathy near the rear full of trepidation. Drugs; they would affect her mind. Up to now the assault had been on her values and standards, and she had altered her behaviour in order to adapt. But always – well, up to this week - there had been the feeling that she was in control, that she knew what she was doing, that she could pull herself back from 'badness' if she wanted to. But now, with drugs; they would take over her mind and she would no longer have control of who she was. She wondered how events had led to this catastrophe.

The room was sparsely furnished. There was a television in one corner, opposite which, against the wall, was a sofa in a faded green cover. Across the sash windows there were drawn, green brocade curtains, also faded and old, but still intact. The carpet was worn, and a light brown in colour - what her mother would have called tan - and which had doubtless been chosen 'so as not to show the dirt'. Along the back of the sofa Kathy noticed some cushions in gold brocade, which served to lift the whole room into a bit of life. Three of the kids sat on the sofa, two boys and a girl; the rest sat on the floor around the room, their backs resting on the olive-green walls. Kathy sat on the only chair to the left of the sofa. Those on the sofa settled well back into its depths and removed the cushions and placed them along the top of the sofa back.

Gary opened a paper bag and poured a few of its contents into his hand. They were white tablets and looked just like one of the aspirin brands her mother used to use, thought Kathy. Gary told them all the drug was ecstasy, and he walked around the circle putting one tablet into each outstretched hand. Tam followed with a glass of water which he had got from the kitchen. Each received the tablet, like the wafer of bread, she thought, and each drank a sip of water - not alcohol, like the wine of the Eucharist to raise the spirit in you, but, ironically, an agent, too, of the spirit, a liquid that would release the spirit of this new bread, this tablet called ecstasy. She put the tablet in her mouth, her normal dose of spirited courage quite absent, an absence reinforced by the thought of what Gary might do to her if he caught her cheating. Besides, in her depressed state it might lift her, she thought. She took her sip of water from the proffered glass, swallowed, and waited like a lamb led to the slaughter.

Conversation continued in the same desultory, inarticulate fashion, with the glottal 't's and the missed out words, so that Kathy still had difficulty in understanding a lot of what was said, and felt these kids no longer spoke English but a kind of shorthand or patois that was compulsory.

After about ten minutes the conversation gradually became more sporadic, interspersed with exclamations of 'wow', 'Christ', and further slang expressions, all accompanied by the usual strange, asphyxiated laughter. It happened to a few of the girls first, then to one or two of the boys. All the while Kathy remained firm as a rock in a threatening sea, unbending on her island, just there to watch and observe. But was it so threatening, she wondered. She was looking at the green sofa and seeing the old faded print of flowers, roses, spring to life. 'They are amazing,' she thought. 'They are so vibrant, alive. I can even see the stems and the thorns on the stems.' Her eye travelled to the curtains. Here were more flowers - beautiful lilies, roses, foxgloves, peonies - all woven into the brocade in various shades of green thread. The leaves were so delicately sewn, and the flowers seemed to be pulsating with life, and even though it was all green, Kathy could have sworn she was seeing the flowers in colour. The roses were in delicate pink, the foxgloves in mauve, the lilies, white, and the peonies a magenta. With what care they have all been stitched, she thought, aware of so much beautiful detail that she could never ordinarily have seen.

'So, my island, my rock has gone,' she thought, 'and I am now in this sea with the rest, with these lotus eaters. And it is beautiful!' She felt all her carefully-erected defences leaving her; she looked at the golden cushions opposite her and they were exquisite; they too were beautiful in their detail; they were so pleasant, so peaceful to behold, so generous in their nature. 'They are indeed alive,' she thought. 'Some spirit moves in them.' And she gazed at the intricate detail of the flowers embroidered into the material, and felt a well-being she had never known before. She felt a generosity of spirit arising in her own being, starting in her stomach and chest and then gently flooding her whole self. It was more than just her body and mind; this golden spirit seemed to inhabit and pervade all the space immediately about her physical body too. She turned her attention to the others, the kids, and felt she loved them with a new understanding she never would have thought possible. She felt a belongingness with them, a keen relatedness, as though she and they were all one, all part of the same creative idea, all undergoing the same experiences in life, the differences being only in degree and timing and reaction. She saw them as they really were – betrayed, lost, brave, struggling – and found them to be lovable human beings. She really loved them, looked at them with new eyes, with an affection that welled deep from within her. She wondered if Jesus had felt like this - had walked over the hills in Galilee, walked among his disciples, taught the woman at the well – all the time feeling in this state of oneness. It was amazing this state, she thought, so full of joy! And she felt she could accomplish anything, love even the most depraved and despicable human being, could love any criminal.

And now Gary was having sex with one of the girls. The tattoos on his buttocks rippled with rhythmic movement. Kathy watched, fascinated, modesty gone; all thoughts of right or wrong not just banished but seen for what they were: erroneous. 'This is entirely right,' she thought, 'just as it should be. Perhaps not what Jesus taught, but perhaps it is what God wants. It must be; it feels so in accord with everything; all is one now, all is a unity; we are in tune now, in tune with nature.' Two or three other couples now joined Gary and his partner on the floor. Kathy watched in quiet wonderment, aware of every small detail, and all seemed perfectly acceptable, perfectly right. And now the couples started breaking up, and forming other partnerships, and now it was no longer boy and girl, but groups of three or four. This is group sex, she thought, and she watched, bewitched, entranced. She had no inclination to participate herself, and sat quiet and comfortable in her chair, no longer feeling that desperate need to belong, to do as the others were doing. She was the only one not participating, but now it did not matter that she was different. She still belonged; she was still one of them; the difference now was that she did not have to demonstrate her belongingness, her sameness, by action. Things had mysteriously moved on beyond the necessity for action. She belonged, and that was now clearly a fact. How could she not have seen this before; how dull she had been; how lost and stupid. And the knot in her stomach began to relax, and she felt the glimmer of life opening up for her again; and she was conscious of this wonderful sense of well-being. Things were going to be alright again. But better than just alright; much, much better!

After about three hours Gary announced that it was all finished, that it was not safe to remain there any longer, since someone might raise the alarm. Kathy was surprised to see that Gary seemed much less affected than she was, that he could still be aware of the time, of danger, of the small vigilances that somehow seemed to be still insinuating themselves into his awareness. He said that they would all meet there again in three weeks' time. The kids sorted out their clothes, dressed, refreshed themselves with water in the small kitchen, and descended the stairs still in a trance state. They all parted outside the house, and went their separate ways. Kathy found herself in the company of Gary. She was hardly aware of him; she was continuing to notice her surroundings with the same raised awareness and feeling of peace that she had experienced in the room. The slabs of the pavement seemed to be glowing and pulsating, alive with some kind of life; the leaves lying in the gutter or on the pavement were a medley of beautiful colours; the fronts of the houses seemed to be alive too, and the shabby paintwork suddenly shone vibrant and bright. The dahlias and michaelmas daisies and asters – what few there were in these tiny gardens – were bright too, and lovely, and seemed to be singing. Kathy walked along with her hand in Gary's and felt suddenly carefree and happy. It was the first time she had felt so relaxed for many months. Not since her mother had become ill two years ago, had she known such peace. She felt touched by God in wondrous blessing and felt hugely grateful.

'In three weeks' time, little sis, my love,' she heard Gary saying. 'In three weeks you will lose your virginity.'

She barely registered what he was saying, but an image of herself in the sexual act with Gary in that room with all those other people looking on came into vision, and she contemplated it with total equanimity. It seemed perfectly right, perfectly normal.

They parted at the Rag, Gary going the opposite way with several of the kids, and Kathy, who now found herself with Nick, walking in the other direction to the children's home, continued to float along in this state of paradisiacal ecstasy. Nick now took her hand, and again Kathy did not object. Vaguely, she was aware of Nick's great need of companionship, love; probably, she reflected, Gary too, and that only by taking a drug could they express this need and have it satisfied. She wondered again about their mothers. What were *they* doing when these guys were little? Where were they? How had these boys and girls grown up into sexual beings without the vocabulary, both in words and behaviour, to articulate the human need for love and intimacy? No wonder these people take drugs, she thought, and no wonder the rate of coming off them was so low and recidivism so high; these kids just don't have the means of getting love any other way. But these thoughts were only sparsely formed; for the most part she was walking along in a haze of happiness and well-being, only faintly aware of her intellectual observations. The friendly paving stones glowed and felt soft and familiar to her feet. The world, after all, was alright.

Chapter 11

───ᨡᨡᨡᨡᨡ───

Ma Riley

'I don't know anyone else who dries their apples,' said Kathy. 'Don't expect you do; folks don't do these things any more,' said Ma Riley, deftly paring thin slices of the apple which she held in her left hand, skilfully drawing her little knife down with her right hand. 'Folks don't do a lot of things they used to. They'll be sorry. It's all banks, insurance, marketing, advertising today. T'ain't natural. So, it can't go on – and it won't!'

Kathy looked at the slices of apple laid out on old dinner plates on Ma Riley's kitchen floor. The sun was streaming through the window and visibly drying out the apple slices, which were beginning to curl at the edges.

'Good day for drying,' said Ma, noticing Kathy's gaze. 'You only do this when there's a good sun.'

'Yes,' said Kathy. 'It's good to have a nice, hot day now and again. Summer's not been good this year.'

'Well, strictly speaking it's autumn now.'

'No, it's not,' protested Kathy. 'It's still summer. Autumn starts with the equinox in September.'

'That's what folk think,' chuckled Ma. 'First of August; that's Lammas, and Lammas is start of the harvest. That's old Celtic, and they're right. Not noticed all the signs of autumn? Bracken's turning on the moor, blackberries are out, ragwort is turning, chestnut and oak turning too. And here am I with my first crop o' apples.'

'Oh, I don't think that means it's *autumn*. It's still summer; it's only the middle of August,' declared Kathy stolidly, wishing to delay the end of summer; after all they had not yet had much.

'Modern folks here never want summer to end, at least not generally; that's because we don't get much in these islands now, specially up here in the north. But, even so, autumn begins Lammas time. Never heard of Lammas bread? Lammas means 'loaf mass'. The Catholics took this old Celtic custom and used it for their own purposes. The first harvested corn went to make their bread for the mass. So, Lammas became important for the Catholics too. Mind you, they didn't know a thing about Lammas, really. You have to go back to the old people for all that.'

'Who are the 'old people'?' asked Kathy.

'Oh, there's a few around,' said Ma mysteriously, paring off a particularly thin slice.

'Where, who are they?' persisted Kathy.

'All over; well, they were; not many left now. And these modern 'travellers' – they ain't the real travellers, the gypsies; give the gypsies a bad name, they do. The true Roma, now, always with their horses. You couldna' part a true gypsy from his horse. And the children loved them too - the gypsy children. Such good little riders, they were, and they had this love of their ponies and horses. Love your horse, and it'll love you all it's life; that's what they used to say. They were wonderful singers and dancers too, and some were good tinsmiths – made copper pans and all.'

'Why did they never settle?' asked Kathy

'I don't rightly know. Came from India originally. Maybe they were an itinerant tribe there. But what few folks know is the gypsies travelled all round Britain all the year. Folks think it was just for the pony switches. But t'wasn't. Appleby Fair now is famous for its horse trading; thousands gather there today. But before then it was something else.' And Ma Riley seemed to withdraw into herself, as though she were revealing too much.

'Go on, Ma,' said Kathy earnestly. 'What did they really gather for?'

'Ah,' sighed Ma, after a good minute's silence. 'They gathered to make the Great Wheel turn.'

'What, what great wheel?' asked Kathy intrigued.

'Why, the Great Wheel of the Zodiac. Someone had to keep it turning, give it energy. If not, the world might come to an end. They gathered in Appleby, all of them – well those that lived in the north. Came from Tara in Ireland; celebrated Taurus there. Then, after Appleby, they went to Durham. Such a lovely time they had there. That was the festival of Cancer, the Moon; the time of the family; oh, all the families would try and be there for that one. And then on down to York. I think the great god of the Sun itself used to be there in those times. Those were the places where you saw most of the Roma, because Yorkshire was where most of them settled. The horses and the trading – that was always secondary. Though it was the horses that many of them went to Appleby for. Great for the horses there! But really it was the twins they went for. They wanted that magic from the twins.'

'What were the twins?' asked Kathy. But Ma did not hear her, and carried on without stopping.

'Oh, those gatherings! The friends and families meeting up again, and then the feasting and celebrating. Very important it all was! News was exchanged about very significant things, like events going on in the heavens, and weather changes that would affect the earth; the women would exchange their herbal lore, and what changes were going on with the plants. They knew so much, the old people. Hardly any left now. Then after York they did a few more places, and then arrived in London. London, again, was another important centre.'

'I can't imagine how travellers on horses and carts celebrated a festival in London. It's just such a big place, and so, well, towny, I think,' said Kathy.

'Oh, I'm talking about a long, long time ago,' said Ma Riley, 'when it was thought the Roma had the Celtic knowledge. London was a nice city then. Not long after the Romans.'

'Oh, as long ago as that?' said Kathy. 'And what is the Celtic knowledge?'

'I'll not be drawn further, lass; I've said too much as it is. Too much for a young soul like yourself. If you really want to know, the knowledge will come later, all of its own.' And Ma again seemed to withdraw into herself, and remained in silence for some minutes.

She continued slicing little pieces from the apples, sitting with her back to the window, so that the sun shone on her white hair, which was caught neatly into a round bun on the back of her head. Her old brown skirt held the basin into which the apple slices fell, and her stout, bare legs, white skinned, were set foursquare on the stone floor. Her old sandals, which she seemed to wear all the summer, come rain or shine, revealed feet that were in remarkably good shape for an old person. No crossed toes, bunions, corns, or yellowed toenails – her feet had retained their form and health, Kathy thought. Her old, blue blouse, on which Kathy could make out some beautiful embroidery of flowers, covered her ample figure comfortably.

'But I'll tell you, my dear, the surest sign, of all that autumn is here, is the robin. It's the season of the robin, and my old friend, little redbreast, knows that only too well.'

'What do you mean?' asked Kathy fascinated. 'The season of the birds doesn't come till spring, surely?'

'Oh, redbreast knows,' said Ma. 'Just you listen out for him. It's about now he starts his singing. Any time of the day you can hear that little song; you don't have to be particularly looking out for it. Short little bursts. People say it's sad, plaintiff; but I think it's something else.'

'What do you think?' asked Kathy, fearing Ma was going to stop again and not reveal something of great interest.

'Well he's doing two things; first he's happy autumn is here because there are plenty of seeds to eat, especially in the hedgerows and my garden; and second if you know how to listen he's singing about the kind of winter we'll have.'

'Can you tell?' asked Kathy. 'Do you understand his song?'

'My dear,' chuckled Ma. 'You are going to get me to give away all my secrets. All in good time; not all at once.'

'Look,' said Kathy. 'There he is; there's robin on your windowsill.' Ma turned and watched with pleasure as a robin pecked at the seeds she had placed there.

'You don't have any bird feeders,' observed Kathy looking out into the garden.

'I don't need any. The birds are happy with the old ways. I just put out a few scraps, like I've always done. And they hunt among all those flowers for the seeds. The tits love pecking at the bark of the wild apple too. Too many bird feeders spoils the birds; they don't go hunting for themselves any more. T'ain't good! Those blue tits - too many now, and they're not strong. A hard winter will wipe most of them out. What did Mr. Darwin say: survival of the fittest, wasn't it? Well, he's right; and now humans are weakening many of the species of birds by spoiling them. Yes,' she mused. 'Mr. Darwin was one of the greatest of our modern scientists; more like the ancient ones. Saw that science is all a matter of reducing multiplicity to unity – finding the pattern in diversity. Science today is obsessed with examining everything, instead of thinking more deeply about what is *behind* everything. That way they would find what they are looking for. Mind you, Mr. Darwin was not right about everything. He didn't get evolution right – the evolution of species, I mean.'

'What do you mean?' asked Kathy, predictably, and feeling she had not understood at all what Ma had just said. But Ma would not be drawn.

An old clock ticked comfortably on the mantel piece, and Kathy began to feel she was in another world, a world where, ironically, time had stopped, where the ticking was more a sign of another time - where there were no clocks; just the sun to mark the time of day and the season. And where the people were all like Ma Riley.

'Do you believe in magic, Ma?' asked Kathy suddenly. She had heard some of the villagers say that Ma was really a witch, that she could work potions and spells. Kathy had thought that a terrible thing to say, for she knew that it was meant maliciously. She had learnt in history how they used to burn old women, or anyone, who practised healing and herbalism, calling them all witches. Some people in the village, she felt, had not moved much beyond those old attitudes.

'Magic? Kathy, my lass, you want to know everything, all in one go. You're an impatient lass. You'll have to go careful. Impatience is inclined to get a body into trouble, sometimes great trouble. But you're intelligent and curious, and they're fine qualities. Just watch them, that's all. Don't be like the hare, be like the tortoise.' Ma went on with the apples; her large pile of rosy, red fruit was dwindling. A silence fell upon them again, which Kathy found very peaceful and had no wish to speak and break it. She fell to wondering about Ma Riley.

'Who is she, really?' she had asked her mother. 'She's not like the other villagers, the ones who've been here for ever. She's been here a long time, but somehow she doesn't seem one of them.'

'No, she doesn't, and I don't think she is,' said Elaine, rinsing another bowl and putting it in the dish drainer.. 'There are folks that say they know all about Ma Riley.'

'What do they say,' asked Kathy, drying teaspoons and putting them away. Elaine took a deep breath, and seemed to be hunting for the right words.

'Well,' she began, carefully. 'There's folks that say she's a Derwent.'

'What, from the big hall up Stanhope way. That's impossible. She can't be a Derwent. They're aristocrats.'

'Nothing's impossible in this world,' replied Elaine, wondering if she should go on.

'Well, go on,' said Kathy. 'What happened?'

'Well, they say,' said Elaine tentatively, very carefully, 'they say that the last Lord Derwent - not this one – the one who died twenty years ago; well his wife - the first Lady Derwent - lay with a gypsy.'

'Lay with a gypsy!' repeated Kathy, incredulous, and quietly amused at this quaint expression.

'Yes, and Lord Derwent would not own the baby when it was born. "Eyes as brown as the chestnut and skin just the same," he said. Said it had to go to its "natural father. Damned if he was going to have a gypsy in his house." He always was a sour bit of work; was and remained so to the day he passed on. A mean old gaffer - that's what they called him up at Stanhope.'

'So, Ma Riley was brought up by gypsies,' said Kathy. 'So, she's a Romany. No wonder she knows so much country lore.'

'Yes, and they say that her mother was devastated by it all (as well she might be) and that she used to secretly visit the Romanies, so she retained some contact with her child. Then when the child was eighteen she managed to put some money her way, so that the girl would have some means of supporting herself, and could leave the Romanies if she wished.'

'And did she leave them?' asked Kathy.

'Well, I don't rightly know. I believe so. But some time later, they say, she just appeared in this village, and bought that tumbledown cottage. Probably with the money her mother had given her.'

'What a great story,' mused Kathy, 'and it all happened right here!'

'But there's other stories,' went on Elaine, emptying the dish water down the sink and enjoying these new confidences with her daughter.

'Oh yes?' said Kathy, who was now agog with interest. 'Tell me.'

'Well, there's others say it wasn't that way at all; that *she*, that is Ma Riley, ran off with a gypsy when she was eighteen, and that Lord Derwent cut her off without a penny. Disinherited her.'

'How awful,' said Kathy. 'And was she pregnant?'

'That, no-one knows.'

'How simply dreadful; it's not so bad to get pregnant, really.'

'Oh, yes, it is,' replied Elaine quickly. 'It's very bad to get pregnant before marriage. It never works out. Look at all the delinquent children; they're nearly all children of single mothers, who can't count, spell or speak properly. Kathy smiled to herself. Her mother was on her soap box. But, for now, she wished to bring her mother back to the sharing of this fascinating piece of country gossip about Ma Riley.

'So, what did Ma Riley do then? An aristocratic girl cast out of house and home.'

'Well, she went to live with her love, went to the Romanies.'

'Oh, how lovely,' Kathy breathed, impressed. 'Like the Raggle, Taggle Gypsies, O.'

'Well, my dear,' said Elaine 'if you think it was lovely, I'm sure Ma Riley did not. Because it didn't last a year!'

'Oh,' said Kathy, disappointed. 'So, what happened?'

'Nobody rightly knows,' said Elaine. 'She just disappeared, and then some time later – nobody knows exactly how much later – she appears again; out of nowhere. Just appeared, they say. Bought that little cottage and there she's been ever since. That must have been about sixty years ago.'

'But her name,' said Kathy. 'It's Riley. Surely she comes from the Rileys in Cumberland.'

'Well, that is a mystery,' said Elaine. 'To be sure, I don't know how she's come by that name. Just took it, I imagine. Did not want to be saddled with the name Derwent or her Romany name. Too many questions. Too much gossip, you know.'

'I wouldn't be surprised if there's a very good reason why she's got that name. I bet she's really a Riley!'

'I've told you too much, my girl. Don't you go telling anyone what I've just told you. Gossip is a bad thing. It's alright in families, but don't you breathe a word outside about this. Ma Riley's a good old woman, and I wouldn't want to see her hurt.

She must be very old now, in her nineties I reckon, and she needs a bit of kindness now. Must have led a very hard life; very lonely, I should think.'

'I won't tell a soul,' Kathy promised, feeling she had just discovered a wonderful source of edifying gossip, and intended to plumb it again. How much more did her mother know about the goings on hereabouts?

She found she was looking beyond Ma's head into the long garden beyond.

'Full of weeds,' her mother had observed. 'I'll have to get Dick to go and give her a hand, gardening. She's probably past being able to start such a big job now. How did she ever let it go so far, get so bad?' But as Kathy looked at all the weeds basking in the warm, afternoon sun, she began to perceive an order among them all, and started to see them as flowers. At the back were the taller ones, the hemp agrimony, and the cow parsley, the white and mauve colours making a good backdrop. And then in front of them the golden rod, just coming out, and the rose-bay willow herb now going over, and the vibrant purple toadflax. Further forward there was verbascum and some orange lilies, fleabane with their pretty daisy heads, comfrey (for tea, Kathy supposed) and feverfew (for headaches). Kathy stood up to see what grew nearer the front. She spotted some ground ivy and self heal.

'And in amongst all that,' said Ma, following Kathy's inquisitive gaze, 'you'll find my herbs – mint, parsley, marjoram, chives. People always underestimate mint. It's the finest of all the herbs. Oh, and there's basil too, somewhere; I forget where. And can you see the marigolds? Such pretty flowers. Such service they give. Never fail. Come up every year, from the seeds.'

'But you've no real flowers, Ma, only the lilies,' said Kathy, trying not to be tactless. 'No lupins, delphiniums.'

'Ah, well,' said Ma. 'Those flowers are all new. Posh, you know. They take so much looking after, I should think. Like spoilt children. They're all show; not much use. Now my flowers – they all have their uses. Take the golden rod; make a tea with that and you do your kidneys a lot of good. In the old days they clapped you in prison for talking like this; terrible time for the old people then.' There, she had mentioned the 'old people' again. Kathy felt she wanted to know much more about them.

A mouse peeped out of a corner, twitched its whiskers and ran towards Ma's pile of apple cores on the floor. Kathy was mildly shocked. Her mother would have reacted in fright, and her father would have been amused by this. Kathy was more interested in the little creature, but still, she thought, it ought not to have been in the house. But Ma did not seem to mind at all; she just carried on with the apples. They watched the mouse in silence. Then Ma said: 'That's Tiddly Wink; he's a field mouse; he's quick, can disappear in a trice, especially when Miss Moppet is around. But Miss Moppet wouldn't harm him.' Miss Moppet was Ma's cat, and had never been known to hunt birds or small animals. 'Not a birder,' the villagers would say, 'just a placid, old, daft marmalade, like its mistress!'

'Don't you mind mice running about your kitchen?' asked Kathy.

'Not in the least,' said Ma. 'This was their land before ever I came here, before they built this house. Can't take their rights away from them; we've all got to learn to live together. And now they have less and less land. I hear new estates are going up all over the place. Well, folks have got to have somewhere to live, I suppose. Too many folks, I think, now.' They both watched Tiddly Wink in silence. He gnawed at the apple in quick little bites, pausing while he digested a morsel, his whiskers twitching and his beady eyes darting around, looking for danger. Suddenly, he turned tail and raced across the room back to the hole in the wall.

'Well, he had a nice bit of tea, don't you think?' laughed Ma. 'Would you like a cup of tea, dear?' Ma rose and took the kettle hanging over the fire which had been burning slowly in the grate in the fireplace. She took some lime flowers, which she must have collected, Kathy thought, and poured the scalding water over them in two large earthenware mugs. Then, after a minute or two, she added some cold water, to make the tea drinkable. 'And I've got some little biscuits cooking in the oven,' said Ma, and opened the blackened iron door at the side of the fire, and took out some shortbread biscuits, perfectly cooked.

'Mmm, these are delicious,' said Kathy appreciatively.

'Yes, that's an old recipe from Scotland. Well, they're the folks for shortbread, aren't they? I got this recipe ages ago.'

'What's that on your windowsill, Ma,' asked Kathy noticing a lump with a tea towel over it.

'Oh, that's my bread, dear,' said Ma. 'It's proving. Resting, you know. Doing what it has to do in its own time. Very difficult to make good bread today; they've changed the flour so much.

Not like it used to be. And they used to ferment the seeds a bit, leave them in water a few days. Now I don't think they do that. It's difficult to make bread that's good for you now. Tastes good; I buy some now and again; but good for you – I don't think so.'

'Oh, look, Ma. Is that a greenfinch on the hemp agrimony out there? It's quite a green bird.' Ma turned round and looked.

'No, dear, that's a siskin. Looks much like a green finch, but it's different. A smarter bird; keen on looking good. Comes from Bracey's wood over yonder by Coker's farm, the pine wood, you know.' Kathy knew it. The family had gone for a walk there once. It was mostly a silent wood, and Kathy had not noticed many birds in it.

'You know your flowers well,' said Ma. 'Who taught you?'

'Oh, Granfy,' replied Kathy. 'He knows so many. But he's getting forgetful now; what he can't remember he looks up in his wild flower books.'

'Well he's done a good thing – getting you interested in wild flowers. Is Susie interested too?'

'Not yet,' said Kathy, loyally. 'But I'm sure she will be.'

Half an hour later Kathy walked down the narrow path of Ma's front garden to the gate. It was lined with primroses, now dormant, wild blue gentian were in flower, and some wild cyclamen waited quietly to pop out in their glorious colour later in the year. A large brown spider was resting in its web that it had woven between the gate post and the buddleia. Kathy looked at it, but could not bring herself to like it. There was something quite horrible about spiders, she thought. She would never bring herself to like them.

'Oh, there's my darling,' said Ma. 'Just look at her, isn't she lovely? So big and strong. And look at that splendid web! Isn't it perfect? That's Sybil, and she's a real pet. I do love her. Now look, Kathy girl; see that little mark in the web – that's her signature. All spiders leave one of those in their webs. They're a bit naughty, a bit egotistical, you know. But they're just like us; they're proud of their work, and they want folk to know who made that web.' Ma brushed the biscuit crumbs from her faded blue blouse and ample bosom onto the garden. 'A treat for the birds,' she giggled. Kathy was studying Sybil. Those legs; eight of them, and seeming to be covered with small hairs. Why did she find such a tiny thing so repulsive? She did not know. No, she would never be able to like spiders, she decided. She would line her doorsteps with conkers, as her mother did each autumn to keep them out. Ma Riley took Kathy in her arms and kissed her. 'Come again, child, any time. And give my good wishes to your family.'

*   *   *

'Did Ma Riley give you anything for Susie's cold?' asked Elaine.

'Yes,' said Kathy, giving her mother a small bundle wrapped up in old newspaper.

'These are the herbs; she said to boil them in water for one minute, then cool and divide into three, and drink each third in the morning for three days.'

'Mmm, I wonder what they'll smell like; the last lot were awful!'

'She didn't say,' said Kathy.

'Oh, and did you ask Ma Riley if she would like your father to come round with his fork and dig up all those weeds? I know they're not her herbs; she goes out collecting those.'

'I think she's quite happy with the way things are,' said Kathy.

'Just as I feared,' said Elaine.

Chapter 12

———⁓⁓∞⦵⧜⦵⧜⦵∞⁓⁓———

Saintliness

Kathy awoke early the following morning, still in a state of bliss, experiencing everything in her room as beautiful and feeling her life was more than tolerable. She had been dreaming about Ma Riley, and that had added to her feeling of pleasure. However, the effect of the drug this morning was not as strong as it had been last night, and she was aware she was going to have to face Mike, and somehow get through a whole day at her special school. But this thought, and indeed all of the daily exigencies of her present life that loomed vaguely before her, did not seem insurmountable, depressing or unjust. She contemplated her day ahead with calm and confidence, and even looked forward to it. Leaving aside the uniform for the previous school, Michael Mount, she donned jeans and tee shirt. Bending to the demands of the kids, the special school, James Arnold, required no uniform, and indeed dispensed with most rules, so that the kids existed in a kind of vacuum – no rules at home and no rules at school – so that, Kathy had reflected over the three weeks she had been there, they existed in a sort of free-form life, with no structure, limitations, and no expectation of how the next bit of life would be. No wonder they were all psychologically damaged, she thought. The school was compounding the earlier problems. Miss Carstairs, the head teacher, was the only redeeming angel in their lives. She seemed a Mother Theresa to Kathy.

Not feeling like any breakfast, Kathy, nevertheless, descended the stairs to the dining room. She noticed the scuffed paintwork of the stairs and the cheap carpet of glaring orange, in a new way. The carpet scintillated before her. Mrs. Dobbs was in the kitchen banging around, as usual, with pans and crockery. What she was doing Kathy had no idea, as breakfast was a simple meal of fruit, cereals and toast, and no lunch was ever prepared in the home on weekdays. She poured herself a cup of tea, knowing that the caffeine would be good for her and helped herself to some cereal. Seeing her, Mrs. Dobbs shouted through the hatch that Mike wanted to see her in his office. The unrelenting ugliness of life here, thought Kathy, was wearing. But not today! It was not just the surroundings, it was also the ugliness of the behaviour of the children and the adults – the staff, the social workers, the other council staff. Mike and Miss Carstairs, were the shining exceptions. How could they bear to work in this level of society? Wouldn't they soon give up, admit defeat?

But this morning, none of this ugliness touched Kathy very much. It floated by her, not because she had developed a thick skin, but because there was something in her now that no longer responded to the ugly, the baleful, the wounding, the unjust. The evil of this place seemed to drift by her in quite an amazing way, unable to find a handle in her on which to hook its tentacles, to knot her stomach, to fill her with dullness, to seed anxiety and anger. Now she had learnt how to manage things. Never again would she allow the influence of this place to encroach upon her. She would stand apart from it all, just as she now did. And again she wondered if this was the state Jesus had occupied for most of his thirty three years on earth.

Nearer to home, she also wondered about Becky Sharp. Perhaps Becky's resilience and courage had been enabled by this ability to be unaffected and brought down by surroundings, by the behaviour of others. But then, she had to admit, Becky had not always behaved *herself.* She had schemed and plotted, even against her own best friend, Amelia. Why, the author himself had called it a novel without a hero. But that was because Thackeray had probably forgotten how Becky had started life. He had written in serial form for Punch magazine, and it had probably emerged as many good stories, rather than as one whole, integrated novel. He had, Kathy decided, probably got carried away with portraying the bad side of Becky. Becky was not really as bad as that. Kathy determined that Becky was a worthy heroine, at least in the main part of the book, and that she would remain a most useful guiding light. And if need be, she, Kathy, would re-invent some of the story. Refreshed by the memory of Becky - her wit and spontaneity and resilience - she felt that now she could lay more plans and execute them like Becky. Perhaps the ecstasy has opened a door that should have been open all the time, but which will stay open now, she mused.

She knocked on Mike's door without trepidation and the usual need to prepare to defend herself, and entered in a state of great tranquillity and confidence and utter defencelessness. She smiled at him sweetly and helpfully. Mike took one look at her and said, 'if you could see how stupid you look, Kathy, you would not stand there smiling at me like last year's Cheshire cat or some village idiot from heaven knows where. You have taken a drug!' Hurt and utterly confused by Mike's response to her, she was momentarily at a loss for words. Nobody had ever spoken to Becky like this. All of them in those days had always remembered their manners. How dare Mike treat her with such a lack of courtesy. And what did he mean by 'last year's Cheshire cat?' She was missing something, and felt at a disadvantage. Was the ecstasy slowing her down, making her brain sluggish? She banished the thought. No, this new state was the answer, the answer to everything.

'What was it – crack?' asked Mike.

'No; it was ecstasy,' answered Kathy.

'Ecstasy! Where the hell did Gary get that. I presume it was Gary who gave it to you?'

'Yes, but not only me. He gave it to a lot of us.'

'Good god! How many were you?'

'About a dozen,' and she was surprised how easily and exactly she recalled the scene of yesterday evening.

'And what time did you and Nick get in last night?'

'About ten thirty,' said Kathy truthfully and helpfully, and feeling very holy. It was much nicer telling the truth.

'And did anything happen?' What could he possibly mean, she wondered. And for some reason of prudence that she did not intend, she decided to say nothing about the events that had taken place after they had all taken the drug. And, at the same time, she felt a regret that it was no longer possible to be open and honest.

Mike gave her a long stare, obviously searching for something and not finding it. She felt he was looking for something like her soul, but her soul just now was cocooned in a cloud of beauty and great lightness, in a magical harbour where Wynken, Blynken and Nod sailed in their ship of dreams - a silver sea of lullabies and fairy stories - and she felt that utter confidence and all-rightness that she had felt as a very small child in her father's arms.

'How low you have sunk, Kathy! What would your parents say? I have failed you! Social Services have failed you!'

'No, you haven't, Mike,' she said, and a feeling of such magnanimity rose up in her, that she felt she could forgive Social Services too. How good it was to feel bathed in this kindness, this light, this forgiveness, even. This Kindly Light, she thought, and wondered where she had heard the phrase. 'No, you haven't failed, Mike. I understand everything now.' And she felt how hard it was for Mike not to be able to understand, not to be able to see things as they really were. And she began to feel a deep compassion for him, and again was astonished at all these beautiful feelings that could arise in her so spontaneously. She looked at Mike in pity that he too could not share in this superior state.

'For goodness sake, Kathy; don't look at me like some silly sheep. You've lost your wits. Frankly, if you could see yourself you would not be impressed. You are good for nothing and no-one at the moment.'

'Well, that was predictable,' she thought. 'He belongs to the uninitiated; he just does not know that there is a better way of being, the way of Jesus. I must be patient,' she admonished herself, in a saintly way. It was nice to be on a superior level. Now all things would be possible. But she must remember to be kindly, patient and compassionate with others; they would need her understanding, greatly. Seeing it was hopeless trying to engage with her, Mike said: 'Are you able to cope with school today?'

'Oh, yes,' said Kathy obligingly, feeling she could do anything now.

'Well, you had better go. I can't think of anything else you could do in this state.'

* * *

A week passed and, to Kathy's surprise and disappointment, so did the new-found superior state she had discovered. 'Was is it just all the ecstasy,' she wondered. 'Was my new way of understanding things no more than the effects of the drug?' Sadly, she found herself returning to her old ways of thinking and feeling – her former idea that her life was intolerable and dangerous; that she had to act always in such a way as to escape this danger; that she had to be constantly on the alert for ways in which to improve her lot. All this was gradually descending upon her once again. And she began to feel the same oppression she had felt before. If only she could ascend once more into that state where she could perceive things as they really were, where she had been in touch with the truth of life. But how to do it? Take ecstasy again? Somehow that did not seem to be the answer. There must be another way to reach that state, that other dimension where everything made sense, and where she had felt so good, so saintly, and yes, powerful, in a gentle and effective way.

One morning she caught sight of herself in a large mirror in the hall at James Arnold, and saw that her expression had resumed its form of the past months. The beatific smile that had adorned her features for the past week had now been replaced with the former look of hardness and anxiety, her mouth and eyes compressed again into that determination to face the challenge to survive, and to survive well. What about Jesus? she wondered. Well, what about him? she thought sourly. Perhaps that was why he got himself crucified, because he went around in that stupid state. That saintly state! Instead of getting real, instead of dealing with people and situations. Perhaps he just didn't 'get it'. She was sure he had not taken drugs; but if he had *behaved* as though he had taken something ...., if he had sort of *pretended*, and then been able to carry it off – well, that was fascinating, but something she would not be able to do. He was just too good a guy, she decided, but unreal, out of touch; and he would have been more use if he had got real. But then she thought of his action in the temple with the money lenders. That was an aggressive act; real, to be sure. Not the act of someone walking around feeling saintly all the time, like she had been doing for the past week. No, Jesus was something else, she decided. Not much help. And Becky. What about Becky? Was Becky something else too, a girl beyond her reach? And, importantly, was she the help she had thought she was? Of course, she was! The problem was she had not thought much about Becky recently, not enough. She must get back to working out how Becky would manage this life, this life at the bottom of society.

Chapter 13

───∿∿◦◖◗◦∿∿───

Into Danger

Kathy was sitting alone on a bench in the park. It was 10 o'clock in the morning, and not many people were around. They were either shopping or still not up and about, she thought. She took another pull on her cigarette and wondered vaguely about her life. This was the first opportunity she had had for truanting at her new (third) school, since Mike took her there every morning, and once there she was closely supervised. However, this morning, she had managed to slip away between sessions; Kathy felt she could not call them lessons; they were more like the waiting rooms for mentally ill children. She was not bored, she had found; she was fascinated by this experience, and observed the children, and speculated on what had caused their slide into this dark level of life, a place that promised no hope, no reprieve, and from which most of them would never recover, she felt; these kids were just too implacably against following the rules, adopting the kind of behavior, that would bring them rewards. They had been trained from a very young age, she thought, to react and behave in ways that were contrary to what is natural, had received no experience of warmth, love, and a predictable, ordered environment. They had probably only been able to develop survival tools, had been trying to survive even as young babies, and their brains had consequently been deformed. She remembered once, with the family on holiday, she had been in a public toilet, and had seen a young mother changing the diaper on her 6-month old baby. The young girl had been handling the baby very roughly and cursing it. The baby was crying so piteously. Kathy was struck with horror and tried to say something to the mother, but she too was cursed. All Kathy could do was to get out of the place. These young people, she thought, in James Arnold, must be the adolescents of those babies. She wondered how many more such severely damaged children there were in the country.

When she had finished her cigarette she planned to go up to the Rag and put in an appearance there. Lisa and Tina might be there, and a few of the boys. Although they were all hardly 'normal', hardly mentally healthy, they at least were better than the kids in James Arnold, and she could have some sort of a conversation with some of them. Lisa was the one who seemed the most intelligent and with whom Kathy could dialogue a little. Also Lisa would tell her more of what went on in gang life, but even then Kathy had the impression Lisa was withholding much, so that she still could not glean much about the other kids. She had the feeling that she was being kept on the 'outside' in a sort of holding pen. And she felt Gary was behind all this. For all their lack of intellectual development and their dysfunctions, they could follow the ethos of the gang very well and keep Kathy just where Gary wanted her to be.

She exhaled and watched the smoke curl up into the air, white against the grey backdrop of an overcast day. Suddenly, she espied Lisa walking along the path towards her, and wondered what she was doing here. She knew she had some sort of job working for Gary, but had always failed to discover exactly what it was. Several of the other girls also worked for him. Lisa sat down beside Kathy, and something in Kathy was grateful for this human body beside her, this little bit of human companionship. Lisa pulled out her pack of cigarettes and the two sat in silence for a short while, inhaling and exhaling tobacco smoke and nicotine, and deriving a great deal of soothing satisfaction from it.

'Gary's got a job for you,' said Lisa suddenly.

'Oh,' said Kathy, surprised at this announcement. She was not used to this directness from Lisa, or from any of the kids. She usually had to prise information from them, and even then she was yielded only morsels. 'I don't need a job. I get everything I need at The Haven. Besides, I'm still at school; I'm not old enough to work.'

'No, you're not at school. We all know that. You truant as often as you can. And, anyway, you don't learn nought at James Arnold. It's not a school at all. It's only for crazy kids. You're not crazy!' Kathy accepted this compliment and noted how far she had fallen that compliments to her were now in the currency of mental illness.

'And,' continued Lisa 'it's not cool to go to school – any of them. They don't teach you nothin'.' Kathy silently thought of her old school in Newcastle, and knew that was not true. But she banished that thought; she had weeks ago surrendered herself to the philosophy of these kids; she must at least try to be consistent.

'I don't truant just now – much!' explained Kathy, 'because I am too closely supervised. There is not the same opportunity.'

'You can always make the opportunity, sis,' said Lisa unsympathetically. 'What are you doin' today?'

'Nothin, really; just thinkin,' replied Kathy.

'I've got something much better for you to think about,' said Lisa conspiratorially. 'Gary's got this job for you.'

'Oh,' said Kathy, wondering what it could be.

'He wants you to lift some things from that sports shop in Hounslow high street.' And she went on to describe where it was. Kathy could not place the shop as she was not familiar with the shopping areas of Hounslow.

'That don't matter. I'm to take you there and wait outside, while you do the job.' Kathy's stomach sank. She had joined their club, compromised so much of herself - her values, her behavior, taken drugs - and now they (Gary) wanted more.

'You mean shoplift?' said Kathy in a low voice.

'Yeah, shoplift, take, pinch - call it whatever you want.'

'But that's stealing,' said Kathy.

'Sis, you're not living in middle-class land now. We don't call it 'stealing'. We call it: taking what is rightfully ours. We buck the system, 'cos we have to. The system never looked out for the likes of us; it was always supervision, children's homes, James

Arnold sort of schools. Well, we want a life like those rich guys. We're not going to spend our days defending ourselves to the police, in detention centres and prisons. We do it another way.' Kathy could not follow the logic of this thinking; it seemed to her they were following exactly the way that would land them in detention centres and prison.

'But they have safeguards,' objected Kathy. 'If I take those things out of the doors, an alarm will go off.'

'No, it won't. I've got a device here. You simply put it in the bag with what you've taken and then walk through the doors, and no buzzer will go off.'

'I couldn't,' said Kathy. 'I don't want to steal.'

'Sis, you got no choice. It's Gary's orders. This is your first initiation. Like I said you don't live in middle-class land no more. Things are different for you now, and we're gonna look after you. You must've seen you're not properly in the gang. Well, this is your first test.'

'And what happens if I fail?'

'Oh, you won't. I'll see you don't. I'm to train you, and if I fail in that Gary'll sort me out,' and she gave a nervous laugh. 'But I won't fail and neither will you.'

Kathy was silent a long while, trying to sort out how to respond to this new onslaught that was being imposed on her world. She realized now she had been congratulating herself for the past ten days that she had at last a place – not the best of places – but still a place in the new scheme of things, and in which she could experience some sort of belongingness. Now, she realized there was a price to pay. Nothing was free. Gary wanted his pound of flesh. Of course! He wanted her services as a common thief. So, she had thought she had achieved status and security in the gang, that she was even a respected member. How mistaken she had been! All these impressions had been courtesy of Gary. He had given her a long rope to play with and she had played with it. She had irretrievably entangled herself in it, and now Gary was hauling her in like a lassoed animal.

'And is there another initiation?' Kathy asked quietly.

"Fraid so, sis.'

'What is it?'

'You would call it 'rape'. We have another name for it.'

'What?' exclaimed Kathy. 'I didn't hear you right. You can't be telling the truth.'

'Calm down, sis. It's not that bad. You get used to it after a while. Better not to think of it as 'rape'.'

'Get used to what?' asked Kathy in a state of shock.

'Sex, the way they do it.'

'You mean raping is the way the gang do it?'

'Like I said, we don't call it "rape". And it don't happen all the time. When we're doing drugs it's nice. But other times .... well, it's different.'

'And who does it?' asked Kathy, unable to bring herself to use the word.

'Gary, and then the rest of them.'

'What, more than one?'

'You heard of gang rape? Well, sis, if you're in a gang you gotta experience it. First hand!'

Kathy thought she was going to be sick. All normal feeling had left her. She only felt shock and panic in her stomach and a strange numbness coursing through her whole body. Seeing how devastated she was, Lisa said gently,

'Honest, Kathy, it gets better. I'll give you a few tips. But for the initiation, well, you just gotta grin and bear it. Hey, look at me; I'm still alive!' Kathy noticed a look of compassion in Lisa's eyes. So she had not been completely brain and body-washed of her humanity. With this unexpected touch of sympathy, she thought she was going to cry. But all she said was, 'but some of those boys are only twelve or thirteen.'

'Oh, Gary likes to start 'em young. He says it's natural. Sis, I gotta leave,' said Lisa suddenly, looking at her watch. 'I'm meeting Gary. Our first training workshop is tomorrow for you and me. Meet me at the Rag at 10 am. And then, afterwards, we'll go and have a burger somewhere.' Lisa winked encouragingly at Kathy. Then she stuffed her cigarettes away, slung her bag on her shoulder, and proceeded to walk quickly along the path again from where she had come, her short, dyed, black hair lying in a close crop on her head, above her purple and black jacket, her hips swaying awkwardly in her too-tight and worn jeans. As Kathy watched the departing Lisa, Gary's words of nearly three weeks ago came back to her: In three weeks you'll lose your virginity.

'Rape, a fate worse than death!' she had heard somewhere. Yet here were all these girls raped regularly, it seemed, and not showing trauma. How was it possible? So that was why they all looked uniformly ugly. They are trying to make themselves look unattractive in order to avoid the sexual attentions of Gary and the other males, she mused. And the new horror of her life gripped her like a vice, and she knew she had to do something.

Chapter 14

―――ᴡᴏᴏᴇᴛᴏᴏᴋᴇᴏᴏᴡᴡ―――

Waking Up

Kathy arrived back at the children's home and let herself in with the key she had had copied at the locksmith. It was still mid-morning. Fortunately, there was no-one about. The cook had not yet arrived, and neither had Mrs. Buller. She stole quietly upstairs, barely took in the shabby surroundings of her room, went straight to her bed and sat bolt upright on it. She was more alert than she had felt for a long time, and her brain, although still in a state of shock, was also thinking very efficiently.

Kathy now saw in crystal clarity what her life had become and what it was to be. She was clearly going to become a drug addict; she had seen how all the kids had taken the tablet of ecstasy offered to them, because they had had no choice. That way, she reasoned, Gary could make them obedient. By craving ecstasy, weed or any other substance, Gary would oblige and satisfy their needs, but in return they were his slaves to carry out his nefarious wishes. They were the worker bees for Gary, the queen bee. They would steal, fight, rape on Gary's orders. They would all fight, the girls too she had been learning, and perhaps kill members of other gangs. She was thinking all this through very rapidly, but very clearly, she knew. All the pieces of the puzzle that had defied her attempts to fit together were now interlocking in an elegance that would have been satisfying if it were not so horrifying. Yes, she thought, this is exactly how it works; this is the way of gangs.

And now she had met one of those gang leaders, a thug who was determined to be a CEO too, by whatever twisted means available to him! And with that realization she felt the last fleeting, delightful flutterings of childhood – that last tenuous link with innocence and the utter trust of a child – leave her forever. She was now an adult! She had just completed an initiation, but an initiation very different from the one Gary had in mind for her!

Her first thought was to go and tell Mike everything. But she dismissed this idea; she felt Mike could do nothing, would not be able to protect her. He might call the police, but the police seemed strangely powerless where Gary was concerned. Hadn't he killed? So, why had he not been arrested, or at least investigated? Perhaps he covers his tracks, she thought, leaves no evidence. Or was it something else? Perhaps he was valuable in some way to the police. Perhaps he even had power over them. She did not know. What she did know was that she needed complete protection from Gary. How could that happen without her being smuggled to another part of the country, another part not of her choosing, and with more gangs she must run the gauntlet of? No, Social Services had tried and failed to understand and to provide for her. They were completely underfunded and out of their depth, she realized. The social problems had escalated so exponentially in recent years that these well-meaning people were now totally powerless, she thought. The downward march seemed relentless, unstoppable now. 'You're your own gel,' she suddenly heard Granfy saying. 'No-one can look after you like yourself and your family.' Well, she had no family now, so it was up to her.

She withdrew her thoughts from these reflections and forced herself to focus on the immediate problem of her life, and very soon she was concentrating hard on the real danger she was in. Her stomach heaved again, and fear gripped her heart. Did she have the intelligence to make a plan, and then the cool nerve to carry it off? She had never had to do anything like this before. Now she was to act like some heroine in a film or a book. Perhaps like Violette Szabo in Carve Her Name with Pride – an old film set in World War II, which her school in Newcastle had recently shown one afternoon for the whole school to see. Kathy had fallen in love with Virginia McKenna, thinking she was the most beautiful woman she had ever seen, portraying a character that was both very courageous, working behind enemy lines, yet compassionate and kind beyond credulity, and which eventually led to a concentration camp and then her execution. The image of Violette Szabo, she determined, would give her the courage to make a plan, and then execute it.

She calculated the amount of time she had for action. It was Thursday now. Gary's initiation, she gathered, would take place next Tuesday. Where, she had no idea. Perhaps in Gary's house, perhaps in Tam's, where they had done drugs. But it didn't matter where. The important thing was not to be around next Tuesday. To be gone by Tuesday! She would flee and she would manage! It was nothing to what Violette Szabo had accomplished! She would escape from her present life which promised only crime, drugs and sex slavery.

She would flee to Somerset, she suddenly decided. Granfy was in Somerset; somewhere. But where was Somerset? She needed a map. There were a few books in an old, scuffed bookcase in the television room downstairs. She peeked out of her room; no-one was about; she crept softly down the stairs. She could hear Mrs. Dobbs in the kitchen, but the kitchen had no view of the television room, so she was safe. There were no maps in the bookcase. 'I will go to the library,' she thought. 'I'm not a member, so I can't borrow anything, but I will find what I need in the reference library.' She collected a pencil and pad from her room, made sure she had her key and slipped noiselessly out of the front door. Now she assumed a different posture. She must amble and slouch a bit, and look as though she had no purpose in her demeanour and posture.. Gary's spies would be everywhere. She must behave in a way that would arouse no suspicion, and she would certainly go to this 'shoplifting workshop' tomorrow with Lisa. She must allay all suspicion. She avoided the Rag, and, instead went the other way. She soon came across a small newsagent, with the usual Asian behind the counter. Yes, he knew where the library was, and directed Kathy across the common in the direction of the old town hall.

She quickly found what she was looking for in the reference library: a map of Somerset in the west of England. She made a list of all the major towns. Bath and Bristol she knew of, and Weston Super Mare she had studied in geography in school – its climate, geology, ecology and agriculture. She had enjoyed those studies; the name had been so evocative and the place so far away from Northumberland and its chilly winds. Somerset - it appealed to her, and even more so now. The name seemed to ring of warmth, comfort, ease, perpetual summer – a state that was receding day by day from Kathy's emotional life; soon those feelings, she felt, would be relegated to memory only. Of the other towns – Wells, Shepton Mallet, Midsomer Norton – she had never heard. Glastonbury she was acquainted with through its festival. Which town to pick? Where, in this beautiful county of rolling summer pastures, of sheep and grazing cattle, of gentle hills and warm sea, are you, Granfy, she wondered. She could not think. Granfy had never spoken very much of his sister, and Kathy had the impression they had not been on very good terms. May seemed a relative in name only, and the families had never had any communication; but, nevertheless, May had undertaken with the social services to visit her brother, and to keep an eye on him. And so Granfy had been shipped off to Somerset, presumably to the town nearest to May. But which town was this?

Kathy pored over her list of names and tried to *feel* which one it might be. She knew psychics were employed from time to time to find missing persons. But her attempts at divination failed. Kathy had no idea where Granfy was. She tucked her list into her day bag, and then set off to find the bus station. It was not far away. Buses were pulling in and out all the time. She went into the office and made inquiries, and came away with another list of buses going to Somerset. They all left from Heathrow, and she would have to buy her ticket there.

It was lunch-time now, but Kathy thought better than to return to The Haven just yet. Mrs. Buller or Mrs. Dobbs might see her, and then the supervision would be very tightly imposed for at least a month. Then she would never be able to make her break for freedom. No, far better, she thought to just stay in the library until 3.30pm. She had no money to buy a burger for lunch, but that was no hardship; she had never eaten burgers before she had arrived in west London, and, besides, she was not particularly hungry.

Returning to the library, she went into the main section and found the fiction shelves. Vanity Fair was there. She took it down and carried it over to a table and looked at the illustration on the front of the book. There was the carriage she remembered so well, crammed full of Victorian men and women, but really men and women of any era. The rich men in top hats and fat stomachs; the poor men without hats; the rich women in long, hooped skirts crushed in the melee of thronging, competing humanity; and others outside the carriage, trying desperately to gain a foothold on the vehicle of life, all terrified of being left behind. But where were they going, she wondered. Did they, themselves, know? She opened the book and flicked through a few pages, reading again about Becky Sharp and her deceitful, selfish ways, her complete insensitivity to others, her only focus, the goal she had set herself - of rising in society. Kathy paused on a few pages, reading intently and with a new objective eye. She experienced a sudden feeling of revulsion towards Becky, and all her sympathy for and identification with Becky Sharp started slipping away. 'Why, this girl is cold, hard; she is a harpy!' said Kathy to herself. 'How could I possibly have thought she could help me? It is because of her that I have made these mistakes. Becky is without values, without a conscience; it is because I have values that I am not joining the gang; it is because I have values that I will not steal, lie, and do drugs.'

At 3.30pm she left the library and started her walk back over the common to the children's home. She felt strangely alone without Becky, without that mentor she had so often called to mind. She affected her usual, disconsolate, slouching style, knowing she would be walking within sight of Gary's henchmen. Just going into the library would seed the thought that she was 'going straight'. No, she must play this part very skilfully right up to the last moment. Then on Monday evening it will all be over, she told herself, for it was Monday, the day before the initiation, that she would execute her plan, and leave for Glastonbury. She realized she had decided on Glastonbury. She could already taste the refreshing promise of freedom, and she felt something of the old Kathy returning to her.

Coming into the sitting room a short while before Mrs. Buller would ring the gong for supper, Kathy found Angelina, alone, sitting in one of the big armchairs. The child smiled brightly when she saw Kathy and ran to her side.

'Hello, Kathy, I haven't seen you for ages. Where've you been?' The child looked fearful and slightly downcast. She was having to learn the ways of the system too, having to learn that here quite a different arrangement of values operated to the one in which she had been brought up.

'Hello, Angelina,' said Kathy. 'How're you doing? Settling down?' Kathy really did not know what to say to Angelina, and felt inadequate to the child's expectations of her.

'They haven't found my mum yet,' said Angelina. 'But I know they will,' she said determinedly.

'I'm sure they will, too,' said Kathy. 'You must be patient.'

'Will you come with us, on our trip on Saturday; please Kathy. We're going to Osterley Park. It's not far. Oh, I would so like you to come with me.' Kathy learned it was in the afternoon, and calculated the workshop would not last longer than the morning, and so immediately assented. She would tell Gary or any of the gang who might ask her, that she had been made to go on this trip. She looked at Angelina and felt quite tender towards this grief-stricken, traumatized little black kid and thought 'Angelina brings out the best in me, how strange. A little kid having this effect on me!'

The workshop passed off without incident. Kathy was shown the device that she would operate when she was ready to leave the shop. Gary told her what she had to take; some of the things were easy – the displayed tee shirts lying on counters and the jewellery. You just pretended to be considering buying an item, and then, with a quick look round to make sure no-one was looking in your direction, you slipped it into a non-see-through plastic bag. The jeans and jackets hanging on racks were more difficult, but Lisa demonstrated how it was done. Kathy was impressed with the thorough training she and some of the other girls were being given. Nothing was left to chance. These gangs – some of them – operate with an efficiency that a successful business might boast of, she thought.

Having completed her training and skipped a lunch of burgers with Lisa, she returned hurriedly to The Haven hoping the party had not left without her. They were just boarding the mini van, when she arrived, and she climbed aboard with all of them. At Osterley Park they all disembarked and lined up into the semblance of a crocodile, as their leader instructed. They walked to the reception area, fees were paid, and most of the kids scattered but only as far from the adults as they were allowed. It was a nice park, but Kathy failed to take in much of the surroundings. She was thinking of the task ahead, the adventure that lay in front of her, the undoubted risk and the threat from both the official authorities and the non-official authority – Gary.

Kathy found herself walking beside Barbara, with Angelina on the other side of her, occasionally darting off to see what the other kids had discovered. As usual, everyone, except Barbara, Angelina and herself, were badly behaved. These kids just do not know how to go on, thought Kathy – running off here and there; are they never still? She felt strange, awkward, being part of this assortment; she felt humiliated and angry. She glanced at Barbara and could see she too felt uncomfortable. They walked together. There was a bond between the two of them, the bond of the degradation they were each forced to endure; the grief and loss which had not been addressed in either girl; and the necessity for adaptation and survival. And there was also the recognition of shared values – they both came from good working-class homes, and had learnt the values that ensure a good life and, possibly, happiness. Barbara was, Kathy knew, a star in sport at her school, just as she was on the way to becoming in her old school. Ordinarily, Kathy would have wanted to become friends with Barbara, but Barbara's situation was so much better than Kathy's. Being still at her old school and retaining her old friends, a large part of her life was still intact and functional, and Barbara could keep it that way if she was strong enough and sensible enough. Kathy had no such advantage. And she felt that twinge of jealousy, or was it hopelessness, that she had never felt in her old life. She was aware of Barbara walking along beside her, slightly smaller than herself, her strong, well-coordinated, athletic body, moving easily along the path over the common. Kathy felt the strength and common sense of Barbara. Overwhelming as this whole experience was for her, Kathy knew that Barbara would get through. In that face, with the fair, wavy hair, that always looked attractive and tidy, and with those big, china blue eyes, Kathy knew that beyond a certain prosaicness of character, that sometimes made Barbara seem boring, there was that steadfastness, that rock-like essence that was going to get Barbara through. She really was so full of common-sense, thought Kathy, that she will transcend in the end.

By contrast, Kathy was on her own and felt an utter stranger in an alien land, and did not trust herself to become emotionally involved with anyone. Real friendship was out of the question. She needed all her strength and all her wits to guide her through this inhospitable terrain. But all that was about to change! If she could pull this feat off, have the grit and the nerve to do it properly, and if luck was on her side, then she would greatly improve her situation and once again have something of a future to look forward to and work for.

Chapter 15

---~~~ɷₒₑ₮ₒ₲ₑₒₒ₩~~~---

Escape

The following day, Sunday, Kathy awoke early, aware she had slept only fitfully. Half the plan had been formulated, but the other half, a vital piece, was missing. Where was she to get the money from for her bus ticket to Glastonbury?

All the kids had labelled jam jars standing on Mike's desk. Into these Mike put their pocket money every Saturday, and when someone wanted money, Mike would give them what they needed out of the amount available. Kathy had just used up most of hers on the new pair of training shoes, and, more recently, on a new day bag. There was only one or two pounds in her jar now. She contemplated stealing from the other jars. Barbara's jar, she knew, was fairly full, as were some of the others. It might prove difficult to get into Mike's office as he usually locked it. But not always, and maybe today or tomorrow there might be the occasion when he left the room unlocked. But she

115

dismissed this idea. To sink as low as a common thief seemed a terrible thing, and a capitulation to this system. After all, the reason for her escape was to avoid this very kind of life. No, she would be heroic and honest. She would not let this environment triumph over her, suck her in as it did so many other young people. How could she face Granfy having become a thief?

She had an idea. She rose, showered and quickly dressed, and, without eating breakfast, she slipped quietly out of the front door No-one was up, so no-one had seen her go. They would soon find the note she had stuck on Mike's door, saying she had gone to the library. She had noticed they were holding a special event there today. She walked quickly up to the Rag, head bent to avoid recognition, and went into the newsagent. The Asian woman, who ran the shop, told her, yes, she did need help this morning. The regular delivery boy had not turned up for work, and the woman's husband was not home to help out. With great relief, the woman put the heavy bag over Kathy's shoulder, and bade her be as quick as possible, because they were late. Kathy was aware one of Gary's spies would probably see her and report her odd activities. Well, it could not be helped now. She should be gone by the time Gary decided to take any disciplinary action.

Kathy worked the whole morning. The Sunday papers were too big to push through letter boxes, so she laid them outside front doors, inside porches, on door steps. In some gardens there were big, fierce dogs, and sometimes rottweilers and german shepherds. Into these gardens Kathy threw her flat plastic packages. Several trips had to be made to and from the newsagent, as there were too many bundles to do in a single trip.

By one o'clock she had delivered all the papers. Throughout the afternoon other jobs were found for her in the shop. By four she had finished, and by then, Lakshmi, the Asian manageress, had run out of things for Kathy to do. She asked if Kathy would like to do the weekend paper rounds on a regular basis, but Kathy declined. Then Lakshmi paid Kathy for her work the sum of thirty pounds. Delighted, Kathy set off for the children's home, her money safely in her pocket. It was more than she had expected and would easily cover the single fare to Somerset. 'Somerset', she thought, as she walked along the street. 'Somerset', she sang to herself, happily. 'Granfy, I am coming to find you.' Just then Steve, one of Gary's mates emerged suddenly from a side-street. The manner of his appearance was somehow threatening and alarmed Kathy. Then, recollecting she was in a busy area with plenty of people around, she relaxed and faced Steve.

'Been somewhere?' questioned Steve.

'Yes, I have,' replied Kathy, volunteering nothing.

'You look happy,' he continued. 'What've you got to be happy about?'

Kathy regretted he had seen her mood, and, more, that she had allowed her emotions to relax. Had she not learned yet that she could never relax here? She was not in Somerset yet, not safe yet.

'What've you got to be happy about?' he persisted suspiciously, as though happiness was a state that was disallowed on Gary's territory.

'Oh, I was just thinking of an aunt of mine,' she said. 'Must be off. Ciao.' She left Steve, standing nonchalantly on the street with nowhere to go and nothing to do.

'None of them have anywhere to go,' she reflected. 'Well, I do. Somerset, here I come!'

Apart from the problem of which town to head for, there was also the problem of *when* to go. She would leave in the morning, she decided, not the afternoon. They wouldn't get concerned until late in the evening, so she would have a whole day to get clear of London. So, by Tuesday, when there was to be the drugs session, and worse, she would be well gone. But she dreaded the discovery by Gary. Would he come looking for her? If he found her, he would know how to bring her to heel, crush her. Well, she would be gone by Monday evening. By late Monday night, or, with luck, Tuesday morning, all hell would break out, certainly, in The Haven, and probably in the gang also, she felt.

She rose on Monday morning much earlier than usual. Again, she had not slept much during the night, such was her state of anxiety. She had decided to take only essentials in her bigger day bag. Everything else she must leave behind, including her mobile phone. She had read that people could be traced by their mobiles. She did not dare pack before breakfast, in case someone came into her room and discovered her packed day bag. Everything was as usual in the dining room – dishevelled-looking kids, using bad and inarticulate language; another 'kitchen' lady trying to supervise; Mrs. Dobbs banging around in the kitchen, but the sounds drowned out by the noise of the kids. Kathy took her place at one end of the table and ate her cereal, hardly aware of it, thinking all the while: 'I will soon be away from all this.'

'You look as though you have something on your mind, Kathy,' said the new dinner lady.

'Oh, do I?' said Kathy and hurriedly masked her expression again.

Up in her room once more, she packed her bag – jeans, sweater, several tee shirts, her wash bag, a framed photo of Granfy and Susie, a notebook and pencil, and her camera. She put the mobile phone into a drawer, closed the cupboard door on all her other clothes, including the school uniform for Michael Mount and a top and skirt she was very fond of. But, like Becky Sharp, who had not completely left her, she knew there was no time now for sentiment. And she recalled Frodo and his companions in the last part of the Lord of the Rings, when they had to ditch all their excess baggage, which then consisted of apparent essentials like pots and pans, in order to be prepared for their last great battle. This is it, she breathed. This is my big battle! This was her opportunity, for it was the one day in a long while that Mike was unable to take her to James Arnold school. He had trusted her to get herself there by bus. She regretted breaking this trust.

When all the noise had died down in the dining room and the kids had gone to school, she opened her door. All was quiet. With a beating heart, she tiptoed downstairs. Mike's door was closed; it was impossible to tell if he was in or out. Mrs. Dobbs was washing up, and as long as she stayed in the kitchen with the new woman, she would not see Kathy. Kathy stole swiftly back up to her room, donned her jacket, felt the money safely in her pocket, picked up the back pack, and carried it downstairs in her hand; better not wear it yet. No-one was in the hall, and no-one could see into the hall. She let herself silently out of the front door. Through the garden gate she went. Then, out of sight of the front door, she slung on her back pack. Still no-one was shouting at her, no-one was raising the alarm. With a thumping heart she walked briskly up the street. She was leaving the children's home!

She gained the Rag; its shops were doing good business at this early hour of the morning. Perhaps she should have left it till later – one of Gary's men was bound to be up and about, perhaps buying cigarettes, and would see her and her big pack. But there were many people about, and she was hardly noticeable, she thought. She walked onto the Rag, and thence onto the common and started her traverse across a corner of it, hoping to merge in with the autumn foliage. Her heart was still thudding in her chest; only the thought of what she had to do next – buy a ticket, board the bus – kept her anxiety at bay.

She completed her crossing of the common and joined the queue for the bus that went in the direction of the nearest underground. She kept her head down hoping to keep her face hidden. This was perhaps the most dangerous part of her escape. If one of Gary's spies saw her, then all would be up, and she might never be able to leave this place. She imagined them 'escorting' her from the stop, quite unobtrusively, so that none of the bystanders would understand what was happening. Gary would know how to do it. Perhaps a knife at her back. The bus seemed never to come. Kathy prayed, over and over again. The pack seemed to get heavier, and with every passer by, she expected to see one of the gang. She kept her face turned to the road, away from the passing pedestrians. Finally, the bus arrived, late. Kathy boarded in trepidation. She passed up towards the back, where she would be more hidden and found a seat. So far, no heavy hand had laid itself on her shoulder and restrained her – the touch she was so dreading. She slung off her pack and sank into the seat, resting the bag on her knees, and still keeping her head low. The last passengers had boarded, and they were off! She breathed a small sigh of relief. The first step was about to be completed.

Alighting from the bus, she slipped swiftly into the underground station and purchased a ticket for Heathrow on the Piccadilly line. She had taken the tube once before to Osterley Park on one of her truanting excursions, and so was familiar with the procedure. She still found it an amazing experience. There was a metro in Newcastle in Northumberland, but she had never used it. Within a short time they arrived at Heathrow. She got off the train at terminal two and found her way to the central bus station. There were many people of all nationalities. For a moment she felt quite lost, and that feeling of alienation from her surroundings, of not belonging to anyone or anything, briefly descended on her. But there was also an advantage in being in such a big crowd – it would be harder for anyone to identify her. She shook off the emotion that, a moment ago, had threatened to overwhelm her, and hurried to the ticket office. There she was informed that there would be a half hour wait for the Bath bus. She returned to the airport and mingled with the busiest and most crowded section of the terminal, and then secreted herself in the toilets for some time. Ten minutes before departure she returned to the bus stop. The bus had not arrived. She found a seat in the bus shelter and with bowed head and hair pulled over her face, waited, counting the seconds. On time, the coach pulled into its bay, its huge bulk negotiating the corner easily, as the wheels turned in a tight lock. Impatiently, Kathy waited while the driver loaded suitcases and bags into the bottom of the bus, and then started taking the tickets of the passengers. Kathy boarded and found a seat at the back; she stuffed her back pack onto the overhead rack and settled into the seat. And waited. This was the moment! If the bus would only start without incident, without her being discovered, then she would be away, surely away from this city, London, which held only misery and captivity for her. Again, with head bowed, she counted the seconds, and prayed.

The bus started! They were off! Gary had not arrived to take her back. The police had not arrived to return her to the children's home. No-one had come for her. She was free; free to start a new life! It had been easier than she had thought. You could just drop out of your life, she mused, and with a bit of planning no-one would ever know, would ever find you. She wondered if many people did this. It was a strange feeling to be so unattached, to have no-one in the world. Well, there was Mike; he would certainly feel sufficiently attached to put out an alert and get the police looking for her. But that was only an official attachment. She felt no attachment to him, although she had liked and respected him, and after a time she felt he would forget her. No, she was absolutely free; she had no ties whatsoever, was responsible to no-one, and no-one now was responsible for her. She thought of all the pop songs forever singing about freedom – and love. Well, she was certainly free. Very free. And to be free of that life felt a profound relief. But to have this freedom all of the time – she was not sure she liked the idea. She wondered if she could cope with it. In a strange way this freedom suddenly seemed to be a huge responsibility. She had got rid of one responsibility – the responsibility of surviving in west London – for something that now seemed a far greater responsibility – total responsibility for herself and in completely new surroundings. Was she going to be able to feed and shelter herself? Any education would probably now be out of the question. That would have to wait. This realization felt almost overwhelming. She wondered if she would be able to carry it. How much easier, she thought, to have, as your responsibility, other people. She returned her thoughts to her plan. This was her responsibility now: to find Granfy. So she did have a life. It was a straw, but a big, firm straw, and it would lead her into a life again - a nice, warm life full of friendly, intelligent, kind people, and she felt hope rise in her stomach.

Glastonbury! Out of all the towns she had seen on the map, Glastonbury seemed to have more appeal. The name was pleasant, she had thought, and as it was in big, bold letters on the map she had assumed it would be big enough to have several care homes. She wondered if Granfy's sister, May, had undertaken her commitment to Granfy, and was visiting him, or if she neglected him, as her mother's cousin, Eileen, had neglected her.

Chapter 16

—◦◦◦◦◦◦◦◦—

Reflections

London slipped by – the rows and rows of identical, little houses, the small gardens, the collections of shabby shops. Then a major dual-carriageway, and then, finally, onto the M4. Now they were passing green fields and cows and hedgerows. It was still London, she thought. But that depressing conurbation with the endless, suffocating streets; the sameness of it all; the tens of thousands of people all packed into that part of London, with no countryside to see, to smell, to be in, no room to live rightly – all that was behind her. The green fields and the hedges covered now with old man's beard and red berries and hips reminded her of Mickle Wood. It would all be looking so lovely there. Autumn had been her mother's favourite season. No more London, thought Kathy determinedly.

But the hard part of her plan was before her. Her first concern was to continue avoiding discovery. She knew missing children got into the news and their photos put up in public places, but she had never heard of a child in care attracting media attention. Besides, she was not really a child. A missing girl of fifteen would not attract a lot of attention. She prayed to Violette Szabo to guide her, help her.

Now, at a safe distance from the threat of the gang, her mind drifted back to her brief, but intense, experience of it. She realised now it was completely male-oriented, extremely chauvinist; the alpha males walked off with all the booty, while the girls were used, humiliated and physically harmed. She had no doubt that gang rape must certainly injure a girl. With her limited knowledge, she couldn't think of an age in European history where it had been this barbaric for women. She knew that in most Moslem countries it was the men who ruled the roost and the women led a wretched life, having to cover up and deny their womanhood, their humanity, even; she was thinking of the little girls, with those dreadful circumcision operations, that she had once read about – clitoredectomies, she seemed to remember they were called. What could be worse than being a woman in many of those moslem cultures? What barbarity they had to endure, being totally under the control of their men – men who functioned no higher than the physical level of life, men who were worse than animals using their ingenuity to devise ghastly forms of torture, mental and physical for their women and girls. And then it was all legitimized by their religious laws. She had read of these heinous practices, she recalled, in a little magazine she had found lying on her mother's desk. It was the newsletter of a charity to which her mother had subscribed, a charity dedicated to educating the women of these societies and also to alleviating their lot.

And the long arm of this malevolence, which had for some reason taken such deep root in those Arab, African and Eastern European countries, was now stretching over the whole of Europe too. The same evil had taken root in the big cities of Europe and now she was facing it, head on. It was not an infection, a virus from certain sections of the Islamic culture, she felt; it was more like an unavoidable outcome of certain circumstances and practices that must now exist in our so-called civilized countries, that bred, called forth an atavistic, perverted sexual instinct in many young males, who were genetically predisposed and then conditioned by their environments to these practices. The law-makers and social services of these western societies had largely thrown their hands up in despair and then turned a blind eye to the whole gigantic, psycho-social problem. They had done nothing, were doing nothing, and would never be able to do anything to counteract these primitive tendencies of these underprivileged sections of society.

She was only fifteen, she reflected, and now she was thinking like an adult, but she had been subjected to a total immersion course over the last few months in the life-style of the ignored and rejected of society; she had been given a bird's eye view of the degradation of her society, and others like it in the west. She had no idea what the cause was, but she was sure this kind of widespread and pervasive degradation and depravity had not existed in European history. What had happened she wondered, to render our 'civilized' societies so suddenly vulnerable to such corruption of essential values and decent behaviour?

'We have no ideals any longer,' her mother had remarked. 'Greed is let loose, and those very people, those men and women of privilege – highly educated and who have all their needs met – are giving no leadership, no example to the rest of us. They only model how to make a lot of money. Then they set up charities. But the harm has been done, and they cannot compensate for that. In fact they give nothing back. Power and money are the ideals today. And I daresay this is what is really the root cause of terrorism. It is not a lack of education and opportunity, really; governments may tout that about the terrorists optimistically but futilely.

'No,' said Elaine, her brow furrowed but excited at the direction her thoughts were moving in. 'No, I'm wrong. It's not greed alone. You remember when Moses smashed the golden calf the Israelites had made under the encouragement of Aaron, his brother?' Kathy could not remember that story; religious education had not been high on the list of priorities at school. 'Well,' continued Elaine 'our problem today is really, fundamentally, the lack of a collective ideal; an ideal to collectively follow. We are trained, and particularly the young today, to follow the golden calf or god of competition, individualism and greed. A dark trinity, one in three, three in one. The Americans particularly worship the aspect of individualism – rugged individualism, I think they call it. Well, Moses destroyed that golden calf. Those Israelites were so lucky! And just as *that* golden calf was destroyed so will ours be. I wonder who or what will do it?'

Kathy did not understand fully what her mother was talking about, but she felt intuitively Elaine had discovered something very important; if it was not the truth, then it was very close to it. Elaine had had very little education, she always said, but enough to train her how to think properly, particularly the training she had received from one teacher, the science teacher. 'But God save us from the fundamentalists and their ideals,' she had added. Yes, her mother was right, Kathy thought. She had often dismissed much of what Elaine had said as 'Mummy on her soap box again!' But she was glad she had nevertheless listened, because now it was proving very useful. Yes, the clever - the CEOs, the bankers and others - had made off with the loot. And money could buy a lot! Pick up any newspaper, she thought, and you would see what an amazing life-style these people had. They could have been living on a different planet. Yes, some loot! But now certain sections of the underprivileged class were demanding *their* pound of flesh; they had waited long enough; opportunity and reward were as far from their reach as ever, perhaps further than for a long time. So now they would react, make off with *their* loot too - yes, a very different loot, but nevertheless a reward – for the alpha males, at least.

She felt she was getting close to the cause of the canker of modern society and was grateful for her mother's thoughtful help. The embracing of such primitive values, as individualism and competition had led to the flourishing of greed, and, because the present climate facilitated this, including, it seemed, those parts of government that were supposed to control it, more and more ordinary men and women, who were not essentially greedy, were being sucked into this new and destructive system.

And thus the gangs, she thought. They are one of the logical outcomes of the abdication of responsibility of the privileged, and not all the public money in the world can solve the effects of this grave malaise, without first addressing the cause.

The bus was travelling along the M4 at a steady, smooth pace, with no interruptions in its motion. She drifted into a grateful, light sleep.

After about one and a half hours, the bus turned off the M4 and, waking up, she saw that the route led through gentle, rolling countryside, which she assumed was the southern end of the Cotswolds. Certainly, most of the villages they passed through seemed constructed of that warm, honey-coloured stone.

They had briefly studied the Cotswolds in geography, and she knew of families who had gone there on walking holidays. The countryside and the villages looked soft and gentle, basking in the weak November sun. There were still some red apples in the orchards they passed, and the michaelmas daisies bloomed in the cottage gardens, behind white gates, picket fences and stone walls. She could love this place, she felt, but would Somerset love her. She dared not relax; she had much to do before the day was out.

The bus rolled unimpeded through Bath. Elegant terraces of beautiful Regency homes arose on either side of her, and, now and again, she glimpsed attractive, little streets off the main route. She gazed with interest, from the bus, into the windows of shops in the smart high streets. They waited a short time in Bath bus station, and then they were off again. Through more little villages and towns, the bus continued its delightful way, and Kathy resolved she would do this journey again, when her life was sorted out, when she and Granfy were set up in a little house, and when she would really be able to enjoy this tour through the Bath and Somerset countryside.

Radstock, Oakhill, Shepton Mallet passed by. They reminded her of Hexbury and Colbridge at home, decent country towns, not spilling over with people. A few minutes later the cosy cottage homes and gardens bearing geraniums and dahlias had given way to hilly fields and grazing cattle and sheep, and woods, now rapidly shedding their leaves. Then it was Wells! A bigger town than the ones she had just passed through, but beautiful with the white, Gothic towers of its cathedral rising majestically and protectively over the market place. And in the centre of the market place rose a graceful, arched town cross, with what looked like a watering trough at its base. Here, too, Kathy resolved to come again in happier times. She also wondered if she had chosen correctly. Perhaps she had been too whimsical in settling on Glastonbury. The name had indeed sounded magical, inviting, but perhaps Bath or Wells or even Bristol, being bigger, might have been more practical. Practicality now was of the essence, she reminded herself, not sentiment.

Finally, at last, the bus passed the town sign announcing Glastonbury. Kathy's heart leapt. Her Glastonbury! Kathy and Granfy's Glastonbury! For she felt sure Granfy was here. She looked eagerly at her surroundings through the bus window. The larger buildings looked elegant and attractive, and the small terraced and semi-detached houses looked pretty and other-worldly, and Kathy felt relief sweep through her. She could live here. Life here would be good! It was all so different to the relentless march of the ugliness of London. She could breathe here; there was less of everything and more air, more space. And somewhere here there was a care home where Granfy lived!

She alighted in the Market Place, which was more of a big, wide street than a square. She noticed a huge ruin of some ecclesiastical building behind a half-empty car park, and at the end of the street stood a modest, but elegant, tapering town cross, with much delicate, carved stone work. She looked at the rows of shops and cafes opposite the ruin; they looked prosperous and inviting; she wondered what this town held for her.

Chapter 17

———————

Glastonbury

Kathy walked towards the town cross, as she felt that would be in the heart of things. And she was proved right. The high street, with all its shops and bustling activity on this early Monday afternoon, stretched up to the east in front of her. She walked up quickly trying to keep herself as invisible as possible, but nevertheless noticing that many of the shops were not what one would expect in a country town. There were several bookshops selling the usual new-age literature that was for sale also in many of the bookshops at home, but here there seemed such an abundance of it. And there were also shops selling what her mother had called new-age bric-a-brac: fairies, angels, wizards, witches, crystals, fairy cards, jewellery, draping cotton and velvet skirts. And what she noticed too, in her walk up the street, were the people. Most of them were in outlandish garb, in clothes all colours of the rainbow and all styles thrown on together without a care for pleasing appearance. She was somewhat shocked. She had never seen so many strange people walking around. And outside the church there was a large group of tattered-looking men, wearing even stranger clothes, but in some subtle way all very similar. These were the homeless, she thought, the drug addicts and the ex-hippies from that infamous age, the sixties, of which she had heard much. She walked quickly on up the street, feeling she had made an error in selecting Glastonbury. It just did not seem to go with Granfy. Everything here was contrary to his style and his values. She wondered if she should take the bus back to Bath. She also noticed she was hungry.

Eventually, she found what she was looking for – a chemist. She went in, found the cosmetics section and bought some eye make-up, a lipstick, and some big, hooped earrings. She then went into a charity shop and purchased, for one pound, a jacket. Then she returned to the bottom of the high street and went into The Knight & Pilgrim. At the bar she ordered a coffee and sandwich and took it into a darkened corner, where she settled herself at the table. The caffeine had an immediate and welcome effect, and she contemplated the next part of her plan with a growing sense of confidence and adventure. Finishing her coffee, she found the Ladies, which, as she had hoped, was empty of other customers. She spent some minutes applying her eye make-up and lipstick, and then began the difficult task of removing all the studs in her ears, and replacing them with the new, hooped earrings. Still no-one else had come into the toilets. Lastly, she changed her jacket. She emerged from the hotel, changed in appearance, but not enough, she felt. When her hair got longer she would undoubtedly look different, but it was *now*, in order to evade detection, that she needed the disguise. And she must get new shoes. These trainers were very eye-catching and might give her away. But she had very little money left. Her next most pressing task was to find a job - and her recent luck in the newsagent's in London gave her added confidence in this – and somewhere for the night.

She walked the short distance back to the town cross. School was out now, and a group of kids occupied the area, lolling on the cross and skate-boarding in the generous space around the monument. Kathy observed them for a short time, inconspicuous in a shop doorway. There was a leader, she saw, so it was obviously something of a gang, but the leader here looked an entirely different animal to Gary, and the gang looked much more loosely organised. The leader was not as powerfully built as Gary, neither did he seem to inspire the same respect and fear in the other kids. He seemed more normal, she thought. After a minute or two, she stepped out of the shop doorway and walked towards the group. She noticed some of them gave the impression of neglect and dysfunction, but a few looked decent kids from normal families, just there to have a good time with their skate boards. Most of them wore the confused, sullen look with which she had become very familiar - the expression of repressed anger that betrayed they knew full well that life was passing them by, that they had not been properly prepared to gain the good things of providence. None of the kids took any notice of her, so she sat down on the steps of the monument. She wondered why she was approaching them. Partly it was because these street folk were one of a kind with her now. She knew their ways now; although not able to feel fully identified with them, something in her now did feel some affinity with these people. Most of them were the outcasts and the semi-outcasts - kids who, through no fault of their own, found themselves outside the normal tracks of humanity; the ones who would probably never have a decent job, never be able to enter upon normal family life, the ones who would drink and take drugs. And she was here also because she just needed to make contact with other human beings her own age; she just needed company. And she hoped from this contact she might find lodging for the next few nights.

The bigger youth was driving his board up and down the curb, hopping and jumping it from the road to the pavement, as though his feet were glued to his board, and then wheeling and turning in sudden, sharp movements on the flat, when the board would suddenly be spat out in front of him. The next moment he actually came to a full stop. He eyed Kathy for a moment.

'Hi, never seen you here; where're you from?'

'Manchester,' she lied.

The boy continued with his antics, showing off his movements. He brought his board up close to Kathy again.

'I'm Paul,' he said.

'I'm Kathy.' (She had thought about giving a false name, but had decided to only falsify her surname.)

He studied her with serious eyes, and she searched for signs of friendliness, but he was off again; restless, she thought. She watched him ride his board; deftly his body controlled it, like a good horseman at one with his mount. He was of a tall, slim build with a head of thick, dark hair, that was not lank and dirty, but well-groomed. None of the kids looked as ill-groomed as they had done in west London. A slightly better system of standards obviously prevailed here, she felt. His face was long, like her own, but pale, and his small mouth was set either in determination or anger; she could not tell. Granfy had always said the mouth of a person was very important; that you could tell a person's character from the mouth.

'Go on,' she said. 'Go on with your skating. You're good. I like to watch you,' and she was amazed at her own spontaneity, and wondered if what she had said had been wise. Paul half smiled and continued with his astonishing antics.

Now a smaller boy joined them. He must have been about eleven or twelve years, she thought, and he had a severe limp. He came up to the monument, where Kathy was sitting, and sat down beside her. The two of them watched Paul and the others circling round, mounting and descending the curb. She wondered what this child was doing here. Surely he was not a stray, like most of the rest of us, she thought; surely he was part of a proper home.

His name was Philip, he told her, and he was twelve. He was in a children's home, a few streets away, and had arrived there when his grandmother had gone into a care home. She had brought him up from infancy, as his parents were both drug addicts. He had never known where they were and had never seen them.

Kathy studied Philip. He was only three years younger than she was, but he looked and felt much younger. His light, hazel eyes looked appealingly into hers, and his blonde hair flopped over his forehead. She reflected he would never be acceptable to a gang, or even a quasi gang, like this one, with his disability, and so, ironically, that injured leg would save him from a possible life of crime and drugs.

'What happened to your leg?' she asked gently.

'I had an accident when I was little; a car ran over me. A drunk. And now that leg won't grow properly.' Kathy imagined the scene, and found herself feeling very sad for him. 'And what about you?' he asked. Kathy repeated the story she had concocted on the bus, half of which she had already told Paul: she was fed up with her family in Manchester, and had decided to leave and look for work.'

'Why Glastonbury?' asked Philip.

'Oh, the festival. Thought I might meet some nice guys here.' She surprised herself with this answer, and wondered if that had been part of the reason she had, unconsciously, selected Glastonbury.

'Are you frightened?' he asked.

'No,' said Kathy, not wanting to admit weakness to this kid.

'It must be hard,' he persisted. 'Being all on your own.'

'Actually, it's nice.' Kathy heard the defiance in her tone, and was again surprised at how her speech seemed to have a life of its own.

'Were your parents really awful?' he continued.

''Drug addicts,' supplied Kathy, getting restless with his questions.

'I know many druggies,' he said, trying to be helpful. She did not respond. She continued to watch Paul in silence, as he deftly manoeuvred his board. He seemed quite oblivious of her, while Philip, on the other hand, seemed acutely aware of her. She was conscious he had edged closer to her, and that he would have liked to continue their conversation. However, her focused attention on the acrobatics in front of them subdued him into a suitable silence.

The sun was sinking in the sky, descending in a pale, blue heaven behind the buildings on the west of the market place and Market Street, lengthening the shadow of the town cross. Suddenly, Paul parked his board on one of the steps of the cross and walked up to the Knight & Pilgrim. Two or three of the others followed. They returned after a few minutes with cans of beer. Soon the town cross area was littered with cans of alcohol and cigarette ends. Kathy felt she was back at the Rag in London, and a gloom descended upon her. She also felt some of the kids were under sixteen, and therefore were consuming alcohol illegally. But did that matter to her now, she wondered. She had broken many rules in the last six months; hardly right for her to sit in judgement on others; hardly right for her to maintain her old standards. And yet she knew she would never take drugs again. She had no-one in the world to turn to, except Granfy – when she found him; her only insurance was her good mind, her sharp brain, and she was going to protect that with all her strength. Granfy! Yes, that was why she had come to Glastonbury - well, to Somerset!

'Heard of an old people's home in these parts?' she unexpectedly blurted out to Philip. He hesitated, looking uncomprehending. 'A care home for the old?' she said.

'Oh, a care home! Yes, my Nan's in one.'

'Where?' asked Kathy quickly, not daring to hope that Granfy might be nearer than she thought.

'Here in Glastonbury, up Chalk Street,' said Philip. 'I'll take you there, if you like.'

'That's great,' said Kathy, standing up.

'Oh, not now,' said Philip quickly. 'I have to be getting back to Tor Edge.'

Feeling she had lost dignity in front of this kid, she pretended to stretch, and settled back again on the hard stone of the step of the cross.

'When, then?' she asked casually.

'Tomorrow?' he offered.

'What time?'

'Five o'clock; I'm going to see my Nan then. You can come with me. I have to be back in Tor Edge at six for supper.'

'Fine. I'll see you here four forty five,' she said, regaining some of her dignity.

'O.K.' said Philip and he moved off.

'Hey,' she added, as he went. 'What's Tor Edge like?'

'It's O.K.' he said. 'They're nice there.' That was all he volunteered. Kathy guessed the kids in the home were probably not all very kind or sympathetic. With that limp, he would be picked on. Not able to join in many of the physical activities, which were timetabled in with regularity for the younger kids, he would be bottom of the popularity polls.

She watched him descend the few steps, slinging his school bag on his back.

'Ciao, Paul; bye,' he called. Paul heard, but took no notice of him. Kathy watched him as he started his progress along

Market Street. On the small side for a twelve year old, Kathy noticed, but he was not under-grown. He had quite a sturdy body, and, apart from that leg, it looked strong. She wondered when his voice would break. He had spoken with a boy's voice. Past the café, he went, with the ruins opposite; past an alley way, where shafts of afternoon sunlight fell momentarily on him, and then past a fine looking, Georgian house; his body going up and down. Kathy again felt sadness for him; she felt her heart opening in compassion. Her problems, though serious and life-threatening in a real way - in that her life could plunge inexorably into even greater difficulty - could, she believed, have an end to them. One day soon, she believed, she would wake up and find that some of her old life had been restored, and that she would find herself once again on track. By contrast, Philip had to get used to the idea that the dull ache, the biting injustice of his life's condition, the taunts of others would never go away, but would be, as it was now, the defining feature, not only of his life and his life chances, but also of his psychological life. There would be no denying it, however politically correct the environment might be; he would always be seen as that limping boy, or man – the lame one.

Paul ran his board up to her and brought it to a sudden, full stop.

'Been talking to yo yo boy?' he asked. She did not answer. So, he had already been assigned a name of ridicule. By now Philip was approaching the end of the street. The sun again fleetingly caught him in a gap between the buildings, illumining his small figure in the blue jeans and green jacket.

'Found anywhere to stay tonight?' queried Paul.

'No,' she replied.

'You ain't been looking much,' he said. Kathy's eyes narrowed and her mouth pursed.

'You can come to our place, if you like. My mum often has folk stay.' Kathy hesitated. She felt she did not like this youth, but she did not have much choice; he had offered digs.

'Thanks,' she replied, trying to disguise her relief. 'That'd be nice, if your family, your mum really doesn't mind.'

'She don't mind,' he said, leaving her, and continuing with his skating.

By now Kathy was bored, and wished to do something else. She stood up, and, picking up her back pack, she decided to take a little turn down the street, keeping Paul and the kids in sight. Then, when she saw them departing she could immediately return. However, on seeing her leaving, Paul picked up his board and can of half-finished beer, and, catching her up, said they should be going now. They walked up the high street in silence, Kathy wondering how much of himself this taciturn youth would be revealing over the coming weeks. But she had tomorrow to look forward to. Would Granfy be in that home in Chalk Street? She felt sure he would be.

Chapter 18

—⌁⌁∙⟨∘⟩⌁⌁—

New Friends

It had been a sheep worker's cottage originally, one of a row of ten or twelve Victorian houses – a pleasing line of homes, adding to the impression that Glastonbury was still a market town. Paul opened the door onto a dishevelled sitting room. Kathy had guessed there would be disorder from the array of inappropriate items on the window sill she had seen from the outside. Rugs lay strewn across the floor and furniture, CDs and cheap books lying everywhere. Whisky and wine bottles, some half full, lay around; dirty dinner plates were piled up in one corner. There were ashes and cinders in the cold grate; a girl's clothing adorned an old rocking chair; a bottle of washing up liquid and a half-full bottle of milk stood on the window sill. Inwardly, Kathy closed her eyes to the disorder, noticing how her spirits sank. On the floor near the centre of the room stood a music centre, and from this came the low sound of reggae on some radio channel. The soft, yellow light from the western sky poured into the front window, casting a warm, ameliorating glow on the disarray, and no doubt curdling the milk on the window sill. At the other end, through the back window, Kathy could see a small, neglected garden rise to a trellis fence, beyond which rose a steep hill in which grew a profusion of different species of trees. The shadowed eastern sky and the thick autumn foliage set a gloom over that part of the room. She stood in the warmer half of the room, in the light, and looked expectantly at Paul.

He looked awkward. He indicated an arm chair for her to sit in. She obediently moved across to it, removed the rug that was lying over half of it, revealing a greasy wing chair (rather like the one her grandfather used to sit in at home), and carefully laid the several CDs on the arm. The smell of whisky was strong, and she wondered who drank, and if there was an alcoholic here. Although still young, she had lately become aware, through the ethics classes at her old school, that people could become alcoholic quite easily and quickly. Paul was making her a cup of tea in the kitchen. She was surprised he was aware of such a nicety. Or perhaps he was preparing supper. Very soon he returned to fetch the bottle of milk off the window sill.

'Are you sure your parents won't mind my being here?' she asked again.

'Me mum won't mind at all; she likes company.' He made no mention of his father. Yes, but will she like *my* company, Kathy wondered. This woman must surely have her own kind. Or was it someone else who was doing the drinking? Well, Paul would not be telling her, so she would have to wait and see. She did not offer to give Paul a hand. She thought he might be embarrassed by the state the kitchen was bound to be in, and then, too, she did not want to depress her spirits even further. Glastonbury had seemed so promising when she had conceived the idea that Granfy would be here. She wanted to hang onto that mood, that tiny thread of hope. After London, she felt she had arrived in a place more like the home of her upbringing, where the air was fresh, and the traffic less, more comfortable; where there were green fields around and prosperous shops in a nice town. But, most of all, she had escaped from fear, drugs and rape. She sat watching the light of the sunset out of the window. Cirrus clouds of pink and gold were catching the last rays of the sun, invisible now behind the buildings opposite. All in all, she was pleased with her progress. This disorder here was only temporary, she told herself. She too would be disappearing from here soon. Everything moves on, she thought firmly.

They were taking tea together, sipped out of cracked china mugs, when Paul's mother arrived. The door was opened with too much strength, and, in a gust of wind, a large, colourfully-dressed woman burst into the sitting room. Her thick, wavy, golden hair was cut in an untidy bob, and swept back from her broad, smooth forehead; her hazel eyes were merry and well-meaning, and her great body, warm and bulky, moved surprisingly easily, Kathy noticed. Without a moment's hesitation she had taken Kathy in her arms and was clasping her in her ample frame. Kathy could feel the mounds of flesh against her own body, and could smell a slight odour on the woman, which was not unpleasant.

'I'm Jenny – Jenny Wren,' and she laughed loudly at this supposed joke. 'What's your name, duck?'

'Kathy Harris,' replied Kathy, trying to get used to this name, Harris, and then waited for the next question.

'Paul brought you? Well, of course you stay the night. I can see you've nowhere to go. Well, we're used to folks like you. You'll be comfortable here.' While saying all this, she had found herself a whisky glass from an oak cupboard that hung in one corner. Kathy thought it was the best bit of furniture in the room, and that it was probably an antique. Jenny settled herself into the armchair across from Kathy, and gazed at her for a moment, allowing the whisky to slowly settle into her and cast its spell of pleasurable sensations all over her large person.

'Where're you from?' she asked

'Manchester,' interposed Paul. 'And she don't talk like she's from there,' he said, as though Kathy were not present.

'Well, I don't know about that. She ain't *said* anything yet,' said Jenny. 'Why are you here, dear?'

Kathy repeated her story, carefully making sure she only imparted what was necessary.

'Well, I'm sorry to hear your parents are addicts,' she said, but cautious, Kathy noticed, not to get herself involved in any discussion around people doing drugs. 'But it's nice to get away,' she said brightly. 'I left home at fifteen, and never looked back since. A nice home, very happy, but I just wanted to be away. On my travels! And never looked back since!' And she took another swig of whisky, and a far-away, troubled look crossed her brown eyes for a moment or two, taking all the merriment out of her face.

'Mum,' said Paul, and Kathy sensed some anxiety in him (perhaps he was watching the consumption of the whisky). 'Mum, we need supper. Shall I go down to the Chinese take-away?'

'Oh, luv, is it supper time already? Yes, it is.' She had looked at her watch and registered surprise. 'It's late! Be a luv and get some chicken curry for me. What'll you have, Kathy?' Kathy had no idea, never having had Chinese food. They only had *tea* out at home, now and again, and never supper.

'Oh, I don't know,' she said, slightly flustered, feeling ignorant. 'You choose for me, Paul.' Jenny opened her purse and gave Paul a twenty pound note, and Kathy knew she must somehow repay Jenny for this favour.

Paul was gone for about twenty minutes – an interval which gave Kathy and Jenny enough time to learn something of each other. Under Jenny's questioning, Kathy enlarged on her story slightly, disclosing the fact she had a younger sister, Ellie, who was still at home, and who was visited by social workers. Jenny looked at Kathy, penetratingly for a moment. Kathy tried to shrink into her eye make-up, and felt she should have applied more lipstick.

'You don't look like one of those kids,' she said. 'You look educated; you *feel* educated.'

'Well, I kinda took refuge in my books,' said Kathy. 'It was a way of getting away from the hell of it all at home. All that doing dope. It's so awful, you know ....'

Jenny was silent for a while, no doubt considering these apparently ingenuous remarks of Kathy's. She contemplated the dead fire in the grate, and, seeming to find no solace there, took another swig from her glass.

'Well, yes, to be sure,' she said. Then, seeming to gain strength from her inebriated state, she began to talk freely and told Kathy she worked in a children's home down the other end of town. She said she would have liked to ride her bicycle there and back each day but it was just too much for her now. So, she walked. That was what was nice about Glastonbury; it was small enough to be able to walk everywhere – and all that walking kept her nice and fit. Kathy asked if the place where she worked was the same children's home, where Philip, the boy with the limp, lived. (She could not bring herself to say 'physically challenged'. Her mother had said those terms were quite stupid and that she could always find a way round them.)

'Oh, yes,' she said. 'He's a love, little Philip. Poor Philip!' Kathy wondered if she knew her son called him 'yo-yo boy.'

'I heard some of the kids down at the skate-boarding place call him 'yo-yo boy,'' she said.

'Well, did they?' said Jenny in a tone that did not quite register the surprise it was meant to. 'You'd think they'd know better. That's just cruel. If ever I catch anyone calling him by that name, or any name, I'll whack them.' But Kathy could see the alcohol had infused her brain with pleasing and illusory ideas about her capabilities, and that in reality Jenny probably heard disparaging references to Philip every day, and did nothing about it – probably could do nothing about it.

Paul returned with the Chinese take-away and found some clean plates from the kitchen. It was a pleasant enough evening. Kathy discovered she was very hungry, and, for the first time since leaving home, enjoyed her food. Jenny was slowly overcome by the alcohol, and by ten o'clock, when she announced they must all go to bed, she was making very little sense. Paul showed Kathy to his sister's room, and gave her two clean sheets to put on the futon, and a bath towel. His sister, Colette, was away just now, he said. No doubt she would find out more tomorrow, thought Kathy.

*   *   *

Kathy slept well that night – the first time in the four months since she had left home. She dreamed of home. Her father was in the shed in the garden, repairing a rocking chair Kathy's mother had found in an auction house in Hexbury. Kathy was in the dining room facing onto the back garden doing her homework. Since no-one was at work or at school it must have been the weekend. It felt like Sunday. There was a stillness in the air, a lack of timed activity, a peace that could hang a little too boringly over life. Perhaps it was church, where they had all undoubtedly been earlier in the morning, that made one feel slightly gloomy like a kind of dampening down of the spirits. And, too, the sky was grey and overcast, and spotting with a light rain. That was *very* Sunday! She gazed dreamily out of the window, the only sound the intermittent hammering from the shed. There were daffodils out, and crocuses. They looked so green and yellow and purple, so fresh - true heralds of the joyousness of spring. Kathy returned her attention to The Mill on the Floss, and the difficult life of Maggie Tulliver at the mill. Would Maggie's fortunes change and finally result in her being able to express herself in the ways she wanted? Would she marry someone who was himself good and spiritually inclined, as she was, and who could provide her with the means for the self-improvement that she so longed for? And what of her brother, Tom – so central to Maggie's life? She contemplated Maggie's life from the warm security of her own, and caught sight of her father moving about at the end of the garden. She forgot to think about Maggie, and for a few seconds rested blissfully in the comfort she had in seeing her father go about his tasks. Her world was ordered, predictable, she thought. She moved from one aspect of it to another, and always securely held in the warmth of her home. A peacefulness and a confidence pervaded her whole self, and she thought when she had finished the next chapter she would like to go and bake a cake in the kitchen. She returned her attention to the chapter in hand, and followed Tom in his efforts to catch a fish. She heard the water in the millstream, and felt the rain coming down on him, and then he seemed to get fainter and she must push him on, make him crawl through the bushes, hang over the edge of the water and catch a fish. She woke slightly, conscious that she was now in that light sleep state, weaving this dream, inventing it, propelling Tom forwards. And then she heard the rain on the window, and the dream vanished.

Fully awake now, she mused on the life of Maggie. A few months ago Maggie's life had seemed problematic and difficult, and, by contrast, her own full of promise and ease – a more preferable life. Now, things had been completely reversed, and it was her life that seemed the problematic one, and – much worse – a desperate one. Her own life had delivered such a blow as to shake her confidence in the very principles of life that she had formulated. She would never want for food or a roof over her head, as the unfortunates of Maggie Tulliver's time would experience; but she might never again move in a class of intelligent, well-behaved, decent people. Her recent experiences had catapulted her into a class she never really knew existed – a class of badly-behaved people and drug-ruined intellects. She was on the bottom rung of British society, and she wondered what the bottom rung of Victorian Britain had been like – the work house came to mind. But, surely, in the work house people still had their wits about them, and therefore could still think and hope. She thought of Gary and the gangs, and knew there was no hope for these people. And she wondered what kind of a God it was that had so cruelly flung her out of her birthright into a world where there was only degradation, and where she was so helpless.

Lying there in the early hours of this Tuesday morning, when she should have been at school, perhaps discussing the Mill On The Floss, she looked around this strange, disorderly bedroom, and realised this was the first time she had looked back on her life and had tried to make sense of it. It seemed like a terrible nightmare that could only happen to someone else. It really could not have happened to her, Kathy Miller, whose life two years ago was proceeding in a very orderly and reliable way. Somehow, she thought, I have to find Granfy. Somehow, he was the key. In finding him, something of her lost life would be restored, her lost sense of self would be healed. And, here in Glastonbury, she felt, it would be possible. Here, from what she had seen, there were none of those abandoned, life-hardened, young people she had mixed with in London, who were beyond the help of teachers and social workers.

The rain must have stopped; it had stopped pattering on the window. And in the garden she could hear a chaffinch singing somewhere on a tree close by. That little orange-coloured bird with the grey head and white wing flashes was singing its heart out - like water cascading down a cliff, she thought, and then finishing with a final flourish. And her spirits lifted.

There was silence in the house when she rose from her bed, which seemed to suggest Paul and his mother were not up. She would have to creep noiselessly about and not disturb them. However, when she descended the narrow staircase, she saw a note on a large sheet of paper and a key. The note told her to help herself to breakfast, and to lock the front door when she went out. It was signed 'Paul'.

She made herself some toast and a boiled egg for breakfast, and ate in the sitting room, looking out of the window. The milk bottle had been removed, but the washing up liquid bottle was still there. Still, she enjoyed her breakfast. She felt free. Free of those institutions to which she had been assigned and confined. Free of the children's home and free of James Arnold school, and free of that other institution – Gary and his gang!

The kitchen had not been as disgusting as she had expected; perhaps because they bought take-aways most of the time, she thought. She washed the few dirty dishes, tidied up, and wiped down all the counters, and briefly re-arranged the fridge. Then she put on her new jacket and day bag and set off to look for a job.

Chapter 19

―――∽✦∾――――

Disappointment

G etting a job and having some money had now become a
priority, even surpassing that of finding Granfy. Amenable
though Jenny seemed, she would some time soon want some
reimbursement for her hospitality. If that was not forthcoming
she mind find herself homeless, Kathy thought. Even with all
my problems I am too smart to let that happen, she mused. After
all, I have run away successfully, she reminded herself. Even
if only for a day! She wondered if they would come looking for
her. She imagined Gary turning up in Glastonbury and making
straight for the town cross, as she had done. She shrank from
the thought, and felt fear deep inside her. That scenario spelt
doom - a life-time of doom; it was a dreadful prospect. She
thought of Nancy being a virtual prisoner of Bill Sykes, and, for
the first time it occurred to her that people, especially women,
by accidents of fate, could have truly, terrible lives.

She was making for the café down at the bottom of the high street, near the town cross. On the way she passed a newsagent and stopped to study the front pages of the morning's press. None of them reported a missing girl; nowhere did she see a photograph of herself. With relief and a heart that beat easier, she continued on down the road. Then she realised it was too soon yet for the press to write the story of a missing girl. Mike would have been bound by the rules to report her absence immediately, but the police would concentrate their search in London first, surely.

She was about half way down the high street, when her eye was caught by a sandwich board on the opposite side advertising the fare of a café-restaurant. The shops on either side of it were full of new-age ware – crystals, models of fairies, books on runes, astrology and meditation. The café was up a narrow alley and looked to be very 'alternative', like the neighbouring shops. She fancied that the 'alternative' establishments would offer better prospects for employment than the conventional ones, and entered hopefully. The café was dimly lit and filled with wooden chairs and tables at which a few customers were eating breakfast. Kathy liked the feel of the place and walked up to the counter, where many different kinds of home-made cakes and scones were displayed in a glass case. No-one was present to serve. She thought they must all be engaged in preparing the lunch. Finally, a young woman, with long, fair hair and pleasant brown eyes, wearing purple and long, jangly ear-rings, emerged from the kitchen. Feeling awkward, Kathy immediately went round to the till and caught the woman's eye, who finished putting some sandwiches in the display case. She then approached Kathy with an inquiring look. Nervously, Kathy asked if she needed any help waitressing, cooking, anything. 'Have you waitressed before?' the young woman asked.

'Yes, a little; in the holidays,' lied Kathy. 'And I learn fast.'

'Well, actually, we do need some help just now,' replied the woman, but we need someone to start right now. Our assistant cook is off ill.'

'Oh, I can do that,' said Kathy, and her spirits rose.

Sensing the brightness in Kathy's face, the woman quickly added: 'but it won't be for long; our assistant will be back.'

Kathy was engaged there and then – just for a few days, she was told - and set to work in the kitchen, cutting bread, preparing salad vegetables and making up sandwiches. She felt happiness rising in her. It was good not to have to spend her day in that dreadful school for delinquent children, or truanting and having to find things to do to while away the time. It was good to be with normal people too, even if she did find them a little strange with their untidy hair and long, draping clothes.

At the end of the afternoon, when the café was almost emptied of its tea-time customers, Emma, the blonde and purple woman, whom Kathy took to be the manageress, told her she could leave. No questions were asked, and she was given twenty five pounds. Kathy had no idea if this was a fair wage, but she was very satisfied. She could give Jenny something. She felt a wave of relief spread over her, as though an important hurdle had been taken. She felt a small sense of security, a pleasing feeling, arising in her stomach.

She tidied herself up in the staff cloakroom, repairing her heavy eye make-up and applying fresh, bright red lipstick. She had never worn make-up before – her mother told her she was far too young for that, and that anyway she would never need to – but, surveying herself briefly in the mirror, she saw how the charcoal black of the pencil and mascara enhanced the colour and shape of her eyes. She thought it brought out the blue in her grey eyes and made them look bigger. But she felt she looked common, too - like some of the kids in the towns at home, that her mother disapproved of.

She arrived at the town cross a few minutes before Philip. There was only a handful of kids there, mostly younger boys. Then Philip came into view, limping noticeably, up and down. He still wore his jeans and green jacket, and, as he approached, she could see his blonde hair still fell across his forehead. He was still smiling too, and, as he drew nearer, it increased. She wished he didn't smile so much at her. She only wanted a sort of business relationship with him. She didn't want anything more friendly. She had her image to think of. Paul would be someone to be reckoned with, and there may be others – Garys. (She prayed this would not be the case.) Being seen as Philip's friend might not be compatible with getting herself accepted. However, she felt more than well-disposed to him this afternoon. He was going to take her to the old people's home to find Granfy. She felt full of hope and her old feelings of childhood security and well-being seemed within reach. They were not yet within the compass of her being, but she felt they soon would be. Soon, soon things will be better, sang her mind. Granfy would be able to help; just seeing him would put everything right, and soon she would get him out of the care home and they would set up house together somewhere. Just a little house, something that was feasible. They wouldn't ask for much. Just a little house the council could afford.

And with these thoughts Kathy watched the lolloping gait of Philip as he bounced along the street – up and down – towards her, smiling his friendly smile. She pondered why the doctors had not done more for him. She wondered why he didn't at least have a built-up shoe.

'Hello, Kathy,' he said shyly.

'Hello,' she replied. And she felt a wave of sympathy for him again, which, in the next instant, irritated her.

'Do you still want to come to the care home?' he asked.

'Course I do,' said Kathy, jumping up and descending the steps. 'Let's go now.'

It was an odd sensation walking along with this young boy with the floppy, blonde hair, and the flopping gait. Up and down he went, beside her. Part of her wanted to take him in her arms, like she might have done with a small, younger brother, and comfort him in his terrible affliction. And part of her warned against becoming a feeling, normal person. In the three months she had been in London, she had learned some valuable lessons in toughening up; she was not about to let these lessons go. She needed all her survival skills; she needed to keep herself hard and defended. Nevertheless, she found she enjoyed Philip's company, despite herself.

They came to the end of the street, and turned left into Chalk Street. The sun streamed up the road. It was a warm day for November, and she felt the heat on her back and relaxed into it. At home, being so far north, at this time of the afternoon it would be dusk, she thought, and the feeling of the approaching winter would be very evident.

'Where did you stay last night, Kathy?' asked Philip.

'At Paul's place.' There was a short silence, while Philip pondered on the implications of this.

'Was it alright?' he ventured.

'Perfectly,' said Kathy. She knew how Paul regarded Philip, the name he called him, and wondered if it also extended to bullying. 'Yes, it was fine,' she added.

'I'm glad,' said Philip after a moment, in what Kathy thought was a gesture of generosity and selflessness. Was he really so pleased and concerned that she had been comfortable last night, and then only through the good services of someone who was so callous towards him? She cast a long glance at him. His child's face was pleasant to contemplate, not troubled by the implications of this news at all, but genuinely glad for her. She imagined again the acute psychological suffering he must have to endure privately, and the long years of suffering in front of him. Just now, she thought, he still had that innocence, that trust of childhood which must mitigate the pain somewhat; but he had something else too, she felt, but could not put her finger on it. He turned to look at her, and his warm, brown eyes smiled at her.

'I like you, Kathy,' he said in his child's way. 'Can we be friends?' Kathy recognised that he would hardly have any friends, and that her friendship would mean a lot to him, but she could not afford to extend this part of herself to him. In these times, in the community she now found herself in, friendship had become a luxury of the past. Everything now was political.

Finer things, like manners and friendship, were for the better-placed; they were privileged things, she thought. Here you took stock of your situation and watched your back all the time. If you're not smart and you don't do it like this, you get really hurt, she mused, even killed, especially in the poor areas of the big towns, like that part of west London she had just left.

'Do you miss Manchester?' asked Philip. 'It must be very different to Somerset?'

'No; it's not that different,' replied Kathy, needlessly irritated.

'Oh, I didn't know,' said the boy, his brown eyes gazing at her in puzzlement, as he tried to fathom why he had irritated her. She regretted that she had been sharp with him, but, really, he asked too many questions. He should know when to keep quiet. He must learn how to be smart. Then, she reflected he was only twelve, and that probably he *was* learning to be streetwise, in his own cripple-boy way. Like her, he too would probably be learning to absorb information in order to increase his hold on that tiny bit of power that would be available to him, and so avoid at least some of the taunts of the other children. In order to deflect the attention from herself, and because he insisted on trying to talk to her, she decided to ask him about himself.

'What do you like to do when you're not at school? Do you just hang out at the cross?' she asked.

'The cross?' he looked puzzled again. 'Oh, you mean the plaza,' he laughed.

'Plaza!' said Kathy. 'It's not a plaza. Do you know what a plaza looks like?' and she laughed too.

'No, I don't, Kathy. Tell me. What does a plaza look like? I only call it that because they all do.'

'Oh, do they?' said Kathy thoughtfully, slotting away this important fact.

'A plaza,' she explained 'is a big square. Like they have in European towns. They have them in London, too, but they're different.'

'Oh,' said Philip. And Kathy could see he had no experience of Europe, not even from books. She had picked up her scanty knowledge from her French books and from a school trip to Paris last year.

'What do I like to do?' repeated Philip, who had been hoping she would return to her question. 'Well, I like looking at the animals in the river; I like to look at the birds in the garden, and at the river too. And I like dogs,' he said finally and with gusto. 'We used to have a dog.'

'When?' asked Kathy.

'Oh, at home,' he replied. And Kathy did not pursue the topic, realising there were memories he could still not bear to face.

'But I'll take you to the river, Kathy, and show you all sorts of things.'

'Thanks,' she said. 'That would be nice.' But she could not envisage that a pleasant trip to a river to watch the wildlife would ever become a reality.

'Oh, here we are,' said Philip, stopping suddenly in front of a big, gracious, Georgian mansion. He opened the gate and led Kathy up the short path that stopped before a blue front door, ornamented with a big brass knocker of a dolphin.

Kathy's heart started to beat. 'Granfy,' she thought. 'Please, dear, dear God, let Granfy be here.' She looked at the big, shining dolphin, and liked it, and wondered if it would be a lucky omen. Philip rang the bell, and after a few seconds a middle-aged woman with short, brown hair and a friendly face opened the door.

'Oh, Philip,' she said. 'Come on in, love,' and she stooped and kissed him on his cheek, and patted his head. Kathy was taken aback; she hadn't seen this kind of affection for a long time. She stared at the woman.

'This is Kathy,' said Philip.

'And I'm Mrs. Craggs,' said the woman. 'Nan's in her room this afternoon,' she told Philip. 'Just you go along, dear. She's waiting for you.'

'Yes, thanks,' said Philip. 'But first, Kathy here; she's looking for her grandfather.'

'Well, come along to my office, dear, and you go on up to see your Nan, Philip.' Kathy followed Mrs. Craggs down the lino-floored passage, which only slightly marred the elegance of the house. She had rarely been in such a house before, and was reminded of the National Trust properties they had occasionally visited as a family. Feeling daunted, all of a sudden, by this grand house and the probable impossibility of her mission, her heart entered a new phase of rapid beating. They entered the office of the manageress. Kathy was not sure if Mrs. Craggs was the manageress.

'Now, dear,' she said. 'What is your grandfather's name?'

'Archie Miller,' replied Kathy.

'Oh, no, dear. We've no-one by that name here; not now. Let me look and see if he was here some time back.' And she turned to a shelf housing a number of large box files.

Kathy felt her heart sinking, and with it the beating subsided, and now she felt rather weak. Her disappointment was intense. For weeks, she realised now, that she had been planning this moment; waiting for it; giving it a life that would give her her life back. And now this nice woman in the pale blue uniform had just smashed her dream.

'Thank you,' she said in a small voice, and she realised she was close to tears. Mrs. Craggs stepped out from behind the desk, and put a comforting hand on Kathy's arm. Kathy felt the tears well up in her eyes, and prayed Mrs. Craggs would remove her hand, because under that hand she felt undone. She felt weak and helpless, with all her loss of the past four months just below the surface, willing a way to come up and spill over in tears. Kathy knew if she cried she would not be able to stop. Mrs. Craggs did not remove her hand, because she was that sort of woman – naturally kind and caring. But, in time, Kathy collected herself, and recalled her new persona from its brief escape, and put it on again, and assumed all its disciplined feelings once more. They were becoming so familiar – these Becky Sharp feelings. Mrs. Craggs removed her hand, and returned to the box file on her desk.

'I'll just have a look through some back files,' she said.

'Oh, that won't be necessary,' said Kathy. 'He only went into care four months ago.'

'Oh, I see, dear,' said Mrs. Craggs and closed the box again. 'And what's your name, dear?'

'Kathy, Kathy Harris,' she said, wondering why she had chosen that name while sitting on the bus, making up the story of her past life.

'So, he went into care four months ago, and here in Glastonbury?'

'I don't know,' said Kathy, feebly. 'Somewhere in Somerset.'

'Somewhere in Somerset! But that could be any number of places – Wells, Taunton, Bath or even Bristol. I tell you what, Kathy, come back tomorrow evening when the manageress, Mrs. Evans, is here. She might be able to help - with the computer, you know. I don't understand these things, but she does; she's good.' Kathy nodded. 'Well, I'm really sorry, dear. If *I* hear of anything, I'll let you know. Where do you live?'

'Oh, I'm just staying with friends. I won't be there much longer,' she said, embarrassed not to have a fixed address. 'Just let Philip know – we're friends.'

'I'll do that, dear. And now do you want to wait for Philip?'

'No, thank you,' said Kathy. 'And thank you; you've been very helpful!'

'Goodbye, dear, and come back tomorrow evening and see Mrs. Evans.' And Mrs. Craggs opened the front door.

Kathy stepped outside again and let her feet guide her to the gate. It was dusk now; people were hurrying about in their lives. What was she to do? She had no life, no plans now; she was not going anywhere now. She had to make a choice here; she could either turn left and go up to Paul's house, or right and go back to the town cross, or the plaza, as she must now call it. But which? Which did she belong to the most? She put her hand in her pocket to feel the pack of cigarettes, and felt the key to Paul and Jenny's house. The decision was made for her. She did have somewhere to walk to, to head for. Lost, hardly able to bear her disappointment, she walked on automatically. But at least she had somewhere for the night, she thought, and she also had twenty five pounds in her pocket. She thought it would be nice to have a cigarette, and looked around for somewhere to smoke it.

Chapter 20

────◦◦◦◦◦◦◦◦────

Disturbing Feelings

She sheltered briefly in a gateway, which bore the name, 'Chalice Well', enjoying the inhaling of the smoke. On either side of the gate rose high, Cotswold stone walls, which did not seem to be forbidding, even in this now darkened hour, but which rather seemed warm and welcoming. She decided to ask Jenny and Paul about this place.

The key turned easily in the lock, and she let herself into the house. It was chilly, like the evening outside had become, and the television was on. She called, but no-one answered, and she felt there was no-one at home. From the dirty dinner plates on the floor, she realised that Jenny and Paul had eaten. Momentarily hurt she had not been thought of, she cleared away the dirty dishes, turned off the television, and let herself out of the front door again. She walked down the high street until she found the Chinese takeaway, and bought exactly what Paul had bought for her last night.

She walked rapidly back to the house. Still no-one was in. She settled herself into the sofa, and began to eat, watching a wild life programme on the television. At ten o'clock the door opened and Paul appeared, a little the worse for drink, she thought. He stood sullenly in front of the door surveying her.

'My mother's at a party; we've both been there. She won't be home tonight, she's staying with her boyfriend.'

So, Jenny had a boyfriend, thought Kathy. She had not considered this before; she thought her over-weight would have put off any man.

'We could have a nice time here,' he suggested in a leering way.

'Actually, I'm just off to bed, Paul. I'm dead tired. Had a tiring day. There's a good programme on television you could watch.'

'I don't want to watch television,' he said, and made a step towards her. All the new fears she had learned over the past four months came flooding back. She realised in a flash she would be no match for Paul. Not a big youth, he was yet sinewy and strong. I can't stay here, she thought. This house is not safe. But she had no-where to go, not at this hour of the night. Then Paul seemed to recollect himself. He moved about the room in a normal way.

'You're gonna be alright, sister; as long as you're here I'll look after you.' A flood of relief swept over Kathy. She could see he meant what he said and that he no longer constituted a danger. But she was puzzled: why had he called her 'sister'? Was there something about her that made these bullies, like Gary and, now, Paul, call her 'sister' or 'little sis'?

She slept fitfully during the night, dreaming now and again of Granfy, of finding him, but always in strange and unreal landscapes. Once he appeared as an old man with a long, white beard high up a mountainside, beckoning her to climb up to where he was. But the path was steep and rough and she was afraid. And she had remained on the lower slopes. In the morning she was perplexed by the dream, and wondered if, after all, she was fainthearted and lacked courage.

When she came downstairs she discovered that Paul had already left for work. She fixed herself a boiled egg and toast again, holding the egg in a paper napkin, because she could find no egg cups. The fridge was filthy, and she decided, if she got time later in the day, she would clean it out. She left for work. It felt strange to have swapped her long bus journey into Newcastle, where her school was, for this walk to work. Only four months ago she had been a regular pupil in a regular life. 'Granfy, Granfy', she called inwardly.

At the restaurant Emma was sweet and kind, Kathy decided, but a little fey and 'floaty'; all those long, draping clothes and earrings and hair put Kathy in mind of some overgrown child who could not give up her belief in fairies. But the shop next door was full of such figures; perhaps people in Glastonbury, she thought, really did still believe in fairies. She wondered how Emma ran the business; she did not look at all business-like. However, at midday, Kathy, her hands deep in dishwater, was introduced to Debbie. 'Debbie is our manageress,' said Emma. An attractive woman, in her mid thirties with alert, appraising eyes and tidy, short brown hair, her presence spoke of authority and competence. Nervously, Kathy withdrew her yellow-gloved hands from the bowl of soap suds, and after an introduction by Emma, repeated her Manchester story.

'I see,' said Debbie. 'Well, if you are to stay with us, and there may be a possibility, I'll need your P45 form.'

'Yes, of course,' Kathy managed to say, as if it had been an expected request, and then she regretted the deception. She had perhaps made the moment of truth harder. She would have to confide to Emma that she did not know what this form was or where to get it.

Having eaten a substantial lunch at the restaurant, in order to make supper unnecessary, and having pocketed another twenty five pounds in cash, Kathy left the restaurant and, with hope once again restored, made straight for the care home. Mrs. Evans was busy with a patient's relative in the office, and Kathy sat in the small waiting room. The walls were lined with paintings done by the patients, some of them quite good, thought Kathy. Eventually, Mrs. Evans saw her visitor out of the front door, and welcomed Kathy, who followed her into the office. Mrs. Evans was an older woman, short in build, with thick, grey, curly hair, and spectacles, who, Kathy thought, looked just like the manageress of an old folks' home should look. Kathy repeated her request.

'Kathy Harris, is it?' she asked, rather formally.

'Yes,' replied Kathy. 'Mrs. Craggs thought you might be able to use your computer to find my grandfather.'

'I don't know where she got that idea from. I can access all the care homes in Somerset, but I don't have access to their patient lists. They're private.'

'Oh,' said Kathy, absorbing this news and feeling despondency descend like a leaden weight again.

'I would have suggested the electoral roll,' said Mrs. Evans. 'But as he's only been in care for four months, his name will not yet be on the register.' Kathy hardly knew what an electoral roll was; she had heard her parents mention it, but did not know its purpose. 'I'm sorry, dear,' said Mrs. Evans, sensing Kathy's disappointment. 'Have you nothing else to go on? A relative or something?'

'Well, there's May Miller, who is his sister.'

'There you are!' exclaimed Mrs. Evans. 'See if you can trace May Miller on the electoral roll. She does live in Somerset, doesn't she?'

'Oh, yes,' and Kathy's spirits lifted a little.

Mrs. Evans led Kathy to the door and saw her off warmly, wishing her luck in her search. 'You're a proper Sherlock Holmes,' she said encouragingly.

It was only five o'clock, and Kathy did not want to go back to the house just yet. Instead, she bought the Daily Mail and went into a café and ordered a cup of tea and a brownie. This felt more like tea-time at home, and some small part of her felt placated. She read the paper from cover to cover, but there was nothing in it about a missing girl. She allowed herself some small congratulation. At least some of her strategy was going well. Then she remembered she had not thought sufficiently of Becky Sharp for some time. Perhaps if she had remembered her things may have gone better. And she wondered again about Becky's feelings. Had Becky ever felt the bitter disappointments and disorientation she was now feeling. She could not remember Becky's feelings ever being described in the book. But if Becky always had her plans and strategies to follow, then there would have been no place for feelings like disappointment. She decided to bring Becky back into her life. She still needed this ruthless, cold, young woman. For a bit longer, anyway!

At that moment she raised her eyes and saw a boy coming into the café. It was Philip! 'Oh God,' she thought, 'he has no friends but me! Can't he find someone else to be his comforter. Not me, please. Go away, Philip.'

'Hello, Kathy,' said Philip, limping up to her table and taking a seat. 'I've been looking for you everywhere.' His boy's hand, not yet hardened into muscle and shape, pushed back his blond hair, and his brown eyes smiled happily at having found her. Kathy tried to return his look as stonily as she could, but Philip carried on in the same jocund, trusting manner, either because he was unaware of her look, or because he was so used to such discouraging signals he could ignore it. And then she hated herself for being unnatural. How had Becky managed these situations, calling for sympathy and understanding?

'I've told my nan all about you,' he said proudly. 'She wants to meet you.' How could an old woman in a care home help me, thought Kathy and she was irritated. Philip changed the subject.

'Was Mrs. Evans able to help you?' he asked.

'No,' said Kathy, abruptly, and disliked herself again.

'Oh, I'm sorry, Kathy,' he said, crestfallen. 'What are you going to do now?'

'Oh, I don't know. I'll think of something,' she said airily, placing her packet of cigarettes on the table, hoping to demonstrate to him that she was not the good, kind girl he seemed to be taking her for. She wished he would go away. He was bad for her image – Paul might see. And he was bad for her feelings; he made her feel soft and kind, when what she had to be was hard. Hard, hard, like steel! she said to herself: kindness is a luxury; I cannot afford it now; later. Just now I must survive. And she compressed her lips and returned his good humour and friendliness with impassivity.

'Kathy, please look after my bag; I'm going to get a drink and a cake like you,' he said suddenly. And he got up, leaving his school bag on the chair, and limped over to the food counter. Kathy watched him, and all of a sudden, her heart softened, as she felt again the full impact of his silent, lonely road and struggle in life, and she was sorry for him, and the tears actually welled up in her eyes. And she felt she did, really, deep down want to be his comforter, and big sister. And, too, she was amazed at the instantaneous change of emotion in herself. One moment she had been intensely irritated by him, hard and unsympathetic; the next, in a flash, full of compassion and understanding. She marvelled at this aspect of herself – the way one emotion could, chameleon-like, give way to another. She wondered which was really her. Which of the emotions more truly belonged to her; and who and what was she really? She wondered if the stress she was going through was making her unbalanced. She dimly recalled her grandmother, who had long been dead, saying of several people: 'oh, so and so's not right in the head!' And again that fear for herself reasserted itself in the pit of her stomach. She felt that Becky indeed was absolutely her only refuge.

Chapter 21

———⟨∽∞⊶⊙⊷∞∽⟩———

Showing Off

Kathy was playing in the main road of Mickle Wood. It was not a busy road and was perfectly safe for the village kids to play there. Her father had just fixed new brakes on the bike, and her mother was pleased she was staying in the village this Saturday, and not cycling over to Hexbury or the riding school at White Hill.

'I'm so much happier you're playing with your friends here,' said Elaine.

'Meaning what?' said Kathy rudely.

'Well, going to the White Hill riding school; it's too far and I do sometimes think, Kathy, those girls are not good for you.'

'What do you mean?' asked Kathy angrily.

'Well, dear, they're not our class. You'll only make yourself unhappy mixing with them. We don't have the money they do.' Elaine looked at her daughter and knew it would be very difficult to guide and advise her. Susie was so much easier. This child was wilful and so independent, and her precociousness sometimes defeated her.

'Maggie and Phyllis aren't rich,' retorted Kathy. 'They live in small houses, probably smaller than ours.'

'Oh, I thought Phyllis's people were well off,' said Elaine, puzzled. 'That time I saw Phyllis, she looked, well, sort of rich, as though the family had money.'

'No, they're not,' said Kathy emphatically. 'That's Phyllis; she gives herself airs and graces and pretends she comes from a rich family.'

'Oh,' said Elaine, deflated. She sometimes wondered if this school in Newcastle had been the best choice for her daughter. She wondered if it made some of the girls ashamed of their backgrounds.

'Only Ellie comes from an upper class background, and I like her; we're friends.' And with that Kathy ended the conversation and went into the garden to collect her bike and leave through the back gate, which gave onto the narrow alley.

'Susie's coming too, dear; do you mind?' called Elaine apologetically.

They pedalled up and down the street on their bikes, sometimes riding onto the green, and performed various little stunts they had learned. Some of the younger boys, who now appeared, were particularly good at getting speed up and then putting their feet up on the handle bars, especially when they came down Well Lane, which ran off the village main road at right angles and then up into the hills. Flying down they came, turning at the corner, feet up, jackets billowing, amid whoops and shouts of sheer abandon. Kathy watched in admiration and felt some anxiety about her turn to do this stunt. Then Tom arrived. Immediately Kathy's feelings became mixed with something else that she did not understand. She was only aware of the fact that she must, at all costs, impress him, and certainly not disgrace herself. Conscious she was about to engage in showing off, she went a good way up Well Lane to give herself plenty of speed, and prayed to God she would not crash and fall off and break an arm or crack her head open, which had been known to happen. She should have worn her bike helmet, she knew, but none of the others were. She set off. Well Lane was steep, and she had given herself a good hundred yards to work up speed. Soon the wind was in her face and on her chest, and she could feel the excitement and panic rising in her and the thudding and vibrating of the front wheel. She had stopped pedalling; there was no need now; the gradient was enough to give her all the speed she wanted. She gripped the handlebars tightly, her mind dominated by the image of Tom at the bottom and the fact he would see her. Garden walls and fences and winter flowers and leaves flashed by unnoticed. All she saw was the tarmac immediately before her and the main road at the bottom advancing by the second. By the time she got to the bottom she was going about forty miles an hour. Frightened, but exhilarated, she deftly swerved round a high garden wall on the right, as she turned into the main road. Then there was that fence on the opposite side which she now had to clear. Two years ago Geoff had crashed into it, and the village residents had almost succeeded in getting this game banned. She cleared it; she had managed the sharp turn and not gone hurtling into the fence in front. She was safe! She had seen Tom out of the corner of her eye standing further up from the fence, and experienced a deep feeling of satisfaction, knowing he had witnessed this escapade of courage. She hurtled on for another fifty yards, coming to a stop beyond the green. Flushed with excitement, she turned to see the reaction of Tom and the others.

'Great, Kathy! That was some ride,' called Tom, as she rode her bike back to the group. She felt praised, and knew she would do almost anything to earn Tom's attention and praise again. A big lad, strong and handsome, all the village kids were somewhat in awe of him. But he rarely came out to spend time with them now; he was usually playing in some organised sport with his school, or else working for his GCSEs, or helping his father with some chore. Soon, he too came flying down Well Lane, but, unlike Kathy, he swerved to the left, which was a much more difficult manoeuvre, because of another garden wall that jutted awkwardly out into the street. His dark hair swept back by the wind and his face set confidently, he swerved easily and gracefully and came to a stop further up the street. He wasn't flushed, as she was, and she thought he hadn't looked in the least bit frightened as he came hurtling down the last part of Well Lane into that difficult corner. Would she ever be able to be as cool and competent as these big boys, she wondered. Her mother thought Tom misled the younger children; she thought it was all Tom's idea that they do these dangerous things, but Kathy knew it was the kids who came up with these ideas.

* * *

It was Sunday, and beneath an alternating cloudy and blue sky, this March afternoon delivered its usual share of sunshine, showers and gusting wind. Kathy's parents and Susie had gone for a walk up the Fell, behind the houses, leaving Granfy asleep on his bed, and Kathy to do an essay on the Mill on the Floss. She leafed through the book again; she liked Maggie; she was intelligent, kind and beautiful, all the things a girl would like to be. She liked Tom Tulliver too; he had his good points. How was she to tackle this essay? 'Describe Maggie's life, and contrast it with a young girl's life today,' was the question, set by Miss Rutter, the English teacher. Maggie's life was vastly different, and she seemed much more mature than the young girls of today. Where to begin? Kathy also had Black Beauty on the dining room table, a book her mother had got out of the library for her. She had been well into this during the evenings of this week, after she had done her homework, and all she wanted to do now was see the story to its end, see this beautiful, distressed horse finally achieve a resting place with kind people. But the Mill on the Floss essay had to be handed in tomorrow. It was just like Kathy to leave it to the last moment. She gazed beyond the round, polished oak dining table, with its marks of age pitting the surface, a constant reminder, if you cared to be reminded, of the other families in olden times who had sat round this table or worked on it, as she was doing. She gazed beyond it into the garden and saw the big cherry tree at the end, which stood bare of foliage and naked to the elements. She wished she could be out walking with her family, her face in the wind, and some sharp showers of rain on her cheeks, with the scared sheep running off before them, as they strode across the moorland.

Now her gaze came to rest on the blue and white bowl of apples on the window sill. These apples were so red and inviting, Kathy could have got up and taken one. If the apple on the tree of Knowledge of Good and Evil was as tempting as these, then she could quite understand Eve. How unfair of God, she thought, to forbid them to eat of this fruit, and then to go and put a bright, red, juicy apple on the tree! She did wonder about God sometimes. In the New Testament it talked about a God of love; this did not seem to be a very loving thing for a father to do to his children. And then all the woes of humanity were said to have sprung from this one original sin. What guilt the souls of Adam and Eve must carry, she thought. Particularly Eve, as she was the one who actually did the deed. And she thought of the millions and millions of humans, particularly women, throughout the world who could all attribute their constant, subtle feelings of guilt and unhappiness to Eve, which must be God's punishment for that sin. But why would God want to punish the descendants of Adam and Eve for that sin? 'And the sins of the fathers shall be visited upon the children unto the seventh generation,' she recalled the vicar of Mickle Wood darkly repeating one bleak Sunday morning. How strange it all was, she thought, and how unjust to blame it all on Eve. And how did a soul carry all that guilt?

Chapter 22

—wₒₒₑₓₒₒₑₒₒₘ—

Becoming Aware of Loss

The days passed. Kathy found herself working six days a week in the restaurant, and was grateful to be able to spend these suddenly enormous blocks of free time in distracting activity. And each day she was earning twenty five pounds in cash. She knew Debbie was soon going to ask for the P45 form, but as yet she did not know how she could overcome that hurdle with an incognito name. With a little of her earnings she purchased a warm woollen sweater from the charity shop, because the November days were turning chilly and thought about buying some other clothes. But there was no need. There was a uniform narrowness about her new life, which did not require she have many clothes. True, she should look decent in the restaurant, and she would get a couple more tops to wear with her jeans, but that would suffice. And then she must save.

Her next task was to access the electoral roll. For this she would have to go into Bath, she was told on the phone, or Bristol, as that city had its own roll. They would be able to tell her if May Ferguson, her great aunt's name, did live in Somerset (but she knew already she did); however, for obvious reasons, they would not disclose the address over the phone. She was told that the roll was organised by streets and that if she wanted to find this person she would have to go through all the pages herself – about eighty thousand names. She would have to think of something else. She looked through the telephone directories kept at the restaurant, both the local one and the Bath one, but no May Ferguson was listed. It was hardly surprising; many single women today were ex-directory, Emma told Kathy. But Emma let her use the restaurant phone to call all the Fergusons in the local area. None of them was called May, and none of them had a relative by that name.

Most days, after work, Kathy went down to the cross, or the plaza, as she was learning to call it, and hung out with the crowd there. She suspected Paul was always pleased to see her, but in his dour way he never showed it. He was such a silent, private guy she thought, with veiled eyes that never expressed the slightest emotion. Eyes that withheld themselves, assessed, gave nothing away, non-trusting. He merely skateboarded, she thought, when he wasn't working, as though that were all there was to life. She watched, with Philip installed at her side, as he usually was these days. The board shot out from under Paul's feet, flipped up and round, and started off the other way with Paul miraculously facing the right way on it. There was no doubt he was very skilled in his sport, and better than all the other boys that gathered there, and this was, she guessed, the reason he had a certain amount of power over them. There was no doubt about that. He scarcely uttered a word; never even gave that kind of look that could say so much more than words. Yet the other kids, she noticed, were more aware of him than anything else. They kept out of his way, but followed his lead in the various movements and stunts. They might look as though they were performing independently, but after observing them for some time, she had realised there was a pattern, a predictability, in their behaviour. Paul was the unsung boss, and silently, obediently, they made him king, like subjects knowing it was the right thing to do. Why, she wondered. Was this fear? Was there some sanction underwriting this division of power? She had not sensed any threat in this gang; not the way she had in London, when she had been cowed into behaviour that had been psychologically damaging, she now realised. It was clear to her that she was much less threatened here in Glastonbury.

And then she wondered why she hung out with these people. After all, they were not her kind. And she did have her mission of finding May Ferguson; she's my great aunt, thought Kathy. Strange to have an aunt, even if it's a great one, that no-one ever mentioned at home. And she wondered what May Ferguson could have done to earn such studied neglect. She came here, she told herself, to the plaza so often because it was just better than sitting in the café every day after work, reading the newspapers for reports of missing children. And she did not like going back to Paul's house; it was not her home, after all. She had no right to use it as a home. That was something else she must do. After the P45 business had been sorted out, she must find a room to rent. Then what, she thought. But here her mind drew a blank. 'One step at a time, Kathy,' her grandfather used to say; 'you are too impatient, girl; you can't have it all at once.' And she remembered the history teacher at school describing Robert the Bruce, hiding on an island somewhere, watching a spider climb its tortuous way up to the roof, trying to fix its web on a beam, patiently. It had fallen six times before it eventually succeeded on the seventh attempt. That was the way to approach his predicament, the Bruce had decided. And then he went on to defeat the English, routing them at Bannockburn in 1314. A long time ago, she thought, but the principle still stands. And that is what I shall have to do. She felt encouraged.

'Come on, Kathy, I'm bored with this; let's go,' said Philip one day, after watching the skaters for about half an hour. She was less embarrassed by Philip these days, but she had no intention of letting him become a 'proper friend', as he seemed to assume, still less of becoming her shadow. She wanted something more. She wanted a boy or a girl of her own age that she could relate to, talk intelligently with; not this handicapped, uncool boy who was four years younger than she was. But the other, so far, had made no appearance, and so she had allowed Philip to sit at her table in the café, and to stand beside her at the cross. But now this appeal to her to 'come on' grated on her nerves. It irritated her that he thought a level of familiarity had been gained in their relationship, and that he could make assumptions about whether she was bored or not.

'I'm not at all bored, Philip,' she said coldly. 'You go; I'm staying.'

'You *are* bored,' persisted Philip, his brown eyes looking up at her. 'I can *feel* it.'

She was caught off-guard. How could he *feel* something about her mood, without her having said a word? This mind-reading unnerved her a little, in the same way that she felt unnerved in not being able to read Paul's mind.

'There's so much I want to show you, Kathy,' he said, impervious to the rebuff.

'Well, it's too late now,' she said. 'It's getting dark.' He had to agree.

'On Saturday or Sunday, Kathy, when you have a free day, I want to take you to the river and show you all sorts of things. There's not so much going on now, as there is in the Spring, but there's still a lot. There are a lot of migrating birds, and the starlings are such a sight.'

'The starlings?' queried Kathy.

'Yes, Kathy; there are millions and millions of them.' On the one hand, she thought, a day out in the countryside sounded very appealing, something she knew she needed and would enjoy. On the other hand, the thought of spending it with Philip was not an attractive idea. How to get rid of this kid?

'Yes, O.K.,' she said, amazed that her tongue had not followed her line of thought.

'Which day then, Kathy?' he said, happily.

'Saturday, I'm free.'

'Oh, that's great; there are more buses running on Saturday. I know a good place we can go to. I'll come and get you at Paul's house.' She was struck by his gallantry, at the absence of thought for himself, limping up to her house and then back to the bus stop. That reminded her of her father. He had been like that; well-mannered, courteous, willing to put himself out for almost anyone. God, she thought, those days seem far away now. And she was afraid she was going to forget her father, and wondered how she could stop that happening.

*   *   *

She was six years and Susie was two, and they were on a beach in Northumberland; on one of those long, beautiful beaches that you only get in Northumberland, where the sand is fine and almost white, and the dunes, covered in marram grass, undulate away into the distance in both directions, and where the sea, always a little ruffled because of the north-east wind and usually a dark blue, but sometimes quite green, comes sliding up the wet beach in smooth, curved lines of white spume. How she had loved those summers. The sun shone brightly enough, and sometimes the sand was quite hot and the shallow water warm. And the wind soon chased away any obstructing clouds. But it must have been chilly because her mother rarely came in bathing, and usually sat with two cardigans on, and her father used to vigorously towel her and then Susie dry after they came out of the water – or perhaps it was Susie first. Then he would push them down on the towel and tickle them. How she had loved that! Her father's big, strong hands knew exactly where to go, so that you couldn't help but squeal with delight, and then laugh helplessly. It was a strange feeling being tickled, a kind of torture, because you could not escape from the tickles. And yet you didn't want to escape. Because it was so good to laugh like that, to really laugh. She could remember pleading for more, even when she was quite tired from laughing. 'More, more, do it again, do it again, Daddy.' And Elaine had sat in the hollow of the dune, bundled up, and laughed and laughed too. All this time little Susie had been jumping up and down, squeaking with delight also, and then had promptly lain down on the towel for her turn - just a baby, really, a plump, blonde-haired baby with those sturdy baby legs and arms. 'Do it me, do it me, Dadda,' she had pleaded in that baby way, not knowing at all what to expect, but wanting to be included at all costs.

And here she was with Philip. Yes, he wanted to be included too. In something. Something he felt Kathy carried inside her, something she could give him, that he badly needed. But what have I to give him, she wondered. What is it about me that seems to offer inclusion? How does he see me? Is it merely company? There must be others he could find for company, surely? But she knew this was unlikely. With his lameness he was an outcast, especially in this neck of the woods, in this desolate level of society, where everyone was something of an outcast; where everyone was either lost, deprived, damaged, neglected or bereaved; where everyone was unready for life, unprepared, unsuspecting, innocent, unable. Yes, truly unready for the shock of life and its brutality, its incapacitating blows, its relentless buffeting; its fun and lightness taken away from you, when you have just been introduced to it; its comforting, parental arms no longer supporting you, when you are only half out of babyhood; its expectability no longer dependable, so that you were disoriented the whole time, as though you were shipwrecked in a cold sea, trying to find a log to hang on to, and all you can find is flotsam. And then she really understood why she and Philip hung out together, and with this crowd. They were all outsiders, and like lost birds of a feather they flocked. She wondered if she could go against what seemed prescribed for them all, what seemed writ in nature's book. Philip could never escape; his disadvantages were too many; but could she? She pondered on her predicament.

Chapter 23

—∿∘⬲⊙⬲∘∿—

Who Are We?

All these thoughts and anticipation of finding Granfy put Kathy in mind once more of home and Mickle Wood, and she wondered now, not about her family, but about Ma Riley. What would Ma Riley be doing now, she reflected. Would she be in her garden or cooking something for her supper? It was almost too much for Kathy. She suddenly felt very homesick for Ma Riley; Ma Riley would, after all, have been able to help her, she thought. She should have thought more of the things Ma Riley had told her, and perhaps less of Becky Sharp. That would perhaps have been the best way forward, after all. But she was not sure. London had been such a terrifying experience and Becky had surely helped, she felt certain. If it were not for Becky she would not be here in Glastonbury where there was a glimmer of hope. Her last conversation with Ma Riley came back very clearly. It might have been particularly helpful, if she had only had the time to think of it. But she was so busy surviving, she had not thought very much about Ma Riley, and probably not at all since her last memories of her in that park in London a few weeks ago. What was it she had been saying?

'Oh, yes, Jesus was a very good man, exceptional, and all those Christian saints were very good men and women too. And they put so many of them to death,' said Ma Riley sadly, 'because they knew the Truth. But to make it all simple, which is what I like to do (and I daresay you have not been taught this in church), first and foremost Deity exists in nature. You see you don't need all these extra beliefs that Christianity and Judaism have (and probably Islam). It seems to me that a lot of that extra teaching could be a bit of a distraction. No, I'm not in sympathy with a lot of what these western religions teach.' Ma stooped down and picked up an acorn that had fallen into her garden from a neighbouring oak.

'Isn't that a marvel, Kathy? Just look at the beauty, the efficiency of this little nut, how it will fall out of its case at just the right moment?' Kathy looked at the small, hard nut and was impressed with the dainty little fruit and thought of the mighty oak it could one day grow into. Ma wiped some soil from her large, honest hands onto her old, blue, faded apron, and continued walking down her garden path, with Kathy following behind.

'Now I don't know anything about those Eastern religions – perhaps they're like the 'old' religion that I know, where we see the Creator in all of nature. Just look at the beauty of a flower; listen to the trees and appreciate all that they do: they give shade to us; often they give food; shelter and homes to animals and insects; they give firmness to the ground – they stop sloping ground from slipping; they give their bodies for our firewood, houses and furniture; and even when fossilized they are still useful to us. Look at the ways of animals. It's all marvellous, isn't it? And the Creator created it all! It may sound old-fashioned, like a fantasy, but he did! And then came man!' And Ma Riley looked sad again. 'Along came man, and all man wanted to do was to exploit all of this beauty and wonder and miracle.' And they both walked along in silence, contemplating, in their own ways, this fact of life. They were now among the raspberry canes and both started picking the ripe fruit and depositing them in the two bowls Ma had produced from somewhere.

'So Deity created man,' she continued. 'Why did Great Spirit then create this highly intelligent, highly complex and dangerous being? I won't say 'animal', because man is not an animal; he is supposed to stand some way between the Creator himself and his animals.'

'Yes, why were we created?' asked Kathy. 'I've often wondered.'

'It's good that you do wonder; most people never give it a thought.'

'Well, we don't get much time for thinking about these things,' said Kathy, feeling she had to say something in defence of her fellow man.

'We have all the time in the world to think about these things,' said Ma gently. 'We don't think about them because we *believe* we haven't got time, we *believe* other things are far more important – like buying a new car or, for a woman, a new article of clothing. It's all a question, you see, of what we consider important. But worse than that, people today don't really care.' Kathy went on picking her raspberries in silence. She did not have much money to buy new clothes, in fact she had no money for ordinary clothes; she liked to spend her pocket money on things for riding or for her bicycle, and she was glad, and resolved never to spend much on clothes.

'And it's all so sad,' Ma went on, 'because man is missing the whole point of his creation, the whole point of his life.'

'And what is the point?' asked Kathy, now thoroughly intrigued, especially as she had just freed herself from the trap of liking new clothes.

'Man was not created like the animals, whose only purpose is to eat, sleep, seek safety, and breed. If that had been our purpose we would not have been created with this fine brain, this great intelligence, these marvellous, dextrous hands, and a heart that can be so sweet and compassionate. No, man was created for something much, much higher than just surviving and breeding.'

'What then?' asked Kathy, sensing she was on the verge of some great truth. 'What?'

'Man,' said Ma very quietly and very reverently 'was created to appreciate all of Great Spirit's creation. That is man's only purpose. And since it is the only reason we are here there is plenty of time for it. Deity wants man to lift his head from the ground, to look up, up; to look round at the beauty of nature: to hear the harmony in the running waters and still lakes, to marvel at the majesty of the mountains, to sense the profound beauty of the rose, to inhale the ecstasy of its perfume, to love his brother animals and to care for and respect them. And when all that is done, then to ask: "Who made all this?"'

'Yes,' breathed Kathy, deeply affected by the poetry of Ma's words. 'Yes. You are right.'

'And when man has asked that question, the answer will soon follow.' Kathy said nothing. She was still allowing this great truth to sink into her mind, to sink and to permeate all her being.

'That's right, dear,' said Ma. 'Just ponder on what I've said. Don't rush with it, like everybody does these days.' Kathy continued reflecting on Ma's words. Sometimes these great truths, she thought, resound like a beautiful trumpet throughout your whole body, awakening every cell.

'And once we know there is a Creator, so many more questions will be asked,' said Ma quietly. 'And so many more answers given.'

That was the last conversation Kathy and Ma had had together. Shortly thereafter Kathy had been taken to London to begin an entirely new life – a life bathed in the amnesia of Lethe, she now realised.

Chapter 24

—⁓∞o⌇∞⌇o∞⁓—

The Discovery

She left work at the restaurant two hours early one day, not long after. Business had been slow, and Emma suggested she take the rest of the day off. She found herself walking up to Chalice Well. It was the middle of the afternoon and there was still enough light on this warm November day to make a visit worthwhile. She paid her entrance fee, which was obligingly reduced to the student rate, and began her walk guided by the leaflet she had been given.

It was all very strange, she thought; so many different gardens all set in a small space, one leading into another. She gazed at the water in the bottom garden, which was mainly lawn, running down in red clay, circular pans, thinking how original it was to create such a water flow, not realising it had been created like this to mimic the flow of a natural spring and restore energy to the water, until she read the description in the leaflet.

192 | MORELLE FORSTER

She wandered on up the garden, following the water's course, and came upon a longish, rectangular pool, which was named the Healing Pool. There was a girl sitting on the low, protecting wall, dangling her feet in the water, her boots lying on the grass. Another hippy, thought Kathy, and the long, wispy hair and dangling earrings and the long skirt, which was bunched up around her knees, reminded her of Emma. Kathy sat on the wall too, near the end of the pool and put her feet in the water also. The water was tepid, and, yes, it did seem to be calming to her nerves, which were so on edge these days. Perhaps it really was good for you, really was healing. The girl got up, and holding the yellow and orange material of her skirt, she began to wade around the perimeter of the pool. When she passed, Kathy could hear she was murmuring something. Perhaps it was a mantra or an affirmation. She had heard of such things at home from the little she knew of yoga. She looked at the girl, and wondered if all this new-age stuff really helped you, really helped your life along. Did all these 'floaty' clothes and the unnaturally soft way some of them had of speaking really put you onto a spiritual plane? She was barely aware of these things, since the only place she had heard spiritual things talked about was at church on Sunday mornings or evenings. Here it all seemed very different, as though God had suddenly become a very female entity; no, entity was what it had been at home, in church especially and in the hymns sung at school. Here it was more a soft, feminine force that seemed to have taken up residence in the denizens of Glastonbury, male and female alike, making them seem abstract, distant, 'saved' even, but which, at the same time, wiped away all precision of action, all desire to will and take control of things and manipulate life, reducing all these people, she thought, to a sort of vapid ineffectiveness, particularly the men – at least the few new-age male followers she had thus far encountered. Only Debbie, the manageress at the restaurant, and one or two others seemed to have both feet in the world of Kathy's background. But if the rest of them were 'saved', as some of them, like Emma, seemed to believe, then perhaps it might be a good route to follow. Perhaps if she dressed in these long, impractical clothes, and just put up with their inconvenience, then her life might start to improve.

But she could not see this happening. Since escaping from the children's home and social services, she had been learning what it meant to be the master of her own life, the architect of her own fate. Without her own powers of decision, courage and considerable effort, without her wile and intelligence, she would still be a prisoner in London – a prisoner in that desolate children's home and a prisoner of Gary. Her 'sensible' approach to life had worked for her! Becky Sharp's energy of character and resolution, which made her invariably look towards the future, not permitting herself useless sorrow and regret for the irrevocable past, were the values that had successfully guided her thus far, but not forgetting the brief use she had made of the war heroine,Violette Szabo. No, she would stick with Becky! Although she was cold, hard and scheming, Becky had done well with the cards dealt her, and when she had fallen short of desirable behaviour, it was because she had not had much choice. If she, Kathy, relaxed her grip on things now, gave out her true name and age, or did not turn up for work, just because she did not feel like work, as seemed the way for many in Glastonbury, then she would surely find herself back in London, in a life so without hope it did not bear thinking about.

She watched the yellow and orange vision in the doc martin boots drift away down the garden and quickly disappear from sight behind a tall hedge, and disappear from Kathy's life like the gossamer thing it was. Still, I can try some of their ways, she thought; it can't do any harm, and it might just work. So, she rolled up her jeans and walked round the pool also, praying to God to help her find May Ferguson and Granfy.

She found herself wandering into a little place which was called the Lion's Head pool. A lion's head had been built into a dry stone wall at one end, behind which was a water source, and from the lion's mouth the spring poured into a little round pool. Odd to have healing water issuing from a lion, she thought, unless it was meant to be a kind of Aslan lion. Two glasses had been conveniently placed on the rim of the pool, and Kathy took one, filled it and drank. The water was cool and tasted different to the water she was used to drinking. Iron, she thought, as she looked at the redness of the water.

Then she found the Vesica Piscis and what looked like the source of the spring in the whole garden. She sat on the low stone wall and studied the wrought iron design on the underside of the round, wooden lid of the well, which was now raised and rested back for viewing. It was a strange symbol, she decided; utterly incomprehensible to her, but which she guessed was of great new-age significance. It looked like two circles intersecting, and creating an oval in the centre, and with a perpendicular rod running through the whole. As she looked closer, she saw that this rod was actually an arrow with the head pointing up to the sky. There was no-one else about, but still, she thought, there was an uncommon quietness; there seemed to be a certain hushedness about this small space, and she felt people would not talk to each other here, but remain in a reverend silence. Well, *she* wasn't reverend. It was a nice place, a sanctuary even, but it could not be about God, not with that odd design. Still, she did feel peaceful here, as though she had discovered some sort of secret haven, and thought she would like to come back.

She left Chalice Well and started the short walk along the street to Paul's house. Immediately out of the garden, her anxiety returned. The brief peace she had experienced walking round the Healing Pool and sitting beside the Vesica Piscis had dissipated, like a brief sunny interval between dark clouds and rain that can suddenly be swallowed up again by all that rolling greyness. Her mind returned to the problem of finding May Ferguson. Not in the local telephone directories, not in the Bath directory, not to be found through the electoral rolls – where could she learn about this great aunt of hers? Social services could certainly tell her, if she revealed her identity, but that would be like an embrace from the enemy. She walked round and round the problem in her mind, as she had done these past weeks, realising she was becoming repetitive about it and that she was locked in a maze, unable to find the way forward. How to find Ariadne's thread, she wondered.

She let herself into the house. An almost empty milk bottle had found its way again onto the window sill. A whisky bottle and glasses stood on the floor. However much she tidied up, no-one seemed to notice. Although, come to think of it, she did remember Paul once or twice remarking on the fact. Jenny never noticed; she was convinced of that. On the other hand, Jenny was as friendly and relaxed about her staying on in the house as ever, and very grateful for the money Kathy handed to her on Fridays, by way of rent. 'Oh, my love, you're like the good angel from Jesus, himself,' said she, putting the notes into her purse and smiling with tenderness at Kathy. 'You could be my very own daughter, you could,' she laughed. 'And a lot better than her,' she added darkly. 'Make yourself quite at home, honey, make yourself comfortable.'

When had she last felt 'quite at home'? She could not remember. At the time that she had had a home, she had never thought about feeling comfortable and 'at home'. Only in looking back did she give those experiences this name. She wondered if she would go through all of life like this – just reacting to life as it came along, and only later dividing it up into experiences and labelling them. This one segment was called: 'Phyllis is a bossy know-all, and I have to go carefully with her'; that one: 'I really enjoy the netball practices; I will always do sport – all my life.' Upon her present experiences she cast no reflection; she dared not. Best to leave them in their uncrystallized state.

*   *   *

And she let her mind wander to the netball matches, some of which they had won and some lost, but all of which she had found exhilarating. She would go into the cloakroom afterwards to shower, and see her face had turned a deep red, and wondered at some of the girls, whose faces just turned a rather attractive pink.

Then she might hurry to the bicycle shed. Ellie, the captain, had said the team was going to have a meeting during the mid-morning break to discuss tactics for the netball match on Saturday morning. It was necessary to sequester themselves from the playground and all the noise and find a place with some privacy and quietness. Behind the bicycle shed had been a notorious place for the few girls who 'smoked'. They had been discovered once, and a big fuss had been made, and they had almost been suspended. And not since then had anyone met behind the bicycle shed. 'They'll think we're smoking,' Kathy had said. 'Well, we're not,' said Ellie. 'So it's alright.'

She was a few minutes late, as her piano teacher had insisted on her playing 'Fur Elise' several times, before she was satisfied.

'Sorry I'm late!' Kathy joined the group and sat down in the small circle of girls. Behind them the rows of bicycles stood neatly chained in their individual sections, most old and worn, some bright and new. Kathy wished they lived near enough for her to ride to school. Her bus ride was long, and seemed to take a precious chunk out of her day.

'Phyllis can't come,' said Ellie.' 'She's got to see Mrs. Greener about some chemistry experiment.'

'Well, we can't discuss much,' said Kathy. 'She's Centre.'

'I know,' said Ellie dejectedly. 'I had this super plan, and I wanted us to go over it.'

'Well, what is it?' asked Maggie.

The bell rang, signalling the end of the break. They got up from the ground, dusted down their skirts, picked up their bags, and hastened off to their various lessons. This was one of the last conversations Kathy had had with her friends at school, and she brought her thoughts back reluctantly into the present. Her school days had been good, she reflected. She may not have thought so at the time, but now she valued them. And how she missed her friends! Ellie, Maggie, Judy, Val, Linda, Julia. How she missed their company, their gossip, their laughs. She felt she even missed Phyllis. She looked out of the window. At the town roofs, not of Mickle Wood, but of Glastonbury. And saw the darkening, grey sky of a warm, muggy November evening; not the sharp, cold, bright skies of the Northumbrian moors.

It would soon be time for her to go into town and get herself a take-away. She was beginning to yearn for some proper home-cooked food in the evenings, but Jenny said the oven did not work, and that it was better to get take-aways. Kathy did not know why this should be the case, as she had boiled eggs on the hob for breakfast. It seemed to be a foible of Jenny's that supper should be take-away, and Kathy did not dare to challenge this.

In the meantime, before supper, she decided to strip her bed and take the sheets and pillow slips down to the launderette she had seen on the high street. She took off the top sheet, saw it was quite stained and wondered why she had not thought of washing the linen before now. Then she took the pillow slip off. Lastly, she started on the under sheet. It would not release itself, even with her tugs, and, not wanting to tear it, Kathy knelt down and discovered it was caught under one leg of the bed. Then she noticed this leg was too short, as though it had been broken at some time. To compensate for the missing bit of leg, an old telephone directory had been wedged underneath it. Forgetting the sheet, Kathy stared at the directory. Then she lifted the bed, and gently pulled the directory out from under the leg. She saw that it was a Bath directory and that it was ten years old. Ten years old! She could hardly believe it! This was what, she realized, she needed – an old phone directory that could have May Ferguson's number listed, before she had gone ex-directory. She put it down on the bed under the light from the naked bulb which hung in the middle of the ceiling, and quickly turned the pages to Ferguson. There were a number of entries under that name. She ran her finger down to the 'M's. There were several listed under M. Ferguson. And then, as she continued to run her finger down the column, it stopped suddenly. There it was, written clearly among all the other M. Fergusons – May Ferguson! She must have, at some later date, had her entry removed and gone ex-directory. A wave of lightness descended upon her, the grey rolled away, and she felt for a moment the old Kathy of her childhood – the Kathy sitting with her family in the garden of their home and enjoying a tea of scones and victoria sandwich cake, all baked of course by her mother. How perfect and secure life was; so secure she never even thought of it, never labelled it with any adjective, nor indeed did she label any of her experiences. She was merely a child who depended on good things to happen in her life, and they did, with regular predictability. She looked at the directory again and thought surely this was the May Ferguson she was looking for. She felt certain May was not a common name; that there was not another May out there. She gazed at the entry in trepidation and hope. Then quickly took her notebook and pencil off the chest of drawers. She wrote down the numbers of all the M. Fergusons too - just in case. She put her notebook safely in the cupboard, which was full of Paul's sister's clothes. Then she carefully returned the telephone directory to its accustomed place as bed support.

A few minutes later she let herself out of the house, as dusk was closing in on the town, and, with a step that was light and full of promise, walked down to the launderette with a plastic bag of bed linen.

Chapter 25

─────⌘─────

A Day Out

It was raining when Kathy woke up on Saturday morning, which was a pity, she thought. Walking on the Somerset Levels beside the river would not be so pleasant in the rain, and she had no rain gear, she suddenly realised. Perhaps she should call in at a charity shop on the way to the bus stop and find something.

The rain sputtered on the dirty window pane and she could hear it drenching the ground outside in the small garden. She hoped her trainers would be sufficiently waterproof. She rose, and moving down to the end of the bed, she knelt, drew aside the grubby, torn, blue curtains, and gazed out onto the eastern aspect of Glastonbury. The Tor hill rose at the end of the small back garden, strange and mysterious, a constant reminder of something; it seemed to define Glastonbury. The real residents – the ones who were not new-age - did not visit it, she suspected, and would not take much interest in it. But it was there, undeniably – big and prominent - with that dark, sinister tower on the flat top, casting its influence over all the town, giving its name to shops, cafes, streets, and businesses. She had been up once and nearly blown off in a wind that was more like a gale, a wind that was quite absent when she had started her climb and also when she had descended into the gentle air of the Levels again. Perhaps there was some force, some spirit that raged against the atrocity of hanging, beheading and quartering Abbot Whiting up there on the hill in 1539, during the dissolution of the monasteries under Henry VIII.

She brought her gaze lower and regarded the ancient cherry tree just beyond the small lawn of the garden. Its ringed boughs were glistening with moisture and dripping large drops of water, and the last of its rather dull, autumnal leaves either wilting under the steady downpour or else falling to the ground to lie on the carpet of leafy, brown mulch which was already compositing nicely. No birds sang, not even the blackbird in the cherry tree, who woke her regularly in the morning. They were all taking shelter, she reflected, just watching the rain. Soon, the cherry would be bare, and it would be winter. Where would she be then? Not here, she fervently hoped. With Granfy; I will definitely be with Granfy. And she thought about the telephone number safely written down and planned to call May Ferguson that evening. She heard Jenny moving about in her bedroom next door, and her reverie came to an end.

At the bus stop, wearing a day bag that was obviously full of things, Philip was waiting for her.

'What have you got in there?' she queried.

'Oh, not much,' he said. 'A little lunch, and a bottle of juice and coke to drink.'

She had not given much thought to lunch. She could go long hours without food, and, anyway, had assumed there would be a visitors' centre where they were going, and where they could purchase snacks.

'There's no refreshments for sale where we're going,' said Philip. So, Gracy, in the care home (a weekend auxiliary worker) had packed him a lunch of sandwiches and juice, enough for two. Philip had negotiated with his social worker to be let out on his own.

'That was good of Gracy,' said Kathy, feeling her powerlessness and dependence on others. 'Here, give me some of those things. I've got room in my back pack.'

The bus was on time. It had all but stopped raining, and now there was a blue sky ahead of them, and, in the clouds, a beautiful rainbow.

'We often get rainbows here,' Philip remarked, as he pointed it out to her on the other side of the bus. The sun shone for a few seconds, now and again, as grey nimbus swirled directionless in the sky, fighting an imminent dissolution. Perhaps they will re-form, she thought, and it'll pour again. And she was glad she had purchased the pac mac.

It was pleasant country, she thought. These low-lying and once-boggy Levels, which had been drained into managed ditches and canals, had become suitable for farming, she had read, and now cows grazed peacefully on the thinning November grass – an archetypal bucolic English scene. This reminded her of the paintings of Gainsborough and Constable that she had once seen when she and her mother had visited an art gallery at home. She noticed all the cows were Fresian or brown and white. 'Devon reds and charollais, those other white cows,' said Philip. A flat and tired green, the autumn fields of Somerset, with huge oak, beech, and chestnut trees standing in the middle of them, passed by, as Kathy watched out of the bus window.

'Will we see the starlings?' she asked.

'Probably,' said Philip. 'We're not going to the place where you get the best view, but I think we'll still be able to spot them.'

They alighted from the bus in the village of Westwick, and Philip led her to a minor road running south to a place called Platwick.

'Platwick Heath is where we're going, Kathy,' he said, and she noticed a certain command in his bearing now. However, the pace was slow, as Philip's leg prevented him from walking quickly, and Kathy wondered how long it would take to reach the heath.

'These are all heaths and moors around here,' he explained.

'That's odd,' she replied. 'Where I come from, heaths and moors are always high up, and often covered with heather.'

'Oh, they're not here; they're low and wet.'

'Well, I think that's more like the fens. The fens round Cambridge are all low and wet like this land – we did it in Geography last year.' Philip made no reply. He had not had these geography lessons.

Kathy noticed the dark clouds had all but disappeared, and the wet road stretched before them, the tarmac shining in the morning sun and blue sky, and the hawthorn hedges glistened with raindrops. The hogweed and jack by the hedge on the verges bore tawdry flower heads and the wild carrot curled its old blooms into neat birds' nests. The long grass was wilting with the weight of advancing autumn, and the red berries in the hedge announced the imminence of winter.

'How far do we go to get to this place?' asked Kathy after some minutes.

'Oh, not far,' replied Philip evasively.

'Yes, but how far, how much time, do you think? she persisted.

'It's about a mile,' he conceded. Kathy felt a wave of anger rise in her. It would take them ages to cover a mile at this pace.

'You fool, Philip,' she blurted out. 'It'll take all morning to get there!'

'No, it won't,' he said defensively. 'I'll try and walk a bit more quickly.'

'You can't,' she said. 'You know you can't. Oh why did you choose a place with such a long walk?'

At that moment a van approached from behind. Kathy had the sudden idea she would hail it and ask for a lift, and so made the hitch-hiker gesture that she had occasionally seen.

'Keep walking, Philip,' she commanded, wanting the driver to see he was disabled. A few yards in front of them, the van stopped and they were invited to get in. They squeezed onto the front seat, and after a few minutes the driver, a local farmer, stopped at the entrance to Platwick nature reserve.

A short walk on the grassy path gave Kathy time to reflect on her outburst. She realised she had been looking forward to this outing, and now had the feeling Philip was going to let down those expectations, through his unreasonable desire to please. But her anger subsided, and she wondered that she could so easily lose her temper with such a defenceless boy, as Philip, who was trying to humour her, even look after her. Her mother's words returned to her: 'Kathy, it's a very bad fault you have; you must curb your temper. I don't know where you get it from.' Granfy had said the only person on his side of the family who had a temper was his sister, May. 'A real paddy she got into when she wasn't pleased,' he had said. But that family revelation had only come when Kathy was little. Contrite, Kathy stared at the information board not far from the entrance to the reserve, and briefly took in the notes on the history and the wild life. But she felt unable to apologise to Philip.

They took the sign that directed them onto the Sweet Track, an ancient way across the Somerset Levels of reed beds and peat bogs, connecting up various settlements, and constructed 6,000 years ago, she had read.

'Goodness, this must have been a very watery place in those days,' said Kathy, trying to picture what it all must have looked like.'

'Oh, yes, it was very watery,' said Philip. 'My nan told me the Tor was an island in a land of water.'

'How beautiful it all must have looked,' she said, picturing a romantic landscape. Perhaps Avalon had been a beautiful island city in the midst of this watery landscape.

'Yes, it must have been very different before they put in all the drains and canals that criss-cross this countryside? Why, we're walking alongside one now.' Kathy looked to the left and peered through the thick vegetation and saw a wide ditch full of deep water, with reeds growing at the side. 'Before that they must have used boats to get from one place to another,' continued Philip.

They started up the Sweet Track, which bore a black drainpipe running alongside them. This performed a constant sucking of water out of the track and conveyed that water to a ditch at the beginning of the track, which they had just left. Even so, the track was quite wet, and, in places, became a bog of spongy peat. Philip had on Wellington boots and was protected, whereas she only had on her trainers, which were beginning to take in water. After several hundred yards, the track became impenetrable. The conservationists had done no clearing work here and the trees and undergrowth grew thick and dense over what might have been the track, and they returned to a wide grassy path they had recently crossed. The wood stretched away on either side full of young oak, willow, and silver birch. Kathy saw there were no large trees, which accounted for it being a wood full of light, and wondered if mature trees fared badly in such water-logged terrain and died young. Certainly, there were many fallen birch trees, lying and rotting in the wet ground, and wrens flitted about in the tangled undergrowth, uttering their surprisingly loud calls for such small birds.

'That's a wren, Kathy,' said Philip. 'Listen! It's saying 'tea kettle, tea kettle tea kettle, tea.'

'So, it is,' she laughed, listening to the frequent bursts of this piercing, rolling call, and feeling the memories of her walks with her parents in the woods and hills of Northumberland. How precious these recollections were becoming. Her father had known a little about the natural life they had encountered

on their walks, but his knowledge had not extended to the calls
of birds, except the few obvious ones.

Philip then pointed out the dying foliage of wild flowers,
the brown straw of fern that had completely gone over now, the
bright greens of the various mosses, and the chiff chaff that
sang its monotonous refrain from a silver birch not far off.

'You know a lot about nature,' Kathy eventually said. 'Where
did you learn all this?'

'My nan taught me,' he said proudly. 'She knows everything.'
Kathy pictured a kindly, old woman, a real country woman, like
Ma Riley, with white hair and apple-red cheeks, and wondered
if these women still existed down here in Somerset. As well as
Ma Riley, she had occasionally seen other such women in the
remoter parts of Northumberland.

'She must be special, your grandma,' said Kathy.

'She is; well, she was,' he said. 'She's not so good now she's
in the care home. I wish they hadn't put her in the home. We
were much happier the way we were. I don't think I like social
services.'

They had come to the end of this dry, grassy track and were
looking across a wide expanse of white water, that was fringed
with reed all around, and, here and there, islands of reeds out
in the deep water. The weak November sun cast its waning light
on the far side of the lake over the flat water.

'Isn't this beautiful, Kathy?' said Philip.

'Yes, it is,' she replied, accustoming herself to this fen
landscape, a type of countryside she had never before seen,
except in photographs or on the television. How warm and
mellow Somerset seemed after the bracing winds and wide

skies of Northumberland; how yellow and gentle was Somerset, she thought, in contrast to the grey, cold clouds that blew across the distant, mauve Cheviot hills and the diamond-hard blue skies you could get on a summer's day or a frosty winter morning. How different it all was! And it dawned on her how serious and challenging were the adaptations she was having to make. Her mind returned to Philip's nan, the old woman with the apple-red cheeks and love of nature.

'How did you do these journeys?' asked Kathy. 'You didn't have a car, did you?'

'Oh, no,' answered Philip. 'Stan used to bring us in his van. He was my nan's friend. He's a plumber. He's nice, is Stan; perhaps you'll meet him.'

Philip had turned to the right and was walking along the wide turf path that skirted the lake. 'I've never seen so many reeds; I suppose they're good for the wildlife.'

'Yes, they are,' said Philip. 'But they are more good for humans; some have actually been planted to be used for thatching. In the summer,' he said, 'these waters are full of swifts and martins.' The only birds Kathy could see were several swans drifting lazily on the calm, flat water. Philip took out a pair of small binoculars and scanned the water and sky. A flock of Canada geese passed overhead, honking emphatically. Kathy laughed.

'They are such funny birds,' she exclaimed. Philip laughed too. She knew her enjoyment was his enjoyment. What an extraordinary child, she thought, and looked at him, his straight, blonde hair brushing the top of the binoculars, his clear hazel eyes glued to some spot on the distant bank of reeds, his generous mouth, still, in expectation, as he sought an answer to some movement he had seen among the reeds, and the hint of a strong chin.

After a few seconds, he gave up, and they continued along the path. Soon, they veered off to the left, passing through a low wood of mainly young, straggling willow, skirting the lake to their left.

'Where are we going?' she soon asked.

'To a hide,' he said. 'Perhaps you saw it just a little while ago.'

They arrived at the hide and Philip opened the door. It was dark and warm inside and smelt pleasantly of wood. They lifted the flaps that covered the glassless windows and secured them back. A draught of warm, fresh air invaded the space, bringing with it the smells of the lake. Kathy looked out over the water but could see nothing but the swans and a pair of Canada geese. After a few minutes, during which they took turns with the glasses, a man came into the hide. He introduced himself as Robin. They learned he came from 'Bristol way' and was spending the weekend in the several nature reserves on the Levels. He slept in his camper van, he said. Kathy noticed he had a strong, west country accent – the first she had heard since arriving in Somerset. That beautiful, rolling of the language, and the burring of the 'r's, that her grandfather had once described to her. Yes, he said, he had lived in Somerset all his life. 'Lots of visitors ask me if I'm from Somerset,' he added.

'Maybe it's because there are so few real Somerset people left here now,' suggested Kathy.

'Oh, we're around,' he grinned. 'Just got to look for us. In the villages, mostly. Where're you from?'

'Glastonbury,' said Kathy.

'Oh, you won't find no Somerset folk there. All left there now. It's full of strange folks, these days. We're the summer people,' he said. 'And we can't live in places like Glastonbury; all those townies. Most of them from London or thereabouts, I understand.'

'What do you mean "you're the summer people"?' queried Kathy.

'Oh, it's an old name,' said Robin. 'Goes way back to the Celts. Some says those that are real summer people still have the powers.'

'What powers?' queried Kathy again, politely. But Robin had said enough and would be drawn no further. He opened a large, ledger type book that lay at one end of the wooden shelf.

'Oh,' he exclaimed. 'There's been others here this morning. A pair were seen yon side of lake.' He took a large pair of glasses out of his back pack and scanned the lake from side to side. But it was Philip who saw the otters first.

'There they are, there they are!' he exclaimed excitedly. Kathy and Robin trained their eyes in the direction Philip had indicated, and saw two otters playing in the water. One moment their heads were visible, and the next they had upended and disappeared, diving for fish, Robin said. A swan nearby glided on the water, uninterested in the activity of the otters. After a few moments the otters started swimming towards the hide. Perhaps there's better fish here, thought Kathy. A few yards away from the hide, and in clear view, the pair resumed their search for lunch. Every so often they would be rewarded and surface to eat their catch in only two or three mouthfuls. Occasionally, they turned onto their backs and fed off their fish in a reclining position. Other times they approached each other, and appeared to be playing, swimming and diving together.

How care-free, they are, observed Kathy to herself, and wondered how it was that humans, even in the most hospitable environments, could not be free of care and be spontaneous like animals. Children could sometimes be like that, she thought. She had occasionally seen such children; they always seemed to go with parents who were exceptionally confident and secure. But seeing such children had not happened often. Most children were like herself and even sunny Susie - inhibited, like their parents. And she thought of her mother, forever worrying, forever tidying up. Dad had been better, she thought, but he was a stick-in-the-mud. Something held him back from what her mother called 'the adventure of life.' Her mother had complained once to Kathy that he could get a much better job than the one in the saw mill, if only he would trust that he could do better. Ah, well, sighed Kathy to herself. It's all in the past now. But was it? She wondered. The mark of her parents was burned into her being, and she was aware she carried this around in her head all day, perhaps in her genes. Would it go on like that forever? She thought of Becky, but Becky seemed a feeble friend today; she had never expressed any interest in wildlife, and would probably not have enjoyed this excursion. Kathy turned her attention back to the otters and their delightful antics, and thought when she got the opportunity to be spontaneous, she would take it. How helpful it would be to shed the burden of her life, if only for a few minutes, and be carefree like these otters.

They left Robin in the hide, and wandered back down the track through the wood, and found a log to sit on and have their lunch. Gracy, in the children's home, had prepared them some delicious sandwiches of ham and salad; Philip said it was so delicious because they were eating it out of doors. As dusk was falling they returned to the road, and managed to hitch a lift back to Westwick and, after a short wait, caught the bus back to Glastonbury. It was well past tea time when they arrived, but their usual café was still open and busy, and happy to serve them with tea and carrot cake.

Philip ate his cake with gusto. He looked happy, Kathy thought, and his country complexion glowed with health; the air by that watery landscape obviously agreed with him. She wondered if she looked so healthy and attractive. Not many weeks ago she had wanted to look ugly, like the other girls in Gary's gang; now she found that idea strange, and hoped that with her lengthening hair, her features would soften again. She watched Philip consume his tea, and felt she was beginning to understand him; to comprehend how he seemed to remain untouched by the sadness and limitation of his life. She felt the unusual strength he demonstrated for such a young person was somehow connected to his enthusiasm for nature, and that his walks in the fens and woods around Glastonbury had nurtured a peace and solace within him that allowed him to withstand, with equanimity, the insults of his life: the taunts of his contemporaries and the exclusion from many of the normal activities of the young. She wished she, too, could learn to develop such a love of the natural world, and then to have the strength and peace and confidence that love seemed to bestow.

'Oh, we didn't see the starlings,' she said suddenly.

'Next time,' grinned Philip, his mouth full of cake.

Chapter 26

━━━∽∾⌒⊙⌒⊙⌒∾∽━━━

The Telephone Call and The Fall

Kathy arrived back at the house after her excursion with Philip, all thought of the day's activities swept from her mind, as she contemplated the task ahead of her. It had been three days since she had discovered May Ferguson's telephone number in the directory. But she had been afraid to call her. What if this May Ferguson was not Granfy's elder sister? Then she would never be able to find Granfy. And without Granfy she knew her life would remain in limbo, on hold. Not even a rehearsal; just a nothingness, an awful mistake, like travelling in a train she had not been meant to take, a train that was taking her in quite the wrong direction, with all the wrong people on board, and the wrong countryside passing by the window. She would become a little, lost nobody, swallowed up in the vast, seething mass of humanity, and nobody would really care if she died, just like so many of the kids, the lost kids, that she was now forced to associate with. She was in the wrong story. She reflected that Susie would care very much if she died, but now Susie would probably never know. Her plaque in some cemetery would merely say: 'Kathy, of unknown name', because by then, in the funeral process, her surname would have been discovered to be false. Her anxiety had increased during these days, as she was faced with this existential crisis. Was she ready for it? She felt she was not, and so had delayed telephoning this number. But now, this evening, the house was empty. Jenny was off somewhere, and Paul had gone out with some mates. He had wanted Kathy to come, but she had politely declined and said next week. And she had yesterday planned to make the call, and she had committed to stick to that plan, even though she had a sick feeling in her stomach in anticipating its failure. She did not go to the take-away for her supper. She did not feel like eating; her whole body felt tense with anxiety. Indeed, she felt herself close to despair, panic even. Would this be the key to getting her out of this unreal life, or not? This was a Rubicon that she was either going to cross or fail to cross, for she had no plan 'b' if the telephone call was fruitless.

With uncertain fingers and fluttering heart, Kathy dialled the number and waited, listening to the ringing tone. An elderly female voice answered.

'Hello, is that May Ferguson?' asked Kathy

'Aye, that's me!' came the reply, and Kathy's heart gave a leap of hope, as she detected a light North Country accent. She went straight to the heart of the matter.

'I'm Kathy Miller, your great niece, I think.' Now her cover was blown. There was a momentary silence at the other end, but only momentary. Then: 'Well, would you believe it? Archie's son's gel, are you?'

'Yes,'

'Well, where are you? In Northumberland?'

'No. I'm in Glastonbury, and I wondered if I could come and see you?'

'Aye, that'd be nice. When d'you want to come?'

'Saturday, next Saturday would be good for me,' said Kathy, planning to speak to Emma about having Saturday as her free day.

'About four o'clock?' said Great Aunt May Ferguson.

'That'll be fine,' said Kathy. Then May Ferguson gave her the address, and some directions for getting there. She lived in sheltered accommodation, she told Kathy, and not far from the Bath bus station, where the bus from Glastonbury terminated.

Kathy replaced the receiver. She felt a huge load was lifting itself from her heart. This was the first time since arriving in the South that a chink of light had appeared in her situation. All her determination to not submit to what fate was trying to work out for her, to not accept the injustice of her new life – all this refusal to yield seemed finally to be working for her, to be resolving itself at last to her will. Like Becky Sharp, she began to feel that you could, with determination and effort, make life go your way. And the wonderful bonus was that Aunt May seemed to be on the ball. Kathy had calculated that she was in her late seventies, because Granfy was seventy five years, and May, she knew, was a bit older. There was a good chance that this old lady might have dementia, but she had sounded very alert on the phone.

All at once, she found herself weeping. It was only the second time that she had shed tears, since her new life had begun, but these tears were welcome and wholesome. Kathy could feel the tension and anxiety of the past weeks and months slipping from her body, and what was more - she knew why she was crying. It was the relief of finding 'family'; your own flesh and blood in the end meant everything. There was an understood obligation amongst relatives that they were there for each other, that relatives were bound to help, as though held by a deep, secret oath. Kathy had never known this, but now she did, deeply and profoundly in her being. Even if the relatives proved useless and disloyal and did not help, there was still this ineradicable feeling and belief of obligation; that you could and should turn to them as first port of call. To have a first port of call was indeed a wonderful feeling, and that was what had been absent all these months, she now realised. Blood is indeed thicker than water, she thought. Aunt May will help me. And she felt her heart flicker to life with this thought and become young again, and felt her blood once more might sing in her veins, as it should in every child and young person's veins.

Even if Aunt May could not help her beyond providing the location of Granfy's care home, Kathy knew that just to be with her family would be profoundly healing. Thoughts of home flooded her mind, as she lay on the futon bed that was propped up by that telephone directory - the directory that had enabled her to find the correct station where she might now board the correct train and might now pass through the right countryside. She had no idea how her meeting with Aunt May and then with Granfy would go, but, undoubtedly, she was about to open the book of her life again. The proper book. A new chapter was about to begin, but it *was* the story of her life; she was no longer stumbling and fumbling around outside that story, lost and stranded and trying to make connections with the previous chapters that would not connect.

It was dark now, that deep November darkness that enfolds the northern world in a restful, comforting embrace, but which few can repose in. But Kathy did. Her repose was sweet and confident, and she felt as she had felt as a small child in bed, listening to the sounds of her parents in the kitchen below. It was sweet to have a relative.

*   *   *

'Kathy, darling, do take Susie; she loves to go with you; she loves the things you all get up to,' said Elaine, trying to be flattering and persuasive.

'Oh, God, not again,' said Kathy, and Elaine winced at her daughter's language. She wished she did not talk like this. She was still only a child of ten years. And where did she get these terms from?

'I suppose so,' said Kathy reluctantly. She was surprised at herself. Usually she did not mind Susie coming at all. If her father or Granfy had asked her, she would have consented immediately and with a good grace. But somehow with her mother it was different, and she could not remember when this difference had started, but she always felt it was necessary to be unforthcoming and somewhat uncooperative with her; that her mother should work for her, Kathy's, favours. For a moment she felt sorry for her mother, but then that's how it is, she thought. It was just a part of life. She loved her mother, dearly, but never told her; there was no need, she felt. And she deeply liked her mother to be there for her, picking up the bits of her life, putting them together again and never asking for gratitude. She utterly depended on her mother and felt this dependence, and sometimes this ungratefulness, to be a necessary part of her relationship with her. An unacknowledged instinct told her this was the way it should be. And to Elaine it also seemed tiresomely correct, for she looked with pride on the way Kathy was developing and blossoming, finding her own independent way in life and knew a lot of it was due to her own patience and desire to be a good mother. 'Bite your tongue and pray', a friend had once advised.

It was a fine Saturday in early May. Most of the primroses on the verges outside the gardens had withered, but Well Lane and the other little side streets had long carpets of blue bells, growing along the roadside, and up in the beech and oak woods that bordered all along the north side of Mickle Wood, there was a purple haze of bluebells under the trees. Kathy had stood with Susie and their father recently at the edge of the wood, and had been amazed by the blue heaven in front of them that stretched away among the trees.

All the village kids were there, even big Tom. They played desultorily in an uncoordinated way, like an orchestra warming up. Kathy did some circles with her bike, because she could not make it sit up and beg, like some of the boys, and six year old Susie just rode in straight lines up and down the road, laughing and happy to be included in the gang. But spring was in the air, and sooner or later the action would start, Kathy knew.

'What shall we do?' Kathy asked the question they were all thinking, and which they all hoped Tom would answer.

'Dunno,' said one boy and rode past on the back wheel of his bike, the front high before him, his face an expression of studied indifference.

'You say,' said Ned, a bright-cheeked boy with reddish hair, leaning on the handlebars of his bike.

'We'll go to the burn,' declared Tom. And that was that! The burn! It had been decided by Tom. It had been a long time since they had been to the burn, the small river that flowed peacefully through some grass meadows two or three miles away. It was a good place to play and hang out. There was a rope there, hanging on a high, overarching bough over the centre of the big stream, and the kids swung from one side to the other on it. Kathy had never done it before, being too small and not strong enough. Now she was a year older, and bigger, and she thought she would have a 'go'. They set off down the road on their bikes to the burn. Soon they came to a sharp descent in the road, where the bikes gathered speed, carrying them down in a thrilling ride. Kathy felt the wind catching her hair and the warm May air on her cheeks, and smelled the scent of the trees in blossom – a lilac somewhere. Susie was the last down, with her brakes hard on all the time, and flushed with fear and excitement. Then came the climb up the ascending hill. This was when Susie became a nuisance.

'Wait for me, Kathy, wait. I can't go as fast as you. Wait, wait, *please*.' Kathy waited in irritation. The gang was getting ahead. She wanted to keep up with them, but most of all she wanted Tom to see her in a good light. This big, handsome lad everyone looked up to, thrilled her in that vague, indefinable way. She hated Susie for crushing her dignity, making her look as though she too could only climb this hill at a snail's pace. She so wanted to impress Tom again.

'Hurry up, Susie, hurry,' she said impatiently. Susie did her best, her hot cheeks getting more flushed by the minute, as she pushed and pushed her blue bike up the hill. She too had her own concerns. She loved being with the gang, even if they were mostly older than her, and she too had enormous respect for this very big boy, Tom. And she needed Kathy to wait for her and help her. But Kathy rarely did. But once she got to the burn, it would be alright. She would sit in the long grass with the daisies and buttercups and watch the other boys and girls swinging over the water.

At the top, the road levelled out. They had all waited for Kathy and Susie, which was great of them, Kathy thought, but not what she wanted. Then they were off again, about ten of them, pedalling and swerving all over the road, talking, laughing, giggling, shouting. Kathy was in the middle of them, and Tom in the lead. Susie brought up the rear, and was beginning to wail again.

'Wait for me, Kathy, wait; WAIT!' The last imperious 'wait' settled it for Kathy. She rode on, without looking back, determined to have her day as she wanted it, and not to have it spoiled any longer by Susie. In a flood of tears, Susie stopped, defeated. She flung her bike angrily onto the verge and sat down and cried bitter tears.

'Your sister's crying,' said Ned, the red-haired boy, to Kathy, as if she did not know. 'You should wait for her.' But Kathy only set her mouth and pedalled faster to shake him off. As the gang disappeared over the next bluff in the road, Susie picked her bike up and started to make her tearful way back home.

They stopped at a farm gate, which Tom opened and they all pushed their bikes through, and then manoeuvred them over a field of thick grass, where cows grazed. Dandelions and buttercups were everywhere, and thistles, which pricked their bare legs as they passed. Soon they arrived at the burn. The stream was quite swollen, as it had been raining all the past week. Still, the banks on either side stood a good three feet above the water, the red clay clearly visible and rising to the blanket of tough grass at the top. Tom retrieved a special branch from a small, coppiced wood nearby, that he kept for the purpose of harnessing the rope. He returned with the long, branched stick, cast the end towards the rope hanging in the centre of the stream, secured it round a knot at the bottom of the rope and gently hauled it in. The kids watched in fascination – and trepidation. This would not be an easy stunt, if you were one of the younger ones, and it called for courage. Kathy assessed the opposite high bank, and the width of the stream; it was wider than she remembered from last year; she would have to have a very good run at it to get momentum to swing her across.

Tom went first. He took a good run and then, as he approached take off, worked his hands quickly up the slack of the rope, and, at the last minute, pushed himself off with force. Kathy watched in some concern. He was big and strong, and his strength had undoubtedly helped. That big push off had propelled him easily over the water. No doubt about that! He sailed elegantly across the burn, his feet resting on the knot, and his face lit by a smile of pure enjoyment. Then he was over the bank, and he instantly jumped down before the rope started returning itself, while hanging onto the rope with one hand. He threw the rope back to the other side and Tony caught it. Then it was Tony's turn. He did all the things Tom had done, except for the powerful take-off, and only just made it to the other side. Then it was Alice's turn. She was a strong girl of thirteen years and made it quite comfortably. Next went Ned. He too made it, but almost missed the bank. Tom caught him and pulled him the last few feet. Soon it was Kathy's turn. Everyone was looking at her, so she knew it was her moment. She had planned her manoeuvre well, but would she be able to do it? She caught the end of the rope, when it was thrown to her and carried it well back into the tufty grass, vaguely aware of some cows nearby, contentedly grazing. She took hold of the rope below the knot, and, with a deep breath and a silent prayer, she started her run. She could run well, even at ten, but this grass was difficult and she found herself stumbling and losing speed. Finally, some nine or ten feet before the edge she got up speed, worked her hands up the rope well beyond the knot, arrived at the edge of the bank, and took off.

But something had gone wrong; she did not know, clearly. At the last minute she saw the opposite bank rise red and high, but too high, and the water she was about to traverse deep and wide, too wide. In a panic and an utter confusion of thought, she let go of the rope half way over the burn, and a second or two later landed flat on her back in the water. Fortunately, because it was swollen, there were no large boulders near the surface, on which she could have injured herself. She sank in, still on her back, completely submerged, and then, finding her feet amongst all the rocks and stones and weed, stood up. The water was up to her waist. She wiped the water out of her eyes and saw that everyone was laughing, hilariously, some doubled over. Tom was laughing as hard as the rest. Of course, she realised, this was also why they all came. It was not just the exhilaration of the flight over the water. Someone invariably fell in, and it was funny, very funny! She had laughed so much last year when Ned had fallen in, when she had come just to watch. But still, it did not help to know that. She picked her tortuous and ignominious way, between all the stones, out of the river. Charlie put a hand down and helped her climb up the bank. She was soaked to the skin and warm river water poured out of her tee shirt and shorts and ran down her legs into her squelching plimsolls. River weed clung to her hair and the water ran down her arms. This sight of her seemed to be the cause of even more hilarity, and soon the kids on both banks were speechless with laughter. Hot tears welled in Kathy's eyes. She ran to her bike, pulled it out of the grass and started to push it back over the field to the gate.

'Don't go,' called Tom. 'Kathy, stay! You'll be fine! You'll dry out soon.'

'Sorry, we're laughing,' said Charlie, as she passed him. 'But it *is* funny! You look such a sight, Kathy!' But she went on pushing her bike. She could not bear to think of these hateful kids, most especially Tom, laughing at her.

Chapter 27

————~•∽•⟡•∽•~————

Meeting Aunt May

Every minute of every day now, Kathy was suffused with the feeling that she was being returned to the fold of life, that the exile she had had to endure, most unfairly, was coming to an end. She had found 'family'. And the old feeling of lying back on life, of depending completely on parents and home and all sorts of other small predictable things – that experience of a deep inner confidence which required no thought, just trust – began to put forth tiny shoots once more in her being. And she began to feel human again, after a long, frozen sleep. There was a new hope in her step now; but not the hope that had been based on sheer grit and a necessary hardness and determination of character. This was a more immediate hope, a hope that wore a little flesh and blood, a hope that surely could soon be clothed even more as events unfolded. True, everything hung on two old people - Aunt May and Granfy. It could be a fragile thing, this trust of hers; what could two very old people do for her? All manner of things, Kathy thought, vaguely. Adults, especially family, can work miracles. Perhaps we can all live together. And then? After that she did not know. It was not wise, she thought, to let hope run too far in front of you. It might get away from you, she thought. One step at a time, Granfy had said. So, the first thing was to make a home for herself and Granfy.

All the week she worked diligently at the restaurant, foregoing free afternoons so that she might have the weekend free.

'Jesus, Kathy,' said Emma one day. 'You're changing. You've got a beautiful smile. I've never seen you smile before. It's because you're seeing your folks isn't it?'

'I suppose so,' said Kathy, trying to be non-committal. Her new hope and trust and plans were not for the world to see and know. That was a deeply private matter. The world must still be treated with kid gloves. She didn't want to be let down in the eyes of the world. The world was not something that took care of you; therefore, never let your guard down, she had decided. Tell a bit, but not much. And so she had told Emma that she had found a lost great aunt in Bath, and through her she was going to find her grandfather, who had been separated from her by the System.

'The System?' Emma had looked puzzled.

'Social services,' said Kathy.

'Oh, I see,' laughed Emma. 'You make it sound like some communist regime.' This was a thought that had not occurred to Kathy before, and she found it interesting.

'Well, splitting up families, and telling them where to live. Isn't that a bit communist?' said Kathy. 'And a bit 1984?'

'I don't know,' said Emma, in her habitual, vague way. 'What would you have done without social services? Probably starved; been homeless; all that.' And both girls considered this prospect and shivered inwardly. Kathy had no response. Should she be grateful to social services? She felt profoundly ungrateful and angry.

Saturday arrived at last! She had slept only fitfully, the anticipation of the task before her, working on her sleeping mind and drawing her continually back into a state of semi-wakefulness and readiness; readiness for action. Also, there was the persistent and nagging idea that events in Bath might lead to nothing, that it would be a false move in the maze. And that she would have to return to the drawing board. But she had no drawing board. Drawing board was another name for resources, and of these she had none. Only character, like Becky.

A song thrush was singing on the cherry tree in the garden outside. She could tell it was a song thrush by its repetitive song. It was one of Kathy's 'good' birds, one of the birds she loved, and she wondered if it heralded a good day. She could hear Paul moving about downstairs, and Jenny snoring heavily in the room next to hers. She rose, went into the bathroom, which was in its usual cluttered and dirty state, showered and dressed. She breakfasted briefly, sitting in one of the arm chairs, on toast and boiled egg, which she had every morning now. The eggs were fresh from the farm where Paul worked, and she enjoyed them. Paul was getting ready to go to work, and was making himself some thickly-sliced sandwiches.

'Coming tonight, Kathy?' he invited. 'There's a gig in town.' His veiled, expressionless, grey eyes gave nothing away, as usual. If she consented to come, it would be the same as if she refused. It seemed all the same to him. He would betray no emotion. She wondered if he had any. She had never seen him mad, bad, angry or happy (except that once, when he was drunk). He lived a half life of feeling. But, come to that, people could say the same of her. Why Emma had alluded to her never even smiling. We all play our cards close to our chest, she thought; we're all vigilant all the time, watching our backs like prisoners in a vicious prison. It's just like this in this neck of the woods, she thought again. It's survive or not survive. Not surviving was the psychological death of the drug addict, which was still a very real death, a dead person walking round in a body. And she had seen plenty of them in London and here in Glastonbury.

'Thanks, Paul,' she said brightly, but not too brightly. 'I've an errand today in Bath; I don't think I'll be back in time.'

'The gig doesn't start till nine,' persisted Paul.

'It's good of you, Paul, to invite me, but I'm sure I'll not be back in time. Another time,' she added, throwing this fig leaf, and then regretting it.

He packed his sandwiches into his back pack. His movements were neat and graceful, and, although, he was still a youth, his hands were strong and his fingers long; he could have been a pianist, she thought. His thick, brown hair curled around his ears and fell over his face, as he bent to do up his trainers. He was so different to his mother, she reflected. There was not that generosity of spirit, that bubbling spontaneity, that indiscipline, that childish, inappropriate trust in things, that refusal to get organised for life, and, latterly, Kathy thought, that turning to drink for solace from all the disappointments of her life. No, Paul was the antithesis of all this. He was careful, measured, disciplined, always assessing, and fairly well-organised – at least for the small things in life, like work and gigs. He said nothing, and swung out of the house, shutting the front door behind him, not slamming it. This worried her, this not saying anything. Was he hurt, angry? Secretly angry that she would not come to the gig with him? It would have been better to know. The not-knowing how he felt was disconcerting, but she was used to that now.

She washed up in the kitchen, made some sandwiches for herself, and let herself out of the house, with Jenny still snoring upstairs.

She was in plenty of time for the morning bus. She thought she would make use of her time off from work by spending the whole day in Bath, and so had decided to go early in the morning. She had her lunch in her back pack, so the trip would not cost her much. After a short wait, the bus arrived. She boarded and found a seat by the window, from where she could enjoy the journey to Bath. They passed through the pleasant, flat countryside of Somerset, the wet fields and roads slowly drying in a weak, morning sun. Somerset! How she treasured that name still – full of summer and high hopes. Friesian cows grazed in the fields; small holdings and pretty pubs and hens on the roadside slid by the window. Further away bigger farms nestled in the folds of wide meadows, and chestnut, oak and beech trees graced the fields, as though in some stately park, spreading their magnificent boughs, now almost denuded of foliage, across spaces of pale grass. Prickly hedges lined the way, and old man's beard trailed across them, its powdery pom poms of down full of seed for the birds.

Great Aunt May, thought Kathy. What will she be like? And she felt herself compelled to take a more realistic view, now that she was nearing the actual meeting with her, and to furnish the dream, that had carried her through the past week, with a real human being, who would undoubtedly have weak points, and, at nearly eighty, certainly incapacities and limitations. Still, she was sure Aunt May would be vital, mentally functioning, and helpful; after all, it was because of *her* social services had decided to move Granfy to a care home near her. She had also pondered on the question of why the family never spoke of her. Clearly something awful, disgraceful, had happened, and the family had felt it very important to expunge May from all family memories. So, there had been no photos of her as an adult in Granfy's room. Just one of her as a small child, squinting at the camera and standing beside an even smaller boy, who was Granfy.

'Who's that?' Kathy had once asked.

'No-one,' said Granfy firmly. And he had directed her gaze to the other people in the photograph – the parents and grandparents.

'Actually, that's my sister, May,' he had said, relenting. 'May Miller, that was.'

'And what's she called now?' Granfy had not expected this; it was a jump too far ahead for him, Kathy intuited, even as the child that she was. She was being given to understand that May Miller was dead and gone. But then he had said:

'Ferguson, May Ferguson, for her sins.'

So, the marriage had not been quite right, Kathy thought, staring out of the bus window at a distant farm. 'For her sins.' So, there was something wrong with the husband, or the family, or the way in which they had got married. Had she been pregnant? She ruminated on this question, and recalled that picture of the young child with the short, blonde hair, in a summer dress, squinting at the camera. It must have been the time of the flappers, thought Kathy, and wondered if May, when she got a bit bigger, had danced the Charleston.

She mooched around Bath all Saturday, exploring the little, unusual streets and quaint shops, and ate her lunch in the public park. She wondered a good deal, while eating her sandwiches, what it was Aunt May had done; why was she an outcast from the family?

At four o'clock she arrived at a small, brick block of flats, that bore all the features of sheltered housing, Kathy felt. Holding her breath, her heart beating with anticipation, she scanned the list of names, found Ferguson and pressed the bell. Would this old lady be of some use to her, or would she be too old? After a few seconds a voice came through the intercom: 'Is that Kathy Miller?' The voice bore a strong trace of that north country, lilting accent that Kathy knew so well, and she felt a rush of relief on hearing it – a voice of her own kind! A second later came the buzzer sound on the door. Kathy pushed it open. She stood lost for a moment or two in the vestibule, confused by her own feelings, and facing a reflection of herself in a long mirror. Briefly, she appraised the image of a never-seen great niece that would soon present itself to this old lady. A typical teenager in jeans and jacket, Aunt May would look beyond that, see the Miller genes in her build, which was slim and of average height. But it would be the face that would give away the family resemblance, looking so much like her father and grandfather, being long and with that slightly long nose, and those slate blue eyes, fringed by dark lashes and well-defined, straight, dark eyebrows. Her hair was no longer cropped in the way it had been when Gary and his gang had ruled her life. It was longer now and untidy; it needed a cut, she thought, as she tried to arrange it again with her fingers into a shapely bob. She had ceased wearing the eye make-up and lipstick some days ago. From some way above, a voice called: 'Come on up. Take the lift to the third floor.'

Kathy emerged from the lift to be welcomed by Great Aunt May. A small, neat woman, well-dressed in a mauve, tweed skirt and pretty blue blouse, Kathy followed her into her apartment. It was very simply furnished with china ornaments of shepherds and shepherdesses on the mantel piece and window sill, and a few pictures on the walls – prints of rural scenes. Simple chairs with wooden arms and legs were arranged round the room, and a fire, giving off artificial flames, glowed pleasantly in the fireplace. In the centre of the mantelpiece stood a clock upon which Kathy's eye rested for a moment. Untutored in antiques, she nevertheless recognised its quality, the oval face set on a base of deep, blue china, which rested on tiny, curved legs, and the whole decorated in ormolu. She sensed the old lady had registered with pleasure her appreciation of this beautiful object, and felt a good beginning had been made. But how could it be otherwise? This was a relative, and there would be a deep, shared understanding between the two of them. Kathy felt the grief of her current misfortune bubbling up, and wondered with surprise and anxiety if she was going to cry.

'Cup of tea, dear?' asked Aunt May, bustling into the kitchen, and Kathy's emotion subsided as quickly as it had arisen, while the formality of the situation was dealt with.

Tea and buttered scones and jam appeared. Kathy wondered if this was as big an event for Aunt May as it was for her. She did not think so; Aunt May looked too practised in social niceties, as though she served tea and talked to friends quite often, and wore nice, pleasant clothes as a matter of course.

'Eee,' she exclaimed, settling herself into a rocking chair opposite Kathy. 'You're the spitting image of our Archie! Those eyes, just the same as his, and same as your father's, I should think. Never met him,' she added. Then: 'do call me Aunt May; Great Aunt May is too long - a mouthful!' They sat in silence for a moment or two. Aunt May seemed to derive great pleasure in contemplating Kathy. 'You've got Archie's hands, too,' she said. 'At least when he was young; a pianist's hands, me mother always said. Yes, me mother wanted him to be a pianist. Sat him down every evening in the front parlour to practise. But he didn't want it, and that was that! Eventually. Not at first. For three years me mother had this idea. Fixed on it, she was! Eeee, Archie,' and she sighed.

Kathy, too, took the greatest pleasure in contemplating Aunt May. She really was very small, as small as Archie was tall, and quite different in facial bone structure. Where Archie had a long face, May had a broad one with high cheek bones, and a short, wide forehead. She may have been pretty in her youth. It was hard to tell. Her face was now creased with a patchwork of lines, like crumpled tissue paper, some lines even running vertically down her forehead into her eyebrows. But the eyes were bright, and the personality reached out, and Kathy felt there could be a relationship here; that Aunt May could in some way be that relation that would be of such necessary comfort to her. And, of course, she was going to take her to see Granfy! And that would just be the start of much to follow. Aunt May sat on the wooden rocking chair with her feet not touching the ground. Occasionally, the chair gently rocked; Kathy did not know how she managed to get it rocking. She wore no make-up, but her silver hair was tightly permed as was the way with many old people, Kathy felt, and on her old hands she wore a wedding ring. Kathy wondered where the husband was, this Ferguson. As if reading her mind, Aunt May looked at her hands, but said nothing. Then: 'Eeee, girl, it's good to see you!' But she stopped short of saying anything else, and Kathy could only guess why it was good for Aunt May. Perhaps it was the same for Aunt May as it was for her; that it was simply good to have, and be with, a relative. They contemplated each other, until Kathy lowered her eyes in modesty.

'Well, dear,' she said, eventually. 'You tell me a bit about yourself. Archie has told me a lot, already. Poor Archie,' and for a moment her own voice trailed off. Then she continued. 'He's shown me lots of photos of you all – you and your parents and your sister. I'm so sorry, dear, about what happened to your parents.' Kathy bit her lip; she felt she was going to cry. Here, at last, was a safe place where she could collapse on a shoulder and cry and cry. But this was not the time; suppose Aunt May could not handle it, could not support her in that way.

'Yes, it was dreadful,' returned Kathy in a controlled voice. And they were both silent for a moment, Aunt May pondering the vicissitudes and insults that life can deliver at any moment to anyone, and Kathy pondering on the terrible unfairness of life, the injustice of fate, of God, and the uncaringness of it all, and the deep, dark pit that some people found themselves in, and which had to be climbed out of with no hand holes and no ladder.

'Well, lass,' she said. 'You tell me about yourse'n; what brought you to Glastonbury, and what you're doing there. Archie told me they got you fixed up in a nice children's home, near to your mother's cousin, and into a very good school. But I thought all that was in London.'

'Nothing worked out as it should have done,' said Kathy simply. 'It was awful. I hated Eileen, my mother's cousin. I think she did drugs. I ran away.'

'You ran away!' repeated Aunt May, and her eyes lit up. This old lady obviously loved a bit of excitement, the unconventional, a good story, thought Kathy. 'What happened then? Oh, I hope nothing awful.' And Kathy could see she was thinking of modern problems, like teenage pregnancy.

'No, nothing awful, nothing like that,' said Kathy. 'No, the children's home was not a nice place, and the school was 'the pits'!' Kathy neglected to say that the first school had not been bad and that she had truanted. Neither did she mention the gang culture that she had found herself a part of, and which was, really, the cause of all her problems, and which in the end had offered no alternative but to run away. There was too much complication in this important detail, and Kathy sensed Aunt May would not be able to understand and sympathise with this aspect.

'Didn't they come looking for you, dear?'

'I don't know,' said Kathy. 'I used a false name and disguised myself a little.' Aunt May regarded her for a moment or two in silence, and Kathy wondered if she was thinking twice about her initial enthusiasm for a niece that was staking her own way, her own independence, in the course of which she was, perhaps, falling foul of the law. But Aunt May's face continued to be animated, her old eyes twinkling, and the rocking chair worked a little harder and faster. And Kathy was encouraged and heartened, if also a little surprised, by this implied insouciant attitude to 'the authorities.' By the time they were old, people had generally become very conventional, and avoided moves in life that could bring disturbance and alarm. Aunt May, she decided, was a game old lady.

'So, how've you kept yourself, dear? And where are you living?' Aunt May was asking all the right questions and at the right moments, and Kathy again felt that, within reason, here was indeed a person that could be of some help. So, she told her where she was working and living, and she also told her that this house was unsuitable, that the woman was alcoholic and the son strange.

'I have to find somewhere of my own,' she finished. Now, thought Kathy, Aunt May has an adequate picture of my life. I wonder what she will do with it. And she felt glad to have been able to put into words some part of her existence. She wondered if Aunt May would have the capacity to understand the full extent and import of her story; she doubted it, but, still, it was good to have told what she had told – and to a relative. Now what would life do? 'What I really want,' ventured Kathy, 'is to see Granfy.'

'Oh, you shall, dear, you shall,' said Aunt May whole-heartedly, 'although I think you'll not find him as he was.'

So, she thought, on the bus ride back to Glastonbury, a prayer has been answered. She had not gone down on her knees or anything like that; she had thought it a waste of time. She had learnt from Ma Riley that the Creator knew every thought, every desire in our heads, so why bother with formal prayer? Just the wish would do. 'Because,' she could hear Ma saying, 'you must at least make the *effort* to talk to God. Why should he work for you and improve your life if you aren't even willing to ask him nicely?' Well, she hadn't prayed, and her wish *had* been answered, and she felt a great feeling of gratitude well up inside her. God must have felt sorry for her and granted her wish, her quick, informal prayer. She made her mind up to pray more often, as Ma had advised. And Ma's words on prayer came back to her now, still fresh and clear. 'Prayer is always, always answered', Ma Riley said. 'It may not be in the way we want,' she explained, 'and it is seldom at the the time we want, but very occasionally it *is* answered in the way we want and at the time we want. And in that case we must give immediate thanks. But however and whenever our prayer is answered we must always understand, must know that no prayer goes unanswered. The Creator gives us what is best for us, always, not what we want. We are, most of us, not wise and therefore we do not know what is best for us.' And then Ma Riley said that we are only on this earth to grow, and that, sadly, we only grow through suffering, but the Creator gives us our suffering in increments, in bits we can manage. Always. We are never overwhelmed, never too challenged. 'And how does one grow best?' Kathy asked. 'By being close to nature, by seeking the treasures nature has to offer, buried deep sometimes,' Ma Riley reminded her. And then, after a short pause in which she seemed to reflect, Ma went on, 'Think of Mr. Churchill; what a great man he was! But he never would have been great if he had not been challenged in the depths of his character. Yes, he certainly had great challenges and much, much suffering. And that suffering is what gave him that strong character, that leadership that brought Europe out of that darkness of the second world war, one of the greatest darknesses the world has ever known. People today,' Ma added, 'want immediate happiness, and they want tawdry things, tinsel, things of no lasting value, things not worthy of a human being.' Kathy could hear Ma Riley talking as though it were only yesterday that she had said all this. How she missed her; how she missed all that wisdom! The vicar at church never spoke in this way; he had never been so meaningful, so wise, so helpful. She gave sincere thanks again to the Creator.

Chapter 28

―ᴡᴏᴄᴇᴛᴏᴏᴇᴏᴏᴡᴡ―

Getting to Know Aunt May

The following Friday, on her day off that week, Kathy stood again at the front door of Aunt May's sheltered housing, and looked forward to her second meeting with her great aunt. She scolded herself for her feelings which were riding high; she could not remember if Becky Sharp allowed her feelings to run so out of control. As before, a buzzer sounded, and Kathy let herself in, and ascended to the third floor in the lift. Aunt May appeared in a flattering, pink blouse and skirt. Kathy was impressed and felt this old lady was still very much a part of the world, still able to cope with the essentials of life.

'Come on in, dear.' She welcomed Kathy warmly, in that friendly, Northumbrian accent, and settled herself into her rocking chair again, drawing a woollen shawl around her shoulders.

'We'll have lunch in a bit,' she said. 'The potatoes are boiling.' Then Aunt May inquired about Kathy's week in the restaurant. Kathy gave her a brief, appropriate outline, omitting details she felt the old lady would not understand. Then, to her surprise, she blurted out, 'It's my birthday next week!' Like a child, she thought; would Becky ever have done that? Then she realised how hurt she was in not feeling able to tell anyone in Glastonbury. No-one would care. Perhaps Emma would, but it seemed an imposition to put on Emma, when she hardly knew her. But with Aunt May it was different. Aunt May was family. A birthday was a matter for families.

'When?' asked Aunt May.

'Thursday,' said Kathy. 'The eighth of December.'

'A lucky day,' said the old lady. And Kathy wondered if she was just saying this, or if it really was lucky. 'Well, you best come over here,' she said. 'We'll have a nice celebration. I can easily cancel bingo.'

'Oh, no,' said Kathy. 'Don't do that.'

'Certainly, I will, dear. Birthdays are very important.' She smiled, and Kathy felt it was a tender smile. Then, choosing her moment, Kathy ventured tentatively: 'Aunt May,' she said, 'why was there no connection between you and our family? What happened? Why did we never talk about you? Granfy hardly ever mentioned your name.' Aunt May paused in her rocking chair, her feet a good three inches off the floor, her lined face pensive for a moment, while a fleeting sadness passed over it. Then the animation returned and the chair set itself in motion once again.

'I'm glad you ask, dear,' said Aunt May. 'It was because I brought disgrace on the family. Well, they thought it was disgraceful that I should marry Billy Ferguson.' And she paused, and drifted off into thoughts of her young life.

'Why, what was wrong with Billy Ferguson?'

'Aye, our Billy,' she continued, without hearing Kathy. 'Been dead and gone these thirty yer.' And she looked wistfully at the photograph of a young man on the mantelpiece. Kathy followed her eye. It was a formal photograph of a young man in a suit, probably his only suit, his Sunday Best. He had a handsome face, indeed - good, fine bone structure and a high, wide forehead and high cheekbones. His blonde hair, neatly parted near the top of the head, was slicked back with grease. The fact of his handsomeness was what struck Kathy.

'Aye, he's handsome, isn't he?' said Aunt May contemplating her young husband. 'All the lasses thought so. In fact all the gels of Blaydon fancied our Billy.' And a satisfied little smile crossed her face. 'Aye, he was handsome! And strong, too. Very athletic. Even me mother said he was handsome as a film star. She admitted that much.' And Aunt May took a little time out again, in which Kathy could see she was arguing with her mother about her relationship with Billy Ferguson.

'Did your family not like him?'

'Like him! They had no respect for him, no respect for the family. They were ne'er-do-wells. No denying it. And they thought Billy would turn out just like the rest of them. Burglars, the old man and his brother were. Done time in clink, too! "How could Billy be anything but what the trade of the family is," me mother kept telling me. Families were strong in those days, you understand,' said Aunt May, as an aside. 'Sons generally followed in their fathers' footsteps. "And all the sacrifices I've made." Oh, my mother kept on about the sacrifices they made for my education. And I did have a good education. Yes, I got a good job in the pensions office in Newcastle.' And she drifted off into more unvoiced memories. Kathy brought her gently back.

'So, did you marry Billy Ferguson?' But Kathy was going too fast. Aunt May wanted to stay with the early days.

'Aye, me Billy! All the lasses in Blaydon were out to catch him. Had a way with gels, you see. Oh, he was charming. A real charmer!' Kathy got up and looked at the photo and saw the charmer - the good looks, the well-shaped, translucent eyes, obviously blue, and the beautiful mouth; but there was, perhaps, a weakness about the mouth, betraying a weakness of character that he perhaps would not choose to correct.

'And he was clever, too. Aye he was clever. His Dad set him to work in the factory. Did well. They promoted him. Said he was a clever lad who would make out. But he didn't last; didn't like standing by a conveyor belt all day. Preferred the family business.'

'So, did you marry him?' Kathy asked again. And again she realised she was cutting in on Aunt May's reminiscences, reminiscences that seemed to dwell on the courting time, the time of May's conquest of this young blood, who was fancied by all the young women, it seemed.

'Sure, I married him! Certainly, I did! I loved him, you see, and he me. But we had to run away to do it. We went to a registry office. And then my parents wouldn't speak to me any more. And all the girls in Blaydon were so jealous. And then soon after that he went away to the war, you see. All the lads couldn't get to the war quick enough. That's how it was in those days. They all wanted to go.' Aunt May paused, before continuing again. 'Aye, me mother was that upset. I was upset too. And she quite turned our Archie against me. I never heard from him again.' And she looked sad for quite a few moments.

'But you had your Billy,' said Kathy, quietly.

'Oh, I did that,' said Aunt May quite fiercely. 'And we were happy for a time. Mostly during the war – on his leaves. And he came home, wounded in the knee; but he came home! Not like so many of the young lads. Went away, and never came home again. Dear me, it was terrible, terrible! All those families without their fathers and husbands and sons. Oh quite dreadful, tragic! I hope we never have another war again. If people only knew.' And Aunt May was quiet again, while she recalled all those memories of wartime. 'But, as I said, my Billy came home. Wounded in the knee, but that was all. And then he had no job; he looked and looked, but nothing, except in that awful factory. So he had to go back into the family trade.' Kathy wondered what it had been like for Aunt May to find out she had married a burglar. 'But he didn't last long in that,' she continued. 'He wasn't as good as his Dad and uncle, and he didn't care for clink. Not like them. They were hard; they could endure a bit of clink now and then. Billy couldn't. It affected him. He wasn't cut out to be an old lag. And the police were soon onto him, watching him, and their methods of detection got better and better. So he gave that up.

'So, what did he do then?' asked Kathy, thoroughly fascinated by this wayward relative of hers, about whom the whole family had never spoken.

'Oh, he worked on the railways, always jobs for men on the railways in them days,' said Aunt May. 'But we moved away from Blaydon after a bit. We couldn't stand the stigma, you see. Folks cold-shouldering us. Not Billy's kin, of course, but I didn't really fit with them either. They were cut from a different cloth. Rough; aye, rough. And Billy wasn't a *bit* rough! We used to say his mam had him by someone else, not by his Dad. He never even looked like his Dad. Perhaps Joe Keble, the manager's assistant at the factory. He looked like Billy. But Billy's mam was not a good-looker. I just couldn't see Joe Keble wanting an affair with Billy's mam, so I never went after that theory much. Aye, Billy was a one-off. And he coulda done so well. But I never held it agin him. It wasn't me place.' Kathy wondered if she was just so grateful he had married her, that she put no demands on him.

'So, you moved away?' pressed Kathy.

'Aye, we moved first to Sheffield, and then to London. Always the railways. Always work on the railways. Then they started sending him away. He was sometimes gone for weeks at a time, then months. And I never knew where he was. Then he was gone for a whole year. I knew then it wasn't the railways; it was something else.' And a look of deep sadness settled on her face. And, despite her young years, Kathy was picking up that Billy Ferguson had become a philanderer.

'Did you have any children?' asked Kathy, wondering if there were second or third cousins in her family.

'No,' said Aunt May. 'And that was just as well! The money by then was irregular. I had to go out and get a job. I worked in a candle factory in Battersea. Eee, the smell!' And her face brightened, as she recalled this quirky period of her life in the candle factory. And the sadness slipped quietly away, replaced once more by her habitual animation that she had obviously disciplined herself into over the sad years. So, as her family had predicted, she had married a ne'er-do-well. And had had to endure the consequences.

A little bell went off in the kitchen. 'Eee, the potatoes! They're done,' exclaimed Aunt May. 'Who would believe the time would go so fast! Good that I have that pinger; I'd never have remembered.' Aunt May slid gracefully off her rocking chair, and disappeared into her kitchen.

Aunt May had 'done Kathy proud'. She had poached two pieces of salmon and served them with new potatoes and peas. For dessert, she produced a trifle, which Kathy felt was a dish Aunt May reserved for very special occasions. This was the first home-cooked meal she had eaten in the past six weeks, Kathy reflected. Ever since she had run away from the children's home, she had eaten light salad lunches and always take-aways for supper. Well, better than little Tommy Tucker, her mother would have said. And so would Aunt May! And Kathy felt they both would have got along together. What a pity they never even knew one another!

Chapter 29

Finding Granfy

'Archie's a bit changed,' said Aunt May, as they put on their coats after lunch. But she gave no explanation, and Kathy wondered in what way he had changed. His memory had been faltering, but her mother had assured her that was normal in old people. But it seemed not to be the case with Aunt May. Aunt May seemed to have a wonderful memory. Perhaps it was all the numbers on the bingo nights!

They walked slowly up and down a few streets, slowly because Aunt May could no longer walk as fast as she used to. She showed Kathy some intriguing little alley ways, where fascinating, half-hidden shops sold exotic Glastonbury-type ware.

'All for the tourists. All rubbish!' said Aunt May dismissively. 'What has the world come to! It's all unnecessary! Still, I thought we might come and just have a look. It's always interesting to see what's going on, how things change. My, how things have changed from my day!'

Soon, they boarded a bus and within ten minutes had reached the outskirts of the town. They alighted, Kathy giving Aunt May a helping hand onto the pavement. A short walk away, they turned into a gracious drive and continued a short distance, passing flower beds of withered plants and seed heads. A few dahlias and pansies were still in bloom.

It was an old Georgian house, which bore an air of bygone elegance, and Kathy tried to imagine what the original occupants would have been like. Wool merchants, perhaps. She was also surprised that Granfy had been placed here. It would not be cheap, she supposed. Perhaps Granfy had had some funds of his own. The warden came to the door and admitted them, warmly welcoming Aunt May and extending her warmth to Kathy on the introduction. Now Kathy felt herself besieged by her emotions again. How far she was from her ideal of Becky! How weak and pathetic and out-of-control she was, more like the weak and foolish Amelia Sedley than like Becky, the commander. But, it was no good; she could not fight these feelings. At last they found Granfy sitting in a high, wing-back chair playing solitaire on a little table in a quiet, small conservatory, facing onto the garden. Kathy rushed forward and flung her arms round her grandfather.

'Oh, lass,' he said after a few moments, 'Lass, it's good to see you!' He was smiling broadly, but with tears in his eyes, and, pushing her gently away 'so as to be able to see you better', he contemplated the sight of his lost and found grand-daughter. 'I could hardly believe it when May said you'd found her. That was clever, Kathy!' And he held out his arms to her.

'Oh, Granfy, Granfy!' And beside herself with the relief of finding her grandfather and all the grief of her situation welling up inside her, she threw herself into his arms and wept. She wept for some minutes, quiet tears, tears of tragedy and release, and was unable to stop herself. But in that quiet part of the mind that is never engaged completely in the emotion, but which only observes, she found herself registering amazement. She had never intended to behave like this, and had not foreseen it. She was younger and indeed weaker than she had thought. But at the same time it felt so utterly wonderful to be in the arms of flesh-and-blood kin, to feel the large, bony frame of Granfy beneath her head, and his hand stroking her hair. She felt the folded, old skin of his neck beneath her cheek and the wetness of her tears on the skin of them both. She was back! She was home! Her whole body signalled the news, and little by little every part of her began to unwind, to unravel the knots of the stress of the past months, and the vigilance and tension began to recede, and that trusting bliss of belonging, of having family, of being in the bosom of some little paradise returned to her in full consciousness, and she was grateful she had this much, this blessing.

Finally, she disengaged herself from Granfy and took her seat in the chair Aunt May had pulled up for her.

'Well, Kathy, lass, you *are* upset! Have things been so bad? May told me you didn't get on in London, and that you ran away.' He looked serious and worried, as though he could not believe that the social work professionals could be anything but entirely trustworthy and competent. He had never, as long as she could remember, questioned anyone in authority, as her mother did. And she realised that, unlike May, he had not that spirit of adventure, that boldness and humour about life that May obviously had.

'Yes, I ran away; and I am glad. I had to, Granfy; it was so awful.' But she did not go into the details of a situation which would have been beyond his comprehension, and which would only have distressed and confused him.

'And why didn't you write? I thought you might come one weekend and visit me.'

'How could I, Granfy, I didn't know where you were.'

'But your mother's cousin, Eileen, was supposed to tell you. She was given all the details of this place, when they got me in here.'

'She never told me,' said Kathy. 'She stopped coming to see me quite early on; perhaps your new address arrived after that.' Granfy absorbed this information with incredulity.

'Well, would you believe it?' he said. 'I wonder why she stopped coming to see you. What a wicked woman! And your mother's cousin! Some people just cannot be trusted! But you're here now, lass, and, oh, it's so good to see you!' And he held out his hand to take Kathy's.

Meanwhile, Aunt May had been surveying the scene of reunion between Kathy and her brother with some surprise. She had not realised that Kathy would be so overcome with emotion, had not understood that Kathy, for all her appearance of young adulthood, was still essentially a child. But then she *was* only fifteen, sixteen next week. That is still very young, she reflected.

'And your hair, lass! What've you done with your hair?' he asked. Kathy laughed, and ran her fingers through the thick, short hair, that no longer stood up on the top of her head. 'It looks awful!' he admonished. 'You need a hairdresser.'

A tea trolley arrived, and cups and plates replaced the solitaire board, and cakes and scones and jam appeared. Kathy felt she wanted to stay there forever. A little bit of happiness had squeezed through the cracks of her lonely life, through the long battle she was fighting that had given no hint of victory. That was until now.

On the bus back to Glastonbury that evening, Kathy felt as though a huge door had opened; a gate had yielded, and, beyond, there was a different landscape, different country. How would her life now change? What would Becky do with this new, better situation?

Chapter 30

———❦———

Sweet Sixteen

I t was her birthday, and Kathy was riding the bus again to
Bath. As before, she had joined it in Wells. Aunt May had told
her that Wells had a beautiful cathedral, and that one day soon
they would visit it together. There was a settled feeling about
this pronouncement, as though Kathy had some degree of order
and control in her life; that there was a work life and a play life,
and in her play life she could take trips with Aunt May. But, of
course, this was not the case. Apart from the relief of finding
Granfy again, there was the huge problem of her life: where
was she to go, and what was she to do? Should she pray? 'Well,
first,' she thought, 'I will have to find a little flat and get Granfy
out of that care home. He will do much better having a normal
life again. I will work during the day, and during my free-time
I will study, and then I'll go to university, and get a grant for all
our expenses.' So, the next step was to find a flat in Glastonbury

or Bath. Perhaps Aunt May would be able to help them. There was still the difficulty in her work life of the P45 form. She was sure Debbie was soon going to take her on as 'permanent', and she would need the P45 form and her proper name. Well, she thought, others have done it before me. I'll find a way.

It was Thursday, the eighth of December, and her sixteenth birthday. A greyness had formed over the softly-undulating landscape, and rain had started to gently fall, spattering the bus window with raindrops. It often rained on her birthday, she reflected. That was the problem with a winter birthday. 'Yes, but just think,' her mother had said. 'The eighth of December is in the sign of Sagittarius. It's meant to be a wonderful sign: the sign of optimism, a cheerful outlook on life, an inclination to happiness and generosity - and much travel and higher learning,' she had added, brightly. Her mother knew nothing about astrology, but she had found this definition of Sagittarius, and of Leo for Susie, somewhere and kept trotting them out at odd moments. So, I am a Sagittarian, she thought. 'Much travel and higher learning,' she repeated to herself, and wondered if she would ever even get back into 'lower learning'.

The rain had become heavier, and was now pouring down onto the little gardens, the stone walls and the cottage roofs. The bus windscreen wipers worked fast, and the window ran with streams of water. The grey sky was low and seemed to hang over the woods and hills, suspended, motionless, trapped, and unable to move on. The kindly breeze that might have blown it all away was quite absent.

And, so on this dull, but still mild, winter day, Kathy stepped off the bus in Bath, and started her walk to Aunt May's for her birthday lunch. In the afternoon they would visit Granfy.

'So, Kathy, dear,' said Aunt May, settling herself into her rocking chair, her feet again not touching the floor. 'So, you're sixteen, sixteen today! Sweet sixteen, and never been kissed,' she said. Not knowing if this was merely a statement or if it carried a vague question, Kathy blushed slightly and looked down.

'I haven't, actually,' she said. 'Is that bad?' She recalled the few girls at school, at home, who had started dating at fifteen years. And wondered now if she was somehow slow in this respect. Her mother had always discouraged her, but her mother may have been wrong. But then she was sure no boy would have wanted to go out with her.

'No, child, it's not bad! Not bad at all. It's good! The longer a girl holds off from all that – within reason, of course – the better the man she'll marry.'

And Kathy felt this philosophy was right. There had been evidence all around her, back at home, that the girls who dated young did not do as well in their studies as the other girls. And then there had been so little time for a boyfriend. Her mother had been adamant that she join one or two of the school clubs and participate in the after-school sports sessions, even if this meant her father had sometimes to drive in and pick her up in the evening. 'You only get one chance at education, Kathy,' Elaine had said. 'I didn't get it; you and Susie will.' Nevertheless, despite knowing May was right, she asked: 'Why, Aunt May? Why do girls and boys turn out better when they don't date?'

'Because,' said Aunt May definitively and with emphasis. 'Because, when you hold off from dating, you develop character, and when you have character, you go through life much better, and that means you have a much better chance of a happy marriage and family – and, today, a career.'

'You didn't have a happy marriage, Aunt May,' said Kathy somewhat presumptuously, she knew.

'Oh, I know, I know,' said Aunt May with a twinkle in her eye, and glancing at the photo of Billy on the mantelpiece. 'Doesn't always work out that way. But I did hold out on dating, mind you; got a good education – as good as the working class could get in those days. My parents kept me at school till I was fifteen. Archie left at thirteen. So, you see, I was always able to get a good job. I had to! That rogue,' and she smiled at Billy's picture. 'He was never going to be able to take care of me.' Kathy was amazed that Aunt May could take such a benevolent and humorous perspective on what, at the time, must have been a tragic life – a childless marriage, a faithless husband. Perhaps she *had* been affected at the time; and perhaps she had had other men. But everything about Aunt May suggested that she had travelled her road on her own; that there had been no other men; that Billy had been her only love. Yes, thought Kathy, a good education is vital, and perhaps it *is* more vital for a woman, but a chill cooled her heart as she tried to envisage her life stretching away before her without a mate, without a family. It would never be enough for me, she thought.

Aunt May had slipped off her rocking chair, and was looking at her watch. 'You pour the water out, dear. I'll fetch lunch!' Aunt May returned from the kitchen with a trolley laden with the meal and a bottle of Beaujolais, and the two celebrated Kathy's birthday over a lunch of lamb, and birthday cake with sixteen candles on it. Kathy was touched. It must have taken Aunt May a great deal of time and effort to make this beautiful cake. Kathy pushed her chair back, and went over to Aunt May and kissed her on the cheek.

'Thank you, Aunt May! This is wonderful! You are so kind.' Kathy was surprised at herself making this gesture. They had never demonstrated their affection for one another at home in quite this way. She realised she had done this quite spontaneously, and felt that it was good. There were tears in Aunt May's eyes. Perhaps she is not used to this either, thought Kathy, and wondered if it was the north of England - if the north produced people who were inhibited when it came to situations of showing affection.

'No, love, it's not kindness,' said Aunt May. 'I did it for myself too. We must take every opportunity to celebrate life; to bring joy and light into our days. It all goes so quickly, you see. Life! You've got to take these moments and make them into little festivals. So, you see, I'm really being selfish!' Then Aunt May sang Happy Birthday. Even though she was old, Kathy could hear that she had a very good voice, tuneful and with good pitch. It was odd, having this old lady sing happy birthday to her; not long ago her family had done this. But she was enormously grateful. It made her feel a little more normal.

After a while, Kathy and Aunt May set out to take the bus to Granfy's. They got off a stop earlier, so that they could walk the last part as they were early. The rain had stopped, the pavements were drying out, but water still flowed quickly down the gutters, and drips dropped off the plane trees.

'Quite a downpour,' said Aunt May.

'Yes,' replied Kathy, taking Aunt May's arm, so that the two of them walked arm in arm up the hill.

The warden warned them that Granfy was not doing too well today. 'Occasionally he has an 'off' day,' she said, 'when he doesn't make a lot of sense. But they're not many, those days, as you know, Mrs. Ferguson,' she said reassuringly.

They found Granfy sitting staring at the television, at the kind of programme he would never have watched at home. Kathy was dismayed, and further concerned when Granfy addressed her. He had welcomed them appropriately with delight and affection, but then seemed not to remember correctly who they were and had gone off into a long, rambling monologue, punctuated now and again with questions they could not answer. But Aunt May took charge of the situation, lovingly and competently. She moved beside him, took his hand, and said:

'Now, Archie, what's this all about? Who wouldn't give you beetroot for lunch?' And so it went on for half an hour – Aunt May trying to soothe and placate Archie, and bring him back into the present. At tea-time they were allowed to move into the conservatory, and a young girl brought in a tray of scones and cake, just as on the previous occasion. Before they started to eat, Aunt May told Granfy in a firm, clear voice that it was Kathy's birthday, and that she wanted Granfy to join in and sing Happy Birthday. Aunt May started singing in her tuneful voice, and, with the first few words, something seemed to click in Granfy's brain. He left the world of dementia, inhabited by strange, illogical beings and events, and returned to his present life, to the understanding it was his granddaughter's birthday, and that he had forgotten to send her a card. He sang with gusto to compensate, and Kathy felt sure a member of staff was going to come into the conservatory and tell these two old folks to quieten things down.

Kathy felt flat on the bus ride back to Wells and thence to Glastonbury. Aunt May had done her best, and it was true she had had a good birthday. There was much to look back on, but life was really a question of looking forward, and Kathy had nothing clear to look forward to. And now the main plank of all her plans was coming adrift; what if Granfy were to sink more and more into these periods of dementia? If that happened then it would be hopeless trying to set up a new home with him.

With this new complication in her mind, Kathy arrived in Glastonbury. It was quite dark now, even though it was only seven o'clock. A cool, fresh wind was blowing from the north, which keened against her face, as she walked up Chalk Street to Paul's house. She felt the cold biting into her through her thin, light jacket. Winter is here, she thought. And then there was that other matter: how much longer could she remain living with Jenny and Paul?

Chapter 31

—⁓꘍◦◯◦◯◦◯꘍⁓—

Respite with Philip and Spiritual Lessons

It was dark these days, when Kathy finished in the restaurant late in the afternoon. Nevertheless, the kids still hung out with their skate boards in the market place, and Kathy still went to hang out with them. Most days Paul was not part of the gathering, working long hours on the farm, and this added to a feeling of relief and enjoyment that she derived from these occasions. She felt she should get herself a skateboard and become a participant. Watching others do what she could do had never been a large part of her life. 'Don't watch others doing it,' Granfy had said. 'You go out and do it.' The boys and one girl twirled and rode their boards, stopped abruptly or ran gracefully alongside them for a few steps, then remounted. The street lights and illumination from the shop and café windows, now filled with Christmas lights and decorations, cast a festive

glow over all these activities in this corner of Market Place –
all blessed, Kathy felt, by the benign and mysterious presence
of the town cross that silently stood as witness atop the fine
sculptured tower, at whose foot she now sat.

'That's great, Kevin,' she shouted, and 'Do that again, Pete!'
She now knew all the names of the boys and they seemed to
value her praise and encouragement. Here was a small place, a
tiny fissure in her existence, where she could experience, to a
small degree, those feelings of community, of peer relationship,
that made her feel human again; returned her to a small part
of her old self. A very small part, but it was something. Yes,
she had Aunt May and Granfy now, she thought, but somehow
she felt she needed the company of younger people also. She
noticed these feelings of being at ease in the restaurant, too.
The other women, who worked there were easy and pleasant.
She wished they would invite her home, share with her the
warmth and glow of their living rooms this lonely Christmas
time. She particularly wished Emma would extend more
friendliness to her, and take her home some evening. But the
other women in the restaurant had told her Emma had trouble
with her man, that he hit her sometimes, and that Emma never
brought people home. Who would have thought it? reflected
Kathy. Emma, who always looked so other-worldly, and above
the beastliness of life, living with a man who did that to her.
Poor Emma, she thought.

Philip, too, came many evenings. He enjoyed the conviviality
and the protection he felt Kathy's presence lent him. 'How do
you manage to get out of your place so much, Philip?' she asked

him once. 'I thought these children's homes were very strict about the young ones, like you, coming and going.'

'Oh, they don't mind me coming and going,' he said happily. 'They trust me; they know I can't get up to much. They think I'm visiting my Nan, and often I am. I'll get my homework done later; it won't take me long. And right now the other kids are watching television or just fooling around.' Kathy could guess he would not fit easily into these activities, and again she was amazed at his resilience and his resourcefulness in finding ways of removing himself from the threatening behaviour of the other children. Paul taunted him, she knew, but she never heard the other boys mocking and ridiculing him here, at the skateboard place. No, this was not a gang in the sense the group in west London had been. That was a real gang - nasty, corrupt and depraved (threatening and dangerous elements of British society), and she marvelled she had not come to any harm. She wondered briefly how Barbara was doing. Then she wondered if Barbara missed her, or indeed if any of them in the home missed her. Angelina, the little black girl, would definitely miss her. Kathy wondered if they had found Angelina's mother yet. She felt that was very unlikely and that Angelina would have to remain in care long term, and Kathy wondered how she would turn out, at the end of it all. Mike also might miss her, when he had got over the shock of her disappearance. But only for a time. He had so many other pressing cases to deal with. She wondered if they were still searching for her. It had been nearly two months now.

The warm light from the street lamp glowed on Philip's young face and fair hair. He had a few freckles across his child's nose, and his pink, healthy cheeks spoke of a happiness on this cold, mid-December evening.

'Do you like it, in the children's home?' she asked. Philip was silent. Then he said: 'I like it with you, Kathy. You're my friend.'

'You must have other friends,' she replied. He made no response and she regretted having underlined his aloneness.

'Kathy,' he said after a minute, in which they had both been staring at the other kids, mesmerised by the antics of the skaters. 'Kathy, I want to take you to Chalice Well. My Nan and I know it very well. We went there so much. My Nan used to work there too.'

'Oh, what did she do?' asked Kathy.

'She was a cleaner,' he said. 'They do bed and breakfast there too, and she cleaned in those houses. It's really a lovely place,' he said emphatically, his warm, friendly eyes filled with fervour, gazing into hers with confidence.

'Yes, I know,' she said. 'I've already been, but I'll come again. Of course, I will. I liked it. We'll have to go on a Saturday or Sunday, I suppose, when you aren't at school?'

'Yes, either Saturday or Sunday would be great for me, Kathy.'

'I'll see if I can get two days off next week; I'm going to Bath again on Thursday.'

*　　*　　*

It was Sunday and a fine, white frost covered all the roofs and gardens of Glastonbury. The late flowers drooped under the shocking chill of the icy crystals, and seed heads stood beautiful and eye-catching in their new white, powdery mantle, particularly, Kathy thought, the wild carrot, whose little, delicate baskets seemed just made to catch the soft rime, as though a baby's blanket had been gently laid around them.

She was wearing jeans and trainers, but also a new, warm jacket she had bought at the charity shop. Philip suddenly appeared in the forecourt of Chalice Well gates, clad too in a warmer jacket and high-necked sweater. He smiled with pleasure at Kathy and indicated his back pack. 'We can have a little picnic up in the meadow,' he said. 'Gracy's done us some sandwiches.'

'It's too cold to have a picnic,' said Kathy.

'No it's not. Nan and me often had picnics in the winter. And there's some hot soup in here too.'

'Here, give it to me,' said Kathy. 'You've carried it all up the street.' And she swung Philip's day bag onto her back. They walked under a long pergola, which Philip said was covered in wisteria and honeysuckle in the spring and summer. Kathy thought it must look lovely. They paid their fee at the entrance, and the young man selling the tickets recognised Philip and told him he did not have to pay.

'Doing O.K, Philip?' he asked. 'How's your nan?'

With tickets in their pockets, they then followed the little path up the hill with gardens on either side of them. Most of the flowers were now dead, but some sedum and lady's mantle and euphorbia, set amongst the shrubs, still struggled to brave the winter. They met a few other people, but in the main they had the garden to themselves. After a few minutes they came into the small garden on the right, with the Lion's head spouting water at one end into the small pool. There were the two glasses on the edge of the pool, that she had seen before and used.

'That water's very red, Philip; full of iron, I should think,' she observed.

'Yes, that's the chalybeate, the iron in the soil. That's what makes the water so red. They say it's the blood of Christ, really.'

'The blood of Christ!' exclaimed Kathy. 'That could only be in Palestine.'

'Well, they say Joseph of Arimathea, Jesus' uncle, brought the chalice of the Last Supper, after the crucifixion, here to Glastonbury and buried it here, or near to this Lion's Head. And now this spring pours out not only water, but also Christ's blood.'

'Hmm,' said Kathy, feeling this story was more myth than history.

'Oh, it could be true,' said Philip. 'This is a holy spring, and therefore it would make sense for Joseph to hide the cup here.'

'And did they find the cup, then?' asked Kathy.

'Yes,' said Philip.

'And where is it now?' asked Kathy, still sceptical. 'Still buried in the ground?'

'No, it's in Chalice Well house now.'

'Really!' exclaimed Kathy, impressed. 'And what does it look like?'

'It's blue and very beautiful,' said Philip. Kathy registered this information and wondered if she would ever see this cup, this chalice. 'And what makes a spring holy?' she asked.

'Oh, all springs are holy,' said Philip. 'But I think this one's holier than most. I think this one's very holy,' he said, knowingly.

Kathy knelt down to fill one of the glasses with the red-tinged water. She wondered if the glasses were ever given a proper wash, and if they were covered in other people's germs. 'It tastes good, very good,' she declared, as the fresh, pure water left its clean taste in her mouth. 'Here's one for you, Philip,' she said, filling the other glass and handing it to him.

'It's so good,' said Philip. 'I always feel much better after drinking it.'

'That blue cup that you say is the holy chalice,' said Kathy. 'Can anyone see it? Do they let people have a look?'

'Yes, but only special people.'

'What, priests?' asked Kathy.

'No, Companions,' said Philip.

'What's that?' she asked, interested in this mystical-sounding use of the term.

'People who pay money'.

'Oh,' she said disappointed. She had hoped it indicated an honour, reserved for something like knights - Knights of the Round Table, the Red Cross Knights, the Knights Templar, something like that. They were all connected, these knights, she was learning, since coming to Glastonbury. 'A lot of money?' she asked.

'No, but you have to be a special person, too,' he said.

'Oh,' she said, and lost interest, feeling she was not a special person.

Behind the drinking pool they passed another small garden, a rectangular lawn set between flower beds. The garden was still in the shade and the frost lay visible and untouched on the grass and on the seed heads and some dead flower blooms. Kathy looked at the subtle, delicate dusting, as though a fine breeze had blown by in the night and deposited a vestige of something beautiful and unreal from some magical land. She stopped for a moment and gazed entranced. The sun's rays were just ascending above the roofs of Chilkwell Street and were resting on the top corner of the garden, and gently warming the melting rime on the grass and on the leaves of the shrubs and dead flowers. How it all reminded her of home! They often had frosts at this time of the year, and the back garden, particularly, would be covered in white in the early morning, and would not melt until about ten o'clock, when the sun was high enough over the hill to the east of Mickle Wood. Then the weak winter rays of the sun would find enough strength, and slowly the drift of white would be withdrawn from the faded, winter grass. The cars, pulling out of their garages or driveways in the early morning, would drive very slowly, not only because it was dark, but also because there was ice on the roads.

How she missed it all! That cocoon of safety, in which she had spent the first fifteen years of her life, now seemed finally and irretrievably over, finished, gone, as though she had lived in another land, to which it was impossible to return, but another land, which was now, for Kathy, filled with loving people and exciting events; with beauty in the countryside, picnics with her family, and challenges at school. But all was fading, becoming less real and receding into crystallised memories. She was not even sure she could accurately recall her parents' and Susie's faces. And this shocked her.

Philip had walked on and disappeared somewhere. She found him in another small garden, higher up, and sitting on a seat beneath a beautiful, stone carving of an angel. His soft, child's face echoed this angelic quality, and she wondered if it was this place, as well as his love of nature, that was the source of his peace and adjustment to his life? Was this place and nature the fount, where he refreshed himself in his mind; did he come here, in thought, she wondered, when times were difficult, when the other kids or Paul taunted him, when he was excluded from physical activities? But, most of all, she wondered if he had been born with this quality. Whatever the case – whether he had inherited this quality or whether he had had to learn it - he had obviously had a steady, guiding hand in his nan that had steered him deftly and skilfully through his early years. He was watching a robin sitting in a bare cherry tree, the strange, plaintiff little song filling this small space, and quite captivating its listener. The song of real winter, she thought, as she observed Philip's face turned towards the cherry tree in rapt attention. To her, the robin symbolised winter and Christmas, and she remembered the bread crumbs her mother had unfailingly put out for the robin every morning on the bird table; and all the Christmas cards her parents would receive with pictures of robins. She stepped along the path, and took her seat gently beside him, his back pack resting on her knees. After a minute, the robin ceased his uncertain song and flew off.

Kathy and Philip continued on up the path to the top, and Kathy saw another discreet notice asking visitors to observe the peace and silence of the garden. Now they entered the circular, terraced corner of the Vesica Piscis. They sat on the low, stone wall, and Kathy studied again the strange symbol, worked in wrought iron, of the two interlocking circles, creating an oval, like a fish, with the vertical rod passing through the centre of the whole design. She read on the small, explanatory notice that here was the holy spring that fed the whole garden. And, indeed, she could hear the water gurgling into the well, flowing down from the steep hill that rose beyond the top boundary of the garden, a few yards from them. She looked down and could see the water, brown and ruffled and bubbling slightly. There was certainly movement, certainly life in that water, she thought. The leaflet told her that the Vesica Piscis was an ancient sacred symbol, its geometry signifying a union of heaven and earth or spirit and matter. She had never heard of this kind of thing, and asked Philip to explain, but Philip knew no more than what the leaflet said. His nan had told him once, but now he had forgotten, and so would his nan also, he said. Another of the mysteries of Glastonbury, she thought. She and Philip sat huddled on the stone wall, Kathy reading the notice inviting them to meditate, and listening to the water in the well and the robin who was again whistling his unfinished little song in a branch of a small tree to their right. Despite the cold, they sat there for a few minutes, allowing their thoughts to rest on the sound of the water and the robin's song. If that was meditation, thought Kathy, then it was very pleasant, and she could understand why so many people in Glastonbury seemed to practise it, although she could not say that she felt it was doing them any good! She studied the symbol again, and tried to feel the meeting of heaven and earth.

It was a beautiful, tranquil space round the holy spring - this small corner of Chalice Well. Perhaps it *was* holy, she thought; the folk in Glastonbury would certainly say so.

They had reached the topmost, north-eastern end of the gardens, and now returned by another way, one of several paths that offered themselves as they descended. They passed through a meadow, and Kathy guessed, in keeping with the spirit of the place, it would be filled with meadow flowers in the summer. Beyond the fence, there was another meadow belonging to the neighbouring property and on which several horses grazed. The morning sun filled this field, resting on the shaggy, winter coats of the animals, who bathed in its warmth and who cropped the winter grass contentedly. She wondered if it made any difference to them living next to this peaceful place, a sanctuary supposed to be full of angels and fairies. She doubted it.

They discovered more small corners of Chalice Well gardens, including King Arthur's Court and the Healing Pool. It was too cold today to take off shoes and socks and walk around in the water, feeling its healing properties. Kathy was glad she had done it the other day. Another opportunity would not come until the warmer days of spring.

Finally, they came into the bottom garden, the end of their tour, by a path on the left, passing by a small, nondescript hawthorn tree. The guide said that it was a descendant of the Holy Thorn, which Joseph of Arimathea had planted on Wearyall Hill, about a mile away to the south west of Chalice Well. Remembering that Philip had said Joseph of Arimathea was the uncle of Jesus, she wondered what he had been doing in Glastonbury. She guessed it was another story these new-age folk had made up, in order to fill their shops and their town with yet more mystery and allure for the tourists. The note also went on to say that according to tradition, the hawthorn flowered twice a year, at Christmas and Easter, and that a blossom at Christmas was always sent to the queen. The fact that it stated this phenomenal occurrence only happened according to tradition, was, Kathy thought, a clear statement that it did not happen in actuality. More Glastonbury fantasising and obfuscation, she thought.

But, still, there was something about the garden that she liked, that drew her, that seemed to speak to a deep, distressed part of herself and to soothe her. And if it helped Philip, gave him his strength and contentment, then perhaps it would help her too.

They had now entered the bottom garden with its large circular lawn, through the middle of which the red stream continued on its merry, purposeful way. At the top end of the lawn the spring fell into the circular pans, that Kathy had already looked at. She watched the figure-of-eight movement of the water, as it fell from one bowl to another, and thence into the circular pools at the bottom, before traversing the lawn. She remembered the falling mountain streams of the Cheviot Hills, and how she and her family had enjoyed drinking from them, when they knew the waters to be safe. So, she reflected, moving water, especially circular, moving water was better for you. They paused a few minutes, entranced again by the water of the holy spring, and Kathy noticed the frost had all but disappeared from the lawn, and that the winter sun had climbed higher in

the blue sky of this December Sunday. Philip found a seat near
the bottom of the garden, in the sunshine, and they ate their
picnic lunch looking at the swirling eddies of the little spring
as it fell and filled the two large circular pools. To their left was
the high wall, on the other side of which was the main road,
busy now with much morning traffic, and on the inside of which
grew more wisteria, its strong, bare, sinewy boughs snaking
along the stone of the wall. Kathy had not seen much wisteria;
it was a creeper that she thought perhaps did not flourish in the
north, but she had seen pictures of it, and felt it was a plant of
summer and ease and prosperity. She would come back here
in the summer, when everything in her life was different, when
everything was good, when things were safe again.

Chapter 32

———✦◦✦◦✦◦✦———

Betrayal and Triumph

S he had seen Gregory before. He had come to the cross once or twice recently, and had ridden his board round the monument with a certain beauty only some of the kids displayed. He was of a sturdy build with wavy, brown hair, worn at a normal length, and good looks, and he moved his body as an athlete would. He was older than the others, but he looked roughly the same age as Paul, and she guessed he was seventeen or eighteen. As well as being older, he was different to the others. He carried himself well, and his expression was pleasant, and there was a ready smile about his steady, blue eyes, which betokened self esteem. He was able to engage with everyone, and the kids not only liked him but they respected him also. Kathy felt that here was someone normal, more normal than any other young person she had encountered since her moving away from the north. She watched intently as he circled and jumped and traversed, his board flipping out from beneath him at intervals, only to return to the soles of his feet, as if pulled by a magnet. She hardly took her eyes off him, and was irritated with herself that she should be in this role of powerless admirer. It was not the way she liked to do things. She wished she was on a board herself, having fun and attracting the admiration of others.

'He's nice,' said Philip, who was sitting on the steps of the cross beside her. 'He goes away to school. Only comes here sometimes.'

It was Sunday again, and she had worked all the morning at the restaurant. The day before she had been to Bath. It had been depressing. Granfy's mind had been wandering and illogical. He kept asking the same questions, and however many times she had given him the answer, he seemed unable to remember. There was a part of her that clung fiercely to her plan to set up home somewhere with him, but also a part of her gazed sadly at this dream that was slowly fraying at the edges and beginning to disintegrate from the centre. Aunt May was spirited and helpful, as usual, and Kathy felt grateful to have found this relative; but it was Granfy she needed; Granfy was the one who could give her back something of her life, her self. She felt the loneliness and isolation of her life creeping into her, and she sought distraction wherever she could. She even sat with Jenny on many evenings now, when she was not working, among the whisky bottles and glasses, watching soaps on the television with her.

'Lord, you're lovely company, dear,' Jenny would say effusively, and Kathy felt the generosity and warmth of the woman, and longed for her to stop drinking, and to embrace her in her large, ample, enfolding arms, but in a sober, meaningful way. A true, motherly clasp, that Jenny had it within her to offer, and so freely, was something that Kathy longed for in the depths of her being. The strength, the affection and the friendship of Jenny could have lifted her whole life out of the bleak struggle she was still engaged in. But Jenny had long ago taken the decision to cave in, to yield to the over-burdening circumstances of her life, to repudiate her adult responsibilities and become as an irresponsible child. So, Kathy sat with Jenny, and the smell of whisky, on these December evenings, and was grateful for the morsels of humanity that Jenny threw her from time to time. And wondered if she too would cave in.

There was a short conversation between Paul and Gregory, while they rested their boards. Kathy wondered what they were discussing. Then Paul announced they were going up the Tor, and who was coming. Kathy did not know how to respond to this sudden proposal, and kept silent. She had only once or twice been up this strange hill that lay above the town, and which rose suddenly and steeply out of the flat Somerset Levels, and which was sometimes mysteriously shrouded in mist. Philip was quiet too. Then, just as suddenly, Gregory and Paul picked up their day bags and sped off up the High Street. The other kids resumed their activities, while Kathy pondered the question of whether she should go up the Tor or not. It was already three o'clock; there would not be much light left. After several minutes Paul and Gregory returned with their day bags laden with cans of beer. They distributed these to those other kids who had day bags, which was most of them.

Kathy did not have her day bag, and so was exempted from this chore. Now they all turned their attention to their boards and stored them against the wall beside the shop on the corner. Ironic, Kathy thought, that these kids trusted the townspeople of Glastonbury, when they themselves were not averse to petty crimes. There seemed to be a basic trust by everyone in the goodness of humanity, in the decency and fairness of humanity, and this trust and expectation even extended to those who did not play fair. Indeed it seemed, she thought, that it was that very thing that made possible the careers of criminals, that without that underlying quality of fair play in mankind, there would not be the organisation and structure to society that criminals relied upon and exploited.

Gregory announced they were ready. Kathy had already decided not to go. She would find something else to do, perhaps with Philip. Then, all of a sudden, Gregory called out: 'Coming, Kathy?' Her heart filled with gratitude that he had noticed her, and a little pulse started to race in her blood.

'Sure,' she replied.

She started off in the middle of the gaggle of youths and boys, the only girl, Philip at her side, running through the gaudy town, festooned now with Christmas lights and decorations.

'It'll be fun,' said Philip, and his limping gait by her side quickened in anticipation of the pace that would be set.

'You'll never do it, Philip,' said Kathy. 'It's going to be too far. Go back.'

'I'll be fine if you wait for me,' he said.

Half way up the High Street the pace quickened again. The gang had lots of energy and wind, but so did Kathy. She had weeks ago given up smoking and felt equal to anything these boys did. They now broke into a gentle run, bantering and joking in loud voices, in their usual inhibited way, as the dozen or so of them streamed up the street, passers-by getting out of the way. Kathy held her position in the middle of the group, jogging easily along, her years of school sports standing her in good stead. She wished Gregory would turn round and see her competence. At least this was something of his world she could do. Philip was no longer by her side, but she gave not a thought to him, as her young body strained in excitement and anticipation to meet this physical challenge.

'Wait, Kathy, wait, please,' came Philip's voice from the back of the group. The words echoed around Kathy, but she hardly heard them. A boy jogged past her. 'Your friend wants you to wait for him,' he said sarcastically. Kathy ignored him; her sights were set on the back of Gregory in his dark, blue jacket, as he ran lightly up the street, Paul at his side in his black jacket.

'Wait, Kathy, please. Wait, Kathy. I can do it, if you wait.........' His voice trailed off, and Kathy heard him no more.

They entered into a small lane passing a notice which indicated an ashram. They ran past the building and its pleasant gardens, but Kathy was none the wiser what an ashram was. Then they passed through a small gate in single file, and Kathy saw that she was running up a path that led across a field of grazing cattle. Then the path led into a little lane of hawthorn and briar, the blackberries long gone; the wild flowers too, except for some dandelions and nettles. Then through two or three kissing gates which again imposed a single file on the gang. Up a road, and eventually through an entrance in the hedge, they came to the bottom of a flight of steps on the north side of the Tor. Kathy had no idea what direction she was heading in; she was seriously out of breath now and needed to take a rest. But none of the boys looked distressed and Gregory and Paul appeared still fit for a marathon, judging by the relaxed gait they maintained.

Gritting her teeth, determined not to let herself down in front of Gregory and Paul, she kept going, making her legs shift, carefully, one in front of the other, ensuring she did not stumble. To fall or stop for breath would be shaming. And now a wind blew from her left. She could not understand why there was a wind here; there had been no wind at all in the town. It blew her hair around her face, but, worse, it buffeted her body, requiring more energy to ascend the steps. Then the steps turned, and she faced the full force of the wind. High up now, the wind blew even more strongly, more like one of those gales, she thought in her weary mind, that blew down from the Cheviots. It roared and punched, and once or twice it nearly knocked her off the path. She was the last of the runners now, a humiliation she had not envisaged.

A strong gust blasted against her again, nearly throwing her over, and she was forced to stop to regain her balance. But only for a moment. Then she was off, panting, flushed, and perspiring freely. Her chest hurt, and she felt she would have to stop, give up, cave in. The rest of her body felt alright; her legs were tired, but they could go on; it was her chest and her breathing that hurt - this enormous pain in the chest, building up with every step up this enormous mountain. She just could not get enough breath. She felt she must stop very soon, or slow down, or something awful would happen to her heart. And all the while the gale poured all its roaring force onto her, buffeting her, pushing at her from the front and the side, thrusting at her light body, vengeful, trying to fell her, to humiliate her. It took all her strength just to stay upright against this monster. She took a moment off from her struggle to glance up, and saw the summit with the dark tower on top not far off. Menacing, it looked as though *it* was the dark force behind this deafening wind. They were all there, all the boys! She was the last, by a long way.

Refusing to yield, to stop, to admit defeat, she focussed on the path ahead, saw nothing else, kept only the image of the last fifty yards ahead of her in her vision. There was nothing else in life now, not even the thought of Gregory and the gang on the top, only this short distance to salvation. She fought on, one step in front of the other, her body fighting every blast of the gale to remain upright and on the path. Slowly the way ahead shortened, but her energy shortened too. She kept focussed; only the end of the path mattered, that goal just ahead *was* attainable. It was all she saw, all she was aware of. She would reach it! And then her body could collapse, but not until then. On, on.

She talked herself through the last few yards, her chest aching, her heart pounding, her legs weak, her whole body about to collapse. On, on; three more steps, two, and then one, and with that last step, she hauled herself up onto the summit with her hands, her legs shaking and weak. She was there! She was up on the top! On the flat! She had made it! The feeling of triumph was paramount. She felt it coursing through all of her body. She allowed herself this congratulation. She needed time and a place to feel it. She crouched down on the grass, and then sat.

Now that she had stopped, all her energy had disappeared and she could move no further. She panted painfully, and now felt the full, sharp, agonising pain of her chest with each inhalation. She felt she was in trouble, and that she would never be able to move from that spot. But, still, she felt that triumph. She had conquered that climb; she had run up to the top of the Tor without breaking for a rest, in a terrifying gale that had tried to batter her off the mountain. She noticed the wind was even fiercer here and blew and thrust at her in vicious blasts, tearing at her jacket, whirling her hair around, roaring across the summit, and in and out of that black ruin of a tower. But, sitting on the grass, she was below its main force. The whole of Glastonbury and the Somerset Levels lay before her, serene and gentle, but the light was waning now, and very little was distinct. Only the lights of the town stood out against the shadowy background of the gloaming evening. But she was not aware of this. The only feeling she had was that she had won, that she had beaten that wind *and* that other thing - that thing which had tried to take her off the mountain, off the Tor.

Slowly, little by little, her breathing began to recover, the pain in her chest remained, but that feeling of collapse was disappearing and each breath was becoming a little easier, as though constricted air passages were relaxing. Her thoughts vaguely returned to Gregory and the gang. She had let herself down! Miserably! What would Gregory think of her? A weakling, a girl! But she was too exhausted to think about it or care about it. She sat staring into the dusk, down into the flat countryside that she could barely see, concentrating on her breathing and lungs, conscious that with each breath she could feel her body healing. She had put it under enormous strain, she thought, and wondered why she was so unfit. Suddenly, she felt someone beside her. She had been unaware of the approach in all the noise of the gale. It was Gregory.

'You did well, Kathy. I've never seen a girl climb the Tor as quick as you've just done,' he shouted above the roar of the wind.

'Thanks!' she shouted, not quite sure if this was the compliment she wanted, but somehow deeply grateful for it.

'You got more trouble from the wind than we did, because you're so light,' he shouted again, and the wind blew his hair all around his face, and his jacket swelled out, and his words were carried off almost before she had heard him. 'Come on, we're having a chill- out,' and he indicated to her to follow him. She didn't believe him saying she was too light to withstand the force of the wind. Some of the younger boys were smaller and lighter than she was. But she did not mind. Gregory had revealed another side of himself, which appealed to her, which she liked. She was quietly amazed too. Here was another youth, another member of this gang, even if only part-time, who was not only good-looking and attractive, but kind. She did not think she had ever met such a boy before. Except perhaps Ned and Charlie back home. But they had been just kids; this was different.

She followed Gregory into the St. Michael's Tower. It was open from east to west, and the gale blew through the passage with a ferocity that Kathy had never before experienced. There seemed to be real malevolence in this wind, an unrelenting power, a will to harm and destroy. Cowering along the southern interior wall, but still feeling the wind sweeping her legs and billowing under her jacket, blasting against her head, swirling her hair round her face and blinding her eyes, she obediently worked her way forward, keeping behind Gregory. They came out at the western gateway and Gregory immediately slipped round to the right. Here on the north western corner they were sheltered somewhat from the full force of the gale.

'What a wind!' exclaimed Kathy to Gregory. 'A pity it had to blow just when we decided to come here,' she panted, with what little breath she had, trying to be conversational.

'Oh, it always blows,' said Gregory. 'My mother says it's on account of Abbot Whiting. Come on, have a beer.'

The dozen boys had settled themselves on the bit of grass by this corner of the tower, some leaning back against the tower wall. Kathy, utterly relieved that the ascent was over and profoundly grateful to be out of the main force of the gale, relaxed. She felt the wetness of her underclothes against her skin, the burning of her hot cheeks, and the pain in her chest that was just beginning to subside. Gregory passed a can of beer back to her, and one of the younger boys placed it beside her. She saw Paul watching this action, saw that he was registering this concern of Gregory for her, and instinctively felt his resentment. But now she was beginning to feel unwell, knew that she had overdone things, strained her body too far. She left the beer untouched. Over the heads of the boys she gazed out onto the Levels, a vast, flat plain encircling the Tor, that was slowly being gathered up into the gloom of the night. She looked at her watch. That jaunt from the town centre had lasted just twenty five minutes. No wonder she felt ill. That was ridiculously fast, she thought, and wondered if any of the others were feeling ill, like herself. But they would say nothing; pride would take care of that. She found a place by the tower wall, leaned back into it and closed her eyes. She remained thus for a few minutes, feeling her breathing returning to a more normal rate and the volume of blood pumping through her heart reducing. She marvelled that the others had apparently, after all, been able to do it without ill-effect, and wondered if they were all super-fit, or if she was not as strong as she believed. Slowly and unobtrusively, she revived herself. Gregory had seen she was struggling to recover, and had come up to her spot and had given her a bottle of water to drink. 'But not yet,' he had said. 'And don't drink the beer for another twenty minutes.' As he returned to his place lower down, she again noticed Paul withdrawing his gaze from them.

She sipped the water and listened to the boys all around her, joking, laughing, sniggering, shouting in the wind. Only a few of them, including Gregory, had a good laugh, a real unselfconscious laugh, a free laugh – a laugh that was good to hear. But they were all having a good time. Something about being out in nature, she felt, and being physical, was refreshing their souls – and, of course, the beer! She listened and rested and watched the light fade from the Levels, pursued by the shadow of evening, until the Tor around her and the glowing, western sky, filled with gold and pink, finally vanished into the darkness of night. And the wind still raged around St. Michael's Tower.

After a few more minutes she began to feel fully recovered and managed a half can of beer. This lifted her spirits, and, like the gang, she too began to feel euphoric, and to join in with the joking and the laughing and the bantering.

In the dark they descended. The steps were still visible by the light of a full moon, and their night vision was good, but the roaring wind still assailed them on all sides. However, they came down much more slowly than they had gone up. The ale and feeling of conquest ensured that. They were all pleased with themselves, they were all happy. And the boys kept up their good humour and their inebriated jokiness until they finally arrived at the cross. Collecting their skateboards, still safely stashed against the wall by the shop, they wished each other good night. A camaraderie had grown up amongst them, Kathy observed; they had ventured something together and had overcome, and that had forged some kind of link between them all. They seemed the better for this escapade.

She had had no need to come the whole way down to the cross, as Paul's house was higher up in the town, but something had made her linger on in the group. Even though not part of this male bonding, she had felt something of a belongingness that she had not felt in a long time.

'Night, Kathy,' called Gregory and he started down Market Street to his home.

'Night, Gregory,' she returned.

She looked around for Philip, but, of course, he was nowhere to be seen. She had quite forgotten him.

'Coming?' said Paul, and, having no excuse, she went with him up to his home.

Chapter 33

———✦✦✦———

Bygone Times

I t was a few days before Christmas, and business was slow
in the restaurant. Lunches were still good, but few people
were coming in for coffee in the morning, or even for tea in the
afternoon.

'It's normal for this time of year,' Emma had said. 'The
OAPs and mothers, who normally come in the mornings and
afternoons, are too busy just now, and the young are having
evening office parties in the Knight and Pilgrim and other
hotels.' Emma looked tired; they were all tired. Perhaps it was
an end-of-year affliction. That English-rose bloom that Emma
had, when Kathy had first met her nearly two months ago,
and which Kathy felt was the kind of beauty the ladies of King
Arthur's court would have been blessed with, was faded and her
cheeks slightly drawn, and Kathy noticed a big, blue and red
bruise on the side of her face, which was unconcealed by the

attempt with make-up. Why doesn't she leave him, wondered Kathy. She must have friends she could stay with, and she's so pretty she'll soon meet someone else. Knights and their ladies! Kathy knew that the whole point of Arthur's court was the practice of chivalry and courage. How strange that Emma, who in so many ways was suited to Glastonbury and its pre-occupation with Avalon and Merlin and all the paraphernalia of Arthur's court, should have landed with someone who was anything but a knight!

Kathy fell to wondering who *her* knight would be: Launcelot, Gawain, Galahad? Not Percival – he was too much the boy still. Galahad? Galahad, the crown prince! No, she didn't feel that connection with him. She had seen a print for sale of that beautiful painting of the knight by Watts, standing with his white horse and gazing into the distance, looking as though he had just been blessed by the Holy Spirit. No, Galahad would not do for her; he was too ethereal. She preferred someone more robustly male, like Arthur himself, or St. George, who somehow kept getting himself involved with Arthur's knights, but who didn't belong there at all, she knew. Perhaps Launcelot? But Launcelot was spoken for. He was Guinevere's and would be forever. Still, she thought, there was that maleness and also such romantic passion about Launcelot that appealed to her. Yes, of all the knights, Launcelot would be the knight for her. She could remain deeply in love with him all of her life. She could give herself for him,. He was her white knight! She could join herself with him, completely – the desired state, as she had heard declared several times in the little church in Mickle Wood during marriage services: 'to join together this man and this woman in holy Matrimony'. At that moment she saw the 'joining together' as something deeply and romantically meaningful, and she hoped that that total love and commitment, that deep binding, almost a losing of oneself in this love, would happen to her. And she fell to wondering about Launcelot, and day-dreaming. But people had come into the restaurant for a late breakfast, and she was forced to break off her ruminations about him and return to the mundane task of work in the world.

Since work was on the slack side, Kathy had the time to go to the café on the other side of the street, after she had finished work - often early - in the afternoons and have a cup of tea or coffee. She went frequently. She was waiting for Philip. She bought a newspaper to while away the half hour or so she would spend there. She hoped in her heart he would come. She fervently wanted to make reparation to him. She had looked back on that scene in which they had all raced up the High Street, leaving Philip to face his shame, alone. For those hours after she had betrayed his trust in her, she knew he would have been left with only the aching confirmation that he was not like other people, not able to have the normal excitement and fun of childhood and youth; not able to joke and laugh with others; not be counted one of them; not belong. He was not normal. She contemplated the loneliness that lay ahead of Philip. A long life of loneliness, and she was appalled.

'You are so unkind, Kathy,' her mother had reproved, on one of those occasions when she had run away from Susie. 'How can you do it? She is such a little girl, and you are her big sister. You should be looking after her, not making her sad and unhappy. You are not a kind person,' and her mother sighed once more.

And here she was doing it again, and to someone who was not only smaller and younger, like Susie, but to someone who was also disabled.

She put the teaspoon in her coffee and stirred it round and round, watching the movement of the brown liquid in her cup. Why did she do these things? Why was she unkind, as her mother said. Why did she always want to keep up with the bigger children, and not help the younger ones? Were all big sisters like this? She knew they were not. Ellie, at home, had a younger sister and she always waited for her, if they were out together. She did not know why she was like this, but she was sorry for it, and wanted Philip to know she was sorry, and so she waited for him in the café, almost every day, right up to Christmas Eve. She even went up to Chalice Well on three occasions, and asked at the office if Philip was in the gardens – they all knew Philip there. 'No, he's not here,' she was told. She decided to go to the children's home after Christmas.

It was Christmas Eve and the whole of Glastonbury was in a fervour of excitement. Even those who were atheist or agnostic were caught up in the spirit. Kathy could feel it everywhere; it was as though a warm glow of happiness and benevolence had laid itself over the town and over the countryside, like a soft blanket. She sat in the cottage at the top of the town and watched East Enders on the television. There was nothing else to do. Suddenly, Jenny walked in through the front door – on one of those few occasions when she was at home the same time as Kathy.

'Hello, love,' she said in her usual, cheerful, distracted way. 'There is something annoyingly insincere about the way she greets me,' thought Kathy. 'I could be anyone, no matter that I've lived here for nearly two months. I'm still just a stranger to her. All this affection she shows me means nothing really to her.' Jenny had put down a big bag full of things she had brought back from the children's home. She picked up the whisky bottle from a small table and poured herself a drink. Kathy turned off the television and prepared to make conversation.

'Ah, that's better,' sighed Jenny, as the spirits warmed her throat and then her stomach. 'Much better,' and, bottle and glass in hand, she plunged herself down into the settee, and poured herself another glass.

'So, sweetheart, how are you? Things going well? Still comfortable here?' And, without waiting for an answer, she reached for a magazine out of her bag, and started flicking through the pages of 'Hello'.

'Jenny, I want to ask you something,' said Kathy. 'It's about Philip. Is he alright? I haven't seen him about town for ages.'

'Philip,' replied Jenny. 'Didn't you know, he's gone? A nice family from Shepton Mallet adopted him. I thought he would have told you. You were friends, weren't you? He often used to talk about you.'

'No, he didn't mention it,' said Kathy, dismayed. 'No, he said nothing.'

'Well then, don't fret. It all happened very suddenly. He met the couple about six months ago, and it took all that time for the adoption certificates to come through. Adoption is very difficult these days. And no-one wanted to say anything to Philip, in case it didn't work out. Then, suddenly, two weeks ago, word came. And so he went, just like that. He was happy about it.'

So, that was it! Philip had gone! Gone to better things, better people, better friends!

*　*　*

Christmas arrived! It was the morning of Christmas Eve! Kathy packed her night things and sponge bag into her day bag. She was going to spend Christmas Eve and the next few nights, sleeping on Aunt May's floor or on the little settee. The robin was singing his song on the cherry tree in the garden outside, and she felt quite cheered listening to it. Paul had left a few days earlier to spend Christmas with his father in Norfolk somewhere, and Jenny was having her man friend round to stay for a few days. Kathy was heartily grateful that Aunt May was able to put her up for those days. The restaurant was going to be shut until New Year's Eve, and she would not have been welcome in Jenny's house – at any time of the day or night, she felt. Jenny would have made out she *was* welcome, but she would have been embarrassingly in the way, she knew. Again she thought she must find somewhere else to live. In the new year!

Kathy arrived mid-morning in Bath. It was a cold, crisp day and the sky was blue and fresh, lifting the spirits. Snow would have lifted them even higher, but Aunt May said they almost never got snow in Bath. That was disappointing, and Kathy recalled the snow over the moors and hills and the Cheviots, which fell every year, and the warm cottages with their cosy lights and fires. And she missed it all.

She and Aunt May went to church on Christmas morning and sang carols and then they both took Holy Communion.

Kathy felt better for the Eucharist, and wondered if she should go to church more often. It was nice to feel the Holy Spirit in you, and to believe it would help you in your life. But the truth was, she thought, that feeling left you the minute you stepped outside the church, and Jesus and the Holy Spirit weren't anywhere in her life just now, and they certainly weren't helping her, she was sure. She felt entirely on her own.

They walked back from the church, along the empty streets, under the bare trees, Aunt May barely coming up to Kathy's shoulder, and Kathy, feeling too tall, tried to alter her pace to keep in step with Aunt May. It was pleasant to have the streets to themselves; you could appreciate the architecture, which, in places, was beautiful, and you were able to see the little shops, really see them, unhindered by tourists.. Some were quite shabby and obviously struggling to survive financially, and others were smarter and doing well. The town was very different on this day, and Kathy wondered if towns, generally, had known such quiet days, like this one, in the past, or if they had always been full of people, as they seemed to be these days. She decided they must have had many more quiet days than modern times allowed with the incessant commercialism and the relaxing of the law that banned business on Sunday. Those days were much quieter, she decided, and more harmonious, probably.

In the afternoon they went to visit Granfy again. He was rambling once more – he looked a sweet old man, yet ineffectual and dependent. But he did immediately recognise Kathy and May; however he was not the Granfy she had known. He was not fit for anything even mildly challenging any more. Soon the day would come when he would not be fit for life, she reflected. She was bitterly disappointed, but there was a new resignation finding a place within her, that permitted her to realise that her plan to get Granfy, her Granfy, out of the home, and take him away to live with her, was now only a hopeless fantasy. Things had moved on; Granfy was settled in the home; it was his life. And she too must move on, replace that dream with another one.

Aunt May was singing along with all the other residents in the sitting room. They were singing God Rest Ye Merry Gentlemen, and a nice man had come in for the afternoon to entertain them all. Kathy listened to Aunt May's lovely voice. She sang with perfect pitch again and it was a pleasure listening to her. She wondered if all May's family had had good voices. She couldn't remember if Granfy's voice was good or not. She thought back to church, but no memory of his voice came to her. After the carol singing, one of the staff put on some old-time dance music, and, to Kathy's amusement, residents seemed to come alive. They tapped their hands and feet, smiled, wore far away looks of happiness, and many actually got up out of their chairs and started dancing with each other or with the staff. Granfy was moved in some deep part of himself also, and, remembering his youth - the feeling of adrenalin and the excitement - he strove to recapture it, as old people do, Kathy thought.

'Come, Kathy, love, let's dance.' And, with a helping hand from one of the staff, he struggled out of his chair. Beaming at Kathy, as though she were his belle, he attempted to sweep a gallant bow, almost toppling over. Kathy steadied him. Still beaming, rather stupidly, Kathy thought, he took her firmly by the waist, and started waltzing her round the room, unsteadily and not always in time with the music. Kathy found this a strange experience. Her grandfather, to whom she had turned for help, had become as a child. She didn't know how to waltz very well; her generation didn't go in for these dances, but she was picking it up, and finding she could follow Granfy's footwork quite well. He held her firmly round the waist, and she had laid her hand on his right shoulder, as she saw the other ladies were doing. It was a strange duet, she reflected - Granfy had gone into another world, left behind the world he was no longer capable of dealing with, and she, the child, was suddenly the adult. She might have felt sad, but there was Aunt May, sitting on the edge of her seat, clapping in time to the music, smiling broadly, urging them on, and with, Kathy saw, tears in her eyes. Kathy had a moment to look round the room. Here were all these old people up out of their seats (almost all of them), to which they normally seemed glued - walking sticks, crutches, zimmer frames, all laid aside – dancing to Ivor Novello, Montevani, Strauss, or just singing one of Noel Coward's songs. It was unbelievable, she thought, how alive they all had become. How utterly dear to them the thought of their youth must be, if it can work a miracle like this, she reflected. All of them, the old women too, had that look of happiness in their faces. They seemed as though they knew exactly what was good for them – not pills, not visits to the doctor, not fresh air and exercise, but this music and dancing - reminders of their early encounters with the opposite sex, of love and romance.

Another of Strauss' waltzes started. Granfy had just been returning to his chair, but was seized with the desire to dance again, and once more, unsteadily, led Kathy back towards the centre of the room. Once again, they waltzed around on the green carpet, avoiding the other couples, to the strains of the Emperor waltz. More and more of the residents had returned to the floor, each managing some of the movements, determined to make their frail, old bodies recapture, if only slightly, those moments of youth, that now seemed to shimmer in a haze of bygone magic. The few unable to get up also forgot their imprisoning lives and clapped time and smiled and laughed. It was indeed a small window of delight and respite for them, all transported back in time to their own individual memories - memories dear to them - and yet they were bound to the present and to one another by this common bond of music. The music not only gave them back their youth; it also brought them together.

'Everything was so romantic in those days', Granfy said. Yes, it was the romance of the music. It was captivating, uplifting. It made her feel a better person. Life must have had a certain quality in those days, she reflected, a hint of beauty that was not present in the world today, especially not present in the lives of the young. And for a moment she was sad about her generation.

Now they were all getting back into their chairs and one of the carers had put on some Glen Miller music.

'You looked wonderful, the two of you,' exclaimed Aunt May. 'That little jig took years off Archie!'

Chapter 34

———✦✦✦———

Acquaintance with Terror

The clock ticked on Aunt May's mantel piece. Ticking life away. Everyone's life, but hers. Everyone, even Granfy and Aunt May, seemed to have lives that ticked in accordance with a plan. Only she seemed to stand outside this great drama of belonging to life. Forgotten, in error, she felt she was watching her time drain away, useless, wasted, like sand running through her fingers. This had never happened to Becky Sharp. But Becky had never stood outside the pale of life. She had been able to implement her plans, utilise her abilities, because, somehow, she was included. There had always been, however unlikely and however unpromising, circumstances that gave her the means of exploitation; the possibility of bending life to her will and ambitions. Kathy had none of that. She ached for a slice of life, the opportunity to move forward again, but she had nothing, no means by which to do this. She felt like one of those homeless people who had let life slip irrevocably through their fingers, who did no more than wait and wait and wait for death, tortured, she felt, by the knowledge that they had tossed away the most precious thing they ever had. How fragile life is, she thought.

It had been good at Aunt May's. She had slept for three nights on the settee, and had slept well. She had experienced light moments, and distraction from her plight, but it had been no more than a respite. Somehow, she felt, she had to make another plan, now that her plan for Granfy was in tatters. But what? Aunt May came into the kitchen and, seeing her lost in thought, asked:

'What are you going to do, Kathy? What's the next step for you? You can't go on like this. You need to be back studying; you are a clever girl.' Kathy wished Aunt May had not asked this question. It was redundant. As if she were not asking herself that question all the time, and working to find a solution!

'I don't know,' replied Kathy, and, sensing her irritation, Aunt May changed the subject.

She had had a good Christmas! Aunt May had done her best, and Kathy had been entertained most of the time. They had even gone to see The Sound of Music on Boxing Day, one of Aunt May's favourite films, and, lost in another world, Kathy had been transported too.

But, on the bus ride home, three evenings later, she fell into a dejection. The gaiety of Christmas seemed to make it worse. Now she was alone again with her life, with a life that did not work. And now it was the period running up to New Year, when everyone seemed to be engaged in deserved celebration. How could she be so outside everything? Yes, she had Aunt May and Granfy and somewhere to go to for visits, but it was no more than that. They could not really help; she could never really turn to them, expect them to be able to change her life. She was still absolutely on her own.

The bus passed under bare trees that were scarcely visible in the gathering darkness - strange, weird shapes, with wet trunks and wet branches. It had become warm again, and it was still raining. It had rained most of the time at Aunt May's. She passed by fields where cattle, just visible, were still grazing, busily grazing, she thought, as if to blot out something dreadful in their lives. She wondered if all the thousands of young people in Britain, who were called 'under-privileged' felt as she did – deprived of life, cheated of excitement and opportunity, shunted off the tracks into special schools, which were just holding bays, into a limbo that could go on and on and on until you were old and it was too late. It was a terrible feeling. She tried Becky again. Out of the ashes of her circumstances she raked up glimpses of hope. She had forgotten she had taken an enormous step back in October. She had acted. She had run away from London. And her life was immeasurably better, she reflected. She was no longer in captive allegiance to Gary's gang, no longer under threat of becoming a regular user of drugs. She had made a plan and had carried it out, and that was only two months ago. Now she must conceive another plan, a second part, and implement that, and perhaps it was just as well Granfy was not to be included. Perhaps it was easier just to look after yourself, she thought; perhaps it was best to put up with loneliness while you were working things out.

It was early evening when she put her key in the lock and opened the front door. Paul was there. Drinking. Alone and quietly. Not even the television was on. He looked awful, she thought. Dishevelled! And when he looked at her, she could see his eyes were bloodshot. She put her bag down and went into the kitchen to fetch a glass of water.

'Where's your mum?' she asked.

'With her friend,' he drawled. 'She won't be home tonight.'

'Did you have a nice Christmas?' she asked, not knowing what to say, or how to manage the situation.

'Nope. Norfolk is a dreadful place. That's why I'm home.' And Kathy thought things must have gone badly between him and his father. 'Nope. I'm home. But things're not much better here. How about it, Kathy? Come on, we're two lonely people; I know you want it; so come on.'

'I don't know what you're talking about, Paul,' said Kathy, horrified. She turned to pick up her bag and go up to her room. 'And, anyway, I have to go out.'

'Out!' he exclaimed. 'Out! You don't have to go out. You've just come in! Always turning away from me, aren't you? Always pretending you don't want it. Well, I know you do.' His words slurred out of his mouth, and Kathy's heart sank as she realised just how much he had drunk. She had a foot on the bottom stair.

'I'm sorry, Paul. I'm meeting a group of friends in the Knight and Pilgrim; they're expecting me, and they'll get worried if I don't show up.'

'Meeting a group of friends! Like hell you are!' He gaped at her sarcastically, with the eyes of a beast. 'You've got no friends here. I'm your only friend. I've seen you around in town, always alone, except when you're with that limping kid. He your friend, eh? That Philip, that kid? That who you like to do it with? Well, know what that's called?'

'You're drunk, Paul. And I'm going out.' She hoisted her bag up again on one arm and made to cross the room to the front door.

'No, you don't, little Miss Prim and Proper. No, you don't.' And Paul raised himself from the sofa with the agility of someone who was as sober as a priest, and grabbed hold of her arm, and pulled her towards him. The force of his pull made her drop her bag. Now he pushed her down onto the settee and then fell on top of her.

'Paul, Paul, stop it. You don't know what you're doing,' cried Kathy, frantically struggling. 'You're drunk, drunk. Stop it, stop it.' He was strong, pinning her down into the soft upholstery, which gave no leverage to push him off. He was slobbering all over her face, reeking of alcohol. And now he contrived to hold her down with one arm while his free arm worked his trousers loose, with a skill that amazed her. It was now or never, she thought. While he was occupied with trying to undo her jeans, she located the solid arm of the settee with her feet, and with an enormous heave she managed to upset him. He paused in his effort with the zip, and laid the full weight of his body on hers again to trap her. She feigned defeat and lay limp, and waited for him to raise himself again and struggle again with the zip of her jeans. And, then, with all her strength, a strength she did not know she had, she heaved again, heaved as high as she could go, heaved against that heavy, strong body lying on top of her. He suddenly seemed to lose balance. She took her opportunity and brought her knee up and pushed him, again with all her might. He rolled onto the floor. In a flash she had slipped off the sofa. But he grabbed her leg, and attempted to pull her down again. Out of the corner of her eye she suddenly saw the whisky bottle, almost empty. She seized it, and, with a crashing blow, brought it down on his head, as she had seen in films. He let go of her leg, and fell senseless on the floor, his dishevelled hair falling over his face. She seized her bag, opened the front door and fled.

She turned blindly into the street, not knowing where she was going. Down the High Street she ran, past the shops and hotels, decked with Christmas baubles, the soft glow of the windows falling onto the pavements; past the flower shop full of deep, red poinsettias. Inside the hotels and pubs people were carousing and celebrating, enjoying themselves. Tears streaming down her face, her body shaking, she ran, not only to get away from Paul, but also to get away from that terrible thing that had almost happened. Overwhelmed with confusion and revulsion, she hardly knew how to think about it. Something had happened to make her feel her power within herself was lost. The vulnerability of her femaleness was now the feeling that took possession of her. How to get rid of this new, terrifying feeling of powerlessness that seemed to locate itself within her, rather than outside? She ran past the restaurant and the café opposite it. Both were now closed. If it had been open, she might have gone into the restaurant for help. Certainly Emma would have been able to help her, comfort her. But it was dead to the night, its sandwich boards withdrawn, and the alley dark and still. The sound of laughter and merry-making in the Knight and Pilgrim reached her. She came to the end of the street and rounded the corner. There was the bus stop from which she and Philip, only a month ago, had taken the bus to the nature reserve. And there was the bus, that very same bus that had taken them to Westwick, waiting for her! That was why it was there! It was waiting for her! To take her away from this dreadful nightmare into somewhere gentle and healing. By some feat of magic, some kindly being, perhaps an angel, had brought the bus to her to take her away from this terrible event, which was engulfing her whole being by the minute. The engine of the bus was running and it was about to leave. Without a second thought, she boarded, paid her fare, and sat down. The driver had given her a strange look, registering her distraught state, but thought nothing of it; these things happened at Christmas these days. The bus started. They were moving. This seemed so right. To move, to get away, to put distance between herself and that thing, between herself and Glastonbury. She noticed she was trembling and sweating. Her teeth started chattering, and she wondered what the matter was. She had never felt like this before. Was it a cold night? She felt sure it had been very warm earlier on, when she had walked back from the Bath bus stop.

Round the several roundabouts that skirted Glastonbury, they went, until they were on the country road. She still had no exact idea why she was on the bus, except that it had drawn her powerfully and that it was carrying her away from that horrifying event, that hideous thing, that thing that wanted to enfold her in its tentacles, engulf her in its blackness and hopelessness and evil. The trembling increased and she felt the wheels of the bus turning, turning, carrying her away from this thing. She was aware she was looking out of the window into a blackness. There was nothing to be seen; the only life was in the bus, save for the occasional headlights of a passing car.

On and on they went. Some passenger was on a mobile phone, but Kathy did not hear it. She was aware only that she was going deeper and deeper into the Somerset Levels, deeper into the countryside, countryside that would receive her with healing, embracing arms. She could even smell that gentle, wet smell of nature that she had smelled that day with Philip. Here, in the bosom of nature, in that warm, gentle, watery place, among the reeds and swans and otters, she would find what she needed, and all that water would wash away this blackness, that now surrounded and pervaded her being. She would lie down in the reeds and let the water suck away the filth that clung to her, the poison that was leeching out her very being. She was not that person, she kept defiantly telling this thing; she was a whole, good person from a good background. But, nevertheless, she felt on some kind of edge; this thing hovered around her, drawing her into some awful, dark world, from which there would be no escape, in which she would leave behind that Kathy that her parents knew, that Granfy knew, that her friends and teachers back at home knew, and which Aunt May knew a little of. But that image of herself in her mind, so inextricably bound up with Becky Sharp now, was so fragile, so intangible, so uncertain, that she was terrified. That Kathy, that she felt she knew so well, seemed on the point of disappearing into an insubstantial dream forever. What had been sure and certain had become blurred and uncertain, without foundation.

Was she just a dream, after all? Was there really no substance, root, to who she was, who she had been? Would she ever get back to that Kathy, that Kathy that had been safe, so safe that she had even been able to offer safety to her own self when she had been going through a challenging time at school? Where was that girl now? Kathy struggled to find a foothold in the darkness that enveloped her. But there was none. Her mother, father, Granfy, Susie – all were beyond the border of darkness and she could not reach them, neither could they reach her.

'Westwick,' called the driver. Kathy stumbled out of the bus into the unseasonably warm air, and found the little road that led down to the nature reserve. Some part of her was functioning very well, she dimly thought, as she stepped forward into the one mile walk.

Walking quickly, able to see quite well in the dark, and encountering no cars, she arrived at the reserve twenty minutes later. It was dark, but she could make out the sign board of the reserve, and beyond she could see the dark shapes of the low willow that bordered either side of the broad track. There was so much light behind the clouds, she guessed it must be a full moon, and knew she would be able to find what she was looking for. She started walking on the track, and was relieved it was dry. Remembering it was made of gravel and scrubby turf, she knew it was resistant to water.

After ten minutes she reached the large expanse of water on which she had seen the swans and otters and moorhens with Philip. At the right hand end there had been that hide. She could not see it now, but she knew it was there, about twenty minutes' walk away. She turned to the right and began the walk on another wide track, but now the tiny stones had given way to grass, and the ground was quite soggy. She needed boots for this, not trainers. Well, no matter; her feet would just get wet. As it was not cold, they would not freeze, and in the hide it would be quite warm.

And now that thing returned, hovering over her, threatening to engulf her. She had forgotten it for a moment. She ran forward over the grass, her back pack bumping on her back, fleeing the thing. 'Leave me alone,' she cried, and plunged forward over the spongy grass, water oozing out of the turf and peat. And now the grass seemed to come to an end, except for hard tussocks here and there in the watery peat that the track had become. Of course, she thought, all this rain has made the path so wet. She kept walking, her trainers sinking into the ground, and water leaking in at the sides. She concentrated on finding tussocks to step on, clear in the light of the moon, that had now appeared from behind the clouds, in order to keep out of the boggy water as much as possible. It was on one of these movements, when her head was turned slightly that she caught sight of something out of the corner of her eye. She did not know exactly what it was, but it had seemed like a flicker of light. There it was again! She saw it as she lifted her foot out of the peat. She turned, but could see nothing behind her, and in front there was only the track with the grass tussocks and the wood on either side, clearly visible by the light of the moon. She continued, every so often, stopping to scan the path behind her, increasingly feeling something was following her. There was definitely something happening behind her, but she could see nothing. Strangely, she was not frightened. This was nature, raw and pure, and it was going to help her, heal her, cleanse her. Of that she was sure; in the morning she would lie down in the water.

She kept going, and then, there it was again, that flicker of light behind her. She stopped, but the light had disappeared. She raised her shoe out of the boggy ground to step forward and was amazed to see a bright, green light encircle her foot. She put her foot down and raised the other foot, and the same thing happened, and now, strange as it may seem, the light stayed. All around her was this circle of weird, green light, and every time she moved her feet, the light moved into the hole where her shoe had been. She became alarmed; she had never seen anything in her life like this, and wondered if the place was haunted. That young man they had met in the hide, Robin, had hinted at some strange powers in these parts. She turned to move forward again and walked a few paces, and now the green light covered her shoes, playing on the tops and even moving up to the bottom of her jeans. Frightened now, she lunged forward. She must get to the hide, she must get out of nature. This was not what she had expected. She had thought that nature would shield and protect, that it was to be her refuge, probably her last resort, and now it was doing alarming things. Nature was different by night, she thought. People at home, in the village, had said dark, bad things happened at night. Her father had told her to take no notice, and Kathy had not, and she had never been afraid of the dark. She turned and saw that her whole path, the way she had come - the tussocks and the peaty grass in between – was lit up by these sharp, green lights, which stretched all the way to her shoes and which seemed about to clamber up her jeans. So, those old folk at home had been right after all; there were bad things in the night. She stumbled forward, hoping to shake off the green thing, that seemed to be alive and extending its tentacles to bring her down into the peat and possibly drown her. Should she continue to the hide, or return to the road? She felt the hide was nearer and would give her protection for the night. The road would only take her back to the village, and the green thing could easily follow there too. And going backwards, to Glastonbury, was something that filled her with terror. That black thing would be waiting for her on the road and in Glastonbury. She must keep going forward. She lurched on, trying to run, but sinking too deep into the peat to gather any speed. There was an especially difficult place, where the water of the reed lake seemed to leak straight into the path and out the other side into the ditch.

She was grateful for the light sky, and kept moving forward, slowly. In the wetter places the green light grew stronger, and did indeed manage to lay hold of her jeans and advance up her lower leg. She was afraid to call out, to order this thing off her, in case she awoke other sleeping monsters. She pushed on and soon came to a parting of the ways. She went to the left, and the ground became even more boggy and the green lights danced all around her, laughing, it seemed to her, playing with her. Terrified now by what was, she was sure, some kind of malevolent nature spirit, she stumbled on, her way just clear enough, illuminated now by only a faint moon lost behind thick cloud. She espied the hide about fifty yards away, and attempted to run the short distance thence, but she sank deeper into the boggy ground, and a panic seized her. Blindly and weeping, she fought her way on, plunging one foot after another into the peaty water, making painfully slow progress, and aware every moment that the green monster could turn malevolent and harm her. She had read that ghosts, on occasion, did kill their victims. Finally, the hide stood just before her, and then she had reached the hard, artificial ground that was part of the hut's foundation. She felt the hardness of solid earth, the stones and turf, and her heart heaved with relief. She ran the last few steps, opened the door and flung herself inside, slamming the door shut. Breathing heavily from terror and exertion, she looked down at her feet. The green light was still there, but it was much fainter; it was dying, like Christabel, she thought vaguely. It could probably only live outside in the bog; here in the hide she was safe. Overwhelmed with relief that she had escaped the clutches of the green monster, she sat down on the bench and leant her elbows on the window ledge and wept.

Chapter 35

―――ﻮﻮﻮﻮﻮﻮﻮﻮ―――

The Next Day

How long she slept, she did not know, but she awoke the following morning to find herself lying on the wooden floor and bright light peeking through the cracks around the window shutters and the door. The smell of the wood was pleasant; it was a smell of deep nature that it had brought from the forest, where once it had grown. She had spread a sweater and her jacket on the floor to lie on, but arose from her hard bed cold, stiff and uncomfortable. She was amazed she had slept at all, but she had, and felt moderately refreshed. The events of the previous evening returned to her in a rush. What she was most concerned about now was not the ebbing away of her sense of self, that she had been so tenaciously trying to preserve last night - the sense of who she was and had been - but of the green thing that had pursued her through the peat bog. She opened one of the window flaps and gazed out over the wide expanse of grey water lying flat and motionless under a still, white sky. The only movement came from two otters that were playing and diving for fish, near enough to be seen clearly without binoculars. Normally, she would have been excited to see them; now she observed them without interest. Two swans rested motionless nearby; these also she did not pay attention to. Her eyes surveyed the reeds around the edge, searching for any strange movement among them. She saw none, neither could she find any unusual ripples or activity in the water that might suggest something like a Loch Ness monster lurking in its deeps. Seeing nothing out of the front of the hide, she then ventured to open the door at the back. This was more challenging, because out there was where the strange, green lights had been. She opened the door carefully and looked out on the wet, green vegetation, and the soggy path by which she had arrived. All was still, all quiet, save for the chip, chip of some little bird flitting among the low willows. A moorhen sounded nearby, and one of the swans reared up out of the water to her right, and spread its wings into a broad, powerful span. All seemed normal - a peaceful, typical December morning, with rain in the air, but no drops falling. She was grateful for the unseasonably mild temperature. She put on her trainers, still wet, and descended the few steps. Perhaps the thing was still there, and all it needed was for her to step on the ground. Perhaps it was related to disturbance of the ground, her own steps disturbing it. She walked a few paces on the soggy track, trying to keep her trainers from sinking too far into the wetness. She stopped and surveyed her progress. No green lights appeared. Perhaps they were there but not visible by the light of day. Perhaps she was still being pursued, invisibly; perhaps she was still in great danger. She looked at her watch; it was ten o'clock. She had slept a long time.

She returned to the hide. The thoughts of what had happened between her and Paul last night now occupied her thoughts. She wondered what she would do for the next night. She had enough money on her for one or two meals, but she couldn't sleep in the hide another night; it was too threatening, and anyway it might turn cold. No, she would have to find somewhere for the night, and that meant returning to Glastonbury. But the thought of returning there filled her with a dread, and a feeling that resembled disgust; it made her feel unclean. That attempt to rape her had made her feel, in a strange way, dirty, and, although she had determined the night before to undress and lie down in the water at the edge of the lake, to cleanse herself, that idea no longer appealed to her; the water would be cold and she had no towel.

She gathered her things up into her day bag and was preparing to leave, having no clear idea where she would go, when she heard low, male voices. She froze, in panic. The door opened and two men appeared, equipped with field glasses and tripods and cameras. They greeted her and asked what she had seen. Awkward, she replied that she'd seen the otters. It occurred to her she might ask them about the green lights, but she did not feel like talking to anyone. To be alone with her thoughts, to work something through, to be alone with the birds and the trees, was where she felt she needed to be. She bid them a hurried goodbye, and set off on the tracks she had traversed the night before. Nature did not seem so threatening now, but she was still unsure about this landscape, and she felt her confidence had been shaken. It occurred to her the road would be a better place to be. It would still be quiet on the roads - there would not be much traffic in these parts. She could be alone and walk and walk. To walk without stopping was what she felt she wanted to do, and so she decided to walk back to Westwick. The village might have a café, very likely a pub, where she could get something to eat. She was in luck; there was a pub, and they served her breakfast of sausages and baked beans and toast.

All day she walked the roads around Westwick. At one point she found she was walking across another nature reserve on a narrow, quiet road with flat fields on either side filled with hundreds of swans. She barely took any notice. Her situation pressed hard upon her now. The near violation of herself had done odd things to her mind, she thought. She was not thinking in the normal way. She was obsessed with what Paul had done to her, or had nearly done, and a strange grief seemed to be making its way into her mind and body. She felt the grief in her heart. She reflected this must be the feeling that all women, who had been through what she just had, must experience; but much worse where an actual rape had occurred. To be violated in this way, she thought, ate at the very essence of yourself. And she remembered how last night she had thought her sanity was slipping away. How fragile a thing is confidence, she reflected; it depended on so many circumstances; most of all it depended on predictability, and when that failed the structures of the mind seemed to be undermined and to crumble.

She walked and walked under the dull, grey sky of this mild winter day, making many tangents from the main road, always returning to it after two or three miles, so as not to get lost. At last, about four o'clock, and feeling hungry again, she returned to the pub in Westwick, and bought herself another meal. There was a bus timetable pinned up near the entrance in the pub and she studied it. At five there was a bus going to Glastonbury.

All the way to Glastonbury she watched the wet fields of Somerset slip by. Not long ago the thought of this countryside, the land of summer, had filled her with a certain hope, a certain delight. Now, it was flat, dull and wretched, and seemed to offer her nothing. She wondered where she was going and what she was going to do. She could go to Aunt May's, seek refuge there and comfort. But Aunt May was very old, her participation in life much reduced, and Kathy did not feel she would be able to cope with this situation. Better not to tell anyone than to tell and have your story not properly understood. She looked at the miserable fields and thought the cattle looked miserable too, and wondered what Becky Sharp would do now. But Becky seemed a world away and offered no solution. She supposed if the worst came to the worst she could find a bed and breakfast - there were plenty around – and put herself up for the night there.

She alighted from the bus, and walked up the High Street as if in a dream. She came to the church on the left and saw one or two people going in for a service. She noticed Evensong was about to begin. Having nothing better to do, she wandered up the path and went into the church, sat down in a pew, and looked about her. It seemed like any other church – dull and the stained glass windows obscuring the daylight. Most of all it seemed devoid of life. The man who gave her the hymn book and order of service had smiled, but he too seemed far away, unreachable, in that world of belongingness, outside of which she stood, exiled.

She sang the hymns desultorily. They were vaguely comforting; they reminded her of her old life and school assembly, and church on Sundays in Mickle Wood. Then there was the sermon. The priest seemed quite nice, she thought. She didn't hear much of what he said, but he bent over the congregation from his pulpit, gesticulating with his arms and hands, enthusiastically and energetically, and she was struck by his spare, lean body that looked young and vigorous. She looked at him properly, and saw that he was pleasant-looking and intelligent, and here and there she caught some phrases before her mind returned to its state of weary dullness, that seemed to cocoon her. But a chink of light was left in this dark emotional carapace, and a small plan began to form in her mind. Afterwards, she could not say what had prompted the plan - perhaps it was Becky Sharp - but after the service she waited until almost everyone had left the church. Only the wardens and other officers remained, and they were busy with hymn books and other duties. Kathy stood up and walked up the aisle and turned into the porch. The vicar was just putting on his coat, preparing to leave, when Kathy approached him.

'Could I come and talk to you, please?' she asked, hardly audible. The priest paused in his movement, looked at her, and said softly, 'of course, when would you like to come? Tomorrow afternoon, three o'clock is good for me.'

'Now,' said Kathy, in a flat voice, entertaining no hope that this would be possible.

The priest looked at her again. 'Alright,' he said. 'Come with me.' He popped his head round the inside door and said goodnight to the wardens, and stepped out into the night with Kathy following him.

Chapter 36

———∽◦◦◦◦◦◦∽———

In The Rectory

The rectory lay just behind the church, and the vicar opened a wooden door in an archway, set in a high, stout garden wall. On the inside ivy clambered up the masonry, thick and green, giving the small garden an old and settled feel. Kathy envied the vicar and occupants of this house the security that seemed embedded in its old stone walls. A short path of paving stones led to another arched, wooden door, set in more thick, stone walls, the arch overhung with some creeper, now bare, devoid of leaves. The vicar opened the unlocked door and Kathy followed him inside. She found herself standing in a short, flag-stoned hallway with white, plaster walls, which were broken up by dark beams curving up to meet in the centre of the low ceiling. Again, Kathy had the impression of safety and assurance. She felt a kind of solidness, which seemed associated with the oldness of the house and a friendly history, and which seemed to emanate predictability, continuity and benevolence. How easy life would be, she thought, if you lived in this house, and she wondered what mysteries lay behind this priest that seemed so favoured of fortune.

He had left her for a moment to put his head round a door at the far end of the hall, while he spoke to someone, presumably his wife. He returned and led her through another door into a small sitting room. This too was structured around strong, dark beams, and all gave onto an open fireplace at the far side, in which a wood fire was burning. One wall was lined with books, and Kathy felt the man, as well as being favoured by life, was also well-read. The other wall housed the curtained window, looking onto the small garden through which they had just passed. Kathy absorbed the warmth and cosiness of this room and felt she had walked into some kind of small heaven. And, then remembering who she was, or rather who she had become, felt she was somehow trespassing in territory that was rightfully debarred her, and felt guilty and inferior. Once, she could have sat happily and comfortably in such a home; now she felt inadequate, an intruder, and again was amazed at the change that had taken place within herself. And then the memory of her situation returned to her: her broken, impossible life with no future in sight, the attempted rape, which still shocked her, the danger she had been in last night in the peat bogs. She averted her eyes from the priest, and fixed them instead on the green carpet, and wished she had not come. This man and she occupied separate worlds; there could be no meeting between them, no understanding on his part of her life, of the world she was now forced to occupy. Her struggle was hers and hers alone, and somehow she would have to find a way to further her cause by herself. She felt she must ask to be excused, to return to her cold world and find a B&B for the night. She would have just enough money. How foolish to have thought this man could have helped.

'Let me introduce myself; I'm Francis Templeton, and I live here with my wife, Caroline.'

'I'm Kathy,' she said. 'Kathy Harris, no, Miller.' She had no idea why she had blurted out her real name.

'I see,' said Francis. 'That's a nice name; they both are. And where do you come from?'

'Manchester,' she said. 'Actually, more Northumberland.'

'Well, they aren't too far apart,' he suggested. 'Just opposite sides of the north of England.' She registered his small attempt at humour, but did not respond. 'And what brought you south?' he continued.

'Social services,' she answered.

'Oh?'

'My parents both died, and social services decided to place me in a children's home in London.'

'Why London? It seems so far away from everything you have known.'

'It was a bad decision.'

'I know all about children's homes,' said Francis. 'I used to be a social worker myself in London. They're very difficult places.' Tears started to trickle down Kathy's face. He had said children's homes were 'difficult places', so he knew something of what she had been through; so he might, after all, be able to understand, and, without thinking further of whether it was prudent to tell this man anything of herself and her life, she felt a fatal dam had been breached within herself, and that she was no longer in control of how she acted.

'Tell me everything, Kathy,' said Francis. And with those kind words, truly kind, truly understanding, she felt her face crumple, and, before she could do anything about it, she burst into uncontrollable weeping. Her breath came in big sobs, her shoulders heaved, and she was unable to say anything coherent. Francis let her cry, handing her a big tissue that materialised from somewhere.

'Just cry, Kathy; take your time. We've all the time in the world.' His words were unbelievably reassuring. This man was saying all the right things. She raised her eyes to seek confirmation that his face too showed understanding; that he could stay with her for the time it took. His face was bent forward, shadowed in intense concentration. Safe, she continued. Listening to herself was a surprise. Things poured out in a jumbled fashion. What surprised her most was the grief she poured out about losing her mother and father and Susie and Granfy; not the shock of the attempted rape. She had thought she had those feelings safely locked away, but now she saw, or rather heard, that nothing was truly locked away. She sobbed and cried and heard herself tell Francis that she did not think she could live any longer without her family, that life was just too difficult, too horrible.

'Of course,' she heard Francis murmuring. 'Of course.' She told him how she missed them all terribly, and that life had been like a nightmare since her mother's death and social services' intervention. She heard herself say she just could not do it; it was all just hopeless, and she could not go on.

'I would feel the same,' said Francis. 'Exactly the same.' Enormously reassured, she went on. She got to her experiences in London, how afraid she had been of Gary and the gang culture, and how she had felt not able to leave the gang, and how she knew Mike would not be able to help her.

'Why did you have dealings with this gang?' asked Francis.

'I had no choice,' she said. 'Everyone over 15 years in the home was in the gang. You have to be in it.'

'Everyone?' asked Francis.

'One girl wasn't,' said Kathy thinking of Barbara. 'But her case was special.'

And so she went on to tell of how afraid she had been all the time in the children's home. How Gary had spies everywhere, even in the home.

'Go on,' said Francis gently. Encouraged, she went on, almost as if in a confessional, and told how she had had to take the drug, ecstasy, and how dreadful that had been for her; how it had really been against all her principles; how she would never have done such a thing if she had had the choice. Now she burst into fresh weeping.

'It was terrible of me to do that; I'm not like that; I'm not that sort of person. They made me do it; I had no choice.' And she listened to herself appealing to Francis to understand and excuse her from any guilt in these transgressions.

'Of course,' said Francis, and Kathy continued in a great releasing of all her grief, all her sorrow for the wrong turning her promising, young life found itself in. How lonely and friendless and desolate and hopeless her whole life had become.

'And what brought you to Glastonbury, Kathy?' he asked gently. Finding a little self-control, she told him of her plan to find her grandfather, who was somewhere a prisoner in a care home in Somerset, and rescue him and set up home together. She told of how she had eventually found him, but that her idea had proved to be hopeless, because he was no longer 'himself,' she said. Being in care had done that.

'He seems to have dementia or Alzheimers, or something, and so we couldn't set up home together.' She briefly mentioned Aunt May, and how much she liked her.

'Then what?' asked Francis. How did he know, she wondered, that there was more. He seemed to have an uncanny ability.

So, she told him about her return from Bath the night before last and the attempted rape by Paul, and how she had fled, had taken a bus out into the Levels, not knowing where she should go and what she should do. She told of how she had spent the night in a hide on a nature reserve. And now, she noticed, she was starting to shake. The tears flowed once more, and the trembling and shaking took over her whole body. She supposed it was because she had got herself all wrought up in recounting all these wretched things. She said as much to Francis, but he said she was in a state of shock over the attempted rape. He got up and left the room and returned almost immediately with a thick rug which he draped around her. He also had a glass of water which he told her to drink. She sipped the water but the shaking continued, and her teeth chattered noisily. Then the door opened and his wife came into the room with a mug of hot chocolate. She drew a small table up to Kathy, on which she placed the mug, and encouraged her to drink it. Kathy noticed that she too had kind eyes, and felt that their children were greatly blessed by fortune in having such parents. Then Caroline stoked up the fire, which had almost died out, and quietly left the room.

Kathy was unable to drink the hot chocolate, and Francis decided she should go to bed and rest, and that if she were no better in the morning he would call a doctor. He called Caroline, who led Kathy up a narrow, winding staircase which opened onto a spacious landing, off which were several doors. Caroline showed Kathy into one of these rooms, not before pointing out where the bathroom was, and told Kathy to undress and get into bed.

'And I'll take your shoes, dear. I can see they're wet.' Kathy took off her shoes and socks and gave them to Caroline. Caroline felt her feet. 'They're cold,' she said. 'No wonder, with those wet shoes. I'll go and get you a hot water bottle.'

Kathy undressed, and put on her night clothes from the back pack, which Francis had brought upstairs – pyjamas which she had worn at Aunt May's just the night before last; it seemed weeks ago now. Caroline returned some minutes later with the hot water bottle and another glass of water.

'Sleep, Kathy, sleep,' she said. 'Rest will make everything alright.'

Chapter 37

—⁓∘⊶⊙⊶∘⁓—

A Chapter Closes

Kathy awoke the following morning after a deep sleep. She did not wake up fully at first. She allowed herself to sleep on in that half world between sleep and wakefulness, just as she used to do at home. A peace embalmed her body and mind, and she kept at bay the thoughts, the structures of her present life, that would chase away this pleasant state of calm. Instead, she rested in this strange, white bed with the soft, white sheets, gently smelling of something beautiful and distantly familiar, and vaguely heard a bird outside, and went on sleeping. At last she allowed herself to awaken properly. She opened her eyes and saw she was sleeping in a small room, with old beams across the ceiling and walls washed in a pale, soft yellow. She sat up slowly and drew back the curtains, patterned with tiny, yellow flowers, and looked out onto a small back garden, which was bounded on either side by high, thick, old, white walls of adjoining houses; or, maybe, one wall was part of this house, she thought. A female blackbird was hopping round on the grass and a nuthatch was very busy on a bird feeder. She lay back on her pillow and wondered what angel had brought her to this house.

After some minutes, this feeling of recuperation waned, and the now-familiar anxiety returned. 'Goodness,' she said to herself. 'I must be at work.' This routine of work in the restaurant was not only a necessary source of income, but also her anchor in her life. All the little things she had gradually been able to structure into her life had only been possible because of the base, the foundation, however precarious, that her days at work gave her. She realised how much she needed the restaurant, how much she valued it. Francis and Caroline were like visiting angels, but, like Mike, they would not be able to rescue her. She must proceed, as before, with her life, alone.

And then the thought of the scene with Paul returned. It had been lurking in the recesses of her mind, trying to push forward into her attention. Now it entered her life again in the full force of its enormity and its blackness, and again she felt her body beginning to shake. She was amazed that the physical power of a male could reduce her to such a quivering state. She was filled with revulsion, and immediately sensed that unclean, dirty feeling again. She rose and went into the bathroom, and turned on the shower. She showered for a long time, and guiltily hoped Caroline would forgive her all the hot water that poured down the plughole. She soaped herself again and again and stood under the cascading water, feeling the dirt of that event, the filth of what she had been implicated in, the near-violation of herself, falling away, sliding through her wet hair, down her shoulders and arms and stomach, along her thighs, her legs, and now washed away in the soap suds, that filled the bottom of the bath before disappearing into the plughole. It was a new experience for her, and she thought again how fragile a thing is confidence, how it was something she had taken for granted. Her confidence, her ability to respond to life in a meaningful and efficient way, she now realised, could be smashed in a matter of minutes.

She turned off the shower. Of course the little bathroom was filled with steam, and she could not hear a ventilator fan, so she opened the window, and saw the steam billow out in the cold air. She wrapped herself in the bath towel and returned to her room.

Hesitantly, she went down the stairs. What right had she, a child of the streets, really, to be in this blessed abode? This house of good people, who would only have good things happen to them? She found the door to the kitchen. There was no-one there. But breakfast had been laid out for her, she could see. Then an old dog, a black Labrador, heaved itself up out of its basket and came over to greet her on arthritic legs, wagging its tail, like a young dog. Kathy felt deeply grateful. She loved dogs, and had always wanted one, but her mother would not hear of it. The dog gave her a feeling of warmth and happiness, and she returned its affection with appreciation. She patted him, stroked him, put her face against his, and thought how wonderful it would be to be part of a family, a proper family and have a dog. How the children must love this dog, she thought; and then she reflected that Caroline must be taking them to school. After some minutes, she began her breakfast, and looked around the kitchen. Again, it was a delightfully cosy room, with the beams across the ceiling and down the walls, and warm too, in a way that these very old houses always seem to be. Perhaps it was those thick walls, filled with wattle and daub and straw. There were some children's paintings, fixed to the fridge, but no other evidence of children. They must be very tidy children, she thought.

At that moment Francis came into the kitchen. He greeted Kathy warmly, taking her hand, and resting his other hand lightly on her shoulder. Was she alright, better? Did she need a doctor? Kathy told him she was much better, nearly recovered. She thanked him for everything he and Caroline had done for her, and said she would get all her things out of the room, and leave the room nice and tidy. She had no idea where she would go, but she knew she must. Her parents had taught her never to take advantage of people's kindness, and never to outstay her welcome. A sinking feeling of dejection came over her again. Like the little match girl, she must forever stand outside the warm, lighted windows and only look in on others' happiness. Cosiness and security and happiness, it seemed, were not her lot.

'My dear girl,' said Francis. 'You are going nowhere. You have nowhere to go. You are staying here till things get sorted out.' Kathy stared at him, hardly able to believe what she was hearing. Here was someone, a stranger (yes, a stranger with resources, but nevertheless a stranger), willing to help her, who was coming into her life like an angel or the Good Samaritan, and taking charge of things in a way she could not, in a way that only an adult could.

'Now, what you need to do today is go up to that house, and get all your things and bring them down here. And here you will stay until we get things organised.'

'Yes,' said Kathy, meekly, having no better idea, and so happy to put herself in Francis' hands. She looked at her watch. It was eleven o'clock. She should be in the restaurant.

'Then I must go to work,' she said.

'You are not fit to work, yet,' said Francis kindly. But Kathy thought she must be firm. She needed that work, she needed the restaurant. She thought if she became dependent on Francis and Caroline, they might tire of her.

'I am fit, Francis, thank you. And I want to go to work.' He agreed without further argument.

On the way up the High Street, Kathy called in at the restaurant, to let them know she was coming in soon, and apologised for her absence the previous day. They were relieved. Things were not busy at that moment, but soon the New Year festivities would start.

She let herself into Paul's house. Thankfully, no-one was there. She stuffed her few possessions, which had grown over the weeks, into her empty day bag and a large plastic bag Francis had given her. She tidied the room and took her money, which now amounted to three or four hundred pounds, from under the mattress, where she had hidden it. She wrote a little note to Jenny and left her some more money. Then she let herself out of the front door, and pushed the key through the letter box.

She walked along the street, past the outlet factory on the one side, and the little Victorian cottages on the other. The day was still moderately warm for the time of the year, but to Kathy it felt cold and brisk and bracing. There was a fresh chill in the sky, she felt, and a new chapter was opening for her. She was with decent people again, people of her kind. Life was going to resume.

Chapter 38

———∿∿⌒⊙⌒⊙⌒⊙⌒∿∿———

A New Year's Eve Party

Kathy was kneeling on the floor of Francis' sitting room, the room, where a few days ago, she had told him the story of her broken life, culminating with the assault by Paul. She was folding up dozens of church newsletters and stuffing them into envelopes. Francis was in his study, in the room next door, making telephone calls and working on his next sermon. This was a lovely room, she thought. The thick, white walls gave a sense of solidity and history, and she began to feel she belonged somewhere again, that she was no longer an outcast, but a part of society, a part of the English people. She felt a confidence returning, but was wary; it had vanished very quickly in the recent past and could do so again. It all depended now on Francis and Caroline. They were her bridge back into normality. Could they do it? Could they work the necessary miracle for her? The fire burned in the grate and she folded

327

one newsletter after another, laying them neatly in a pile, aware of the fire crackling in the large, open fireplace, sending out warmth and comfort to envelop her. The green carpet was old and faded, and in some places looked very worn. She liked that too. It made her feel more secure than a new carpet would have done; it heightened the feeling of history. This was the time when, after her hours working in the restaurant, she would be in the café drinking a cup of coffee or tea and reading a newspaper. With nowhere to go and nothing to do.

Francis came into the room. He must have finished working on his sermon. He knelt down also and started stuffing the folded pages into their envelopes.

'Do you always do this on the floor?' asked Kathy.

'Not always. Sometimes. When the kitchen table is free, we do it there. But, as you've seen, it's full of Caroline's shoe boxes of gifts to Africa at the moment.'

'Yes, I've seen,' giggled Kathy. 'She's got a lot. I'm going to help her when I've finished here. Who pays for all the soap and toothpaste and tins of beans she is putting into them?'

'Oh, the parishioners. *We* don't. In fact the parishioners bring the shoe boxes already packed. We're just re-organising them a bit, because some boxes have too much in them, and others too little.'

They worked in silence for a while. Then Francis said: 'You had a bad time in west London, Kathy. It sounds as though you were very afraid all the time.'

'I suppose I was,' she replied. 'I was trying to make out, be tough like the rest. And I *felt* tough too and equal to things, but, yes, underneath I was afraid, very afraid.'

'What were you afraid of?'

'Gary and the gang.'

'But gangs can't extend their power everywhere.'

'Oh, Gary could. He had spies everywhere. Even in the children's home. There was Nick. He would tell if I refused to go up to their meeting place.' There was a pause while Francis pushed a couple of newsletters into their envelopes.

'And you still think you had no choice; that you had to join that gang?'

'Yes,' said Kathy, emphatically, wondering what Francis was driving at.

'Did you ever think about it?'

'What do you mean?' asked Kathy, feeling a little defensive. 'It was survival. I had to, otherwise Gary would have taken against me, and then done something awful to me. The girls in his gang were very submissive, obedient. He had made them afraid of him. I didn't want that, so I decided to play the game.'

'But you were very submissive, obedient, as you say, weren't you?' There was a pause. 'And Gary had done nothing to you. Do you think all the girls were thinking like you? Thinking that something awful had happened to some of the other girls, and that therefore they had better knuckle down and cooperate, to prevent that awful thing happening to them?' Kathy went on folding the newsletters. She was struggling. Francis was attacking her. He did not believe her, did not believe how unutterably dreadful it had all been in London. She felt her mouth tightening, her stomach tensing to fight this new battle. Not another battle! Something inside her groaned.

Francis must have seen the gathering of her defences. 'Kathy, you are a remarkable girl; you have weathered a dire situation. The social services made a grave error in removing you from your background. They obviously thought your aunt, your mother's cousin, would kick in with a lot of care and responsibility. She must have deceived the social worker who did the preparation and the visits to her. Intelligent drug addicts and alcoholics are very adept at this kind of deception. But, despite all this, through your strength and courage, you triumphed and made a good decision in running away from the home. Things had come to a dead end there for you – a dangerous dead end.' Francis paused, allowing this affirmation of her character to find its target.

'Mmm,' said Kathy, reassured, but not knowing how to respond. She felt complimented, as though Francis really did understand after all.

Francis went on silently stuffing the envelopes. 'What if you had gone to Mike, the father of the home? You said he was nice.'

'Gone to Mike?' she said, shocked. She was offended, and again felt attacked. 'Mike could do nothing. He was powerless, quite powerless. Gary was the one with all the power.'

'I see,' said Francis, carefully. 'How did you come to know that?'

'I could see it, all the time, all around me. Everyone was afraid of Gary.'

'Even Mike?'

'No, of course not. They would have got the police out if anything had happened to Mike.'

'And not for you? No police for you?'

'No, of course not. I was nothing. I was a nobody. If anything had happened to me, the police would not have bothered.'

'So, you joined the gang?'

'It was the most intelligent thing to do. It was survival, like I said.'

'And you always do the intelligent thing?'

'Yes, of course. Wouldn't you?' Kathy had never talked in this aggressive way to an adult before, except in the children's home, and especially not to someone who could offer her so much. Miserable in some deep part of herself with the way her relationship with Francis was going, she desperately wanted to end the conversation, to make it alright between the two of them, but she seemed unable to control the dialogue, and felt compelled to continue. What was making her act in this way, she wondered. Francis ignored her question. 'Did you try going to Mike? Did you give that option a thought, before you decided to join the gang?'

'No, I didn't. Like I said I knew it would have been hopeless.'

'What makes you so sure, Kathy?' She was touched by the tender way he said this, so touched she wanted to cry. She felt she was breaking down. This conversation was breaking her. She must get out of this room, get away from this effect Francis was having on her. She was weakening. She must at all costs get away, re-orientate herself. Get back to Becky Sharp. Yes, that was it; find herself in good, hard, surviving Becky.

But she did not leave the room. She stayed, kneeling on the floor, on the old, faded, green carpet with an arm chair in old, faded chintz off on her right, and the setting sun slanting in through the window, folding newsletters, and fighting hard in her confused mind to understand what was happening to her.

'And what about that other girl – Barbara? She didn't join the gang.'

'I told you Barbara was different. She still had so much of her old life; her old school and friends. It was a lot different for her.'

'I wonder,' said Francis, quietly. 'She must have felt pretty helpless too. No home, no family. School and friends are not everything. They don't give you that kind of support, that security. I'll bet she felt powerless and vulnerable too, like you.' Angry at this new attack on her character, she quickened her folding of the newsletters, laying one side sharply down on the other, and slapping it down on the pile. She was amazed at this insubordinate behaviour in herself, and, again, miserably thought Francis would ask her, as soon as was decently possible, to leave, to find somewhere else to stay.

She knew Francis could see how discomfited she was; it was obvious, but, for some reason, he persisted. She wished he would shut up. She felt like saying: 'Francis, shut up; it's none of your business.' But it seemed it *was* his business.

'Do you think, Kathy, that, despite all your courage and all your fine intelligence, you got some things a little wrong? Do you think you saw more threat and danger than there really was? Do you think things may not have been as hopeless as you thought? Do you think it was at all possible that a lot of the power Gary had was more illusion; that everyone just *thought* he was powerful; that all the kids in the gang just thought Gary had done something to the others to make them afraid and obedient to him? Do you think it could all have been an illusion, or most of it? A great con trick? Did you know bullies are always great con artists? And you said you were very afraid, underneath, all the time. Fear and bullying make a very strong cocktail. Now, I am not saying it was *all* illusion. I happen to know what happens to a good many of the girls in gangs; but even then they do have a choice. Yes, a good bit of the way you saw things *was* illusion.'

Kathy listened in a state of shock at these amazing revelations of Francis, and was greatly hurt. She was not so much interested in the cleverness of his analysis, as in the fact that he simply had not believed her side of things. Not believed the truth of the situation. She felt disbelieved, invalidated. She felt so disconcerted and confused, she could not marshal her thoughts. Becky was nowhere to be found. She was frightened by this mental disarray, appalled that she was sinking into a mental abyss, where she was no longer sure of anything. Structures, things, thoughts, she had been sure of, began to dissolve.

'I have to go. Excuse me,' she said, dropping a newsletter and rushing out of the room. She stumbled upstairs to her room. Her room. 'No, it is not my room; I have no room, no place here. Soon they will come and tell me to leave.' She threw herself onto the bed, as she had used to do occasionally at home, when she did not get her way, and burst into bitter tears. How dare Francis talk in that way? He was expounding on things, expressing opinions, that he just did not understand at all. She felt angry and betrayed, and in her mind she saw herself hitting him, hurting him.

After some time the crying stopped. She was lying in the dark. A street lamp, some way off shone into her room, its yellow glow fixed on the pale yellow wall opposite the window. She could hear the traffic distantly in the High Street. It was New Year's Eve. What did that matter to her? She was nobody. Nobody cared what happened to her on New Year's Eve. And Francis now would certainly not care. She had cooked her goose, she thought; had burnt her boats. Why had she not been more intelligent in that conversation? Why had she not linked with Becky Sharp and made all the right responses – yes sir, no sir, three bags full sir – and circumvented this dire situation she now found herself in.

There was a gentle knock on the door. 'Kathy, dear, are you coming down for supper? We can't eat it all ourselves and we so want your company.' She was impressed with this gentle approach, these kind words, but knew Caroline was just making the farewell decent, civilised.

'Yes, thank you, I'll come,' Kathy replied with the good manners she had been brought up with, but without enthusiasm.

The shoe boxes in the kitchen had all been cleared away to somewhere; where? Kathy wondered. And a New Year's Eve supper had been prepared. There were several other place settings round the table, and she wondered who else was coming, and wished she had stayed in the bedroom; the last thing she wanted was to be sociable. Then the three other guests arrived, an elderly lady, stout and with a dominating personality; her daughter – a wan-looking young woman – and the granddaughter, who, Kathy guessed must have been about ten. She was introduced to them all – Edna, Vita and Mathilda,

Tilda for short. She gathered it was a family without men, and that Francis was doing his best to supply a little New Year jollity for them. She seated herself where Caroline indicated, and then, thankfully, found she had a role in helping Caroline bring dishes from the stove to the table.

Francis served a little red wine to go with 'the absolutely divine nut roast' as Edna kept saying. Soon everyone was a little merry, a little more relaxed, and crackers were pulled and a toast or two drunk to the New Year. Everyone put on a paper hat and after the plum pudding Francis opened the lid of an old piano that stood in a corner of the kitchen, and began to play Auld Lang Syne. Kathy felt her spirits reviving somewhat. She laughed occasionally and ate her vegetarian meal, but in the back of her mind, for the duration of the meal, she was acutely and painfully aware that she was somehow separated from herself, from her personality. However, she was able to field, adequately, Edna's curious questions about her past, and what she was doing in Glastonbury. That was until the questions became intrusive and difficult to answer. And that was when Francis intervened and turned the attention onto Edna herself, something she seemed to enjoy, and for a time the whole table must listen to a long anecdote which Edna recounted about an earlier episode in her life.

'Now, Francis, dear,' said Edna, turning to him after she had come to the end of her story, 'Francis, darling, you never told me what you did before this, before taking orders. I don't believe you've been a priest all your working life. You are far too wise for that. Don't you think so, Caroline? You were definitely something else!'

'You're right, Edna. How right you are, although I don't know about being wise. I sometimes think I'm the least wise of people,' said Francis.

'Oh, tush, Francis; you're wonderfully wise for such a young man. What would the parish do without all that wisdom? But come, tell us what you did before.'

'What I did before,' said Francis ruminatively. 'Well, I did several things, but the most important was as a social worker.'

'Really!' said Edna. 'How awful! Social worker! How perfectly awful for you, Francis! Poor boy!'

'No, no, not at all, Edna. I was the manager of a children's home. It was the best job I ever did – till I came here, of course.'

'And where was the institution, Francis?'

'Brixton!' Edna looked appalled, and decided to say no more. But Vita was very interested, curious to know what it had been like, what experiences he had had, what black kids were like to work with, and were there gangs?

'Gangs, oh yes,' said Francis. 'Some of the worst in London, in the country - if not *the* worst. Very violent, very dangerous!'

Chapter 39

---~~~∽◦⌒⊙⌒◦∽~~~---

Confessions

The wine had had an effect on Kathy. When she went to bed, she slipped into an immediate, but fitful, sleep and awoke early in the morning, not feeling rested. She quickly remembered the conversation with Francis and the unwelcome feelings it was creating. The feeling was the same sensation she had had on the bus after the attempted rape by Paul. Francis, her saviour and hope! How could he have said those things? How could he have knowingly created such turmoil in her mind? For she felt he had done it knowingly. And it wasn't just her mind. This dark encroaching shadow seemed to extend beyond her mind into her body, her whole being. She felt some kind of mental disintegration at work, and became afraid for herself, again. What she had taken for granted within herself now seemed unstable, unavailable, even. Before, when she had sought and found a certain bit of her personality, a certain

337

reach of her mind, a certain old experience that had created some piece of vital landscape in her mind to enable mental negotiation, she now sought in vain; it was now no longer there. The budding, settling down of her teenage mind into wholesome and helpful pathways that she could traverse, like she had done on her computer, were now sinking, disappearing into a brown, sludgy morass, rather like the paths through the Levels a few nights ago. Vital things were being deleted from her mind, as you might delete things on a computer; but this was not just unwanted files; this was as though whole programmes of needed software were being erroneously erased.

She sat up, feeling a change of position might help, might stop this frightening, erasing process. What was it Francis had said? He had said a number of things that had shocked her. He had said that Gary may not have been as dangerous as she thought. Francis just did not understand. But now she knew he *did* understand; he had worked in exactly the same environment! He had been the manager of a children's home! And in Brixton! Vita had seemed to think that the most challenging place in the world for social work, except perhaps Glasgow. Had she made a mistake in her assessment of her situation in London? Had Gary really been more of a con-artist? She could not believe it. Had she really based her whole time in the children's home on a false premise? Had she really been safer than she had thought? She remembered Barbara and how sad and insecure she had looked, how unsafe she was. And she thought of all the times she had not seen Barbara in the home. She had thought she was in her room, being sad; but one of the younger ones had mentioned once that Barbara was at school during these times, playing in netball matches, or at her tennis club, practising for some tournament. Had she misunderstood Barbara too? Was Barbara actually not so miserable and frightened as she had thought? And then a strange thought occurred to Kathy. Was she looking at Barbara through something like a pair of glasses, through which she, Kathy, viewed the world? Perhaps she saw the world in a particular way, saw other people and their situations in a way which was inaccurate. If this were true – that people did not see the world correctly, but through a pair of glasses, which differed from one person to the next - then that meant there may be no such thing as one reality. There may be lots of realities. What was real for her may not be real for Barbara – or Mike or Gary, and, come to that, Paul. She knew people were different because of their background experiences, but she had never before developed that knowledge, carried it any further forward; had never realised that it could affect the way she saw reality, or, rather, what she once believed was reality.

She started attempting to drag up some kind of stepping stone from the murky confusion of her mind. But each time she was forced back into confronting the possibility that she may have been living in some kind of illusion, as Francis had suggested. Had she been wrong about the children's home, wrong about so many things there? And, if so, how could she trust herself now to make correct judgements of people and situations? She sank back, shrank away from this fearsome thought that seemed to be leading into a nightmare situation, which was dark, black, and where she could not exist, did not have an identity. But what she sank back into was worse; it was stagnant, and also with no exits. And again she wondered if she was becoming mentally ill, or, at least, having a nervous breakdown. What did people do when they were having nervous breakdowns? Scream, jabber, behave like a lunatic? Should she do that? No, she couldn't possibly; she was a guest in this house. Guests didn't behave like that.

She returned to the black morass of no-thinking, from which there were no exits, and decided to return to her thought process, where at least there had been movement, and thus hope of an exit. So, she may have been wrong about Gary, about Barbara. So, Mike may have been able to offer her protection, after all; and, so, playing the gang game with Gary and getting suspended from that good school may not have been necessary after all. And so her flight to Glastonbury and this hopeless mission to rescue Granfy, and her dumb job in the restaurant – all this might have been avoided, and for some real gain: an education. There was an exit here; she could feel it, rather than see it. It was a dim awareness that if she had the courage to stay in this place, this dark, uncomfortable place, then this exit would grow, or she would get nearer to it, and then it would become really available.

In dejected spirits she dressed herself, moved automatically through all her routines, feeling that if she could just protect herself for the time being, she might not become mentally ill; might somehow be able to recover her personality, her sense of identity. Please, God, she thought, let me get my self back.

She was alone in the kitchen. Breakfast had been prepared for her. Fruit, cereals and toast lay invitingly on the table. She ate, without enthusiasm, automatically.

All day, at the restaurant, she pretended 'normality'. She could not laugh when the others occasionally laughed, but she could smile – a weak smile. Emma said she was concerned for her, and wondered what the matter was.

After a week her spirits lifted a little. Not in the old way, but in a new, fragile way; a way she was not sure she liked, because it prevented her from coming to quick and sure assessments of the situations in her life. She was unsure of everything now; unsure of herself; she had lost her map. But, still, she was in a better place than a week ago. She was in a place where there was movement, there was hope, and Kathy put all her faith on that exit coming nearer – the exit that held a more accurate map.

She had not told Francis of the group sex thing. She had not been able to bring herself to do that. She had always seen herself as a 'good' person in this strange area of life, that she knew she was now approaching in her mid-teens. She had never had to think about it very much, as it did not interest her and she simply had not had the time for boyfriends. So, to participate in group sex, even as only an observer, to experience sex in this way - surely the lowest form of the sexual act - was a thing of great shame to her. She wanted to tell someone, to get it out of her system, to go to a confessional, as the Catholics did. Perhaps she should find a Roman Catholic priest. No, she must tell Francis. But she did not want to tell Francis. She did not want to sully herself in his eyes any more than she already had. But the feeling that she must tell Francis was overwhelming.

One evening, she found herself alone with him in the kitchen. They were washing up together; Caroline was out at a Spanish evening class.

'We're not a big family, you see, Kathy, so we don't have a dish-washer. There's no need. We don't have children, as you've discovered. So, we do the dishes in the old fashioned way.'

'So did we at home,' said Kathy. Then, venturing to probe a little, she asked: 'Why don't you have children?'

'We're not able to,' said Francis, matter-of-factly. But Kathy detected sadness in his voice. 'So we enjoy other people's children,' he said brightly.

After a pause, Kathy ventured again into foreign waters. 'Francis, can I talk to you for a bit?'

'Of course, you can, Kathy. What is it you want to talk about?'

'Well, you know I told you I took ecstasy, because I was made to; well…….' She corrected herself: 'Well, because I *thought* I had to. I probably did have to at the time, but perhaps I need not have gone with them all to that house.' Francis nodded encouragingly. 'Well, the ecstasy, actually, um, it went to, um, more than that.' She felt she was getting embarrassed, and wished she had blurted the sex thing out at the time she had told Francis everything else. It would have been much easier. Now it was going to be very difficult. She felt herself blushing. 'Well, um, yes, it went into other things.'

'What things?' asked Francis gently.

'Well, sort of sex.'

'"Sort of sex", what do you mean?'

'Well, um, the others, some of the others, took their clothes off and started having sex. On the floor. That's all. That's all I wanted to say.' And she felt the surprise again that she had felt, not at the actual time, but afterwards when the drug had worn off - the astonishment that she could have been present at such an event. She marvelled at the incredibleness of it.

'I see,' said Francis. 'Did you join in?'

'Oh no, no,' she said, bringing herself back to the present. 'I just watched.'

'That's bad enough,' said Francis. 'But I understand.'

'Yes, it's bad, I know,' she said. 'Horrible! And there must be pregnancies from those sessions.'

'Undoubtedly,' said Francis, gravely.

'No, I just watched. I didn't want to be there, Francis. It's just the way things worked out. The way I *thought* things had worked out. I mean I thought I had to be there; perhaps I didn't.'

'What do you mean, Kathy?'

'Well,' she said, pausing. 'Well, actually, I've thought a lot about what you said, and I think you're right. Gary really was a bully; I really had to be careful of him and his gang – and that was a fact, Francis; but, well, yes, I think I had a lot more choice in those months than I realised.' Francis put a pile of plates away very carefully, very gently in the cupboard.

'I'm glad, Kathy, very glad,' he said, and put a protective arm round her shoulder.

'I just wanted you to know everything,' she said.

'And is that everything?' he asked, smiling.

'No,' she said. And then stopped, feeling unable to continue, and regretting she had begun to reveal more. But, despite herself, she continued: 'I have been horrible, cruel even, to a young boy, a boy who is disabled. I have behaved so badly.'

'What did you do?' Francis looked troubled, more serious, much more concerned than when she had told him about the group sex.

'We were running up the Tor – a whole group of us. He thought I was his friend, and that I would wait for him – because he was slower, you see, because of his leg.'

'Were you his friend?'

'Yes, very much. But I didn't take it seriously at the time. Oh, how I wish I had.' And she stopped in her account of the incident, and heard, again, that forlorn cry: 'Kathy, wait for me. Wait for me, Kathy.' And then she heard little Susie as well: 'Wait for me, Kathy. Wait; you're bigger and stronger than me. Wait. I want to come too. PLEASE.' But she hadn't waited. For either of them. In her mind's eye she saw little Philip and little Susie, smaller, weaker than she, pathetic, pleading for her help. And she had refused, ignored them. She began to cry. She was imagining what it was like to feel as they must have done – left behind, ignored, betrayed. She cried a gentle cry of true sorrow, true remorse. Francis had led her to a chair at the kitchen table, and her tears of repentance flowed down her cheeks into her tissue.

'I am so sorry for this,' she whispered.

'Really sorry?' asked Francis, gently.

'Really and truly sorry,' she said. 'More sorry for this than for anything else. More sorry for this than Granfy's alzheimer's; than the group sex; than my awful time in the children's home.' There was a pause. Francis did not break the silence. The only sound was Kathy's sniffing and the central heating rumbling in one of the pipes.

'I wish I wasn't like this,' she said. 'I wish I were a different person. I wish I were kinder.'

'You are a lovely person, Kathy,' said Francis. 'You are a good person, and strong and courageous. And you will learn kindness. We all have to. Like everything else kindness has to be learnt. And you must learn to pray,' he added. 'The worthwhile life cannot be lived without prayer and a strong belief in God. Do you pray?'

'Yes, I do,' said Kathy quickly. And then she added: 'Well, not properly. I just didn't have time. Actually, I was too distracted. No, Francis, in fact I do not pray.' And she felt another load lifting off her chest with this introspection and honesty. She could hear Ma Riley right beside her – don't forget to pray, Kathy; she could almost see her, certainly she could feel her. Her old friend, her old teacher! How she had betrayed her! How she had forgotten all those lessons! Francis gave her a fresh tissue, because the other one was sodden. And again he placed a steady, reassuring hand across her shoulders.

'Prayer is so important,' he said. 'Proper prayer involves a direct, conscious and intended conversation with God. A vague wish, a mistaken notion that because he knows our every wish, our every desire, he will therefore tale care of us, when we don't even have the awareness of his presence, the interest to realise that he is a living being watching over us and waiting for our attention, waiting for our request for help – to live blindly and ignorantly like this is the biggest error of our lives. When we don't even request his help, why should he help us?' Some time ago, Kathy could not remember when, they had moved into the sitting room. Kathy had ceased to shed tears of remorse, and now listened intently to Francis. He paused and the fire in the grate sizzled now and again, as it consumed a resinous piece of wood, or spat out a spark or two. Apart from that, there was silence in the room. Francis broke it.

'You see, Kathy, proper prayer is the most important activity a human being can perform. It sets in motion all sorts of things – humbleness for a start, trust, patience, reliance on God, which is what he wants of us.'

'Yes, I can see all that following on from the practice of proper prayer,' answered Kathy quietly.

'And another reason why the habit of getting to know God is so important,' continued Francis, 'is that God has the unenviable task of weaving a beautiful tapestry out of all the messy strands of our life. We offer him the untidy threads of our life and he takes them and starts to weave. If we are not in the habit of talking to God, we don't realise this and we keep initiating foolish changes in our lives, when really we should just be sitting still. If we are forever undoing God's work, unpicking the strands of our life, snapping the threads, how can God create a coherent, beautiful tapestry? Relying solely on ourselves, which is what many, many people do, is the greatest mistake we can make. That is what eventually leads an individual to experience bitter fruits at the end of his or her life, instead of sweetness and reward. Work hand in hand with God. Pray all the time to God. Put all your trust in him, Kathy.' A slight breeze rattled at the casement of the window, the walls of the old house exuded solidness, the beams spoke of ageless trees. Kathy felt safe and secure; at peace.

Chapter 40

———ww~o<e>o~ow———

Finding the Way Back

The festivities had come to an abrupt end. It was several days after New Year and now a quietness lay over the town. Denuded of its Christmas regalia, the new-age trend that dominated Glastonbury was revealed once more in all its medley of colourful and philosophical confusion, in its bewildering display of mythical artefacts in the shop windows, and in the outlandish garb of the denizens. The sleeping dragon of fables once more breathed freely, as the new winds of January cleared away the conventional garb of a modern Christmas, and blew fresh and cold through the town, as it settled down once more to its accustomed eccentricity. Kathy, walking down the High Street, was very aware now of the strangeness of Glastonbury, as though it were a town that inhabited some odd time warp and had become cut off from the rest of society. It had been a town which had grown up around the abbey, and had been dominated by the life of the abbot and monks and their Christian philosophy. It also lay at the foot of the Tor, that solitary, mysterious hill, that rose in the morning mist like some mythical mountain out of the fens of the Avalon marshes, and which bore the lonely, haunting tower of St. Michael, like some prize stolen from its Christian heritage and now possessed by the magic of this other pagan ancestry of Glastonbury. A forsaken hostage, the tower stood lonely, but courageously, buffeted by the gale of vengeance that swept the Tor, waiting its time.

Part of Francis' parish was also waiting its time. It gathered on this cold January morning, as it did every day, outside the church, and spread itself out on rugs laid on the pavement, and prepared with cheerful resignation to spend the day, every day, in this attitude, talking to each other or greeting passers-by who were good enough to toss them a coin for their guitar or accordion playing. The donor knew it would go on drugs, but, still, it was the giving season! Old men, young men, sat there, with their Rastafarian hair and woolly hats, and their sad, still dogs, and a few women with their pitiable children. Weren't they cold, thought Kathy. She assumed they just had to get used to a life of considerable discomfort.

She was troubled by these people, not so much because of the wretched lives they led, but because of the fact they had lost their sanity, lost the will to live, lost that wonderful delight in life. Once upon a time, she caught herself thinking again, these people were little boys and girls, and were dear to their mothers. She felt sure their mothers had loved them. What had happened, she wondered, to wreak this mental death in them? Again she felt that fear gripping her heart. She had so recently experienced the fragility of sanity, the delicate thing that her sense of her self was - her identity, her confidence. And she realised again how dependent these things were on external factors, like life being predictable and ordered.

But this new January morning was clean and cold, and there was a blue sky and sunshine, and she felt a freshness in the breeze that had blown away the habitual warm, wet air of Somerset. She noticed a lightness in her step. She had a home at last; well, if not a home, then a base from which to re-think her life. And she was with people she could trust.

She walked up to the restaurant where her life had settled back into its usual routine. Curiously, business was not slack as was customary after the Christmas season and for the next few days she worked hard serving vegetarian breakfasts and lunches and home-made cakes and biscuits for tea.

She went down to the town cross once or twice, but walked straight past on errands beyond. Some of the kids were there, including Paul. One or two of them called out to her, remembering that brief, exhilarating dash up the Tor. She called back to them, but walked on quickly, not looking in Paul's direction, who seemed bent on ignoring her. Gregory was not there.

One evening, soon after, she was sitting in the small sitting room with Francis and Caroline. Caroline was knitting baby clothes that she would give to Oxfam, who would send them off to troubled and persecuted parts of the world. Francis was reading. The fire burned warmly in the big fireplace, and some beautiful music was playing. The Pearl Fishers, Francis had said. Kathy was re-reading Vanity Fair, which she had borrowed from the library. But she was losing interest in it. Somehow Becky was not as real and believable as she had been. Thackeray seemed inconsistent in his portrayal of her. One minute she was nice and quite human, and the next she was despicable. But it was still a good story, she thought. She put the book down and gazed into the fire. Francis also put his book aside.

'Kathy, can we talk a little?'

'Yes, of course,' she said, less fearful now of what Francis might say, more trusting.

'I wanted to ask you if you have thought of what you want to do now with your life?' Kathy paused a moment.

'Well, I can stay on and work at the restaurant, tell them my real name – now that I'm sixteen years social services will no longer be interested in finding me. Then I can get that P45 form, and actually get work anywhere. I'll not be a fugitive any more!' and she giggled.

'And what about your education?' asked Francis.

'Yes, I've been thinking about that; I could go to night school. Bath will have some decent classes.'

'What about going back to school?' Kathy thought about this. She had envisaged working in order to pay Francis and Caroline some rent, so that she could continue staying with them. She desperately wanted to stay with them. They had become like her lost parents. She was sure they liked her around too.

'Going back to school?' she queried.

'Yes, getting back into full time education?'

'What, here in Glastonbury?'

'Anywhere; here, Bath, even Newcastle. I rather think not in Glastonbury; there isn't a school good enough for you.'

'You mean I could go back to a good school?' She thought about it for a minute. It was a good idea, but she was not sure it appealed to her now. She was not used to studying full-time now, and, anyway, there was the practical side. Where would the money come from for all the expenses education involved?

'I don't think so,' she said. 'It's not possible; there isn't the money.'

'I think it would be possible,' said Francis. 'I think you have some funds that you don't know about.'

'Funds?' said Kathy. 'What do you mean?'

'Your parents owned a house, didn't they? I understood this from what you've told us. When that was sold, the mortgage would have been paid off, and the rest of the money, I am sure, would have been put in a trust fund for you and your sister, probably to pay for university. That money could be used now for your education. True, there will be much less for university, but without proper schooling now, university is not even going to be on your map. I am sure this is the way your parents would see your situation.'

For the first time in months, Kathy saw herself making new friends and studying. She saw the sense in Francis' suggestion, but was not sure. She felt she had moved on in life, was on another path.

'If you don't get a decent education now, when you're young, you will always regret it,' said Francis.

'That's very true,' said Caroline, quietly, looking up from her knitting over the top of her spectacles.

'You can never make up for education missed at the proper time. People do it when they're older, yes, but it's not the same. You need to get to a decent university when you are young to meet decent, young men. That's how Caroline and I met. At Durham university,' said Francis.

'Oh, Durham,' said Kathy. 'That's close to where we lived.' The idea of university appealed to her. That life – students rushing here and there, activities to take part in, lectures to attend, so many bright, young people to mix with, have fun with. 'Yes,' she thought. 'I like that idea. How wonderful if I could go to university!'

'How about going back to your old school?' suggested Francis.

'My old school?' said Kathy, fascinated, trying to understand this new idea. 'I would be too far behind. It's been too long now.'

'No, it hasn't, Kathy. You only came south in the summer. You've only missed one term, and with your intelligence you would soon catch up.'

Only missed one term! It seemed more like a life-time since she had left Mickle Wood. She was still unsure. Unsure that Francis had understood all the practical problems.

'But where am I to live? And that is always supposing there is enough money for the school fees, because that school is independent, and charges quite a lot.'

'Good question, Kathy,' said Francis. 'But I remember you telling us you were on a scholarship at your school. Perhaps it could be restored.' Kathy was silent, the impact of all these new possibilities taking some time to register in her mind. 'Do you, by any chance, know the name of your parents' solicitors in Newcastle?' Francis asked hopefully. 'It would be good if I could talk to them.'

'Yes, I can remember the name of Dad's solicitors at home, I mean in Mickle Wood, but I don't know the telephone number.' Kathy wrote down the name of her parents' solicitors: Braithwaite and Sutchley.

'Ah,' said Francis looking at the name: 'a typical solicitors' name!'

'What do you mean?' asked Kathy.

'Oh, you'll understand when you get older,' replied Francis. 'And don't worry about their phone number; with a name like that they'll be easy to track down. Tomorrow I will call and talk to them about your education.'

'But, still, where am I to live? There's nowhere I could live,' she said sadly. 'That's why I got sent down here to London, to be near my Aunt Eileen.'

'I have a colleague,' said Francis. 'A priest in Newcastle. I am very sure he and his wife would have you to live with them. After we've settled the matter of the trust money, I'll call him.'

Kathy lay in bed that night, listening to the winter silence outside. An owl hooted, and somewhere she heard a fox barking. Strange, she thought, to hear a fox in town. The quietness of the still, resting house, stole upon her, and a peace and relaxation entered her body, a peace that she had not felt for months. Her life was finally changing, and changing for the better! For the best! This proposal by Francis was the best she could have dreamed up herself. Going back to school; Ellie, Julia, Val, Linda – all the old crew, some her friends, some not. But how much easier to take up with people she had been with, rather than try to forge new relationships with a whole set of new people. None of them had written to her, and she to none of them. She reflected on this, and felt one of the things she would do in future would be to have close friends, who cared for her. She had spent a spell without friends and she realised how lonely life was without them. She closed her eyes, while sleep stole silently upon her. Somewhere, she thought sleepily, there really *is* a God, and he has heard my prayers, at least my wishes, and he has answered them in his own good time and in just the way that is best for me - not in the way I had wanted, but in the very best way! Yes, whispered her soul, and do you remember just three months ago you were praying that Gary would like your shoes? And she knew Ma Riley had been right! She fell into a deep sleep where excitement mingled with this new peace and trust, and she felt it coursing around all her body, and slept as she had used to do at home.

*   *   *

She was on the bus to Bath, going to Aunt May's to tell her the good news! She had been to Aunt May's once since Christmas, and Aunt May had been so pleased, delighted, that Kathy had 'moved in with the vicar and his wife'.

'This is a start, dear,' she had said. 'A start of some big changes, that you need in your life. I really believe things are going to change and get better .'

'Aunt May,' exclaimed Kathy on this windy, January morning. 'Guess what? I'm going back to school in Newcastle, and I'm going to live with another vicar and his family.' Aunt

May had just shut the front door of her flat and had not yet sat herself down, when Kathy blurted out her news.

'Oh, my dear, I am so pleased,' she said. 'So very, very pleased,' and Kathy could see tears glistening in her eyes. So Aunt May really cares what happens to me, she thought. Aunt May did not hug Kathy, as Caroline had done, and Kathy knew it was because Aunt May had not been brought up to do that. 'People in the north,' she thought, 'my people, don't show their feelings, their affection in that way.' And she was a little sad.

Aunt May was sitting in her rocking chair, her feet endearingly hanging above the floor. 'I am really pleased, dear,' said Aunt May again, surveying Kathy, seeming to take in this new state that Kathy felt had settled over herself. 'My clever, beautiful niece (that's what you are to me, dear) is now getting on track again, getting onto the track of life.' Then Kathy told her everything.

'So, when do you leave, dear?'

'Soon, next Thursday. I'll miss the beginning of term, but only by two days.'

'My goodness, all this is so fast,' said Aunt May.

'Well, some things have to go fast,' said Kathy, feeling excited by the whole prospect now. Then Aunt May suggested they go to Granfy's and let him know the good news.

Walking along the streets of Bath to the bus stop, Kathy prayed that Granfy would be in a lucid state, and able to recognise her properly and able to understand how her life was changing. She so wanted to say goodbye to him properly, for she had a feeling she might never see him again. She tossed her thick, dark brown hair back. It was cut in a bob now, the haircut she used to wear at home, and walked beside the diminutive Aunt May. She felt she was taller than when she had met Aunt May, and wondered if she had grown. She would make a better goal shooter in netball, and perhaps run faster on the hockey pitch. Oh, how wonderful it was all going to be! And the books she would be reading for English literature! She instinctively quickened her pace to match her mood, her blood surging through her veins, but then realised Aunt May could not keep up with her. Slackening her pace, she wondered if, had she continued walking at that pace, Aunt May might have called out: 'wait, Kathy, wait for me'. She smiled to herself and they walked together.

At the home they found Granfy playing patience alone in the conservatory, which was filled with afternoon sunshine. He looked contented, at peace with his life, and Kathy felt how wrong it would have been to have moved him out of here into a flat with her. What a stupid idea it had been! Totally impractical! He recognised her and Aunt May immediately, and they both embraced and kissed him, as people do kiss and embrace one another on meeting again, Kathy thought. He asked how they both were, and Kathy was enormously relieved to see that he was normal, that he could properly understand what was being said.

He began to collect the cards together, tapping them into order on the table in a gentle, thoughtful way with his large hands. It was a pleasing movement, and Kathy liked it. He had been that way at home, always taking his time over things and doing it all in a mannerly way. 'He has an elegant way about him,' her mother had said. 'That's what makes it nice to have him around.'

'Archie,' said Aunt May. And Kathy thought her tone sounded mischievous. 'Archie, Kathy has something to tell you.' Granfy looked at Kathy, curiously, expectantly.

'Yes, Granfy, I've got news for you!'

'What news, lass? Have you heard from Susie?'

'No, Granfy, no. It's something else. I'm going back to school, to Newcastle, to Jesmond High!' She paused, waiting for Granfy's reaction. His face creased into a big smile. He looked relieved, she thought, as though in his lucid periods he had worried about her.

'Kathy, lass, that's the best news I've had since finding May and you again! It's right; right you should be in school. I never thought it right you should be running round waitressing, not going to school and not having a proper home. Not with all the education you've had.'

'Well, I haven't got much of an education yet,' she said.

'No, but you will have; you will,' said Granfy, still beaming at her. 'But where will you live?'

'With a vicar and his wife and family. And guess what? They live in Jesmond too, so I won't have far to go to school. I'll be able to go on a bicycle!'

'Eee, lass, I can't think of a nicer thing to have happened to us.' And his voice took on that sing song lilt of the Geordies that Kathy now felt she loved so much. 'And you'll be seeing Susie again,' he went on.

'Yes, I will,' said Kathy, her eyes bright with happiness.

'I never thought it right that you two should be split up; sending you down to be near that woman, Eileen, that we knew nothing about – well, it wasn't right, wasn't right at all, and I said so at the time.'

'Well, that's over now,' said Kathy. 'I'm going home; well, sort of. I'll be near Susie and I'll be in my old school. And we'll both come to see you!'

'Eee, it's wonderful,' said Archie again. 'Isn't that right, May?'

'The Lord has certainly had a hand in all this,' said Aunt May.

Chapter 41

—∿⌒⌒∿⌒⌒∿—

Endings

She had one last thing to do before leaving Glastonbury. She wanted to say good bye to Chalice Well, the gardens that Philip had shown her round, and where she had been several times since, to enjoy the peace and tranquillity it seemed to bestow. Perhaps, here, she could say good bye to Philip too; perhaps in some strange way her soul could reach his soul – after all, it was meant to be a sacred place – and thank him for his friendship and for their visit to Chalice Well and to the nature reserve.

She walked under the long, wooden pergola, strewn with the thick creeper, and thought in the summer it must look very beautiful. Had Philip said it was wisteria? Her feet were silent on the cobblestones beneath; new, of course, laid when the garden was created, but they had the unevenness of old things, of history, and she felt comfortable and secure. She walked slowly up the paths. Where should she go first? She found her feet repeating the route she had taken with Philip, and stood in the garden of King Arthur's Court and the Healing Pool. It was cold now, but in the summer she could envisage people walking up and down here, in the water, to heal themselves of their ailments. She had been sceptical of this, at first, but now the idea grew upon her.

It was still early in the morning, so she had the garden very much to herself. She sat for some time on the low, stone wall opposite the opened lid of the round well, with the symbol of the Vesica Piscis on it. She listened to the gurgling of the spring down in the well, the surging, bubbling waters - the holy spring, the source, around which the whole garden had been created. And she felt herself agreeing with the idea that there, in those waters, was life, mysterious and self-enhancing, a life that could even heal. She sat and studied again the symbol of the Vesica Piscis, hoping some light, some dawning of its secret would reveal itself. The middle part, she could see, where the two circles intersected, was a fish – perhaps the fish that represented Christianity. She contemplated the whole design; yes, it was a very beautiful, geometric pattern. She read again that the two circles represented the union of heaven and earth, or spirit and matter. But she could not understand the symbolism of the vertical rod that bisected the design. She must ask Francis and Caroline about it all. Then, she thought, perhaps if she sat long enough looking at it, it would bring about some mystical change in her. She liked that word 'mystical'; it was a new word for her, and seemed full of magic and mystery. She sat for a long time. Finally, too cold to tarry any longer, she rose and in a simple inward way she bid the Vesica Piscis garden goodbye.

She thought she would now go to the Lion's Head and drink some of the holy water, and fill a plastic bottle she had brought with her in her day bag. There were voices in that small garden, and she was disappointed she would not be alone. A small group of people were taking turns drinking from the glass, which stood by the lion's head.

'Philip, your turn now,' said a girl, about Kathy's age, and she turned and gave a glass full of the holy water to a boy about eleven years, who had on jeans and a blue jacket. He moved forward, limping heavily, and gently took the glass. Kathy watched him drink, slowly, because the water was cold, but also because he was concentrating on something.

'Philip,' she said softly, moving out of the shadows. 'Philip.' Philip had handed the glass back to the girl, and now looked towards the entrance from where he had heard his name uttered. 'Philip,' said Kathy again. Philip stared, and Kathy looked at him, across the small expanse of garden that lay between them. He looked just like the Philip she had known - the young boy with the kind, gentle face and the blonde hair that hung over his forehead; but now he also looked happy, excited even, as though some heaviness had been lifted, and he could behave more like the child that he was. Had he forgiven her, she wondered, for her betrayal of him as they ran up the High Street all those weeks ago, before Christmas? Would he be able to forgive her?

'Kathy, Kathy,' he said, disengaging himself from the group of people, and coming forward to greet her. 'Kathy, I've been wondering about you, but I didn't know where to find you.'

'How are you, Philip? I hear you've been adopted.'

'Yes, I have. They're a wonderful family. I'm very happy, and so is my nan. Come and meet them. This is my ma and pa.' Mr. and Mrs. Christopherson introduced themselves and their daughter, Esther. Kathy was momentarily distracted by Esther. She had short, fair hair, and a pretty face, but what struck Kathy most was the softness of her face and her kind, confident eyes. But then her attention returned to Philip.

'Yes, Kathy, so much has changed for me. We live in Shepton Mallet and I go to a new school, smaller than my other one, and we're doing lots of new subjects, like physics and chemistry and biology. Oh, and Kathy, I've got a dog. A little puppy. He's called "Gypsy".'

'Philip, that's wonderful, great! What sort is it?'

'Oh, I don't know; we got him from the dog home. What sort is it, Mum? The puppy?' called Philip to his new mother.

'He seems to be a bit of labrador and a bit of spaniel and a bit of fox terrier,' replied Mrs. Christopherson, laughing.

'And he's just like a gypsy, Kathy; he wants to get out and run off all the time. Oh, you must come and see him. Mum, can Kathy come and visit us? I want her to see Gypsy and tell her all my news.' Philip had indeed changed. He was more child-like, more spontaneous. Now, instead of being more like a young adult, he was his own age, and behaving with that exuberance and excitement typical of a child. Kathy was fascinated by this metamorphosis, and wondered if her own change of circumstances could give her back her lost childhood and innocence, and ability to behave so spontaneously, and less warily.

The five of them walked round the garden together, taking in the various sites, and Kathy and Philip exchanging news. Soon, Kathy and Philip found themselves sitting on the angel seat, the Christophersons discreetly withdrawing for a time to leave the two of them space for a reunion. Kathy took her opportunity.

'Philip, I want to say something,' she said tentatively.

'What, Kathy?' asked Philip, expectantly.

'I want to tell you, Philip, I am so sorry I left you that day we all ran up the Tor.' A fleeting look of pain crossed the boy's face, but it was only a moment. He brushed his hair off his forehead, and laughed in the old way, she thought. He had trained himself to laugh about pain and misfortune, and that would probably never leave him.

'It was nothing, Kathy, nothing. It was stupid of me to think I could get up the Tor with all you lot. You were all going so fast. Did you make it? Did they slow down? They must have slowed down some time.'

'I made it in the end; I nearly didn't, and I was last.' Kathy felt better for having told the whole truth, for having admitted to weakness. It was a hard job always being up there with the best. Sometimes she thought it's good to come down a bit and be with the others, be a bit ordinary for a little while. Philip laughed.

'I don't believe you were last, Kathy.'

'Oh, I was, I was. I was even behind that little Will.' They both laughed.

'I suppose Paul and Gregory were the first; they're big,' said Philip.

'Yes.'

'And all the cigarettes Paul smokes,' said Philip.

'Yes,' said Kathy reflectively. 'I suppose it'll tell one day. But, Philip, you do forgive me? It was not a kind thing of me to do. To leave you like that.'

'Of course, I do, Kathy. There's nothing to forgive.' They sat for a moment in silence, looking out across a lawn to some trees at the far side, the quietness broken only by some low, human voices and a solitary crow.

The Christophersons suddenly reappeared. 'Do you two want to stay on your own, or would you like to come with us?' asked Mrs. Christopherson. Philip looked at Kathy.

'Oh, we'll come with you,' said Kathy.

*   *   *

Ever since she had met Francis and Caroline Templeton, she felt as though she were being drawn back again into the warmth of the family circle of humanity. Here she was, in the family of Francis and Caroline and Betsy, the dog, and all the friendly parishioners who seemed to keep constantly coming to the house. It was a home filled with people and warmth and kindness, where good things seemed to happen with great regularity. And soon she would be joining another family in Jesmond, in Newcastle, and she was sure she would feel at home there too. Since he was a vicar also, he must be like Francis. And then there would be the reunion with little Susie. Not so little now, she thought. Susie would be eleven now. But their mother had always called her 'little Susie'.

She finished packing her few belongings into a small travelling bag that Caroline had lent her, and went downstairs to put a sandwich lunch into her day bag. Caroline had now gone to play the piano for an infants' music morning in the church hall. She and Kathy had exchanged a warm and affectionate farewell. Kathy had even shed tears, and Caroline had taken her into her arms and told her she would be coming back soon, and that they would write and telephone each other regularly; perhaps e-mail, Caroline had suggested. She was glad she had the Templeton's travel bag. That meant she would have to return it, would have to come back soon.

Francis put her bags in the back of his estate car, so often full of paraphernalia for parish and charity events. Kathy went back into the kitchen and said goodbye to Betsy, putting her face to the dog's face and giving her a kiss. 'I'll miss you, Betsy,' she sighed. 'Even though I've barely been here any time.'

Francis pulled the door to and they crossed the back garden to the waiting car, and climbed inside. They were going to Bath to pick up Aunt May and Granfy, so that they could see her off on the train too. Francis had said there were too many changes going by bus, and it was nicer, anyway, to go by train on important journeys. So the last time Kathy had been in Bath she had bought herself a train ticket to Newcastle. A return! They passed through the green January fields, not yet clothed in that bright green that April would bring, and wet from a heavy rainfall in the night. She wondered if there were peat bogs in any of those fields. Then suddenly a thought occurred to her.

'Francis,' she said.

'Yes,' he replied, negotiating a bend in the road.

'When I was walking that night in the peat bogs on that nature reserve not far from Westwick – the night before I met you - I saw a very strange thing.'

'What was that?'

'Green lights. Horrible, little green lights all round me, especially behind me, and even on my shoes. I felt they were chasing me and they were very threatening and I was so scared.'

'Oh, that's Fairy Fire,' said Francis. 'You get it sometimes in the peat bogs. It's a chemical reaction in the peat. I don't know exactly what, but I'm sure you can look it up on the internet.' So, that was it! A chemical phenomenon, she thought; nothing more, and she had been so frightened. The danger it had seemed to pose was all an illusion, just like her impression of much of her life in London. Illusion, she reflected! How quickly she had jumped from unsafe impressions to conclusions that had served her ill. In fact her whole life in London had been based on illusions. How many people, she wondered, lived out their entire lives like that. She would have to be more careful in the future, very, very careful. And kind, she reminded herself.

They passed through several villages. Kathy knew them well now from her journeys on the bus. The houses and gardens were still enchanting, but no flowers bloomed, except for the occasional sturdy geranium. They were the survivors, she thought.

They arrived at Aunt May's first. She must have been waiting by the window of her flat, because a minute after they arrived, she appeared at the entrance downstairs. She looked beautiful, Kathy thought, in a blue, woollen suit and matching blue hat, as though she were going to a wedding. Kathy introduced her to Francis.

'So, you are the kind vicar who is doing so much for Kathy,' she said, looking gratefully and tenderly up into Francis' eyes.

'It's been a pleasure,' said Francis. 'Both my wife and I think she's a wonderful person, well worth helping!'

'Thank you!' said Aunt May, as though Kathy were her own daughter.

Next, they went to Granfy's place, and he too was all got up in his best, in his green sports jacket and beige trousers, that Kathy remembered so well. Just like the old days, she felt, and a pang hit her heart, and, for a moment, she felt the tears rise in her eyes. Why feel like this, she thought, when I am so happy? The four of them walked slowly down the wide drive to the car, the two men tall in their lean frames, and the diminutive Aunt May walking beside Kathy. Blackbirds hunted for worms in the large lawn, which was streaked with sunlight glancing through the chestnuts and oak that bounded the property. A cluster of blue tits occupied a bird feeder, and terracotta pots stood near the large front door, in which grew some winter plants. Over all stood the stately Georgian mansion, looming bigger than Kathy remembered it and more elegant, the sunlight reflected in its windows. They had allowed plenty of time for the old people, so there was no need to hurry. Granfy's large feet crunched on the gravel. Aunt May's small shoes carefully negotiated the bigger stones.

They found the platform at the railway station, and Francis insisted on carrying Kathy's bags onto the train and stowing them on the luggage rack. Kathy felt like a queen. After all these months of fending for herself, she was now being looked after in every way. Francis paused for a moment, before preparing to get out of the train.

'Francis, I just don't know how to thank you,' she said.

'Then don't, young lady, don't. And, anyway, all the good things come from him,' and he pointed, in that familiar way he had, to an unseen world above.

'But, Francis, it has also been you. You had to be there too, you and Caroline.'

'Well, perhaps; but that too was by his design,' and he smiled.

The train was soon to leave. They walked back up the aisle and alighted onto the platform. Kathy gave Aunt May a hug, her long arms enfolding Aunt May's small frame. She kissed her on the cheek, and Aunt May kissed Kathy gently.

'Kathy, I'm so pleased to have found you; my niece; well, my great niece, my clever, beautiful niece. You'll go far, dear, if you take care. Always be careful in life. Be adventurous, but be careful with the decisions. They often change our lives.' Kathy bent and kissed Aunt May again.

'Aunt May, I'm so happy to have found *you*. My aunt, my only real aunt,' and she laughed happily. Then she turned to Granfy and he embraced her as he had used to do, stroking her hair, as though she were a distressed little girl.

'It's going to be alright for you now,' he said. 'Come and see us, when you can, and bring Susie. Little Susie.'

'I will, I will,' said Kathy, and shed a few tears onto his green and tan jacket. Then she turned to Francis.

'I think you'd better get on the train,' he said, smiling. 'It's about to depart.' Kathy stepped up into the train, and hung out of the open window.

'Good luck with your GCSE exams,' said Francis.

'Thanks.'

And good luck with the Greens. They're a nice family; you'll fit in easily. Remember me to Geoff.'

'Of course!'

'You'll be thinking of university next,' he grinned, mischievously.

'Oh, I have, I have already!'

'Oh?' he said, raising his eyebrows in surprise.

'Yes, I'm going to try for Bristol.'

'Bristol? Not Oxford?'

'No, Bristol, so I can be near you and Caroline, and Aunt May and Granfy.' Francis laughed. A good laugh, she felt.

'We'll see! We'll see, young lady! And don't forget to pray. Prayers are always answered!'

The train pulled out of the station, Kathy still hanging out of the window, waving to the three figures on the platform, two tall and one small. Her family! And then, as the train rounded a bend, they disappeared from view.

THE END

Printed in the United States
By Bookmasters